MW01485545

Crystal Lake

© 2022 George John Black

Paperback ISBN: 978-1-66786-509-6

eBook ISBN: 978-1-66786-510-2

Crystal Lake

Gardner, Mass. Boat Club House, Crystal Lake.

For mom and dad

GEORGE JOHN BLACK

PROLOGUE

My earliest memory of Crystal Lake is riding my bike along the narrow, tree-lined lanes that meandered along the water's edge as my father sat on the rear bumper of our Volkswagen's open hatchback, legs crossed, leaning against his cane, watching me and at once looking out across the lake with that thousand-yard stare.

As a child, I didn't think too much about it. I was more focused on my bike. But as I grew older, I began to wonder, *what was my father thinking about?*

After I rode for an hour or so, we'd typically walk side by side down one of those lanes, kicking the acorns that had fallen from the oak trees, until we came to an open space near the lakeshore. There, we pulled out our baseball gloves from the knapsack that my father carried, separate forty feet or so, and have a game of catch. This continued for thirty minutes or more until Dad announced it was time to go home for dinner.

We repeated this routine at least once a week for many years until I outgrew that open space. We then moved to the baseball field of the local community college, where I'd more space to run under Dad's long fly balls.

But even then, we returned to those tree-lined lanes a few times every year, no longer to ride my bike or play catch, but instead to sit together on a wooden bench overlooking the lake.

Always the same bench.

There, I began to know my father. The stories he told were enthralling, even for a young teenager who was struggling to find his own path.

As I grew up and moved away to different cities, states, and countries, I would almost always return summers to see my Dad. We'd take a drive out to Crystal Lake and sit together on that same bench. Sometimes we talked only about the Red Sox. But sometimes it was deeper. He was my rock. And no matter what I threw at him, he never flinched. His answers were not always what I wanted to hear, but they were always what I needed to hear.

I returned to Crystal Lake a few months ago with my wife and children, proud to show them my father's engraved name upon his favorite bench. He had passed away the week before.

At that moment, I stood with my family and fully understood what that bench had truly meant to my father. There, he had shared with me his life's story, our family's history, and above all else, he had expressed his love for me, in his own stoic way. And now, I was passing on that history to my own children.

They stared at me, not quite sure why I was tearing up.

But it was simple: I'd come full circle.

If I've learned anything in my life, it's a lesson that my father taught me early on: If you get knocked down, get right back up, and keep moving forward.

Always forward.

He always liked that saying by Satchel Paige: *Don't look back because something might be gaining on you.*

I've tried to pass on that philosophy to my own children, probably with mixed results. When you're a child, you don't really understand it. You just reply, "Yeah, whatever, Dad." But when life knocks you down for the first time, then you begin to understand. You either heed the advice and keep moving forward, or you don't, choosing instead to always look over your shoulder, filled with regret.

Did my father have regrets?

Undoubtedly.

We all do.

But did those regrets define him?

Have my regrets defined me?

Only now am I beginning to answer these questions.

PART ONE

LEAVING HOME: *FROM NORMANDY TO AFRICA*

CHAPTER ONE

George was determined to calmly listen to his mother without firing back. After all, she had raised him to be respectful and polite, although sometimes it could be difficult.

"You should at least wait until you're drafted, Jimmy," she said, her voice cracking with emotion. "You'll leave me all alone in this big house."

Jimmy was George's middle name, used by his mother to avoid confusion with his father. For generations, since the family had first arrived in America from Yorkshire, England, first born sons had been named George.

"Enlist?" pressed his mother. "Why the rush?"

George looked past his mother, out the bedroom window of the family's eighteenth century, ten room farmhouse, and across their expansive front yard. He could see Crystal Lake between the trees. "You'll be fine, Mom," he dismissed her concerns. "Anyways, there's nothing for me here. No work. No future."

"The factories are coming back," said Elizabeth to her tall, gangly nineteen-year-old son. "Heywood Wakefield is reopening the two buildings that were closed five years ago," she continued, referring to the small town's main employer, a textile mill that now making military uniforms as part of the war effort.

"You can't expect me to spend my life working in a factory, mom," replied George, his back now turned toward his mother as he continued to organize his duffle bag.

"You don't have to, Jimmy. Your father never did. He found other ways." She was now pleading.

George abruptly turned around. "I'm not my father, Mom! He never worked a regular job in his life."

As soon as he had said it, he regretted it. His mother didn't deserve that.

"Do not talk about your father like that, George! God rest his soul," scolded his mother. "He did his best."

George knew it was a losing game to continue the conversation. His mother would never understand. He needed to get out, before it was too late. Before he found himself growing old in the same small town where his father had been born and had died only a few months earlier at the age of seventy-eight from colon cancer.

It'd been hard on George growing up with an older father. He couldn't play with his Dad like the other kids. He couldn't enjoy a game of catch in the backyard with him during the summer, or go sledding with him on the nearby hill during the winter.

The family house was located on five acres of land within easy walking distance of Crystal Lake, where George would spend most of his days, standing along the shoreline skipping stones over the lake's calm waters, or borrowing the neighbor's skates in the winter to join a game of ice hockey.

But all the while, his father remained inside the house, usually in his study. A voracious reader, George, the father, could read an entire book in one afternoon. He spoke multiple languages, including Latin and French, which he forced his son to study each day after school.

One of George's clearest memories of his childhood was sitting alone in his father's study, reviewing the day's Latin lesson, as his father watched him through the window while engaged in a conversation outdoors with their neighbor, a rabbi. The two grey-haired, bearded men could talk for hours, passionately debating the ancient translations of the Bible and the Talmud, going back and forth between English, Hebrew, and Latin.

At times, George was in awe of his father. Or maybe just scared of him. But he knew that he always had to do well on his daily Latin quiz— otherwise he wouldn't be allowed outside to run free through the corn fields that surrounded the family house.

As an only child, it could get lonely. But George never thought about it that way. He was happiest when he was alone, especially when riding his bike around town. Sometimes he'd ride through a part of town known as Little Canada, where French-speaking Canadians had settled generations earlier. Other days he'd ride through downtown, past the Napoleon and Acadian clubs. Each section of the little town had its own ethnic flavor, reflecting the town's diversity which had developed at the turn of the century when the textile mills and furniture factories were still booming.

But the Great Depression had ended all that.

Now old men with little hope and thousand-yard stares sat on their porches watching George fly by on his bicycle.

As he grew older, George swore that he would get out—that he would see the world that his father seemed satisfied to only read about in his precious books. That he would belong to something greater than this. And after his father died, the war seemed to provide that opportunity.

But George felt genuinely sorry for his mother, leaving her alone. She had spent many years caring for his ailing father. Although nearly thirty years younger, she still loved him dearly.

Long before he was born, his father had used an inheritance to invest wisely in the stock market, but had then nearly lost it all in the crash of '29. The last ten years had been particularly hard as his health began to fail. He retained just enough of an income from his investments to provide for the family. But it was barely enough. And while he spent most of his days in this study pursuing his passion for academics, George and his mother did all of the chores needed to maintain the old farmhouse.

George knew that his mother respected his father's passion for academics, but also sensed that she still yearned for the more glamorous life that she had once enjoyed in Boston and New York, before they were forced to sell their brownstones and move back to the family estate where George's father had been born during the Civil War.

Despite it all, George would often hear his mother say how much luckier they were than most families. Each Friday, for example, he would accompany his mother to volunteer at the town's small soup kitchen, serving those who had lost nearly everything in the Depression and were now barely able to feed their own children. This made a lasting impression on George.

Despite the hardships that many local families endured, George's mother often said that the small town of Gardner was a good place to grow up. But as he packed his bags and prepared to leave home, he still couldn't wait to get out of the working-class town.

"I'll come back to you, Mom" he said, trying not to react to the tears from her wrinkled eyes. "Anyways, I'll probably never even leave the country."

But as he hugged his mother and wiped her tears, George quietly hoped otherwise. He wanted to see Europe, above all else.

But nothing could prepare George for the shattered world that he was about to encounter.

Despite all the stories that my father told to my sister and I as we were growing up, he rarely spoke about the war. As a teenage boy, I would watch all the documentaries on TV, my favorite being *The World at War*.

But can children really understand?

To them, war is little more than an elaborate video game. I wanted to understand, though. I wanted my father to tell me stories of his time in Europe. But he rarely did.

I knew little about his experiences other than what was revealed by a few medals that I found one day tucked away in my mother's desk drawer. One was a Purple Heart, the other some sort of a medal given to riflemen. It was enough to get a young mind worked up, fascinated by the secret tales of war. I sensed a mystery I wanted to solve.

On one rare occasion when I was perhaps ten, my father inadvertently revealed a bit more than he meant to do. We were sitting together in the den watching John Wayne's *The Longest Day* when my dad suddenly blurted out, "It was nothing like that, for Christ's sake."

It caught me off guard. I wanted to ask him why, but I was afraid.

Then, later that night, I awoke suddenly to the sound of my father yelling. I got up from my bed, opened my bedroom door a crack, and peered down the hallway, past my sister's room, toward my parents' room. They almost always left their door slightly ajar. I could see my father sitting up in his bed as my mother put her arm around him, whispering something into his ear.

The next morning while Mom made our breakfast, I asked her about what I'd heard and seen. Her back was turned to me as she whipped the eggs, but I knew she heard me. A few minutes passed, and I asked again.

"Your father just had a bad dream, Johnny. He's fine," she said finally, though unconvincingly, before turning around to face me. "But don't say anything to him. It's better if he doesn't know that you heard."

"Was he dreaming about the war?" I asked.

My mother remained silent.

CHAPTER 2

Located on the west coast of France in the famous region of Normandy, Cherbourg was one of the first places that the Titanic visited on its fateful maiden journey. Nearly three decades later, it was overrun by the Nazis in the days following the fall of Paris. In June of 1944, it was among the first cities to be liberated by the Allied forces in the weeks following D-Day. As George walked the streets with Yvette, he noted the nineteenth-century Fort du Roule that crowned the summit of the Montagne du Roule, their favorite place in the city from where they were afforded a magnificent view of the sprawling port city below.

They descended the hill and enjoyed perfect afternoons together, riding their bikes beyond the city's limits, past the many checkpoints, to explore the coast of the Cotentin peninsula. It was a beautiful mix of high cliffs and sandy beaches, all seemingly far, far from the warfront. But they were right in the middle of one of history's greatest battles.

The frontlines were little more than an hour to the east. A few times they ventured too far, wanting to see more of the rugged cliffs and the rustic moorlands. Each time they were stopped by military police and told to turn around. Going any farther wasn't safe, as small pockets of German resistance still remained on the peninsula's northwest tip.

"Allons un peu plus loin, George. Je pense que c'est sûr," said Yvette to George. She was always the more daring one.

"No, I think we should turn around," replied George, looking over his shoulder at the guards who were still watching them.

Yvette giggled. "Pourquoi parles-tu parfois anglais avec moi?"

Her smile always had a way of lightening the mood.

"I sometimes speak English with you because your English is better than my French. Ai-je raison?" asked George.

"Tres vrai. Tres vrai." She took his hand, and together they walked back toward town

They'd met only a few months earlier at one of the US Army's training bases near Woolacombe Beach in Devonshire, a rural county in southwest England that had an uncanny topographical similarity to Normandy. George had arrived in early 1944 from Fort Benning in Georgia, where he had completed his basic training following a short stay at Fort Devens in Massachusetts, not far from his mother's home.

Yvette had been born in Sainte-Marie-du-Mont, a small village about ten kilometers south of Cherbourg along the English Channel and a few kilometers north of Carentan. Her father was a World War I naval veteran turned fisherman who knew the waters of the channel better than most.

As the German Wehrmacht had swept over the peninsula from the east following the fall of Paris, he instructed his oldest son, Luc, to take the family's fishing boat and bring Yvette to England. After arriving in Bournemouth, they contacted one of their father's oldest friends, Jacques, who had become an engineer and married an English woman following the Great War and now lived most of the year in Bournemouth. But unbeknownst to Yvette and Luc's father at the time, Jacque's wife was actually an intelligence officer for the British Army.

Had he known, perhaps things would've been different.

But for the next three years following their escape to England, Yvette and Luc lived with Jacque's family in Bournemouth and gradually became intertwined with the wife's top-secret missions, often asked to use their fishing boat to bring supplies back and forth to the Isle of Wight. With its proximity to German-occupied France, the island hosted English observation stations and transmitters, as well as an RAF radar station at Ventnor.

But as 1944 approached, Jacque and his wife's involvement in something called Operation PLUTO would eventually bring Yvette and Luc back to France.

Pipe-Lines Under The Ocean, or PLUTO, was a British operation but also employed many French engineers, including Jacque, who were familiar with the Normandy region. The plan was to construct undersea oil pipelines beneath the English Channel between the south coast of England and western France, presumably in support of an Allied invasion that everyone knew was imminent. As the operation continued well into 1944, Yvette and Luc became more and more involved, often using their fishing boat as cover for the Army divers working the pipeline below.

In March of 1944, Yvette and Luc were brought to one of the US Army's training bases near Woolacombe Beach in Devonshire. They met with American Army officers tasked with planning one part of what was being called Operation Overlord.

"Vous venez d'une ville appelée Sainte-Marie-du-Mont en Normandie," asked one of the officers in broken French.

Yvette smiled. "It's okay. You can speak English. My brother and I speak a little."

The officer nodded. "We're told that both of you're from Normandy and have been helping with a project on the Isle of Wight."

"Yes," replied Luc. "My sister and I've been living with a friend of our father's in Bournemouth since we were forced to leave our home in 1940."

"Do you want to go back?" asked another officer matter-of-factly.

Yvette and Luc looked at each other. "The invasion?"

Both officers nodded. "Yes, Operation Overlord, and we need translators who are familiar with the area near your home."

"Why the area near our home?" asked Yvette.

The two officers looked at each other, not quite sure of how much they were allowed to reveal.

"Tell us," said Yvette.

"The beach near your town."

"Oui," answered Yvette. "Sainte Marie du Mont beach."

"We're calling it something different," he replied. "Utah. Utah Beach."

Almost immediately, Yvette and her brother joined at least a dozen other young French citizens from Normandy who resettled in Devonshire, each assigned to a different unit of the US Army's 4th Infantry Division.

Luc disliked the arrogance displayed by the majority of the Americans in his unit, but Yvette was attracted to their swagger. But in the weeks that followed, she became drawn instead to a quiet, skinny soldier named George. He was more reserved than many of the other Americans, and he and Yvette had little in common. But as the weeks passed, and March became April, and then May, they became almost inseparable.

The problem was their relationship was forbidden, and their constant interactions with one another had caught the attention of George's unit leader, Sergeant Cummings.

"I see that you speak French," said the sergeant one day, seated at his desk in his tent, as George stood at attention.

"Yes, sir," replied George, "But not very well."

Sergeant Cummings sized him up. "I could easily kick you out of this unit and send you back stateside, you know."

"Yes, sir. I understand," replied George, realizing the sergeant knew about him and Yvette.

But the sergeant seemed to have something else in mind. "How did you learn French? School?"

"Yes, sir. Four years in high school, and my father taught me after school."

The sergeant laughed, lightening the mood. "I know how that is. My father used to hound me after school, too."

"In French, sir?"

"Hell, no! My old man didn't speak anything except military," barked Sergeant Cummings. "I spent my afternoons listening to his stories about the Great War. He fought near here, in the Somme and Verdun. I think I know more about France than just about anyone else here. All those stories. In another month, I expect to be on those same fields where he fought a generation ago."

"Yes, sir," answered George, who had no idea where the sergeant was going with this.

Cummings seemed to stare off into space for a few minutes before continuing. "George, I got a proposition for you."

"Sir?"

"How would you like to be *allowed* to spend time with that pretty little French girl?"

In early June, Yvette and George relocated with their new unit to Southampton, as preparations for the invasion reached a zenith. It was nearly impossible to move through the narrow streets of the shipbuilding town as tens of thousands of troops continued to arrive, doing their best to release the tension in the days leading up to the invasion. Yvette and George had learned that they would not be departing with the first ships, but instead in the days following that first wave.

Years later, George came to understand that this had probably saved his life.

The sergeant had reassigned Yvette to be a translator for a small group of soldiers, including George, all of whom spoke French to varying degrees and who bore the responsibility of establishing contact with the

French underground near Utah Beach. Yvette was the logical choice, given her knowledge of the shoreline. Other soldiers in the small unit also had clear purposes, with demolitions and diversionary tactics. But George had little to offer, other than his attraction to Yvette, which the other men in the unit understandably envied.

But something that the sergeant had said back in Devonshire stuck with George.

"Understand this, private," said Sergeant Cummings before he had dismissed George from his tent, "these translators are critical to the success of this mission. They'll be our eyes and ears after we land on Utah beach, move to secure Cherbourg, and head east to connect with the first Infantry Division at Caen. From there, it's on to Paris, then across the Rhine, and all the way to Berlin. Then we all go home. But it all starts in Normandy." The sergeant stood up from behind his desk and walked over to George. "You keep that lady of yours alive, George, and we all have a better chance of getting home before Christmas. She, and others like her, are the key to us breaking out from Normandy."

On the night of June 5, Yvette and George climbed to the top of Cottington's Hill just outside of Southampton overlooking the docks where the last of the troops and equipment were making their way along the "hards," the cement docks that had been constructed only recently to hasten the loading of the warships, supply ships, and troop carriers that would join a fleet of more than a thousand ships crossing the English Channel to smash into Hitler's Atlantic Wall.

"C'est un spectacle," said Yvette, as she pulled George's arms tight around her.

"Quite the sight."

"Can this be the turning point?" she asked, as her gaze moved west toward the George V dry-dock where she could see the Mulberry Harbours that continued to be constructed, later to be floated across the channel to serve as docks on the beaches of Normandy.

"The Russians are already in Poland and could enter Germany later this year. It's going to be a race to Berlin."

For a moment, Yvette sat quietly before saying, "Mais Berlin semble si loin de la Normandie."

George understood as he squeezed her tighter. "You'll be home soon enough to see your parents."

"Mais qu'en est-il de nous? What if the Army doesn't let you stay with me? What if they make you go across France, all the way to Germany?

"Then I'll come back to you when the war is over," said George, matter-of-factly.

"Promettre?" She looked into his eyes.

"Promise." They kissed.

Just then, a tremendous roar approached them from behind. They stood up and looked to the night sky to see one of the most awe-inspiring sights that either had experienced. Flying at no more than a few hundred feet above the fields of Southampton were hundreds, if not thousands, of British and American warplanes, all headed in one direction: east, across the channel.

It'd begun.

"They must be coming out of Upottery," said George, barely audible over the deafening sounds of the invasion force. "A guy in my unit was stationed there last year. It's where the 101st was training."

"The 101st?" yelled Yvette.

"They're the paratroopers, landing in Normandy ahead of the fleet."

"Son passe, George! Son passe! Viva la France!" exclaimed Yvette, waving her arms as the massive air armada continued to fly overhead. "Viva la France!"

George and Yvette remained on that hill throughout the night, watching as the lights of the ships moved away from the docks and headed out into the channel. There was little to be said, both knowing that many of the men on those ships would never return, sacrificing themselves on the beaches of Normandy for a higher purpose not likely fully understood by the nineteen-year-olds who formed the tip of the Allied spear.

History would later refer to them as the Greatest Generation, but as two of its children sat atop the hill watching history unfold before them, all they could do was to hold each other tightly and dream of a day when the world would again be at peace.

CHAPTER THREE

In the summer of 1990, I returned home following my graduation from Bethany College in Lindsborg, Kansas, to inform my father I'd joined the Peace Corps and would be leaving for Africa in a few weeks. I expected that he would do his best to talk me out of my decision. And I was ready for it. But his reaction was quite different, and it surprised me.

"You know, Johnny, I left home when I was nineteen. I couldn't wait to get away from my mother," he said, as we chatted on the front lawn of the house, beneath the maple trees.

"You joined the military," I said, remembering his stories.

"Yes, my way out," said Dad. "Just as your way out is to join the Peace Corps and go to Africa."

I looked at my father. He seemed unusually at peace with my announcement. "You never talked much about the war when we were kids," I said, not really expecting a response.

But something was different this time.

"It wasn't something that your mother needed to hear," he said, looking down.

"You never talked to her about it?" I asked, surprised.

"Very little," admitted Dad, sitting down on the front doorstep and resting his cane against the side of the house. "She knew about my injury, of course, but not the details of how it happened." He rubbed his left leg. "I was definitely fortunate to make it back alive. This leg has been a nuisance over the years, but could have been a lot worse."

I was confused. "But you told Andrea and I that you had been shot by a German sniper while in France. Didn't Mom know that?"

"Yes. But it wasn't the real story."

I was stunned. "But why? Why not tell her the truth?"

Dad motioned for me to sit down beside him. "When I first met your mother more than thirty years ago, we had so many obstacles to overcome. She was Catholic. I was Protestant. Both of our mothers were devout in their churches and struggled to accept the other's points of view. I was basically a small-town boy. Your mother, a big-city girl. She was nearly thirty when we met, and I don't believe she had any prior relationships." He paused, seemingly collecting his thoughts, before continuing.

"So I decided it was best not to talk with her about any of my prior relationships. We had enough against us."

I knew a little about my father's life before he met my mother, but he had kept that part of his life mostly a secret from my sister and me.

But didn't our mother at least know about it?

"I don't understand. What does your injury have to do with prior relationships?" I asked. "I know you were married before Mom. But that was after the war. Right?"

We all keep things hidden, tucked away in the deep recesses of our memories. My father was no different.

"You're *choosing* to go the Africa, Johnny," he began. "It may be the right choice, or it may not. Either way, you'll deal with the consequences. But one way or the other, it's likely to be an experience that'll change you, that'll shape the rest of your life. And when you return, you'll share some of those experiences with others. But some, you'll keep inside, if for no other reason than you believe it's the best way forward. I chose to keep things from your mother, because I thought it was the best way for our relationship to move forward."

"But maybe Mom could have handled it."

"Maybe," replied Dad. "But it would've always resurfaced, and I didn't want that. As I said, your mother and I'd enough to overcome. We didn't need to be burdened by the past."

Burdened by the past. What the hell did that mean?

He looked at me. "You're at the beginning of your life, Johnny. I'm sixty-four and in the twilight of mine." My father reached for his cane and put his arm on the front doorstep to give himself some extra leverage as he stood up. "Come on, let's take a drive."

As we drove down the street from our house atop Bickford Hill, turning left onto Lawrence Street and then right onto Cross Street, we passed by Stone Field, where I'd played baseball throughout high school.

At the corner of Cross and Elm Streets sat my elementary school, which had previously been the high school where my father had taught French and Latin for nearly twenty years until his retirement in the mid-seventies.

We then continued on Elm Street until we entered the rotary near the town's museum and turned left onto Central Street. It took us past the local skating rink and Greenwood Swimming Pool, packed with families looking for some reprieve from the summer humidity. Before turning right onto Crystal Lake Drive, my father pointed at his childhood home.

"That was the place I needed to get away from. The Army was nothing more than my way out. On the day I left my mother, I came to this lake and stared out across her calm waters, wondering what life had in store for me. If I'd known, maybe I would've stayed, although eventually I would've been drafted." He paused. "Maybe everything would've been different, maybe not."

Dad parked the car off one of the narrow lanes that ran along the lakefront. As I got out of the car, I looked across the lake and saw the pump station that still provided the town with its water supply. The water was always clear and calm and no different on this day.

Dad and I walked a few hundred feet to his favorite bench and sat. A light breeze lifted my father's cap.

"Before you leave for Africa, Johnny, I want to tell you a story. The story of my time in France."

CHAPTER FOUR

Since 1940, the village of Sainte-Marie-du-Mont had been occupied by nearly one hundred German soldiers who used the local church tower as an observation post to survey the surrounding countryside and coastline. The Germans suspected that the expected invasion would occur near Calais, much farther north where the channel was narrowest.

But in the early hours of June 6, 1944, this small garrison of Axis fighters were undoubtedly surprised to see members of the 501st Parachute Infantry Regiment of the 101st Airborne Division slowly descending from the sky. These elite American soldiers were tasked with securing what was called Zone C, immediately inland from Utah Beach, in charge of clearing a route for the tens of thousands of soldiers arriving by sea.

Also looking up into the sky in those early hours of June 6 was Yvette's mother and father, who for more than four years had collaborated with the French underground to disrupt the Germans as they attempted to build their defenses along the coast. While their efforts hadn't succeeded in stopping the completion of the coastal fortifications, they'd been successful in the days leading up to June 6 in destroying many of the bridges and railroad lines leading onto the peninsula, hindering German ability to resupply once the invasion was underway.

But as the Americans descended from the sky, they were completely vulnerable to German machine gun nests. Yvette's mother and father understood the danger and ran from house to house in a call to arms. Any local inhabitant with a gun was expected to engage and distract the enemy, giving the Americans time to land and secure a foothold.

It was shortly before 2 am when the first shots were fired.

The fighting became fierce. Most of the locals were armed only with old rifles and were no match for the Germans. But they held out for as long as they could, focusing on the area around the church where the majority of the paratroopers planned on landing. The surrounding villages, including the nearby St-Mere-Eglise, had also risen up against the Germans and were waging similar battles.

Yvette's house was only a few blocks from l'Eglise St. Hilaire—the smaller of the two local churches—at the intersection of Rue D'Eglise and Rue de Mont, right in the center of Zone C. The latter ran perpendicular to Sainte Marie de Mont beach—which history would rename Utah Beach—continuing inland to the center of the village at l'Église Notre Dame, where the paratroopers were landing. The former ran horizontally to the beach, and although it was by no means a main road, it was extensively used by the Germans to bring supplies in and out of the village.

The Allied paratroopers were charged with securing these roads and meeting up with the landing forces shortly after dawn as they made their way off the beach. Yvette's father, who had been in continual contact with his old friend, Jacques, knew the Allies' plan and understood that its success depended on the ability of the paratroopers to secure these two roads. If they failed, then the landing forces would be vulnerable, perhaps leading to catastrophe. Yvette's father knew the significance of the moment. Liberation was close at hand, and all hands on deck were needed to ensure its success.

Crouching behind a stone wall on the edge of his property with a view of the church, he glanced back toward his house and motioned for his wife to descend into their cellar. On the other side of Rue de Mont he could see three of his neighbors taking up similar positions behind walls and barns. From the center of the village, near Eglise Notre Dame, emanated the relentless sound of gunfire as the paratroopers continued to land. Yvette's father could only hope that his fellow villagers were able to provide enough cover for the majority of the brave liberators to land safely.

Nearly an hour after the first paratrooper had landed, the gunfire grew louder, and Yvette's father knew that the battle was moving in his direction. Soon he could hear men yelling in German.

Were they retreating or fighting their way to the beach?

He listened, hoping to hear English, proof that the paratroopers had landed successfully and had moved into position to cut off the Germans. He cocked his rifle and prepared himself for the engagement, signaling to his neighbors to do the same.

But just then, the early morning skies were lit up like a noon-time sun. Yvette's father covered his eyes, temporarily blinded by the flashes. He had been told to expect this. Tracer fire to warn the resisters. The battleships had arrived offshore, preparing to begin their bombardment of the coastline in advance of the beach landings.

It was just before 5 am on June 6, 1944, when the massive guns opened fire. The onslaught continued for nearly an hour.

When it was over, little remained of the coastal towns.

CHAPTER FIVE

Yvette and George crossed the English Channel on June 8 aboard the USS *Bayfield* along with more than a thousand other troops and support personnel. The five-hundred-foot war vessel had already made four crossings since the June 6 landings, continuing to follow the same route each time.

After leaving Southampton, it joined a larger flotilla about thirty kilometers southeast of the Isle of Wight. From there, the ships broke up into five convoys heading for the different landing beaches.

On this day, the *Bayfield* headed toward Utah Beach.

The crossing took about three hours. The waters of the channel were choppy but calm compared to the harsh conditions that the first wave of the invasion force had endured a few days earlier. Nevertheless, George and Yvette still held tightly to the guard rail as they stood on the main deck of Bayfield's starboard side.

"Qu'est-ce que tu crois qu'on va trouver là-bas, George?" asked Yvette.

George knew how worried she was about her father and mother. Had they survived the battle for the beachhead? George had his doubts, but he did his best to reassure her, nonetheless. "Je suis sûr qu'ils vont bien. They know the area well. They would've found a place to hide."

But Yvette knew her father would never have hid. He would've been right in the middle of the battle.

The *Bayfield* set anchor about a kilometer offshore. George, Yvette, and the other members of their small unit waited their turn to climb down the ropes into the Higgins boats to take them ashore. In the coming days, most troops crossed the channel aboard troop transports that then docked with the giant Mulberry harbors that George and Yvette had seen being readied at Southampton. But they'd yet to be floated across the channel.

"Es tu effrayé?" smiled George, trying to lighten the mood as they and the other members of their unit prepared to descend the rope ladder.

Yvette shook her head, but her expression said something different.

Once they were in the Higgins boat, they began the short trip to the beach. With so many other small boats headed in the same direction, the waters became even choppier, causing many of the passengers to vomit uncontrollably. George could see that Yvette was covering her mouth.

About fifteen minutes later their boat arrived ashore, lowered its ramp, and gave them their first clear view of Utah Beach.

It was almost unrecognizable to Yvette, who had spent much of her youth playing on the sandy beach. Unlike Omaha Beach to the east, which had sheer cliffs and narrow beaches, Utah was made up of sandy dunes filled with hare's tail grass and sea holly, which gave way to beautiful tidal wetlands.

But now those pristine dunes had been flattened and transformed into a giant command post of hastily erected tents along sandy roads filled with half-tracks and tanks moving inland. An endless stream of soldiers flowed ashore, passing the bombed-out remains of the German gun emplacements. One of George's unit members flagged down a passing jeep that was headed in their general direction. At first, the driver hesitated, but then he saw Yvette.

"Jump in," he said. "The lady can ride in front with me."

George sat immediately behind Yvette and kept his hand on her shoulder as they passed over the dunes and entered the tidal wetlands, which extended for nearly a kilometer inland. During high tide, they could only be traversed along the few roads that the paratroopers had been tasked to keep open.

On this day, some of the tanks and half-tracks coming up from the beach had assumed that the current low tide would allow them to move off the roads. They had been mistaken, and dozens had become mired in the quicksand-like conditions as George and Yvette's jeep passed them by.

Continuing to move inland, Yvette kept an eye out for any familiar signs of her childhood home.

But few could be found.

As a child, she often rode her bike along Les Granchettes, bordered on either side by eight-foot-tall hedgerows, until she came to the Bay of Veys. On some days, she turned left and pedaled toward the beach, and on other days she turned right and rode along the edge of the Canal de Carentan a la Mer, before circling back home along the Douve River.

Along the way she passed by manor houses, farms, and castles. One of her favorite places to stop was the Sainte-Marie-du-Mont manor with its hipped slate roof, expansive gardens, and friendly jardinier, who would always let her refill her thermos with rainwater from the cistern. Nothing seemed familiar now. It was all gone. All in ruins. As their jeep moved slowly down the street, Yvette squeezed George's hand and pointed in the direction of bombed-out building shells just ahead.

"Est-ce l'église?" asked George, knowing that Yvette's house was near one of the town's oldest churches.

"Oui." Yvette's response was barely audible

"You can drop us off over there," said George to the driver.

"Why?" he answered incredulously. "Nothing here. This whole area was leveled by the naval barrage just before the landings began."

"It's okay. This is where we need to be," said George.

As they climbed out of the jeep, George and the other members of the unit surveyed the surrounding area.

The driver was right. Not much left.

It was apparent that the Navy had indeed targeted the area with a heavy bombardment from their sixteen-inch guns in an attempt to destroy the German gun emplacements scattered along the coastline near Saint Marie du Mont. In those early hours of June 6, a heavy fog layer over the area had made it nearly impossible for the shelling to be accurate. Some of the shells had found their mark, but most had gone astray, landing on nearby buildings, including L'eglise St. Hilaire near Yvette's home.

"Maybe they got out in time," said George, doing his best to console her.

"Non, ils étaient là. Mes parents étaient ici," she replied sharply, sifting through the ruins of her childhood neighborhood. "Je veux voir leurs corps."

George glanced at the other members of the unit.

They all shrugged.

"Maybe a mass grave?" whispered one, trying not to let Yvette overhear.

George shook his head. *Now what?*

"We need to get to Cherbourg," said the unit's leader, a corporal not much older than George. "That's our mission. Nothing we can do here."

Yvette glared at him. "Baise toi. This is *my* mission. Ma famille."

"With all due respect. It's not," countered the corporal. "Your job is to translate for us and help us make contact with the Resistance near Cherbourg."

But Yvette waved her hand dismissively and walked away, and George had no choice but to follow.

"Let her go!" yelled the corporal to George. "We have to get to Cherbourg."

But George kept after Yvette.

CHAPTER SIX

The Allied commanders in charge of developing the plans for the invasion of Europe understood that one of the keys to its success would be their ability to secure deep-water ports. This would allow reinforcements and supplies to be brought directly from the United States.

Cherbourg, at the tip of the Cotentin peninsula, was an essential capture.

But to land forces near the port on June 6 would've made it too easy for the Germans to cut off the peninsula, trapping the Allies. So it was decided to secure the beachheads along the Normandy coast first; link up the five main invasion forces that had landed at Utah, Omaha, Gold, Juno, and Sword Beaches; and then move to take Cherbourg before the end of June.

But in the hours and days following the landings, that plan seemed in jeopardy.

Although the landing forces on Utah experienced little resistance, as soon as they'd moved inland to link up with the airborne forces that had fought their way out of St. Marie du Mont and St. Mere Eglise, the fighting had become much more intense, especially around Carentan.

The Navy's efforts to destroy the majority of the German garrisons on the morning of June 6 had failed, although Resistance fighters had fought bravely alongside the paratroopers in an effort to secure the roads moving inland from Utah. Vicious house-to-house fighting continued for days until the Allies got the upper hand and took the towns between the beach and Carentan.

The Germans counterattacked near the Douvre River, but were unable to maintain the offensive when supplies couldn't get through, forcing the German commanders to abandon the eastern peninsula and turning their efforts to holding Cherbourg to the west and Caen to the east.

The mission of George and Yvette's small unit, along with dozens of other similar units, involved rounding up Resistance fighters from across the eastern peninsula and following behind the Allied forces advancing toward Cherbourg.

Once these forces had cleared the German garrisons surrounding the city, the specialized units and the local fighters would move in, establish contact with Resistance fighters laying low within the city, and work together to drive out the remaining German forces, in hopes of avoiding the bloody, house-to-house combat that was seen in Carentan.

But as Yvette continued to search for her parents in the ruins of Saint Marie du Mont, it became uncertain whether she could continue the mission.

The other unit members were growing impatient and had threatened to inform the regiment commanders of the situation.

George was stuck in the middle.

He understood his role, as Sgt. Cummings back in England had laid out for him. He had no particular expertise. He was no saboteur. Neither was he a particularly good marksman. But what he was, was the boyfriend.

Perhaps the sergeant had known what would happen when Yvette returned home. Perhaps he knew that she would lose sight of the overall mission. So George understood now that his role comprised keeping her focused on the reason she had been sent back to France after more than four years in England.

"I don't care about Cherbourg, George. I never did. I wanted to come home. That's all. But now look at it. Tout est détruit," she said, wiping away the tears as she continued sifting through the ruins of her childhood neighborhood, quickly losing hope that she'd ever find her parents.

George sat down on the remains of a stone wall that had once surrounded L'eglise St. Hilaire and motioned for Yvette to join him.

Reluctantly, she did.

"I know how difficult this is," began George, reaching out to put his hand on Yvette's leg. But she pushed it away.

"No, tu ne comprends pas. None of you do," she said. "You don't know anything about this place. This is my home. I grew up here. Went to school just down the street. That's where I learned to speak English." She looked off at the ruins in the distance. "I used to go to this church with my parents and brother every Sunday, sometimes volunteering to help clean up the grounds." She paused. "How would you feel if your home had been destroyed and your parents probably killed?"

George thought about his mother, the house he had grown up in, and about Crystal Lake, something he hadn't often done since arriving in Europe six months earlier. He had wanted so much to get away from his mother, and from the memory of his father. But mostly he had wanted to stand on his own two feet.

But as he sat next to Yvette on that stone fence, it all seemed so surreal. Less than a year earlier he had graduated from high school and had only turned nineteen a few weeks ago. He hadn't thought too much about what would happen after the war. But as he watched the tears falling from Yvette's eyes, he knew that he wanted to be with her.

"This will all be over someday, Yvette—"

Yvette cut him off. "And what, George? Then we can be together? Do you really think that's possible? After Cherbourg, you'll move on with your regiment across France, and I'll be left here to pick up the pieces."

"I told you, I'll come back for you. This war will be over in a year, maybe earlier. I'll be back."

"Back to what?" replied Yvette, incredulously. "Look around. It's all gone."

"Then you'll come to America with me."

She stood up. "You don't understand, do you? *This* is my home."

"And we're fighting for it. We're here to liberate all of you."

She laughed. "Liberate! So now you're saviors" she said incredulously. "You didn't even know anything about my home before this war began. Don't pretend you care. All of you just want to win the war and go home. We'll be left here to rebuild our lives."

"That's not fair, Yvette. I *do* care. I care about *you*."

"That's my point. If you really care about me, then you'd understand how I feel. This place is who I am."

"But it doesn't matter where we are, so long as we're together."

"No, ça compte. Home is all that matters. You're running away from yours, right?" Her gaze was sharp. "It's why you joined this war. But anyone who runs away from their home, is lost."

And then she walked away.

My father paused in telling his story and stared out across Crystal Lake as we sat together on the bench beneath an old maple tree. I could tell that it was difficult for him to share all of this with me.

But at that moment, I felt closer to my father than I ever had before.

He was sharing a part of himself that had been long buried, and he had chosen this moment to open up. Maybe it was my pending departure with the Peace Corps to Africa, or perhaps not. But whatever the reason, I was hearing a story that had been long hidden, but never forgotten. A part of me felt that he was telling me just for that reason, so that it would never be forgotten.

"I've thought about her words a lot over the years. It was hard to hear, but she was right," said my father, nodding. "I'd run away from home looking for myself. But until I came to terms with the way that I'd been raised by my mother and father, I would always be lost."

He turned to me. "It took another twenty years after the war ended before I really made peace with my mother, and unfortunately it was toward the end of her life. It wasn't that she had ever done anything wrong. But when you're raised by two strong-willed people who have a very fixed way of looking at things, it's hard to find your own space. My mother's focus was always caring for my father, because he was so much older. It's not that she forgot about me. But I often felt that I was in third place in her heart. First came my father, then her church, then me. I realize now that she found comfort and purpose in her faith, and I regret not understanding that sooner. And trying to raise a child and care for an older, sick man was made ten times harder by the reality of the Depression. So I turned inward and learned to do things myself. It was the start of that fierce independence that drove me away from home and into the Army."

"Did your mother ever understand why you left?" I asked, not really sure what to say to my father.

"Oh, I think she understood right away but was never able to tell me. And that's why I'm telling you all of this, Johnny, now, before you leave."

My dad put his hand on my leg.

"It's ironic that we hate certain things about our parents, but then when we become parents ourselves, we do things in the same way as they'd done. It doesn't make much sense, but you see it over and over again. And I guess I've been no different. But I've always loved you and your sister very much, perhaps more than either of you could ever understand."

For one of the few times in my young life, I saw my father's eyes begin to water. Then he composed himself and continued. "But in many ways, my approach with the two of you has been very similar to how I was raised by my parents. Probably too strict. And now you're leaving for very much the same reason why I left home before the war."

I was speechless. I sat there with my father on that bench, the same bench that we would share many times over the next thirty years, hearing a confession of sorts. I was too young to really understand the entire matter of what he was saying. But it stuck with me, and was a small piece to a much larger puzzle that I would continue putting together for many years.

My dad continued. "Anyways, you go to Africa, Johnny. I can't say I want you to, but I do understand it. I hope someday, perhaps while I'm still alive, you'll come to understand what Yvette said to me that day. Anyone who runs away from home is lost, until they're able to confront the reason why they run."

Unfortunately, it would take me many, many years to arrive at that understanding.

CHAPTER SEVEN

The final assault on Cherbourg began on June 22.

Although German resistance had been initially strong, Allied forces systematically cleared them from their concrete pillboxes and bunkers, while the Navy shelled their fortifications on the edge of the city. Days earlier, George had pleaded with Yvette to accompany their unit to a small suburb of Cherbourg called Octeville. In the end, she had reluctantly agreed, but had made it clear to the commanders that once Cherbourg was liberated, she would return to her hometown and continue the search for her parents.

Upon arrival in Octeville, she had contacted members of the French underground who had been operating in and around Cherbourg since the Germans had first arrived in late 1940. These operatives knew the location of the German Kriegsmarine naval intelligence headquarters, which had been responsible for overseeing much of the German Navy's operations in the Atlantic, including U-boat activity.

Using this critical information, British and Allied commandos raided the headquarters on June 26, capturing dozens of German officers and more than five hundred men. The success of the mission brought Yvette to the attention of Allied commanders on the peninsula, the sort of attention that irritated the other members of their small unit, all proud men who didn't take kindly to the fact of the unit's only woman getting all the glory.

"Ignore them," said George one afternoon following a particularly big blowout between her and other members of the unit in the mess hall. "Ils sont juste jaloux."

"Bâtards!" yelled Yvette, loud enough so the others would hear as they left the hall. "Ils se soucient seulement de leur propre gloire."

One turned around and snapped back at Yvette. "You French bitch! We're here because you couldn't protect your own land. Without us you'd still be slaves to the Krauts."

"Et vous êtes tous esclaves de votre propre ego," snarled Yvette, never one to back down.

George knew that was probably the final straw that would put an end to their unit. But it didn't really matter.

In the days that followed, Yvette's sources provided more information that was used by the Allies to force the surrender of the main German force in Cherbourg who had made their last stand at a fortification near the harbor. By early July, all fighting around the city had ended, save for small pockets of German resistance mostly on the northwest tip of the peninsula near Auderville.

Not wanting to risk any casualties with a direct engagement, the Allies ignored these forces, knowing that they would eventually surrender once their supplies were exhausted. Nevertheless, military police were careful not to allow anyone past Éculleville.

It was near this line that George and Yvette often walked during the first few weeks of July, as George awaited the orders that he knew would send him elsewhere, and Yvette prepared to return to Saint Marie du Mont. But despite everything happening around them and not knowing what would happen next, they took solace in each other's company, exploring the coast's rugged cliffs and rustic moorland landscapes.

"I wish you could have seen this countryside before the war," said Yvette, sitting beside him on the outer grounds of the sixteenth-century Château de Nacqueville and gardens, her long dark hair falling over her shoulders, released from the confines of her military helmet. "Il n'y a pas de lieu plus beau."

It was hard to argue with her.

George hadn't traveled much growing up, except for a few trips to New York City on the train to see his aunt. But it was hard to imagine a more beautiful and tranquil place in the world than the Cotentin peninsula in summer. And unlike the destruction found in cities such as Cherbourg, the surrounding countryside had remained mostly untouched. Although the Germans had occupied the chateau for much of the war, even they had appreciated its beauty, save for some of the trees, which they felled in order to fortify their Atlantic Wall.

"Tell me about your home. What are the summers like?" asked Yvette, leading back to get the full sun on her face.

George's mind went immediately to Crystal Lake. "During the summer, I would always awake early in the morning to do my chores around the house and then have the rest of the day to myself. I loved riding my bike along the edge of this small lake near my home. Sometimes, when it was hot and humid, I'd lean my bike against this big tree near the dam, climb to the top of this huge boulder that sat at the water's edge, and jump in. I never told my mother because I knew she wouldn't have approved. But it felt so good to jump from that height into the cool waters."

Yvette smiled. "I don't see you as much of a daredevil."

George smiled back. "No, I guess not. But it made me feel free."

She understood. "Oui, my parents were always very protective of me, too. My brother could do anything he wanted. But not me. I was always supposed to be the dainty girl who would grow up to marry someone from the village."

George looked away. "Do you think you'll still do that? Marry someone from the village?"

"Je ne sais pas," admitted Yvette. "Who knows if we'll even survive."

"Don't say that. You'll live a long life. Both of us will." George paused, remembering their blow-up a few weeks earlier. But then he continued, cautiously. "I just wish we could live that life *together*."

Yvette took George's hand in hers. "One day at a time. Tout ce que nous pouvons faire est de vivre un jour à la fois."

George felt a tingle of hope pass over him.

They sat there together on the grounds of that chateau for most of the afternoon watching the birds feeding from the purple lilac, yellow mimosa, and blossoming cherry trees, seemingly so free and unencumbered by the world around them.

Not yet ready to return to their base at Fort du Roule, they left the chateau's grounds and ventured west along the narrow Rous Des Douanes, moving closer and closer to the security line near Éculleville, beyond which the Allies didn't maintain complete control. As had occurred multiple times already over the course of the previous few weeks, they were stopped by security guards just to the east of the town, usually the same security guards, a couple of kids even younger than themselves.

"How about letting us pass into the town?" asked Yvette. "We'll come right back."

"You always ask. Why would it be any different today?" replied one of the guards.

"There hasn't been any sign of Germans for days, has there?" persisted Yvette.

The guards looked at each other. "No, but we have orders not to let anyone pass. Anyways, what's so important here that you keep coming back?"

Even George wasn't quite of the answer to that. "You see that church just down the street?" she said, pointing to the steeple that rose above the small shops that lined both sides of the street up ahead.

The guards nodded.

"My parents were married in that church, and I haven't seen it in many years. So how about it? Just a quick look, and we'll come right back."

"We can get in a lot of trouble, you know," said one of the guards, looking in the direction of the small command center that the Allies had set up nearby.

Yvette shrugged and smiled. "Je promets. Right back."

It was hard to resist her charm.

The small town of Eculleville was eerily quiet as Yvette and George walked her narrow, cobblestone streets. During normal times, the cafes would've been filled with people sharing the latest village gossip and enjoying an afternoon coffee and croissant. But now, not a soul. The locals had evacuated the town but had been promised by the Allies that they could probably return in less than a month after the few remaining German units either surrendered or slipped away between the checkpoints.

"This probably isn't a good idea," said George as they tried unsuccessfully to open the front doors of the church.

"Allez, trouvons un moyen à l'intérieur." She was always stubborn.

They found an open window around the back of the church, climbed through, and made their way around the back of the altar to the nave. From the pillows and blankets that were strewn about the pews, it appeared that the church had served as a shelter, perhaps as the Germans were retreating to the far corner of the peninsula following the landings at Omaha and Utah.

George and Yvette found a place to sit down and stared at the crucifix hanging above the altar.

"Do you believe in Him?" asked Yvette.

"I suppose so." Religion was definitely not a topic that George was comfortable talking about.

"You said that both of your parents were religious, right?" asked Yvette, admiring a few of the stained-glass windows that had somehow remained intact.

"My mother always went to church, but my father was more of a scholar of the Bible than a believer."

"So which are you? Scholar or believer?"

"My father made me read the Bible in Greek and Latin. To me, it was just homework."

"But you believe in God, don't you?" pressed Yvette.

George chuckled.

"What's so funny?" asked Yvette.

"In all those afternoons I spent with my father translating the Bible back and forth between languages, never once did he ask me if I actually believed any of what I was translating."

"But I'm asking you now," said Yvette pointedly.

George thought about it as he stared at the crucifix hanging just above them. "After what we've seen over these past few months, I don't see how there could be a God."

Yvette nodded, as if she had expected the answer. "But I do."

Her answer surprised George. "Even after what happened to your parents and your home?"

"Especially after that."

"I don't get it," admitted George.

"I think this war either drives people closer to God or farther away from Him. Je me sens plus proche de Dieu."

George couldn't disagree with that logic.

After a few minutes of sitting silently together, Yvette and George walked out of the church and began slowly strolling back toward the checkpoint when suddenly an all too familiar sound approached them from overhead. George heard it first.

"Incoming!" he screamed, as the shell came in over the town. He pushed Yvette into the doorway of a nearby cafe and dove on top of her.

They both covered their heads as the shell landed just down the street from their position.

And then another came in, landing a little closer and covering them with dust and debris. And then another.

CHAPTER EIGHT

I arrived in the east African city of Bukavu, on the Zaire side of the border with Rwanda, in the late summer of 1990 to begin three months of intensive language training and become a Peace Corps volunteer teacher.

Teaching of any kind had never been on my radar, even though my father had been a high school teacher for nearly twenty years. But like many twenty-two-year-olds, I'd no idea what I wanted to do with my life, despite having completed my bachelor's degree in economics. Sensing my indecision, one of my college professors recommended the Corps as a way of seeing the world and "finding myself." But since the Peace Corps wasn't interested in economics teachers, I became a math teacher.

Rwanda was still years away from the genocide that would capture the world's attention, and Zaire was still under the decades-long authoritarian rule of Mobutu Sese Seko. But revolution was definitely in the air, and even a naive kid could feel the tension building, sometimes spilling into the streets of the lakeside city of Bukavu.

During colonial times, it'd been described as a lost paradise, a misted Shangri-La of wide, bougainvillea-laden streets and villas with lush gardens along the shoreline of Lake Kivu.

But the city where I spent the first three months of my African adventure was a far, far cry from that paradise.

Once part of the ancient territory of the Bushi Kingdom, Bukavu had been first colonized by Arabs, and then Europeans at the end of the nineteenth century. The city was officially established in 1901 by Belgian colonial authorities who remained for more than a half century. They were attracted, in part, by the subtropical climate and picturesque setting, the city built upon five peninsulas that jetted out into the lake, and often described as "a green hand, dipped in the lake."

But mostly, the colonialists were attracted by the area's natural treasure trove of gold and diamonds. Sadly, those riches had served to create a seedy—often violent—underworld that had financed countless tribal wars and revolutions.

My first glimpse of that underworld came within days of my arrival at the colonial-era Catholic boarding school, built by Belgium missionaries along the shoreline of Lake Kivu in the early twentieth century. The departure of the colonial powers had left the expansive compound in ill-repair for decades before it was acquired and renovated by the Peace Corps to use as a French-language-immersion school for their volunteers who would serve throughout central Africa.

Each morning, following the first period of language instruction, the other volunteers and I were met near the school's main gate by dozens of local teenagers who had come from a nearby slum called Goma to sell candy and little trinkets to support their families.

One of those teens was named Jean-Pierre. He seemed a bit older than the others, and stood out for the basic English skills that he had acquired over the years by coming to the school each day to sell his wares to the American volunteers. At first, though, I assumed he was no different than the other local kids who were all dressed in torn jeans and dirty T-shirts. Some were barefoot, others wore sandals, and most carried their products in wooden trays that were tied around their necks and rested near their wastes.

But something else was different about Jeanne Pierre than just his ability to use English slang. Maybe it was the way his eyes darted back and forth. Or how he seemed to personally know the guards who always lurked nearby, supposedly there to protect the young American volunteers from the ubiquitous pick-pocketers.

On one particular day, I saw Jeanne Pierre engaged in an intense conversation with one of the guards, clearly a supervisor of the others.

They were both looking intently at a small shiny object that Jeanne Pierre was holding between two fingers. It definitely wasn't a piece of candy.

I looked around to see if any of the other volunteers were observing the same encounter. None were. Suddenly, the object in Jeanne Pierre's hand caught the reflection of the sun.

Jesus, I thought. That can't be a diamond can it? How could a poor kid get his hands on something like that? And what was he trying to do? Sell it to the guard?

When Jeanne Pierre saw me staring, he quickly dropped the shiny object into his wooden tray and hastily covered it from view with another piece of thin wood upon which he spread-out various trinkets and candy.

Not knowing what else to do, I awkwardly smiled, nodded, and quickly walked away.

But that would not be the end of it.

During that first month of my French-immersion training, I followed a very monotonous routine of attending classes for six hours each day. I found the schedule as distasteful as I'd found college, so I took every opportunity to experience the local culture beyond the compound's walls.

When the final class of the day ended around 4 pm, the other fifty or so volunteers-in-training would typically hang out together in the school's canteen playing American music and rejoicing in tall tales of their college glory days.

But I'd not traveled halfway around the world to have an extended college experience. Instead, I would typically head into town with one of the local language instructors, Serge, who also welcomed the opportunity to practice his English. In a combination of English and French, we shared our life stories while walking the unpaved streets of Bukavu, always careful to return to the compound by 6 pm, just in time for dinner.

But after helping to clean up the canteen following our meal, we'd head back into town. We'd often meet up briefly with other volunteers who had ventured out to visit one of the many bars playing American music that lined the main street near the school's main gate. We'd only spend a short time with them before moving to one of the many back-alley spots that were frequented by the locals.

I never considered the danger of doing this, despite the many sideways glances I received, figuring that Serge would step-in if a situation got out of hand. Which sometimes it did.

The cause was almost always some local girl who wanted to sit with the American guy. Her local suitors didn't find the competition to their liking, especially after a few bottles of Ngoma beer, the region's most popular drink.

Usually before midnight, we'd return to the compound, give the guards some money to look the other way at our late arrival, and then find our way to our respective dorm rooms.

I shared my room with a guy from Florida who, like me, had recently graduated from college and was also trying to "find himself." I came to hate that expression. But like so many of the male volunteers, he was mostly intent upon getting as many of the female volunteers as drunk as possible, then seeing which one would follow him down to the lakeshore for a romantic, late-night rendezvous.

Occasionally, he'd skip the walk down to the lake, and choose instead to bring the girl back to our room. I'd have no choice but to wait on the balcony overlooking the lake until they'd finished. Other volunteers sometimes joined me. We shared a cigarette and had a good laugh as we listened to the grunts and groans. Once they fell silent, we all returned to our rooms.

My favorite time of the day was unquestionably the early morning.

I'd awake around 5 am to have the communal shower room all to myself. I'd then step out onto that long balcony that ran the length of the dorm building overlooking Lake Kivu. I'd sit there on the ledge, my feet dangling over the edge, and watch the fishermen take their boats out. In the distance, I could see them casting their nets as flocks of birds circled above.

A part of me envied the simplicity of their lives. But if the early morning was my favorite time of the day, then the daytime was my least favorite. Of all the volunteers in the immersion program, I'm sure I was the worst. I didn't necessarily lack the motivation to learn, but I definitely lacked the skills. Even though I'd taken four years of French in high school and had endured endless after-school lessons with my father, it was as if I was starting from scratch. It got so bad that the program's director called me into this office one day to warn me that I might be sent home if I didn't quickly improve.

I could barely make eye contact with him as he outlined my possible fate.

I went back to my dorm room that night and mentally prepared myself for the possibility of failing the program and being sent home in humiliation.

But I then found some much-needed inspiration from a letter that my father had tucked into my duffle bag before I'd left home a month earlier. In the letter, he recounted his own experiences in France during the war and, perhaps anticipating my struggles, told me not to give up. I then recalled that last conversation I'd had with him on that park bench overlooking Crystal Lake as he shared the incredible tale of he and Yvette. I figured that if he could make it through that experience, then I could certainly make it through an immersion program.

The next day, I re-dedicated myself to learning French.

Besides befriending a few of the language instructors, I also became close with another volunteer who, quite remarkably, was a recent retiree who had spent much of his life as a very successful contractor, building homes for the wealthy back in the States.

But he had long yearned to share his skills with the less fortunate.

Ron and I often walked along the shoreline of Lake Kivu admiring the architecture of the colonial homes that had been built by wealthy Belgian expatriates during the heyday of the colonial era. But like me, Ron struggled to reconcile the injustice that allowed these extravagant homes to exist in such close proximity to a slum like Goma, where Jeanne Pierre was from.

Our route often took us from our school's hillside compound overlooking the lake, down a winding road that continued along the shoreline until arriving at the southernmost tip of the lake where the wealthy neighborhoods were located. Just a short walk through those neighborhoods, and up over a hill, brought us to Goma, stretching for miles down into the valley on the other side.

At one location atop the hill, you could literally look in one direction and see Beverly Hills–like homes extending down the hillside to the lakeshore, and then turn in the other direction and see the shantytown of Goma with thousands of small, mud-brick homes amid a maze of narrow, dirt lanes that, when the rains came, would become a sloppy mess of mud and human feces washing down the hillside.

Ron and I would sometimes walk down those lanes into the heart of the slum, crossing over makeshift bridges that arched over open sewer canals. The smell of feces and stale urine filled the air, at times making me gag. Yet seemingly oblivious to the filth that surrounded them, shoeless children ran amok, unsupervised by parents or older siblings who had gone in search of a day's work to bring food home.

Jean-Pierre was one of those older siblings, coming to the language school each day to earn money for his family by selling candy . . . and perhaps other products.

I'd shared with Ron the story of what I'd observed weeks earlier with Jean Pierre. At first, he dismissed it, telling me not to worry about it. But one day when we saw Jeanne Pierre walking the streets of Goma, we were both hesitant to approach, thinking it was best to turn the other way. But before we could, he turned around and saw us. There was just no place for two white guys to hide in the middle of one of central Africa's worst slums.

"Que faites-vous tous les deux ici?" asked Jeanne Pierre, squeezing through our ever-present entourage of small children pulling at our pant legs, begging for some Chiclets.

"Juste marcher," replied Ron, whose French wasn't much better than mine.

Jean-Pierre studied us for a moment, and I couldn't help but think that he knew I suspected him of doing something illegal.

"It's not safe for you to be here," he said finally in French. "Let me walk you back to the school."

"We're okay, Jean-Pierre," I answered, resisting his pull on my arm to follow him. "We've come here before."

"You have?" He looked me straight in the eye. "Maybe following me," he said with a straight face.

I swallowed hard.

But then a sly smile came over Jean Pierre's face. "Maybe you want to buy some more of my . . . candy," he added, with a wink. "Come."

Jean-Pierre proceeded to bring us to his house. It was there that we learned his story

I'd been right.

It was indeed a diamond that he was trying to sell to the guard that day at the school.

Ron and I listened with fascination as Jean-Pierre explained his trade. How he, and so many others like him, would receive raw, uncut diamonds from locals, mostly teenagers, who had gone to the river beds following the rainy season to look for diamonds that may have been left behind as the floodwaters receded.

Occasionally, the nuggets were sizable. But mostly they were so small that they could barely be held between two fingers. The local kids would then handover their findings to sellers like Jean-Pierre who would sell the smaller nuggets at places such as the language school, keeping a small profit for themselves, and giving the rest to the child prospector.

For larger nuggets, Jean-Pierre explained that he would use his contacts at the language school to locate buyers, often Belgian expatriates, who would then smuggle the contraband out of the country, sometimes back to Europe, but most often to the adjacent nations of Rwanda and Burundi, where they would be resold by warlords to replenish their war chests.

It was certainly easy to accuse people like Jean-Pierre of financing the numerous African revolutions which were most often fought by child soldiers even younger than he was. But when Ron and I saw the conditions in which he was living, we dropped all pretenses.

Like the other surrounding huts, Jean-Pierre's home was made of mud-brick with a tin roof that looked as though it would blow-off in a strong breeze.

There was only one room with large pieces of cardboard serving as the beds for him and his siblings, the youngest of which couldn't have been more than five. He was barefoot and dirty and playing some sort of a game on the dirt floor.

Jean-Pierre then invited us to sit on the only two wooden chairs in the room. He proceeded to serve us two cups of murky water in dented, aluminum cups. It was probably a mistake to drink the water. But neither of us wanted to reject his hospitality. We sat there in that dingy hut for the next hour listening to Jean-Pierre tell us about his family. We learned that his father had left a few years earlier in search of diamonds near the Rwandan border but had never returned.

We learned that his older brother had recently gone to Burundi looking for work, and had also not returned. And we learned that his oldest sister had been raped and beaten by one of the many gangs that rampaged the streets of Goma. Jean-Pierre had discovered the identity of the person who had initiated the rape, and had exacted his own form of justice, the details of which he had left to our imagination.

When our visit was complete, Jean-Pierre escorted Ron and I back to the compound. We said our goodbyes and watched him disappear into the night, but not before stopping to chat with one of the guards at the compound's entrance. Under the dim lights we could see that Jean-Pierre had given them something and had received something in return.

Business as usual.

In the days and weeks that followed, I remained committed to improving my French and tolerating the monotonous class schedule. But I also continued my daily excursions into Bukavu, sometimes alone and sometimes with Ron or Serge. One day, realizing that all the volunteers needed a break from the daily grind of instruction, the center's director announced a trip across the lake into Rwanda to see the mountain gorillas.

We departed in the early morning as the sun was rising, first taking fishing boats across Lake Kivu to Cyangugu, just across the border into Rwanda. From there, we boarded two buses bound for the Nyungwe National Forest, home of the silverbacks. Only a few years earlier I'd watched a movie about the life of Dian Fossey, who had committed herself to saving the endangered mountain beasts. Her original compound was our destination.

After transferring from the buses to a half-dozen or so jeeps, we continued our journey along winding roads, passing through huge tea fields before ascending into the rainforest.

We eventually had to continue on foot along the Igishigishigi Trail, at one point crossing over a high suspension bridge with views over the valley's forests and marshes. A huge waterfall in the distance had created its own small rainbow. Many of the volunteers paused to admire the beauty that surrounded us, as birds soared free, high above the orchids that grew plentifully along the trail.

Continuing still deeper into the rainforest, our guide began chopping his way through the thick foliage using a machete that he swung confidently back and forth. Above us, we could hear the myriad of nature's sounds, all mixing together to create a symphony for the senses. Then, almost without warning, we saw them up ahead in a clearing.

Three silverbacks.

The giant beasts had stocky builds—broad chests, long muscular arms much longer than their legs, and wide feet and hands. Their fur was thick and shaggy, and matted from the moisture of the forest. These three males each appeared to be well over six feet tall and probably in excess of three hundred pounds.

Our guide immediately knelt down and motioned for us to do the same.

I looked around and saw the fear in the other volunteers' eyes. I could definitely understand the temptation to turn and run, but we'd been warned against doing so during an orientation at the school prior to our departure.

For some reason, I'd no such urge.

I recalled being told that they were generally calm, quiet, nomadic animals, constantly on the move in search of food.

As I stared at these mammoth animals, and it seemed almost incomprehensible that these close relatives of ours were being hunted to the brink of extinction. As they stared back at us, their eyes seemed so expressive, reflecting a long life of perhaps more than thirty years lived in the presence of humans, which was probably their downfall. They'd become too trusting.

A part of me wanted to scream at them to run away. We seemed almost unworthy to be in their presence. And then, almost as suddenly as it'd begun, the stare-down ended as the three behemoths turned and disappeared into the forest.

In the years to come, I would think often about my encounter that day with the silverback trio. How they'd made me feel insignificant. How they spotlighted my own insecurities. My own shortcomings.

We've all had similar experiences, I suppose. Events that cause us to question our own purpose. Our own sense of being. Did my encounter that day with the trio change the course of my life? No. But it was one of the first experiences since I'd left home that would result in extensive personal reflection. I suppose it was part of that process of "finding myself," a process which my African adventure was supposedly meant to hasten.

Could I have "found myself" closer to home? Probably. But my experiences in Africa became central pieces of my life's tapestry. Some of those experiences would unquestionably become loose threads of regret. But I would also come to understand that if you pull too hard on those threads, the tapestry of your life begins to unravel.

As I headed back down the mountain with my fellow volunteers, our guide continued to slash through the undergrowth, taking a slightly different route that led us to the edge of the Gisovu Tea Estate. In the years prior to our visit, part of the Nyungwe Forest had become a national park, most of the plantations purchased by the government—except the Gisovu Estate, one of the largest tea plantations in the world. The area's altitude, soil, and rainfall made for ideal conditions for growing some of the world's most sought-after tea, ironically called silverback tea.

On the edge of the estate, we emerged from the forest to a truly incredible sight, as the plantation extended down the side of the mountain, partially terraced and completely green. At the very bottom we discerned a small shack, dwarfed by the massive green expanse surrounding it. We all sat on the edge of the tea field, awed by nature's beauty.

Then, two of the volunteers stood and began running down the hillside. A few others followed, and before you knew it, we were all dashing down the slope. Some slipped and tumbled onto the terraces, splashing in the mud. Others continued their sprint to the bottom.

As I neared the shack, I caught my toe on something that sent me flying through the air and landing in a heap. Almost immediately, I knew that I'd done something to my ankle. As the other volunteers made their way down the hill, they gathered around me, concerned, but still laughing from the thrill of the downhill run. I tried to stand but immediately felt the pain shoot through my foot. I was hoping it was just a bad sprain. A broken foot would probably send me home.

With the help of a few volunteers I was able to make it to the nearby dirt road where our jeeps waited to take us back to the base camp. Our guide had already called ahead to inform the park rangers of my injury. As we approached the base camp, a doctor waited to examine me, along with his young female assistant. The doctor was Belgian and asked me a few questions in French, which I struggled to answer.

Thankfully, the assistant spoke English.

"You're lucky," she said, taking my blood pressure. "It doesn't appear to be broken."

I was relieved, but annoyed. "Stupid thing to do," I said.

She laughed. "What exactly *were* you doing?"

I explained my accident to her and became more embarrassed as I did. She was very attractive, her smile infectious.

"It's okay," she said. "Beautiful place. Everybody gets carried away."

"How long have you been working here?" I asked, trying my best to sound engaging.

"Oh, I don't work here. Just a volunteer like you," she replied, as the doctor wrapped my ankle. "I've been here for a few months learning French, and then I'll be assigned somewhere in the CAR."

"Really?" I said, unable to hide my excitement. "I'm also going to the Central African Republic after I finish my training in Bukavu." I paused. "At least I hope I am, if I'm able to pass the language exam."

She laughed again. "I'm sure you'll do fine. What are you going to be doing in CAR?"

"Teaching math," I replied. "You?"

"Medical assistant in a SIDA clinic, although I don't know where exactly."

I remembered that SIDA was the French acronym for AIDS.

"Wow, I'm not sure if I could handle that," I replied honestly.

"To be honest, I'm not sure I can, either. But it was part of my under-graduate studies, so I guess they think I'll be okay."

"You're going to be a doctor someday?" I asked.

"Something in medicine. Not sure exactly what, yet. I guess that's why I'm here. To figure it all out."

I nodded. "Me, too," I said. "I'm John, by the way."

She extended her hand, again with that big smile. "Nice to meet you. I'm Maria."

We spent nearly an hour together that day in that little clinic on the edge of the Nyungwe National Forest. The attraction was immediate and mutual. I could hear the other volunteers playing soccer outside while they waited for all the jeeps to return and load the gear onto the buses. I was hoping it would take a long time.

In the few months that I'd been in Africa, I'd finally found somebody my own age who seemed to understand me, even though our backgrounds were so very different. Maria came from Puerto Rico and was committed to a career in medicine, using the Peace Corps as a sort of stepping stone. I'd absolutely no idea what I wanted to do with my life.

But I wanted to see Maria again.

CHAPTER NINE

George and Yvette had barely escaped Eculleville with their lives.

When the shells began falling, they'd dived together into a nearby vacant store. The shrapnel had shattered the windows, leaving Yvette with some nasty cuts on her arms, and both with a temporary loss of hearing. They'd been found dazed and rattled by the same checkpoint guards that had reluctantly allowed them to enter the mostly abandoned town just a few short hours earlier.

As best as anyone could surmise, George and Yvette had been spotted walking the deserted streets by a small pocket of Germans who had continued to operate in the nearby towns, and who probably had welcomed the opportunity to target the two young combatants who were foolish enough to venture into unsecured territory on the northern tip of the Cotentin peninsula.

Following a short stint in the Allied field hospital near Cherbourg, George was discharged and given a good tongue-lashing by his superiors, while Yvette was moved to a French hospital in Granville, nearly one hundred miles to the southeast near the Brittany peninsula. At first, George assumed that their forced separation was the Army's method of punishment. But it would soon become clear that just the opposite was true. The Army was already looking ahead to their next target in the ongoing liberation of western France.

One of France's most rugged regions, Brittany was always a mix of spectacular coastline, medieval towns, small islands, and inland woods, rich in culture, tradition, and history. Originally a Celtic territory, it'd been conquered by Julius Caesar in the first century BC and not annexed to France until the 16th century.

For those first sixteen centuries, the fiercely independent people of the region fought off invasions by the Norse and Normans. Even after its annexation, it maintained much of its old social and religious practices. That independence was on full display throughout the Second World War, as local Resistance fighters refused to succumb to the Germans who were intent on securing the French naval base at Lorient to launch their U-boats and surface raiders for the Battle of the Atlantic. The Allies wanted that same base in order to land the vast amount of supplies they needed to feed the breakout from Normandy to the north.

In the early summer of 1944, in the weeks following the D-Day landings, the Americans assumed the responsibility of liberating Brittany, securing Lorient, and opening those northern supply lines which would allow the Allied advance through Caen, into Paris, across eastern France, and eventually into Germany. With the liberation of the Cotentin peninsula nearly complete—save for the northernmost tip near Eculleville where George and Yvette had barely escaped with their lives—the American commanders had turned their attention to Brittany.

The US 8th Corps led by General Middleton would move along the northern coast of Brittany, with Brest as their main target. The 20th Corps led by General Walker would tackle the southern coast starting at Nantes. The two units would then converge on Lorient from opposite directions.

Like the battle for Normandy, success would depend largely on the ability of the Allies to coordinate with the local Resistance fighters of the French Underground. Yvette had been moved to the hospital at Granville, a staging ground for the Allied push into Brittany, for this reason. Given her invaluable help at Cherbourg, it was hoped that she would serve as an intermediary between the Allies and the French Underground near Lorient.

But when she resisted from her hospital bed in Granville, the Army turned to George to change her mind.

"You understand your role, private, correct?" asked Colonel Montgomery, an assistant to General Walker. "I don't much care for the French, but we need this girl to do what she did for us at Cherbourg."

"Yes, sir, I understand," replied George, barely able to control his glee at the prospect of reuniting with Yvette

"And what happened at Eculeville—" began the colonel.

"Won't happen again, sir," replied George, truthfully.

The colonel studied him. "Look, son. I talked with Sgt. Cummings this morning. You remember him?"

George was surprised. "Yes, sir. Of course, sir. He was my commander in England during our training."

"He put you and Yvette together."

"Yes, sir. He did."

"I wanted to know what kind of a man you are, so I contacted him," explained Colonel Montgomery, carefully studying George. "He said you'd be a team player. That you'd get this done."

"Yes, sir. I'll do my best," answered George, not realizing he had made that kind of an impression on Sgt. Cummings.

Again the colonel stared at George, and then softened his tone. "What are your plans after this god forsaken war is over? You think you'll get together with that little French lady of yours?"

George relaxed a bit. "Yes, sir. I'm hoping."

"So she'll go back Stateside with you?"

"Don't really know, sir."

"Or maybe you'll stay here," said the colonel. "There's going to be a lot of rebuilding to do."

"I know that, sir. But . . ." George hesitated, not sure if the colonel approved of his relationship with Yvette.

The colonel could see that George was conflicted. "It's all right, son. I understand. In the middle of this hell, we all need something to hold on to. Something to live for."

George arrived alone at the hospital in Granville in early August. His unit from Normandy had already been disbanded and its various members reassigned. So he had traveled south from Cherbourg with a group of French-speaking Americans who, like him, would be assigned to the different Allied units of the 8th and 20th Corps as they moved across Brittany. But George knew that his role was very different. For practical purposes, he was being used by the military to secure Yvette's cooperation.

So he was going to take full advantage of the situation for as long as he could.

As he entered Granville and made his way toward the hospital to see Yvette, George saw a city largely untouched by war. Occupied by the Germans since early 1941, they'd abandoned the city without a fight, choosing instead to move their forces north to Normandy and south toward Lorient. But the hulking concrete block houses that they'd built still remained, standing in stark contrast to the Gothic church that rose just outside the walled Ville Haute.

As George passed through one of the main gates of the ancient, walled city, he emerged to see solid stone mansions, boutiques, galleries, creperies, and restaurants.

It was surreal.

Life inside the city's walls had continued much as it had before the war. The central square was filled with locals, mingling casually with the thousands of Allied troops who had descended upon the town in preparation for the assault on Brittany.

At the far end of the central square was the hospital, rising five stories above the wall that surrounded the city, a wall built during the 14th century's Hundred Years War between France and England. As George entered the stone building, he was surprised to see a modern medical facility under civilian authority. Again, it seemed untouched by war. But with the assault on Brittany only days away, he wondered how long that would last.

George climbed the stairs to the third floor and proceeded down the long corridor until he came to room 306.

He could feel his heart beating and his palms sweating. He opened the door.

Yvette was sitting-up in her bed speaking with a young man who George immediately recognized from a photograph she had once shared with him.

Her brother, Luc.

Yvette's eyes teared-up as George entered the room. "Tu m'as manqué. I wasn't sure if they'd let you come."

He walked over to her bed and they embraced.

"I guess I'm still your babysitter," said George, wiping the tears from Yvette's eyes. "It's so good to see you again. Comment allez-vous?"

"Much better than the last time you saw me." She smiled.

George turned to Luc. They shook hands and hugged, kissing each other on the cheeks. "Comment es-tu arrivé là?" asked George.

"Luc has some amazing news, George," said Yvette. "Nos parents sont en vie!"

Separated from Yvette in England prior to D-Day, Luc had been assigned to an American unit landing at Omaha beach, while George and Yvette had landed at Utah.

But Luc's road to Granville had been far more dangerous. He had landed on Omaha in the afternoon of June 6, avoiding the meat-grinder of the early morning hours. But in the days and weeks that followed, he found himself right in the middle of Operation Cobra, the Allied effort to break out of the beachhead they'd established near Omaha, pushing south into Brittany through bocage country. Like Yvette, his role was to establish contact with the Resistance forces working behind the German lines to disrupt their supply routes wherever possible.

But unlike Yvette, he constantly found himself under fire. Bocage country, with its mix of woodland, hedges, and pasture, proved a significant obstacle for the Allied forces. When tanks proved largely ineffective, commanders resorted to intense aerial bombardment to open passages between German lines in the direction of Brittany.

Beginning in late July, B-17 and B-25 American bombers dropped more than three thousand tons of bombs northwest of Saint-Lo. Due to multiple days of bad weather, the majority of the bombs fell far from their targets. Many landed in close proximity to friendly forces, both American and French. And right in the middle of the chaos had been Luc.

"I'm not sure how I got out of that situation alive," Luc told George, as he continued to share his war story in Yvette's hospital room.

George could see the intensity in Luc's eyes as he recounted the events.

"My unit had taken-up position by the Madeleine River near Saint Lo along with the rest of 116th Infantry but became separated from the division. We found ourselves near Martainville Hill under continuous bombardment by German artillery." He paused to collect himself as Yvettte reached for her brother's hand.

Then he continued. "It was nearly an entire day and night before the 3rd Battalion finally arrived at our position. For a brief time, we felt saved. But then the bombs began falling. At first we thought it was more German artillery. But then we realized it was American bombers missing their targets. We did our best to dig foxholes to protect ourselves, but there was just no place to hide. At one point, there must have been four of us huddled together in that hole. They tried to blame me, the French guy, for misdirecting the bombing. But we just tried to survive together."

Yvette squeezed her brother's hand. "C'est bien, Luc. Vous êtes en sécurité maintenant. Tell George how you found our parents."

Luc took a deep breath, seemingly relieved to change the subject.

"As bad as Saint Lo was, it was still the key to the Normandy break-out. The carpet bombing opened a corridor that led to Coutances to the west, not far from here," said Luc, referring to Granville. "But by the time we arrived there, it'd been mostly leveled by the bombers, and the Germans were long gone. It gave us some time to unwind and prepare for the push into Brittany. As other units started arriving from up north, I met up with some Resistance fighters who knew of the events around Utah. A few even knew about Yvette's work in Cherbourg." He looked at his sister and nodded approvingly, clearly proud.

"And one of them was from Blosville, just down the road from our parent's home in Saint Marie du Mont," continued Yvette, retelling her brother's story. "They remembered seeing our Mom and Dad on the road heading south toward Carentan."

"That's incredible," said George. "But wasn't Carentan . . ." His voice trailed-off.

"Yes, some bad fighting took place there on the days following the Utah landings," admitted Luc. "But they may have passed through there after the worst was over.".

"And then where did they go?" asked George, sitting on the edge of Yvette's bed.

"We have an uncle who lives in Lorient," answered Luc. "Or at least he did before the war began. We think our parents may have gone there."

"But that's exactly where . . ." George caught himself, not wanting to yet reveal the reason why he had been allowed to reunite with Yvette. But it didn't matter.

"C'est bien, George," replied Yvette. "We know why they let you come here to see me. They want you to convince me to help with the Brittany offensive. How ironic is it that our parents may be in the exact place that the Army wants me to go."

"So you'll go to Lorient?" asked George.

"Of course," she replied with a smile. "I could never let the American Army down," she added facetiously. "But tell them that Luc must go with us."

George looked at Luc and then laughed along with Yvette. "Something tells me that they might go along with that."

CHAPTER TEN

After saying goodbye to Maria in the clinic on the edge of the Nyungwe National Forest, I returned to the language school in Bukavu with a renewed focus to pass the language exam, go to my assigned location in the Central African Republic, and see Maria again.

But unforeseen events would soon interfere with that plan.

In our final week at the language center, we were awakened one night by the sounds of gunfire. Despite being told by the guards to remain inside the dormitory, a group of volunteers and I nevertheless used a side gate to venture out into the streets.

A stupid decision, to say the least.

At first, there was little to see. But then a large crowd appeared over the hill that separated the wealthy and poor areas of the town, presumably coming from Goma. We watched anxiously as the local gendarme established a security-line to prevent the crowd from coming down the hill toward the lakeside residences near our present location. But their efforts were proving unsuccessful.

Soon, the shouts became louder, and the gunfire more frequent.

"We need to get out of here," I shouted to the other volunteers.

But as the crowd reached our location, we quickly became separated.

I panicked, but just as soon felt someone pulling at my arm.

I turned around to see Ron.

"We're leaving," he said, calmly but sternly. "Let's circle-back toward the lake. I think I know a place where we can wait it out."

A part of me wondered how Ron had found me in the crowd. But as I continued to be jostled about, it just didn't matter.

Instead, I gratefully followed Ron along the Grand Corniche that ran parallel to the Baie de Nyofu, one of many small inlets of Lake Kivu. We passed by the Hotel de la Roche where the Peace Corps volunteers often met after class to enjoy a Ndovu lager. Just behind the hotel, down a dark, dirty street there was a good-sized house surrounded by a wall topped with barbed-wire. Ron walked right up the main gate and spoke with a guard through the wrought iron. Their body language seemed to indicate familiarity, which was confirmed when the gate opened.

"Who lives here?" I asked, as we walked through the courtyard toward the front door of the stately home.

"His name's Gaspard," replied Ron. "A Belgium diamond merchant."

"Diamond merchant?" I repeated, surprised. "How do *you* know him?"

Before Ron could answer, the front door opened, and there stood a tall, dark-haired man who greeted Ron in heavily-accented English. Just as he extended his hand to shake mine, my eyes shifted to the figure who stepped out from behind the Belgium diamond merchant.

"My friend," said Jean Pierre with a big smile. "Il est bon de vous revoir," he said calmly, as if nothing was occurring outside walls. "Comment était votre voyage pour voir les gorilles de montagne. And I hear you met a girl."

I was momentarily speechless. A violent mob was likely making its way toward our location. I was in the house of a Belgium diamond merchant who not only knew Jean Pierre, but seemed to know Ron. And Jean Pierre seemed very familiar with our recent trip to see the mountain gorillas.

Gaspard seemed to sense my confusion. "S'il vous plaît, entrez et asseyez-vous. Puis-je vous acheter une bière?"

The four of us sat in Gaspard's large living room which boasted an unobstructed view of Lake Kivu through the floor-to-ceiling windows that ran the length of the room. I watched as Gaspard's guards positioned themselves at the estate's various gates, undoubtedly preparing themselves to repel the riotous crowd if they got too close.

I tried to calm myself down as I sipped my beer and began listening to Ron explain the details of our current situation.

"Jean Pierre was mugged a few weeks ago while returning home from the Language Center," began Ron. "All of his money taken. Gaspard's money, in truth. He came to me asking for help to pay it back. I agreed, but only if I could meet Gaspard and pay him directly."

"I don't understand," I admitted. "Jean Pierre works for Gaspard?"

"Indirectly, but yes," replied Ron. "Gaspard is one of many foreign diamond merchants in Bukavu, but he specializes in the trafficking of diamonds that are found mostly by local teenagers searching the nearby river beds. The teenagers bring the diamonds to him, and he then uses other kids like Jean Pierre to sell the smaller ones around town. Jeanne Pierre had just sold some at the compound before he had been mugged. He was scared of what Gaspard would do to him if he couldn't hand over his earnings."

I was still struggling to understand. "Jean Pierre never told us about Gaspard. I thought the kids from the rivers brought the diamonds they found directly to Jeanne Pierre to sell."

"Some," explained Ron. "But most bring them to people like Gaspard. He's like the middle man, using other kids like Jeanne Pierre to sell the smaller diamonds around town. The larger ones he peddles himself."

Gaspard nodded. "Oui, I've nearly fifty boys." He paused, and smiled at Jean Pierre. "But Jean Pierre is moi best."

I'd been in Bukavu for nearly three months and had interacted frequently with Jeanne Pierre. Not once had he mentioned Gaspard. And why had he gone to Ron for help? Why not me or another volunteer?

"And what do you do with the profits," I asked Gaspard. I realized immediately it was a stupid question. But I wasn't thinking clearly.

The diamond merchant's smile momentarily disappeared, but just as quickly returned. "TIA, mon ami. TIA."

I'd heard that expression before, usually in reference to questionable business ethics and dealings. TIA. This Is Africa.

"So you're using the profits to buy weapons." As soon as I said it, I realized it was another stupid remark.

Gaspard sat forward in his chair and responded angrily. "Fuckin américain! Cette fausse impression de justesse, comme votre meilleur que le reste du monde."

Ron reached across the table and put his hand on Gaspard's shoulder. "Tout se calme. My friend means no disrespect. We're all a little on edge."

"What's happening out there, anyways?" I asked, jumping at the opportunity to change the subject. "What are the people so angry about?"

"Most of the people living in the slums are Hutu," explained Ron, who had clearly learned a lot about the local culture. More than I had. "They're opposed to the governments in both Zaire and Rwanda, which are run mostly by Tutsi. It's a class war, plain and simple."

Ron continued to explain that it was the Tutsi who rose up against Belgium colonial rule in the 1950s, forcing many Hutu—who had allied themselves with the colonial government—to flee to Uganda. Belgium was forced to abandon its colonies in central Africa, and the Hutu refugees struggled to remain relevant as the Tutsi gained control of various governments. In recent decades, many Hutu have returned to the region, mostly living in the slums like Goma."

"And the mob outside?" I asked.

"They are mostly Hutu, protesting against the local Tutsi rule. This whole place is about to explode. The Peace Corps will be leaving soon."

"How do you know all of this, Ron?" I asked. "I thought you were just a construction guy who had retired and wanted to build houses for the poor in Africa."

Ron looked at me, clearly trying to determine how much he should tell me. "I spent most of my career in construction. But before that, I was in the Marine Corps, stationed mostly in this part of Africa at different embassies . . . before being sent to Vietnam."

"And the Peace Corps knew that when you signed up?" I asked.

"I honestly don't know. But a few weeks ago, not long after we visited Jean Pierre's house for the first time, I was approached by someone from the American embassy in Kinshasa. They were looking for someone to give them more information about what was happening here. They explained the tensions between the Hutu and Tutsi, and that things might soon blow-up. I'm sure they saw my file," explained Ron. "At just about that same time, Jean Pierre asked me for the money to pay back Gaspard."

Jesus Christ, I thought. What had I gotten myself into?

But then I thought about Maria. "What about the Peace Corps volunteers in Rwanda? Are these riots happening there, too?"

"Probably," responded Ron. "But the Peace Corps protects its people. So try not to worry. If we're evacuated from here, then I'm sure the volunteers across the border will also be evacuated at the same time."

I didn't feel very reassured, but realized there wasn't much I could do. "So what about this guy?" I asked, motioning toward Gaspard. "He's giving you information?"

Gaspard stood up to refill his drink, glaring at me as he walked to his bar. Jean Pierre followed him.

"You have to understand," said Ron, as we continued to sit side by side. "Everyone is to blame for what's happening here. Belgium abandoned this place long ago, but continued to profit from its natural resources, especially diamonds. But so did America. When I was here in the early seventies, we knew that diamonds were exchanged for weapons by both the Hutu and Tutsi. But we didn't do anything to stop it. In fact, we allied ourselves with these corrupt Tutsi governments, thinking that they would help us to stop the communists who were starting to win too many seats in the provincial governments. Anyways, right now, this house is the safest place to be."

"Why?" I asked. "Don't these people understand that merchants like Gaspard are to blame for all the weapons?"

"Sure. And that's why we're safe here. They won't hurt Gaspard because his diamonds are funding their uprising."

"It doesn't make any sense."

"Gaspard was right, John," said Ron. "TIA. This is Africa. It doesn't make any sense. But it never has."

Three days later, just as Ron had predicted, they evacuated us from Bukavu, traveling overland by bus to Bujumbura at the northern tip of Lake Tanganyika in Burundi. The journey was a little more than one hundred kilometers, but with no paved roads, and it took nearly six hours along muddy, winding roads that traversed Mount Bisoke on the eastern edge of the Virunga National Forest.

We were accompanied on the buses by members of the Belgium military who had come down from Kisangani overnight to provide protection in the event that the riots continued and spread into Burundi. During one of our stops along the way, I noticed Ron chatting with one of the soldiers, and then using his radio. I wanted to ask him who he had been speaking to but never got the chance. An hour later we arrived in Bujumbura. I looked for Ron, who had been riding on a different bus. But he was gone.

I never saw him again.

Many years later, a web search revealed a short obituary saying that he had passed away in 2008 following a "long life of military and community service."

I never saw Jean Pierre again, either.

I'd like to think that he had lived a long life. He was a street-smart kid, after all. But in the years that followed my time in Africa, as I watched the horrific images of Rwandan genocide on the worldwide news, it was hard to believe that anybody could have survived that hell on earth. One particular image showed our language school. Part of it was in ruins. Another part had become a field hospital tending to the brutal injuries suffered during the civil war.

TIA.

CHAPTER ELEVEN

Largely frozen in time thanks to decades of corruption and neglect, Bujumbura was a steamy city of grandiose French colonial planning, with wide boulevards and imposing public buildings. Like Bukavu had been during the height of the colonial period, Buju—as the locals always called it—was a common destination for the wealthy who enjoyed the many high-end resorts that fronted Lake Tanganyika, one of the deepest freshwater lakes in the world.

Most of the resorts had either long ago closed or fallen upon hard times and disrepair. But in the Peace Corps' haste to evacuate us from Bukavu, they'd limited options for housing the near one hundred volunteers. So, for nearly a week, we all enjoyed the posh surroundings of one of the city's few remaining luxury resorts, the Dolce Vita Resort, located just a few blocks from the American embassy, a fact that helped to calm everyone's frayed nerves.

We'd arrived at the resort late in the evening, and we had all been happy just to find our rooms and fall quickly asleep. The next morning, we awoke to knocks on our doors informing us of an important meeting in one of the resort's many conference rooms. The Peace Corps' Country Directors of both Burundi and Zaire stood beside the American ambassador of Burundi, and beside them were American and French soldiers. The room quickly fell silent as the ambassador began speaking.

He explained that we were safe in Bujumbura and would be flown to our posts in the Central African Republic as soon as our visas could be processed. His voice was calm and reassuring. One volunteer raised his hand to ask whether we would still be required to pass a language test before being assigned a post. Much to my relief, the answer was no. How ironic, I thought. Bukavu's street riots may have very well saved me from getting sent home.

As the ambassadors and directors continued speaking; I looked around the room and realized that it was filled with many more volunteers than had been with me in Bukavu. It became apparent that other training and language centers from across the region had also been evacuated.

And that's when I saw Maria.

When the riots had broken-out in Bukavu, there were concerns that it could spread across the border and affect Maria's training-site at the base of the Nyungwe National Forest in Rwanda.

It had not.

Nevertheless, her group of volunteers had also been evacuated. Later on, we discovered that the evacuation orders had come directly from Washington, following a warning from the French and Belgium governments that the situation in the region was becoming increasingly unstable as tensions grew between the Hutu and Tutsi.

"So good to see you again," I said to her, as we finally met up and embraced in the courtyard outside the meeting room. "I was worried that something had happened to your group." It was an understatement. In truth, I'd not stopped thinking about her.

"It sounds like our bus caravan wasn't far behind yours," said Maria. "We didn't have any riots, but they were still concerned."

"Do you know yet where you'll be posted in CAR?" I asked.

"Only that it'll be near Bangui," she answered, referring to the country's capital. "What about you?"

"Not sure yet," I replied.

The Peace Corps always followed a prescribed pattern of training its volunteers. Following a short orientation Stateside (I'd been sent to New Orleans for three days), volunteers are then flown to a regional language center where they remain for upward of three months completing an immersion program in the language they will be using during their two-year volunteer stint. Upon successfully completing the language training, they're informed of their postings. In some instances, volunteers are given additional training in-country prior to being sent to their post. As I spoke with Maria, it was unclear as to whether or not our large group would receive such in-country training, which usually focused on local customs, traditions, and laws.

Not knowing how much time we had together, Maria and I became inseparable in the days that followed our reunion at Lake Tanganyika. While many volunteers were becoming frustrated at not being able to leave the resort, we took advantage of all it had to offer. Whether walking hand-in-hand along the many palm-tree-lined paths that wandered through the expansive property or sitting lakeside together on the sandy beach as the orange glow of the sun gradually faded and dropped below the horizon, we'd both found some peace in each other's company.

Years later, I would understand that our comfort with each other was mostly the result of the traumatic events that we'd lived through. But at the moment, it didn't really matter. Despite our very different backgrounds, we'd found something in common: the adventure of living in Africa.

"Do you miss home?" I asked her as we sat lakeside together one evening watching giant hippos rise from beneath the water to survey their surroundings, and then slowly disappear beneath the surface once again.

"I miss my mom," she replied, looking off into the distance. "She has always been my rock."

"Did she approve of you joining the Peace Corps?"

"Approve?" Maria responded, giggling. "Not really. But she still supported it."

"And your Dad?" I asked.

Maria fell silent for a moment. "He left when I was very young. It's always been just me and my mom."

"Sorry."

"No, don't be," she replied firmly. "I never knew him, and my mom never talked much about him. In truth, there's a lot of that in Puerto Rico. Men behaving badly."

"What do you mean?"

"I don't know." She shrugged. "I guess I've never had much luck with guys." She seemed to want to say more, but then thought better of it, perhaps not yet trusting me.

"What about you?" she asked instead, probably hoping to redirect the conversation. "Any girlfriend back home?"

"No," I responded, looking down at the sand. "I never dated much, not even in college."

"Really?" she replied, looking at me curiously. "Why not?"

"Not sure really. I guess I never found the right person." *Until now*, I thought, but knew better than saying it aloud.

She nodded. "I can understand that. What about your parents? Were they supportive of you coming here?"

"My Dad was mostly supportive," I answered. "I think he understood why I needed to leave home. But my sister thought I was crazy."

Maria laughed. "You and your sister are close?"

"We are, yes. But very different people."

"And why did you need to leave home?" Maria asked, moving her bare feet in the sand. "You weren't happy?"

Complicated question.

"I was happy," I replied. "But I guess I needed my own space, away from my father."

I could feel Maria looking at me, as I continued gazing across the lake.

"You always talk about your dad, John," she said finally. "What about your mom? Does she still live with you?"

The answer to that question has, in many ways, defined my life.

CHAPTER TWELVE

George, Yvette, and Luc departed Granville in early August of 1944, traveling south toward Brittany in advance of General Walker's 20th Corps. Their task—along with other French-speaking US soldiers, such as George, and French nationals, such as Yvette and Luc—was to establish contact with the French Resistance fighters along the southern coast of Brittany and begin coordinating efforts with the approaching 20th Corps.

The same would be occurring along the northern coast of the peninsula in advance of the 8th Corps led by General Middleton. The goal was for the two forces to meet-up near Lorient, driving the German forces from the peninsula and capturing the strategic ports which the Allies could use to supply their offensive across France, and eventually into Germany.

With the Germans in disarray after D-Day, the drive into Brittany should have been relatively easy, at least in comparison to the battle for Normandy and the Cotentin peninsula.

However, disagreements between the American generals, Bradley and Patton, as to how Brittany should be taken complicated matters. Bradley preferred a slower push south, ensuring that supply lines were properly secured. Patton, as was his nature, preferred a blunt-force attack, but one that risked the advancing forces moving too fast for the supply lines to keep-up.

In the end, General Eisenhower allowed Patton to manage the assault as Bradley continued to prepare for the push east toward Paris. Both 8th and 20th Corps, now under Patton's command, advanced rapidly into Brittany, overwhelming the German defenders. But the speed of their advance created problems for the French resistance. Short on modern weaponry, they were dependent upon Allied airdrops to remain supplied. And as the American forces continued their rapid advance, the weapons were frequently dropped in areas already taken by the Americans, forcing the Resistance fighters to wait for it to be moved up to them.

Such dependence on the Americans didn't go over well with the proud French fighters. This became George, Yvette, and Luc's main challenge as they arrived on the outskirts of Lorient, just outside the German perimeter, with preparations underway for the inevitable American attack that the Germans were convinced was coming soon.

But it would never come.

When 20th Corps entered Nantes—about fifty kilometers east of Lorient—on August 6th, they found its port facilities in ruins. On the same day, 8th Corps reached the outskirts of Brest to the west, following their rapid advance along the northern coast of Brittany, despite some heavy German resistance near St. Malo. Reconnaissance showed that any attack on the heart of Brest—which had been heavily fortified upon Hitler's orders—would come at a high cost.

In late August, the attack on Brest nevertheless began.

George, Yvette, and Luc, meanwhile, were among those coordinating efforts near Lorient for the Allied attack to follow the fall of Brest. But as the battle for the city dragged on into September, British forces under General Montgomery reached the port city of Antwerp in Belgium, secured it, and opened its docks to receive supplies coming across the Atlantic.

The capture of the city changed the situation in Brittany.

No longer were its port cities critical to the Allied advance across France, as Antwerp provided a better option. Once Brest finally came under Allied control in mid-September, Allied command decided to simply surround the port city of Lorient for the rest of the war, keeping the German garrisons at bay and out of the wider war. The Allied perimeter around the city became known as the "Atlantic pocket."

But for George, Yvette, and Luc, the change in the Allied plan had caught them—and much of the French Resistance—by surprise. Yvette and

Luc grew concerned that their parents may very well be trapped within the pocket along with more than twenty thousand other civilians and nearly thirty thousand German troops. The contours of the pocket extended over fifty kilometers from the Laïta River just west of Lorient to the Etel River in the east. The line was defended by approximately five thousand American soldiers of the 94th Infantry Division and another ten thousand free French soldiers.

Getting into—or out of—the city was nearly impossible, as both sides had mined the roads and bridges and strung row upon row of barbed-wire across the farmland that surrounded the city, including an area to the east of the city called Le Cosquer, near where Yvette and Luc's uncle lived.

By late August of 1944, artillery duels were a daily occurrence, often targeting enemy observatories, barracks, and gun-batteries. Right in the middle of these duels were George, Yvette, and Luc who had been assigned to an American unit along the Laita River near the seaside village of Saint Julien, west of Lorient. Day after day, they were forced to take cover as shells flew overhead, many originating from the German-held village of Guidel, just on the other side of the river.

Doing their best to remain calm during the barrages, Yvette and Luc would tell George about their trips to the region as children to visit their uncle. They recalled long walks along the peaceful coastline near Le Fort-Bloque where the landscape would casually change as the wooded shores, sandbanks, and river met the Atlantic tides. They recalled picnics to the east of the city on the grounds of the Port Louis citadel with views of the Tour de la Decouverte signal tower and nearby shipyards where, nearly three centuries earlier, a ship named Soleil d'Orient had been built with the nickname L'Orient, giving the sleepy, nearby village its name. It was a ship that would become part of the French East India Company, which would transform the region into a center of world trade.

"Sounds like a great childhood," remarked George, as they huddled together in their bunker on the outskirts of Saint Julien. "How often did you come here?"

"Almost every summer," replied Yvette, her long dark hair tied in a bun and tucked beneath her helmet.

"Like our father, our uncle was a fisherman, out of Port Louis," continued Luc. "The two spent endless hours together on the open seas. Sometimes they would take me along. It was where I developed my love for the ocean."

"How certain are you that your parents returned here after escaping your hometown following the landings at Utah?" asked George.

"Our uncle and his wife would never have left Lorient. And knowing that, I'm certain our parents came here," said Yvette resolutely.

George could see that Luc was less confident. "But how can we get into the city? I doubt the military will allow us to leave here unaccompanied to enter the city," he reasoned.

"They still need us to coordinate with the Resistance," replied Yvette. "They're very active in this area. When this dies down," she continued, joking to the artillery barrage which had started up again, "we'll somehow use the Resistance to get inside the city."

George looked at Luc, who shook his head ever so slightly, before adding, "Any attempt to enter the city will have to wait until the situation stabilizes. In the meantime, we're stuck here."

So in the days and weeks that followed, George, Yvette, and Luc had little else to do but share their life stories, and wait for an opportunity to enter the Atlantic pocket of Lorient.

One story that George took particular pleasure in telling was his summer trips to New York City as a teenager to visit his aunt who lived on the Upper East Side. As a child, he would travel with his mother, taking the train from Boston, through Hartford, and arriving at Grand Central Station where they'd take the 4 train to his aunt's apartment on East 79th Street.

By the time he was in high school, he made the trip by himself, relishing the time away from his parents. While he enjoyed growing up in the small town of Gardner, Massachusetts, he preferred the big city and all that it had to offer, particularly enjoying Broadway shows that he would see with his aunt.

"I loved my mother," said George. "But I always preferred being with my aunt. She seemed more interested in what I'd to say. Maybe it was because my mother was always caring for my father."

"Ton père était malade?" asked Yvette, as the trio emerged from their bunker, the most recent shelling having subsided.

"He was nearly sixty when I was born," responded George. "By the time I was a teenager he was already ill, unable to do anything other than spend the day in his library reading his books."

"Il avait un cancer?" asked Luc.

"Yes, but it's something that my mother never talked about much. Even after he died."

"Horrible disease," said Yvette. "Our grandfather died from it. The last time we were here was for his funeral. He was very close to our uncle."

"You were both close to your parents?" asked George.

"Oui," answered Yvette, as they walked down to the riverside, near to where its waters met the Atlantic Ocean. "We were lucky. Our parents cared for us very much. They could be tough, but they were always fair."

"I'm sure they're both very proud of you," said George, gazing across the river, knowing that some Germans were probably staring back.

"I'm sure your mother is proud of you, too," responded Yvette.

"Probably," answered George. "But when this war is over, I'm not sure I can live with her again. She always wanted to control me."

Yvette reached for George's hand, as Luc walked on ahead. "When we were in Cherbourg you told me that you wanted us to be together when the war was over."

George stopped suddenly. "Is that what you want?" he asked.

Yvette dropped her head and kicked the sand. "I think so. But I need to find my parents before I can really consider anything else."

George and Yvette embraced. "Don't worry," he said. "We'll find them."

"I just want to live a quiet life, surrounded by people who care for me. I'm so tired of seeing the worst in people. Sometimes it's just so hard to imagine a world without war"

"I know," replied George. "When you're just trying to stay alive, it's hard to think of anything else."

Yvette hesitated. "But what if . . ." Her voice trailed off.

"If we don't find your parents?" finished George.

"Or if one of us doesn't . . ."

She didn't need to finish her sentence. It was understood by both of them. Understood by nearly every soldier and Resistance fighter that surrounded them. It was the need to stay alive. The need to maintain hope.

In the weeks that followed, the daily shelling that had become the norm along the perimeter of the Lorient pocket had quieted, if not completely subsided. Word spread through the ranks that the British-led Operation Market Garden in the Netherlands might bring the war in Europe to a quick end.

The Germans were in full retreat on both the western and eastern fronts, but it soon became clear that they would fight on through the fall and winter.

Victory still proved far away.

Meanwhile, George, Yvette, and Luc remained inseparable, allowed by their superiors to move freely around Saint Julien in return for Yvette and Luc's participation in plans to begin squeezing the German pocket. Concern was increasing that the civilians inside Lorient were running low on food and fresh water, so it became clear that a supply route needed to be established. And with that, Yvette and Luc saw a means of getting inside the city to search for their parents.

They'd already been trying, albeit unsuccessfully, to get messages through the German lines, using their local contacts to serve as conduits, contacts which were part of the so-called Lorient Group, a mix of local Resistance fighters and French Forces of the Interior, known as the FFI. But ordinary civilians within the city had hunkered down, realizing that their liberation was still many months away and knowing what mattered most was to simply stay alive. Getting messages to them proved difficult.

Yet, resistance movements were becoming progressively better structured in and around the Lorient pocket, a structure that Allied commanders hoped would eventually help establish the much needed supply line. The least likely point of entry was unquestionably south of Lorient along the coastline where the Germans had built a heavily fortified U-boat base at Keroman. For nearly three years, Allied bombers had targeted the base but had been unable to penetrate its twenty-foot-thick concrete fortifications. While U-boat activity had nearly ceased by August of 1944, the Germans still maintained heavy-gun emplacements south of Keroman where the Le Blavet River reached the sea. The majority of their thirty thousand troops within the Lorient pocket were stationed in this southern area, with the next largest contingent north of the city where the main roads converged from the east and west. As a result, the Resistance was convinced that the supply lines needed to be established either east or west of the city. With the Scorff River to the east, and bridges over that river heavily mined, all efforts were directed to the west of the city.

And it was there that Yvette and Luc would continue the search for their parents.

CHAPTER THIRTEEN

I arrived in Bangui, the capital of the Central African Republic, in the fall of 1990 to begin my two years of service in the Peace Corps as a math teacher in a little village called Boda, just to the west of Bangui. Maria arrived a few days later to prepare for her service in a medical clinic only a few kilometers away, in the slightly larger village of Mbaiki.

Our departure from Bujumbura had been without incident, and everyone was relieved to get away from the instability of east Africa. But following just a few days in Bangui while we waited for transportation to our posts, it became evident that CAR had its own problems.

The European colonization of central Africa had begun in the late nineteenth century when the French, Germans, and Belgians arrived to begin stripping the region of its plentiful natural resources. The Ubanqi-Shari territory was established by the French, who subsequently handed over most control to private companies, which then forced the locals to harvest the rubber, coffee, and other commodities for little to no pay, often holding their families hostage until they met their quotas. From the time the French first arrived to 1940, the population of the region had declined by nearly half, due to diseases, famine, and exploitation by the private companies.

Following the First World War, the local population finally rose-up against their colonial rulers. Although the insurrection was eventually quelled by French soldiers, it was perhaps the first sign that France, along with other colonial powers, were losing their grip on the central African nations.

But during the Second World War, following France's capitulation to the Nazis, many of the same locals that had rebelled against colonial rule a few decades earlier were encouraged to join the Free French army fighting the Germans in North Africa, in return for the promise of free elections following the war. To reinforce the promise, Charles de Gaulle arrived in Bangui in late 1940 to review the troops.

The irony of this French connection didn't escape me.

As my fellow volunteers and I were taught the history of central Africa while learning French in Bukavu, I often thought of my father and the stories he had told me about his time in France during the war. There was little comparison, of course, between the life of a Peace Corps volunteer and that of a soldier. In most ways, they serve opposite functions. But just as my father had joined the military to get away from home, I had, for practical purposes, joined the Corps for the same reason. Nearly five decades later, I found myself in a part of the world that was still heavily influenced by the ghosts of French colonialism.

Soon after the war, France kept its promise and adopted a new constitution that granted full French citizenship to residents of the Ubangi-Shari and allowed for the establishment of local assemblies. A decade later, Ubangi-Shari obtained its independence from France and changed its name to the Central African Republic. But in the decades that followed, a series of corrupt rulers would plunder the CAR and it became one of the world's poorest nations, despite its wealth of natural resources. Military coups became the norm as Christian and Muslim rebel groups vied for control of the country. On multiple occasions, France sent soldiers to the country to reestablish stability. When I arrived, one of these stabilization missions was winding down. But the tension on the streets of the capital remained palpable, just as it'd been in Bukavu only a month earlier.

As all the volunteers awaited transportation to their assigned posts, each mission was housed at a different hotel in Bangui. All of the teachers were at the Hotel du Central along the Avenue de la Victoire near the Ubangi River, while all of the medical officers, including Maria, were at the Hotel Ledger Plaza, near the American embassy.

We'd been advised by the French military to remain inside our respective hotels as they could not yet guarantee the safety of so many foreigners. But such warnings are typically ignored by naive twenty-three-year-olds who think that no harm can come to them. Maria and I left our hotels and met at the Le Grand Cafe near the Jardin Publique as our second day in the city was coming to an end.

As I walked from my hotel to the cafe, I saw a city reminiscent of Bukavu, and most other central African cities, for that matter. The wide boulevards—punctuated in the French style of chaotic roundabouts—were filled with motorcycles and pedestrians, along with countless street vendors selling all sorts of trinkets, which made me remember Jean Pierre. The air was filled with a pungent mix of gas fumes and barbecued beef, the latter served wrapped in yesterday's newspapers.

As I wandered toward the cafe, I immediately became the center of attention, the only white person foolish enough to be walking the streets unaccompanied. Small children surrounded me, tugging on my pant legs, begging for "pipi." I continued walking, and I could feel little hands touching my back pocket, searching for my wallet. Fortunately, I'd already learned to carry my money and passport copy in my front pocket.

I did my best to reply to the children's requests with my limited French, but soon realized that few of the children were actually speaking French. Instead, they all spoke their native language, Sangho, and that pipi was their word for candy. Although in retrospect, I suspect they were more interested in my wallet.

I finally arrived at the cafe, relieved to get off the street. I was even more relieved to find a few white faces who looked up from their beers to nod as I passed by. I soon discovered that most of them were employees of the American embassy down the street and were ending their day with a cold Castel, a popular local brew.

Maria sat by herself at a high table in the far corner of the cafe, her medium-length, black, wavy hair tied in a ponytail that emerged from the rear of an UPR baseball cap, her Puerto Rican flag proudly displayed on her T-shirt, which was partially tucked into her jeans as her feet dangled just above the floor, reaching for her sandals.

"Estas aquí," she said with a sly smile as I approached the table, further confusing my already confused language palette. "¿Fue difícil?"

"Sí, muy difícil," I replied as we hugged. "¿Usted?" That was the extent of my Spanish.

"Muy bien. Ahora eres trilingüe," she said, making fun of poor language skills. We both sat down.

"Did you notice that nobody was speaking French on the street?" I asked as I ordered a beer from the waitress.

She laughed. "What did you expect? These people don't exactly like the French."

"True," I answered. "But all of those French lessons . . ."

"Don't worry about it. You'll still use it while teaching, and I'll use it in the clinic," said Maria.

"I guess so. But I don't think I can learn Sangho," I said.

"Just learn a few phrases, like 'tonga na nyen.'"

"Which means?" I asked.

"How are you," answered Maria, sipping her beer. "Anyways, what do you think of Bangui? Better than Bukavu?"

"Not much different, really" I answered honestly.

She laughed. "You sound disappointed."

I looked at her curiously. "What do you mean? You like it?"

"I've seen worse."

"Really? Where?"

"Near my home." She laughed.

I wasn't sure how to respond to that.

She continued, "There are some really poor neighborhoods in San Juan, Maybe not as poor as this," explained Maria, looking out the window at the Bangui streets. "But close."

"I guess I've never seen anything like this before," I admitted, probably sounding like a naive American. "It's pretty bad."

Maria studied me. "These people probably don't see it that way. It's all they know."

I smiled. "You're judging me."

"No, just still wondering why you came here."

"The Peace Corps sent me here," I shrugged.

"You know what I mean," she countered.

Yes, I did.

Maria had joined the Peace Corps because she actually wanted to help people, and was in a position to do so. She had seen poverty up close and wasn't turned off by it.

I, on the other hand, looked at the people on the streets of Bangui and thought of myself as superior, a reflection of my own insecurities. I should have been ashamed of those feelings, but wasn't yet sufficiently self-aware, and I wouldn't be for many, many years. In the short time that I'd known Maria, I think she understood me better than I understood myself. And perhaps that was the attraction. She forced me to look within myself. And I didn't care much for what I saw.

"Maria, can I ask you a question?"

"Of course," she replied, continuing to drink her beer and play with her sandals. She seemed so relaxed.

"I've seen how the other guys in your group look at you. Why don't you want to spend more time with them?"

She shrugged. "Why didn't you spend more time with the volunteers in your group when you were in Bukavu? Didn't you say that they reminded you of the people you knew in college. Always in search of a party?"

"So I'm different?"

She laughed. "You are. I feel like I can talk to you and you don't want anything in return."

That wasn't necessarily true, but I lacked the self-confidence to make my feelings more transparent.

"Now, let me ask you a question," said Maria. "And tell me if you don't want to talk about it."

I looked at her, waiting for the ball to drop. "What is it?"

"When we were in Bujumbura I asked you about your mother, but you didn't really answer."

I nodded meekly. "I remember."

Maria waited for me to say something more. When I didn't, she continued. "You know, I've come to understand that I'm the person I am because of my mother. I sometimes resented her, even blamed her, for my father leaving us. But I knew that was unfair. She did her best to be both a mother and a father to me. It was probably hardest for her when I was college and began dating and wanting my own independence. But I still lived at home because we couldn't afford a dorm room. Some of my relationships were tough and ended badly. My mother watched all of this, and it was hard on her. Maybe it reminded her of her struggles with my father." Maria dropped her head.

I wanted to ask her more, but wasn't sure if it was the right thing to do. I also wanted to open up to her the way she had opened up to me.

But I couldn't.

Over the years, I've occasionally thought about that conversation with Maria. Something tells me that our relationship may have taken a different path had I been able to open up. But I didn't, so there remained a distance between us. I could see the disappointment on her face as I changed the subject.

But to her credit, she didn't push me.

CHAPTER FOURTEEN

One of my best memories from my childhood remains our family trips to Cape Cod each summer. We always stayed at the same place, a little condominium, owned by the Cassas family, just down the street from the Chatham lighthouse, across from the beach.

Each morning, the four of us walked together into town to have breakfast at Sandi's Diner, followed by a stroll down Main Street so my sister and mother could visit all of their favorite gift shops and clothing stores. My father and I typically waited patiently together on a bench near the bandstand in Gould Park which, conveniently, was near our favorite candy shop.

Afternoons were spent at the beach, usually Lighthouse Beach, where Mom and Dad sat together on two folding chairs in the sand while my sister and I played in the surf. In the evening, it was on to Veterans Field to watch the Cape Cod baseball league which I aspired to play in one day.

Usually once during our week-long vacation, we would take a drive north along Route 6 toward the Cape Cod National Seashore, stopping for the afternoon at Nauset Beach which always mesmerized me with its huge waves breaking just below Nauset Lighthouse, which rested stoically upon a cliff overlooking the Atlantic Ocean.

We were certainly not a wealthy family, but were comfortable. My father had retired from teaching not long after I was born, choosing to enter the investment business, using the money he had inherited from his mother who had died a few years before. We lived in a nice part of town, just over the top of Bickford Hill, in a little red house that my father had built in the early 1960s.

My friends, the Atters, lived just across the street, and my sister's best friend, Anne Frie, also lived just a few houses away. We all walked to school most days, even in the middle of snowstorms. When it rained, our father dropped us off, and then continued on to the local library to review his investments in the *Wall Street Journal*. The proceeds from these investments would allow us to take our annual trip to Cape Cod.

My sister was four years older than me, so we were never in the same school at the same time. But we spent a lot of time together, especially when we were young children. It was a good time to be a kid. Parents still felt safe about their children playing outside until it was time for dinner. And families always ate together.

Sometimes my sister and I played together in the front yard beneath the giant oak trees, and other times we'd walk down the hill in back of our house, through the woods, until we came to Betty Spring Road. Carefully crossing the rural backstreet, we came to Dunn's Pond, a popular fishing hole with a few docks where you could sit and dangle your feet in the water. In the winter, the pond froze over and become the local skating rink. But our mother always forbade us to skate there, fearing the ice was never thick enough.

I have many memories of my mother, but a few stand out and have remained with me all of these years. I remember her always having a snack prepared for me when I came home from school. My favorite were her brownies, served with milk. I'd sit at the kitchen table devouring as many as I could before she took the plate away, my sister laughing at the chocolate mess on my face. And I remember my mom sitting in her favorite green chair in the living room, a cup of tea on the side table, intently knitting away.

Her best friend was Mrs. Cormier, whose husband was a local newspaper writer, often covering the baseball games I played in elementary and high school. She came to the house every Friday morning while my sister and I were in school to join my mother's Friday Morning Tea Club. There were five members in the club. Besides my mother and Mrs. Cormier, there was Mrs. Atter, Mrs. Frie, and Mrs. Healy, who lived across the street from the Fries. The club would gather at a different house each week, but I could tell that my mother was proudest when they came to our house. She served her friends using her best china, setting-up a small biscuit buffet in the dining room which was otherwise only used for special occasions such as Christmas, Thanksgiving, and birthdays.

While my mother entertained her guests, my father would be careful to remain outside, working down in the woodlot to thin out the trees, rake the leaves, and fight off the mosquitoes. In the winter, I made a sledding-run through those woods, using the trees like poles in a slalom run. One time, I didn't swerve fast enough and slammed into one of the trees, cracking my sled but luckily not my head. My mother came running-out to see if I was okay, then sent me to my room for doing such a stupid thing.

The next day I was outside doing the same stupid thing again.

It was a good childhood, probably better than most. But it certainly wasn't perfect. Although my mother could be strict, my father was the disciplinarian, often yelling to make his point. Age has given me a different perspective on his approach. But at the time, the fear of his wrath caused me to find ways to hide the truth, a habit which plagued me for much of my early adulthood. Mind you, I don't blame my father for any of my own shortcomings. He did the best he could, and much of what he did was a result of how he had been raised by his parents.

In the end, most of our deepest struggles are inherited ones.

CHAPTER FIFTEEN

In fall of 1944, Yvette and Luc finally entered Lorient, assisting the Army to establish a supply route to bring much needed food and water to the city's civilian inhabitants . . . and to continue the search for their parents.

For this particular mission—which was to last only a matter of days—the Army had concluded that George wasn't needed. To distract himself while he waited for Yvette and Luc to return to San Julien, he joined other soldiers in the canteen each evening to watch newsreels of the Allied advance across France.

By then, Patton's 3rd Army had smashed their way across the country, approaching the German West Wall, the so-called Siegfried Line. Early reports were positive, and there were again rumors of an early end to the war if Patton could break-through and make an end-run for the Rhineland.

But it wasn't to be.

The German Wehrmacht was holding firm in the Hurtgen Forest on the border of Belgium, and Hitler was already planning the counter-attack that would become known as the Battle of the Bulge. With no end in sight, the 66th Infantry Division that surrounded Lorient as part of the Atlantic pocket was starting to make plans for a long, cold winter, one that would turn out to be among the coldest of the first half of the twentieth century.

To make it possible for the supply line into Lorient to be established, the air force had begun mercilessly pounding the German positions between Guidel—across the river from George's location in San Julien—and Lorient, forcing the Germans deeper into the city.

As the Germans retreated, Yvette and Luc's unit advanced, arriving on the outskirts of Lorient along the Rue de Gaillec. From atop a hill near the Eglise Sainte Therese, Luc and his sister looked down upon the city they knew well, shocked to see the destruction.

"Comment ma et par ont-ils pu survivre?" asked Yvette of her brother. "Il n'y a que de la dévastation."

"Ils sont vivants. Nous devons y croire."

Yvette shook her head. It was difficult to believe that anyone could have survived.

The plan, when first developed, had been relatively straightforward. A small Allied unit would enter Lorient under cover of darkness and link-up with Resistance fighters inside the city, most of whom were believed to be hiding out on the west side. The Germans had retreated deeper into the city, focusing their forces on the southern quarters near their U-boat base at Keroman, which remained operational despite constant attacks by Allied bombers. Once the link was established, plans could be developed for bringing much needed supplies to the city's population.

A week earlier, Yvette and Luc had forcefully made their case to the Allied commanders that they be allowed to join the proposed mission. Given their familiarity with the city, it hadn't taken long for their request to be granted. George's request, though, had been denied.

Now, a day into that mission, Yvette and Luc were well inside the city, cautiously making their way through the rubble near the Eglise Sainte Therese.

At one point, they passed a wrecked German half-track, keeled over on its side. Nearby was a four-story brick apartment building whose facade had been completely sheared off, leaving the rooms inside exposed. Mangy, emaciated dogs and cats roamed free through the rubble, foraging for food and water. But despite it all, not a single human being was in sight. Luc and Yvette's unit continued its advance toward the Scorff River which divided the city into eastern and western quadrants, remaining on high alert, prepared for snipers or an ambush.

But nothing came.

"Where are all the people?" asked Yvette, as Luc and the other members of their unit stopped and knelt down, surveying the area in all directions. She then removed a map from her backpack. "This is where we need to get," she pointed. "Where the Avenue de Normandie crosses the Boulevard du Scorff before continuing over the river."

"We know the bridge is destroyed," said one unit member. "There is no way across."

"We don't need to get across," countered Yvette. "If we can find a clear route to the river, then the Army can use it to float supplies into the heart of the city."

The various unit members looked at each other, puzzled. "That's not the plan," replied one. "We get to the river, link up with Resistance units nearby, and then head north until we get to the perimeter of the pocket. If it's clear, then more units will be sent to secure the route."

Yvette protested. "Oui, but if the route is already clear, then let's hold it ourselves and wait for the other units to arrive."

"Tu es fou," answered another member of the unit, a Resistance fighter who had escaped the city as the Allies were establishing their perimeter nearly a month earlier. "We can't *hold* territory. Ce n'est pas notre mission."

Luc stared at the man angrily. "Then go north. My sister and I'll reach the river alone."

"Seul? You'll never make it.".

"Pourquoi pas?" answered Luc. "Do you see any Germans?"

"Vos deux fous!" said the Resistance fighter. "The riverfront is destroyed. There is nothing there."

"Exactamente" replied Yvette. "There is nothing there. So we hold it ourselves, signal other Resistance units to join us, and then send word for the military to begin sending supplies down the river."

Nearly all the members of Luc and Yvette's unit shook their heads, flabbergasted. "Do what you want," said another. "We're following orders. Once we see the river, we're heading north."

And that was exactly the reaction that Yvette and Luc had hoped for.

They'd never intended to follow the Army's plan. Once they had confirmed that the northwest quadrant of the city was reasonably secure, they intended to find a way across the river, following its eastern banks southward until they reached the Le Blavet River. Near the confluence of the two rivers was their uncle's home, and perhaps residing with him, their parents. It was a huge risk, to say the least. They were going against the Army, and the consequences could be severe.

But in their minds, they had no other choice.

CHAPTER SIXTEEN

Maria and I rode together to our posts in the back of a Peace Corps pickup truck, a three-hour drive from the capital of Bangui, traveling over rugged dirt roads while holding on to anything within reach to avoid being thrown from the truck.

An hour or so into the journey, the monsoon rains arrived, turning the roads into a quagmire. At one point, I jumped out of the truck to help free it from the thick mud. In the process, I lost one of my sandals in the sloppy mess and was forced to continue the trip barefoot, much to the amusement of my travel companions.

About thirty minutes before arriving at my post in Boda, we stopped in Mbaiki to drop off Maria at a small clinic and providing AIDS education throughout the village of perhaps ten thousand people. Although not as prevalent as in east or west Africa, it was estimated that five percent of the population in equatorial Africa had contracted the deadly disease. Without any cure, governments were encouraged to focus on prevention, which meant convincing people to revise their sexual behavior, including the use of condoms.

But governments were slow to respond, fearing backlash from religious authorities, particularly in the Muslim community, of which Mbaiki had a large contingent. As a result, local clinics had turned to NGOs and Peace Corps volunteers to conduct much of the public relations. But with the country already teetering on the edge of conflict, such work had become very dangerous. Along with two armed security guards, the clinic's female supervisor, Jeanne, was waiting for us when we arrived, helping to offload Maria's duffle bags as the rain continued to fall. She was also kind enough to find me a new pair of sandals.

Jeanne was a French missionary—although she prioritized her medical duties over her religious beliefs so as not to alienate the local Muslim population—and had been in-country for nearly two years. She spoke some English but immediately insisted that Maria communicate with her only in French, and that she begin learning as much Sangho as possible.

Outside the capital, only students and business owners spoke French, she explained, and certainly no one spoke English. But despite these various instructions, what Jeanne had failed to tell Maria on that first day was that the clinic's previous Peace Corps volunteer had only stayed in-country for a few months, before returning to America. We wouldn't discover the reason for that early departure until months later.

After a few hours in Mbaiki, Maria and I said goodbye, as it was time for me to continue on my way to Boda, not far down the road. It was hard to part ways. Admittedly, probably harder for me, as Maria was always the stronger one. But we'd been through a lot together in a relatively short period of time. So we promised to see each other as frequently as possible, since our villages were not far apart.

As my journey to Boda continued, I rode with another volunteer who was to be my postmate. Like me, Lisa was going to be a teacher at the village school, having completed her language training in Liberia. And also like me, she had already gone through some adventures.

Regional instability in the west African nation had forced the Peace Corps to hastily abandon the country, resulting in the redistribution of volunteers to other countries, including the Central African Republic. But unlike me, she had always wanted to be a teacher and had completed her bachelor's degree in curriculum & instruction to fulfill that dream.

Lisa and I were dropped off near the village school in a compound where many of the teachers lived. Appearing more like military housing than an accommodation for educators, we learned that the school had once been run by Christian missionaries, harkening back to the French colonial era when so much of central Africa was run by France and Belgium, both of whom had sent many missionaries to the region in an effort to spread Christianity throughout, what they considered to be, a pagan population.

Lisa and I were immediately met by the headmaster of the school, Mr. Sivori, who quickly made it clear to the others who surrounded our pick-up truck that he wasn't particularly enthralled by our presence.

"Regarde ici, deux autres américains viennent nous apprendre à enseigner," he said sarcastically. "Montrons leur à leur nouvelle maison."

Fortunately, a young boy who would be one of our students was kind enough to show Lisa and I to our accommodation. "Ignore le," he said "Il déteste juste les américains. Mais la plupart d'entre nous sont heureux que vous soyez ici."

"*Most* of them are happy we're here?" whispered Lisa to me as we followed the young boy, carrying our own duffle bags. "Guess that means that some wish we *weren't* here."

I shrugged my shoulders but then recalled the two security guards at Maria's clinic in Mbaiki. There was no such security presence at our compound, and it quickly began to dawn on Lisa and me that we were very much alone, nearly a three-hour drive from the capital where the Peace Corps maintained their in-country offices, and in a village that had only a few telephones.

Nevertheless, we immediately began making the best of our situation, understanding that the next two years would be like living in a fishbowl. We wouldn't be able to do anything or go anywhere without being the constant center of attention. Since Lisa was much more sociable and affable than me – a personality that reminded me of my sister – I thought her adjustment was in some ways going to be easier.

But she had her own challenges.

American women, or Western women in general, had come to expect equal treatment in all ways that mattered in their home countries. But such wasn't the case throughout most of Africa where women were expected to be subservient to men. I could tell almost immediately that Lisa was insulted by the way men were looking at her.

Undoubtedly, her instinct was to make some crude gesture in response. To her credit, she resisted that temptation. But her anger certainly didn't subside. As we settled into the compound for our first night in Boda, the men all sat around drinking, while the women cooked, supervised the children, and fed the drunk men. As they did, Lisa seethed with anger.

But we had other challenges to overcome.

First and foremost, we had to explain to the school's headmaster that we didn't want to live together in the same apartment. Whether he had assumed that we were a couple, or did it just to spite us, we were assigned to a one-bedroom apartment at the far-end of the compound, slightly down the hill from the school. The entire compound consisted of perhaps a dozen buildings, each with three or four apartments. Some had one bedroom. Others two. They all had a kitchen (although there was no running water), and they all had a bathroom (although the toilets didn't flush). When we complained about these issues, the headmaster laughed, telling us to use the bucket in the kitchen to fetch water from the nearby river.

Later that first evening, Lisa and I walked down to that river to find that it was being used to wash clothes, to swim, and as an outdoor latrine. We filled our bucket with water. But needless to say, we were intent upon boiling it. Yet, even that posed a challenge since there was no electricity or gas. So, Lisa committed herself to making a fire in the wood-burning stove of our apartment's kitchen. But we soon realized that the stove had no ventilation. When we later emerged from the apartment coughing from the fumes, the other teachers in the compound began to laugh hysterically.

By midnight, the mostly male teaching staff had succumbed to the effects of their drinking binge, and the women had gotten the children to bed, so Lisa and I turned our attention to figuring-out our sleeping arrangement. We were both so tired that it was tempting to just sleep together in the one double-bed of our partially furnished apartment. But not all of the windows had shutters, so we realized that the next day would likely begin with the compound's kids peering into the bedroom to observe the two white people. Wanting to avoid that situation, I decided to sleep on the floor. Within minutes, I was asleep.

We'd survived our first day. Barely.

The next morning, Lisa and I awoke early to the sounds of chickens and roosters running free throughout the compound. As we emerged from our apartment to walk down to the river to refill our bucket for a shower, we were immediately met by dozens of the children tugging at our pants and saying, "Enseignant . . . enseignant."

This again brought lots of laughter from the adults who seemed to be viewing us as a new form of entertainment. When we arrived at the river, we found some women bathing topless in the shallow, muddy waters near the river's edge. This seemed to embarrass me more than Lisa, who removed her sandals and waded into the water to fill the bucket. One of the bathers, perhaps feeling sorry for us, approached us and said something in Sangho. Lisa and I looked at her blankly, at which point the young woman switched to French.

"Vous êtes les deux nouveaux enseignants?" asked the woman, making no effort to cover herself.

"Oui," replied Lisa. "Nous avons besoin d'eau pour une douche."

The woman laughed, but then motioned for us to follow her. "Viens avec moi," she said.

Still topless, the woman guided us upriver along the riverbank until we could hear the sounds of water falling. She pointed for us to continue onward. "Une cascade pour votre douche," she said. And then added, "Attention aux serpents."

"Snakes?" I said, stopping in my tracks.

But Lisa didn't care, her patience clearly running thin. "Let's just go. I really need a shower."

We continued a few hundred feet further, making our way through some thick undergrowth and muddy ground until we arrived at a pool of water at the base of a twenty-foot waterfall.

Lisa looked at me for a moment, before beginning to remove her clothes, save for her bra and panties. I shrugged and followed suit, our shyness quickly fading as we enjoyed the cool, clean water of the falls.

We would return there frequently over the following months, coming to learn that it was known locally as Les Chutes de Boali. At first, we couldn't understand why more of the villagers didn't use it for showering and collecting water. But we later learned that a child had drowned in its shallow waters a few years earlier, so the locals had come to consider it a cursed site.

CHAPTER SEVENTEEN

As Lisa and I slowly settled into our new surroundings, we began exploring the small village of less than five thousand, known as a center of diamond mining. Like Mbaiki, the population of Boda included both Christians and Muslims, each controlling their own section of the town, separated by the main street which started on the hilltop near the school and continued down toward a small hospital. Along the sides of this road were scattered various shops, restaurants, and bars, mostly owned by the local Muslim population. Near the hospital was the village's largest residence, owned by a French diamond merchant.

Eric, we were told, came to town each year during the dry season to buy diamonds, some of which he sold in neighboring countries, and some—presumably the larger pieces—he would bring back to France where they would be recut and eventually find their way to jewelry stores throughout Europe, and perhaps even the United States.

With his own generator and car, he enjoyed an elaborate lifestyle, one that reminded me of Gaspard from Bukavu. Later that year, Eric would become an integral part of our experience in CAR. But during those first few weeks of our stay in Boda, every time I passed-by his walled compound I couldn't help but remember Jean Pierre, wondering what had become of him. It seemed as though all of equatorial Africa had become slaves to the diamond trade.

Toward the end of our first week in Boda, Lisa and I attended our first staff meeting at the school in preparation for the start of classes the following week. This was our first time actually going inside the school and seeing our classrooms, and it became immediately apparent that we had our work cut-out for ourselves. The school consisted of six buildings, all constructed of cinder-blocks with rusty, tin roofs. The majority of the doors and window panes appeared missing, and the classroom furniture consisted of little more than wooden benches and tables.

One of the teachers must have seen us standing in a classroom agape, so approached.

"Not exactly what you expected?" he said, in perfect English, with a distinct British accent. "At one time, this school was one of the best in the area," he continued. "But that was a long, long time ago."

Lisa and I stared at him, surprised to hear English in the middle of Boda.

The teacher laughed. "Jafari," he declared, extending his hand in greeting. "I teach English and world history here."

"Your English is very good," I said. "Where did you learn it?"

"London," he replied. "My parents own the local discotheque. Have you been there yet?" he asked with a wide smile. "It's the place to be!"

Lisa and I shook our heads, but remembered walking past such a place as we explored the town.

"Not to worry," he continued. "I'll take you there as my guests. As for my English, my parents sent me to live with my aunt in London so I could attend college."

"And you came back here?" I asked, genuinely surprised. "Why not stay in the UK?

Lisa elbowed me.

"It's okay," replied Jafari, laughing deeply. "I'm not sure how long I'll stay, but I thought I should give something back to the community. It's not much to see now, but when I was growing up, actually a pretty nice place."

"Why did it change?" I asked.

"About ten years ago the Musulman began arriving from Bangui," said Jafari, a notable tone of disdain in his voice. "They bought many of the stores and restaurants that the locals could no longer afford to operate. Resentment ran deep, and the violence began."

"We haven't seen any violence," noted Lisa. "And the teachers seem to be a mix of Christians and Muslims."

"They are," agreed Jafari. "Mr. Sivori, our headmaster, has made an effort to demonstrate to the community that the two groups can co-exist."

"He doesn't seem to care for us," I said, remembering our greeting as we arrived in Boda.

Jafari laughed again. "Don't mind him," he said, putting his hand on my shoulder. "He's a real leader in this town, but doesn't care much for whites. He sees you as mainly responsible for the country's historical hardships."

I nodded. "He's probably right."

"But if anyone mistreats either of you," continued Jafari, suddenly becoming very serious. "He'll be the first to stand up for you. Good man. But complicated one."

"Do you know anything about Mbaiki?" I asked, thinking of Maria. "Is it safe?"

"No more or less than here," he replied. "But take my advice. Don't walk around at night alone here. Especially you, Lisa. And tell your friend in Mbaiki the same, especially if she's a woman. The teenagers here are tough, always desperate for money and empowerment. Dangerous mix."

"I'll be fine," said Lisa, shrugging her shoulders. "They're just kids."

"Don't be foolish," snapped Jafari, looking over his shoulder to see if anyone was listening. "This place could explode at any moment. Do your job as teachers, but watch your backs."

Lisa and I looked at each other, unsure of how to respond.

Sensing our discomfort, Jafari then softened his tone. "Now, why don't both of you join me tonight at the discotheque. We'll have some beers, meet some people, and enjoy each other's company." He slapped me on the back.

How could we refuse?

Later that night, Lisa and I joined our new friend at his parents' bar, Afrozila, sitting around a large table with other members of the school's staff, including—somewhat to our surprise—Mr. Sivori.

Unlike most of the other bars and restaurants in Boda which were little more than residential houses with front-rooms transformed into bars, Afrozila was very Westernized. The menu included hamburgers and fries, and the music was mostly American top-40. At the center of the bar was a large dance-floor above which hung a disco-ball. I felt as though John Travolta was going t at any minute.

"How long have your parents owned this place?" I asked Jafari, as Lisa leaned in to hear me over the pulsating music.

"My grandparents started it as a small restaurant serving missionaries and their staff. Then my parents took over, made it bigger, added the dance floor. Ever since then it has been a place where everyone felt comfortable drinking, dancing, and talking about everything, even local politics," answered Jafari, taking a big swig from his pint of local beer. "But when my parents sell it, who knows what will happen."

"They're going to sell it?" asked Lisa. "Why don't you take over?"

Jafari laughed loudly, as he pushed his empty pint to the center of the table and motioned for one of the pretty waitresses to fill it up again. "Oh no! This is not for me! It takes a special kind of person to run a place like this."

"But it seems like the town really needs a place like this," I added, as the waitress poured more beer into our glasses.

"True. There is no other place like this in Boda," replied Jafari, already beginning to slur his speech. "But I'm not the one to keep it going. Perhaps our favorite headmaster should consider it," he added.

Sivori turned to us, and for the first time since we'd met him, actually smiled. "Je suis un écolier, pas un barman," he said, drinking down a shot of something green. "Personne ne peut remplacer vos parents," he continued, holding up his glass in salute. "Cette ville a besoin d'eux pour rester."

"What do you know about that local diamond merchant," I asked Jafari, changing the subject. "Does he ever come here?"

"A few times. But he mostly stays in his house behind those big walls."

"Not your favorite guy?" I said, responding to Jafari's tone of voice.

"No, he's not. But that doesn't matter. If you get yourself into trouble, you're better going to him than the police," said Jafari very purposefully. "Remember that."

"Any kind of trouble?" I asked.

"Any kind." confirmed Jafari. "Complicated guy and very unpopular with most people sitting at this table," he continued, looking around. "But I've known people who have gone to him with problems. He helped them, and discreetly."

I wanted to ask more questions, but I could tell that Jafari had had enough and wanted to enjoy the music and the company of his friends. He stood up with his beer in-hand and made his way to the dance floor.

I turned to Lisa and motioned to the dance floor. "Let's dance," she agreed.

CHAPTER EIGHTEEN

In the days that followed our night-out with Jafari, Lisa and I continued to gain more confidence in navigating our surroundings. But one issue remained to be dealt with: our living arrangement, specifically, the sleeping part. We'd concluded that it would be better if I found my own accommodation, separate from the teachers' compound. While we had no problem living together, it was clear from the reaction of the other teachers that they considered us to be together.

I also wondered if Maria would feel the same way.

In retrospect, I doubt that she would've really cared. She was very independent and far more mature than I.

Just before the start of the school year, I moved into a thatched-roof hut on the outskirts of the town. A previous Peace Corps volunteer had lived there for two years. During that time, she had painted the inside and outside white, planted a garden, and installed a perimeter picket-fence. It was unquestionably the only painted mud-hut in Boda.

Unlike in the teacher's compound, where the water source was the river, my little neighborhood had its own well which produced reasonably clean water for bathing and washing clothes. The bathroom, however, was a hole in the ground behind the hut, surrounded by a short fence. During my first use of these facilities, I was startled when I looked up and saw many little faces peering over the fence. Needless to say, the next day I prioritized the building of a higher fence.

On my second night in the hut, the night before Lisa and I began our teaching duties, she and Jafari visited. We sat outside the hut beneath the moonlight drinking beer and eating fruit. Jafari had already cautioned against Lisa and I living apart, insisting that we were safer together, despite the gossip.

"It doesn't matter what anyone thinks," he said to us, as we each sat in a wooden chair near the garden. "What matters is that you're both safe."

"But the teachers won't respect me if I live with John," replied Lisa, reaching for the plate of mangoes and pineapple. "I need to establish myself."

Jafari shook his head. "Take my word for it," he said insistently. "No matter what you do, they won't respect you."

"But what about Kelly," I asked, referring to the previous volunteer whose hut I'd taken over. "From what we're told, she really became part of the community."

"True," agreed Jafari. "But she spoke nearly fluent French and had learned a lot of Sangho."

"My French's pretty good. Although I'm not sure about John." said Lisa, looking at me and smiling.

We all laughed.

"Seriously, though" continued Jafari. "We teach these kids French in school, but most will never use it. Not to mention that we teach them calculus and chemistry, information which has no value in this village. They'll speak Sangho their entire lives, and most will never leave this village. Kelly understood that and learned Sangho so she could tutor the kids in their own language. She talked to them, not over them."

"So she was respected," said Lisa.

"She was respected for her effort to learn Sangho, but she was white and a woman," said Jafari. "No matter how much she tried, she never had their full respect."

"Are women really treated that badly here?" asked Lisa.

Jafari looked hard at Lisa. "You haven't traveled much, and don't know much of the world . . ."

Lisa sat forward abruptly. "Excuse me!"

"Don't get me wrong. You deserve a lot credit for coming here. But you'll soon learn that women throughout most of the developing world—the so-called Third World—are oppressed. Men look at them as sexual objects. Not equals. In fact, if you spoke with every woman living in these huts," added Jafari, "nearly all of them would tell you that they've been raped by their husbands at one time or another, if they even understand the concept of rape."

Lisa sat back. I could see that she was processing what Jafari was saying.

He continued. "It's true that education is important, especially for girls. But they don't need to learn calculus or physics. They need to learn new ways of farming and caring for the land. They need to learn how to start a small business. And most importantly, they need to learn that they deserve the same rights as men. But that message needs to come from other Africans, not white foreigners."

"So you don't think we should be here ?" I asked Jafari, pointedly.

"You're here for your own reasons, and I for one respect that. But Kelly was what I think you call a *true believer*," said Jafari. "Like the missionaries of long ago, she thought she had come here to save everybody. And believe me, African men will not respond to that."

"Was she harassed?" asked Lisa.

Jafari took a big swig of his beer. "She was assaulted. More than once."

"What?" said Lisa, incredulously. "No one told us that."

"Common knowledge around here," replied Jafari simply.

"But why would the Peace Corps let her stay here if she wasn't safe?" I asked.

"To be honest, I don't think they knew," answered Jafari. "I don't think she ever told them. But I think you need to know. It's why I think you're better off living together."

In the days that followed, I could tell that Lisa was rattled. She still insisted that we live apart. But she was quieter and constantly looked over her shoulder. And the first day of school certainly didn't help to improve her disposition.

My walk to school along a dirt path took me over the hills and through little neighborhoods. People were pleasant in greeting me.

"Tonga na nyen," they would say. "Ye ake ape," I would reply, using the extent of my Sangho.

But I couldn't help but think about what Jafari had said to Lisa and I. I was worried for her, but even more worried about Maria. I'd already decided to visit her in Mbaiki that weekend. But first, I'd to get through my first day of school.

As I approached the compound from the rear, I could see many of the kids playing soccer behind the buildings. Even some of the teachers had joined the game. It was a popular sport throughout Africa, mostly because it didn't require any expensive equipment. As I passed by the players and student-spectators, I caught the attention of one of the teachers playing goalie.

"Joue avec nous," he yelled. "C'est comme ça qu'on commence tous les jours."

I hesitated, realizing that I wasn't properly dressed to play. But then I remembered something that Jafari had said to us. How important it was that we looked for ways to gain the trust and respect of the community. So I threw down my backpack and headed out onto the field.

It was only 7.30 in the morning, but the humidity had already set-in. After less than five minutes of running back and forth on the field, I was dripping in sweat. But the high-fives I received from the students and teachers made the effort worthwhile.

It was then that I heard a hand-bell ringing. It was the headmaster, Mr. Sivori, announcing the start of the school day.

The game ended almost instantaneously—to be continued during the school-day's first break—as the kids went running toward the flagpole in the central courtyard. I saw Lisa standing with some of the teachers near one of the classroom buildings. I joined her, and listened to Mr. Sivori rally the "troops" for another year of learning. I learned later on that nearly half of those troops were not in attendance on that first day because they were still working the nearby diamond mines and panning the riverbeds. When the rainy season returned in a few months, so would they. At the start of the school year, education wasn't their priority.

Following Mr. Sivori's remarks, we all made our way to our respective classrooms. My room was toward the front of the school, not far from the main office. As I entered the room, the students were already waiting for me, rising in unison as I entered.

"Bonjour professeur," they all said.

"Merci," I replied. "Asseyez-vous, s'il vous plaît." They all sat down, having no idea just how nervous I was.

The school's secretary had left a roster on my table which I used to take attendance. It took some time, as I'd more than fifty students in my class, sitting three-by-three on the benches that filled the room from front to back, with another twenty standing outside the classroom, wondering how the new, white teacher would fare on his first day.

To my own surprise, I did pretty well.

Ironically, I was teaching high school math even though I'd done poorly in most of my high school math courses before turning things around in college. But unlike the textbooks and calculators that American kids took for granted, these students had nothing more than a single notebook into which they copied everything that I wrote on the blackboard.

The classroom itself had no shelves or posters. No technology of any kind. No AC. Not even any lights. But I found the kids willing to learn, enthusiastically raising their hands to answer questions. As the day progressed and different sections came through my classroom, I began to question if Jafari was correct in his comments about the students' lack of respect for white teachers.

Then came lunch.

There was no cafeteria where the students could purchase food. So many went home for the hour-long break. I looked around for Lisa, expecting to see her in the little staff lounge where some of the other teachers ate their lunch. But when I didn't find her, I walked over to the teachers' accommodations and found her alone in her apartment, in tears.

"What happened?

"They kept screaming," she said. "No matter what I tried, they wouldn't listen to me."

"Which section?" I asked.

"All of them," she replied, trying hard to control her tears.

"I'm so sorry. Is there anything I can do? Maybe I can come into your classroom," I suggested.

She wiped away her tears, and said defiantly, "No, I need to do this myself. They're just kids. Maybe this afternoon will be better."

It wasn't.

Before leaving school that day I checked her classroom and found a few of her students sitting on the floor talking to each other. They were also my students for math. When I asked them about Lisa, they started laughing. I wanted to respond to their disrespect, but knew it wasn't what Lisa would've wanted me to do. So I just shook my head, and left the room.

Later that day I visited Lisa and half-expected to find her sulking. But she wasn't. She was preparing for the next day's lessons.

"You're something," I said, smiling. "You don't give up."

"After just one day, I don't," she replied, but then added, "maybe next week." She looked up from her table and smiled.

"How was *your* day?" she asked.

"The tenth-grade class was the worst. I think they knew more than me."

"I doubt that. Probably just testing you."

"Probably," I agreed, and then changed the subject. "Have you thought more about what Jafari was saying to us the other night?"

"About living together?" she answered, with a wink. "You want to move back in?"

"No," I answered, smiling. "About Kelly. Do you really think she never told anyone about what happened to her?"

"I don't know," replied Lisa, putting down her pen and sitting back in her chair. "If she had told the Peace Corps, I'm sure they would've informed us."

"Maybe."

She looked at me quizzically. "You don't think they would hide that from the volunteers replacing her, do you?"

"I don't know, honestly," I admitted. "But remember the security at Maria's clinic in Mbaiki? It was almost as if they were expecting problems."

'You're worried about her, aren't you," she said. "Are you still going to visit this weekend?" Lisa and I'd grown close, and genuinely cared for each other.

"I think so, yes," I replied. "It's just hard not having any communication."

The days that followed were a bit better for Lisa. On one occasion, Jafari was walking by her classroom when the students were acting up. He stepped inside and spoke firmly with them in Sangho. Lisa wasn't quite sure exactly what he had said, but it seemed to have had the desired effect.

On another occasion Jafari stepped into my room and observed a few moments of my lesson. He nodded in approval before leaving.

It was the positive reinforcement I needed.

But my mind was on Maria and the trip to Mbaiki that Friday night. It was the first of many such trips that I would take during my time in Boda, each one was memorable than the last, if for no other reason than for the dangers of traveling even that short distance between towns.

There were no busses or taxis. Instead, you did your best to catch a ride in the back of some random pick-up truck carrying supplies back and forth. On that first trip, I was fortunate enough to find a ride in *un camion* carrying cases of beer, some of which were from the bar of Jafari's parents. When I went to pay the driver, he refused, telling me that the transportation had actually been arranged by Jafari.

He had become a good friend, always looking out for Lisa and me.

After bouncing around in the back of the pickup for the duration of the thirty-minute trip, the driver dropped me at Maria's clinic. The two guards stopped me at the main gate, asking for identification. I showed them a copy of my passport, having been told many times by the Peace Corps to always carry a copy, never the original. Then, just as the guards were letting me pass, Maria emerged from inside the clinic with a big smile on her face.

"I can't believe you're here!" she exclaimed. "I've missed you."

"And I've missed you," I answered simply, as we embraced. "I've missed you so much."

CHAPTER NINETEEN

George was livid with frustration.

Yvette and Luc had been gone for weeks with no communication. At least none that he was aware of. When he was finally called into his commanding officer's tent, he was expecting the worst, barely able to breath.

"At ease, son," said Sergeant Broninsky, who was in-charge of overseeing the plans for establishing the supply route into Lorient. "Be seated." He gestured to a chair in front of his desk, which was little more than a piece of wood resting upon cinder blocks.

Privates rarely sat in the presence of a superior officer, so the informality of the moment made George even more apprehensive.

"I've been reviewing your file," began the Sergeant. "Unusual, to say the least."

"Yes, sir."

"How do you explain it?"

"Sir?" replied George, unsure of how to respond.

The sergeant looked down at the file in front of him on his desk. "Says here that you've been tasked with providing language support for two Resistance fighters. One of them, since Cherbourg."

"Yes, sir," replied George. "Yvette and Luc."

The sergeant continued reading the file. "A Sgt. Cummings gives you high marks. Says to contact him with any questions about you and the woman."

"Yes, sir." George replied. "Sgt Cummings was my commanding officer back in England."

Sgt. Broninsky nodded without looking up. "But your language rating is low," he said. "Lower than most translators."

"Yes, sir, my French could be better."

The sergeant looked up and stared at George before continuing. "Look private, the Army has clearly allowed you to operate outside of normal boundaries for many months, even before Normandy. I realize that your relationship with the woman is, how should we say, not necessarily sanctioned."

"Yes, sir," replied George. "But has something happened, sir?" asked George, unable to contain himself any longer.

"You realize that I don't agree with what the Army has allowed you to do?"

"Yes, sir. I understand," replied George. "But, please . . ."

The sergeant sighed and put up his hands. "But I don't make the decisions around here. I do as I'm told."

George sat there waiting for the sergeant to continue.

"I've been ordered to send you to Lorient," said the commanding officer, finally.

"Sir?"

"Your girlfriend and her brother are still alive. But they've gone rogue."

George closed his eyes, thankful for the good news, but then thought more about the sergeant's words. "I don't understand, sir. What does that mean, gone *rogue*?"

"Their recon unit is returning now to the perimeter. But your friends stayed behind, continuing deeper into the city," said the sergeant. "And nobody seems to know why."

But George knew why. They were looking for their parents. "Why do you want *me* to go?" he then asked the sergeant.

"Ordinarily, we wouldn't care what they're doing. They're not US Army. If they want to get themselves killed, that's not our problem," replied Sergeant Broninsky. "But in recent days there's been a significant uptick in communication from the Resistance. It's allowed us to target some specific Kraut command positions."

"Other units?" questioned George. "So Yvette and Luc are not alone?"

"Again, nobody knows," answered the sergeant. "But we want that communication to continue."

George tried to process what he was being told. "So what am I supposed to do exactly, sir?"

"Find them," said the sergeant, simply. "Find them, and get them to be a conduit between us and the Resistance."

Something didn't add up. "You'd still trust them after they abandoned the recon unit, sir?" asked George.

"I don't, no," admitted the sergeant. "But somebody up the chain of command must."

George nodded. "Okay, but how do I get into the city?"

The sergeant stood up and walked over to a table with a large map of Lorient. "This is where your lady friend and her brother separated from the recon unit," said the sergeant, pointing at the map. "You'll be taken to this same location tomorrow night."

"Tomorrow, sir?" asked George, surprised at how quickly things were moving.

"Yes," replied the sergeant. "We'll try to get a message through that you're coming. We're guessing that your lady will be there to meet you."

George thought about the plan for a moment. "But how do I know that you won't try to nab Yvette and Luc when they arrive at the rendezvous point?"

The sergeant stared at George, not looking happy about the private's tone. "Why would we? We want them to keep operating in the city."

George nodded, but didn't completely believe the sergeant, or the Army, in general. But he knew it was his best chance to reunite with Yvette. "Where are most of the Germans?" he asked, continuing to look at the map.

"Most have been pushed to the southern part of the city, defending their sub-base at Keroman," said the sergeant, again pointing at the map. "A few clicks to the south of your rendezvous point, along the Scorff River."

George leaned over the map, looking for the area where Yvette and Luc had thought their parents might be. The sergeant watched carefully. "You know where they're going, private?" he asked.

George looked up. "No, sir. I have no idea."

But George had a general idea.

Before leaving, Yvette had told him that they believed their uncle was staying with other relatives who lived near L'eglise Saint Joseph du Plessis, near the Parc du Plessis, on the east side of the river. If they could find their uncle, maybe they would find their parents.

"So, you'll go in?" asked the sergeant.

"Yes, sir."

"Then good luck to you, son," said the sergeant. "But just remember, your relationship with the girl is not permitted and you could still be brought up on charges for fraternization," he warned. "Unless, of course, she continues to be useful to the Army. Understood?"

"Yes, sir," answered George. "I understand."

In the months since the Allied perimeter around Lorient had been formed to create one of the so-called Atlantic pockets, the Allies had slowly been shrinking the pocket, moving closer and closer to the outskirts of the city. Meanwhile, the Germans focused all of their efforts on protecting their base at Keroman. But by the early winter of 1944, any attempt to move their U-boats into the open Atlantic was immediately met with overwhelming

Allied power from the air and sea. There was little the Germans could do to stop the Allied supply lines that stretched from America to Europe.

As Winston Churchill had so famously said, the New World had indeed awoken and come to the aid of the Old World. But the war was far from over.

As George prepared to enter the outskirts of Lorient, events were unfolding around the world. President Roosevelt had just been elected to an unprecedented fourth term, but would not live to see the summer of 1945.

The American Army had reached the outskirts of Metz in Eastern France and were within striking distance of the German border.

On the Eastern Front, the Red Army had broken through German lines in the Ukraine and had Poland in their sights. German V2 rockets continued to hit Britain at a rate of nearly ten per day. In Asia, the island of Peleliu had fallen to the Allies as American B-29 bombers began using their new bases on Tinian Island to conduct bombing raids over Tokyo.

Hitler himself had left his headquarters at Rastenberg to descend into his bunker beneath Berlin. Eight months later he would be dead. But for George, it all seemed so far away. Only one thing mattered.

Yvette.

The sergeant had assigned six men to accompany George to the rendezvous point where they expected Yvette and Luc to be waiting. Three of the six men had just returned from the city following their separation from Yvette and Luc. So they were not overly thrilled about the order to return.

"You must have some kind of pull with the brass for this escort into the city," said one of them as they walked along the edge of the river and darkness began to fall. In the distance, they could see flashes of light, as Allied bombers continued to hit German targets near the port. "Far as I'm concerned, they should just be left to fend for themselves."

George was tempted to respond, but thought better of it, realizing that he needed these men to guide him to the rendezvous point. So he tried to change the subject. "What's it like in the city?" he asked. "Did you see any civilians?"

One of the younger soldiers replied. "Not many. Few we saw were scavenging for food. It must be tough. No electricity. No running water."

"Are we able to get supplies to them?" asked George.

"That was the whole point of going into the city," said the first soldier. "Open a supply line. At least that's what I thought we were doing, until your friends decided to do something different."

"Maybe they had a good reason," said the young soldier. George guessed he was barely eighteen.

"FUBAR," said another. "Total FUBAR. Why should we risk our lives for two Resistance fighters? No Germans in the northern part of the city. Supplies can easily be brought in without any communication with the Resistance."

"But once the supplies get to the northern part of the city," said George, "don't we need the Resistance to help get those supplies deeper into the city where many of the civilians are unable to escape?"

There was no response.

George understood that the Resistance was crucial to the Allied plans. The sergeant had also understood it, even though he had been reluctant to admit it. The Germans controlled the southern part of the city, and only local Resistance fighters could move about without being singled out by the Germans. They would have to be the ones to bring the supplies down from the north. He had no doubt that Yvette and Luc were trying to coordinate these efforts. But he also knew that they were simultaneously looking for their parents.

Shortly before midnight they arrived at the rendezvous point, the western side of Le Pont des Indes which crossed the Scorff River just to the west of L'église Saint Joseph du Plessis, near the Parc du Plessis, where George believed Yvette and Luc had gone.

But the other members of the recon unit were not aware of this.

Even George was unsure as to how the rendezvous would play out. Would Yvette and Luc risk showing up? If they did, how would the unit react? Would they simply welcome Yvette and Luc back into the fold as if nothing had happened?

"Are we in the right place?" asked one of the unit members, struggling to see anything in the dark. "Maybe we're supposed to be on the other side of the river," he considered.

The older soldier looked toward George and waited for a response. When none came, he ordered two of his men to the other side of the river, using what remained of the bridge that appeared to have been hit multiple times by Allied bombers, or perhaps even blown up by the resistance attempting to limit the ability of the Germans to be resupplied.

George looked eastward across the river toward the Parc du Plessis which wasn't far from the bridge. He suddenly became more confident that perhaps Yvette's parents could have survived. But that was assuming that they had even made it out of their home near Utah Beach months earlier.

George had not wanted to think too much about everything that had happened since D-Day. He tried instead to focus on each day, doing whatever it took to stay positive. The past few days had perhaps been the hardest. He knew he wanted to spend his life with Yvette, but it seemed almost pointless to think about it. You never knew if you'd even be alive the next day. Still, he had no doubts about entering the city to look for her.

But as he stood near the ruins of the bridge waiting for any sign of movement, he also understood the risks. The Germans were probably a few clicks to the south, but were known to send snipers into the northern sectors. And even though the Allies would not bomb the center of the city out of fear of hitting the thousands of civilians that remained, bombing was nonetheless inaccurate, and mis-drops were common. At any moment, a bomb could drop on their location.

Just then, one of the two unit members who had crossed the ruins of the bridge thought he saw movement near a building to their immediate left. "Over there," he whispered to his partner, pointing toward a bank at the corner of the Le Boulevard Niemen and Le Rue Raymond Guillemot. "See," he said again, a bit louder. "There. Upstairs window."

"Flash," one of them said, using the most current password the soldiers used to avoid friendly fire. When there was no reply, they said it again. "Flash."

Minutes passed, and then the response came. "Thunder."

By then, George had also made his way across the partially frozen river, hopping from one concrete chunk to another that had fallen into the water when the bridge had been mostly destroyed. He was now close enough to the eastern bank to hear the exchange of passwords.

"Stay where you are!" shouted the unit leader to George from the other side of the bridge, immediately regretting the volume of his voice.

George had already reached the corner of the bank. He crouched down for a moment, looking back at his unit leader, seemingly considering his next move. But then he sprung forward, disappearing around the corner.

"Son of a bitch," said the unit leader. "Damn fool."

"What do we do, sir?" asked another. "Should I go after him?"

The unit leader was clearly reluctant, but knew that George was his responsibility. "Yeah, go after him. We have no choice."

Two more men crossed the bridge and joined up with the other two on the eastern side of the river near the bank. The four men then moved slowly forward, doing their best to remain in the shadows. They approached the side of the bank where George had disappeared, and called out his name in hushed voices.

No reply.

They then tried the code. "Flash," one of them said.

Again, no reply.

The foursome looked toward their leader across the river and threw up their hands in a gesture of futility.

George was gone.

CHAPTER TWENTY

Over the months that followed, Maria and I spent most weekends together. Sometimes she would come to Boda, but mostly I would travel to Mbaiki, as her work schedule at the clinic often included weekends. Such was the case that first weekend when I surprised her by arriving at the clinic on a Friday evening with the help of the driver provided by Jafari. It must have been nearly nine o'clock at night, and she was still working.

"Seven days straight," she said, as we sat together in the clinic's front-office. "And usually twelve hours per day. It's exhausting."

I could see the dark circles beneath her eyes.

"Why don't you talk to your supervisor and ask for fewer days and less hours," I suggested. "You have to take care of yourself."

She shook her head. "I need to prove myself. It's difficult enough to be taken seriously here."

It reminded me of Lisa's struggles. "But you need time for yourself, Maria. If you keep this up, you'll burn out," I insisted.

She shrugged her shoulders. "Not much different from college, really. If I wasn't studying, I was working part-time jobs to pay my tuition. Who has time for themselves?"

She sounded tired, but not sorry for herself.

"But still," I pressed.

She interrupted, clearly wanting to change the subject. "How about you? How are you and Lisa doing?"

"I'm okay," I replied honestly. "But it's been hard for Lisa."

Maria nodded. "It's definitely harder for women here. Even worse than Puerto Rico, and that was pretty bad."

"I guess I've never seen that kind of sexism before," I admitted. "My sister is four years older than me and never said anything about experiencing it."

"Yeah, I think it's different in the States. My aunt lives in New York and would always tell me that I should leave the island as soon as I graduated. I think any place where there's a lot of poverty and poorly educated people there's likely to be inequality."

"I guess education is the big equalizer after all," I replied, thinking back to the many talks my father gave me about the importance of finishing college. "But first you have to actually get people to go to school."

"What do you mean?" she asked.

"When classes began last week in Boda, probably a third of the students were absent because they were mining for diamonds."

"You can't really blame them," Maria replied. "What they're learning in school is not going to help them much in their village. They need something that teaches them a particular skill."

Just as Jafari had said, I thought.

"I think most of my work here will be teaching," continued Maria. "And I'm sure that's why they wanted a woman volunteer."

"How so?" I asked.

"The biggest problem in these villages is SIDA," she said, referring to the AIDS epidemic that was spreading like wildfire throughout equatorial Africa. "Without any cure, the only hope is to get these women to insist that men use condoms."

"Will your clinic provide them?" I asked.

"That's the idea," replied Maria, wiping the sweat from her face. "And I think it's the main reason why my boss is always so irritated," she continued. "She doesn't believe it's the right thing to do."

"Why not?" I asked. "That's the only way to slow the spread of the disease?"

"She's a missionary, and her faith opposes birth control."

I shook my head. "Hard to understand."

Maria nodded in agreement. "But we still have to do what we can. That's why we're here, after all."

I thought about that for a moment as we watched some villagers walk past the clinic, most of them women with heavy loads balanced upon their heads.

"You know, Maria, the college professor who encouraged me to join the Peace Corps once told me that I needed to go to Africa for myself, not with the intention of making any profound changes. Because when we leave, most of our work will be undone. So there has to be another motivator. Something more personal."

Maria considered my professor's words, and I thought about something that my father had told me before I'd left. "Good intentions are one thing," he had said. "But lasting change will only occur if there's consistent follow-through over a long period of time. Do the best you can, but realize that if someone else doesn't continue your same work once you leave, it's unlikely to have any long-term impact."

"Anyways, we have to try our best while we're here," said Maria. "It all has to be for something."

I nodded. "We have to find satisfaction in the work itself, regardless of whether it actually changes lives."

"Probably right," she said, looking over her shoulder to see if any early morning patients had arrived at the clinic. None had. "So what about you, John? Are you satisfied with your job at the school?"

"It's okay," I said. "But I'm much more satisfied when I'm here with you."

The next morning, we both awoke to the bustling sounds of the village. Like Boda, life started early each day in Mbaiki. The women were always up first, heading down to the river for water or down to the local market for the day's food. Maria's modest accommodation was located in the same compound as the clinic. She shared space with the clinic's tough director, two local nurses, and one local doctor. Remarkably, that small handful of people were responsible for the health and well-being of the entire village.

I spent the night on the floor outside of Maria's room, not wanting to cause her to lose the respect of her co-workers. As the day progressed, I did my best to stay out of the way, but was fascinated by the interaction between the clinic workers and patients, nearly all of whom were women. Some came to the clinic with minor lacerations, while others came to receive the various vaccinations that the clinic provided free-of-charge. But most came for the prenatal care that was nearly impossible to find elsewhere. Maria took a lot of pride in the fact that the clinic had seen an uptick in the number of pregnant women who came in, just in the few weeks since she had arrived.

She was clearly having an impact.

"Did your predecessor get out into the community as much as you have?" I asked, as we again sat outside the clinic during her lunch break.

"When she first arrived, I believe she did. But as time passed, she spent more and more time inside the compound, reluctant to venture out."

"What changed?" I asked, remembering Jafari's warnings.

Maria hesitated.

"Did the director tell you something?" I prodded.

She looked down and nodded. "I always move around the village with a security guard," she said. "The director won't let me leave the clinic without one."

"Why? Something happened to your predecessor?" I asked, starting to get concerned.

"I've heard a lot of different stories," Maria said, continuing to look down. "Who knows what's true."

"But *something* happened," I said. "Maybe you shouldn't . . ."

She cut me off immediately. "Don't, John." She looked hard at me. "Don't tell me what to do. I want to be successful here, and I can't do that if I have restrictions. From you. From the director. From anyone."

I could tell she meant what she said. And I respected her too much to push. So I did my best to change the subject. "Do you ever go out with your co-workers?"

She seemed to relax, appreciating the change of topic. "Sometimes," she replied. "After a long day at the clinic I don't mind a cold beer."

"Me too," I answered. "The parents of one of the teachers at my school owns a local bar in Boda," I said. "Sometimes Lisa and I'll stop by after school. It has air-conditioning, believe it not," I added.

"Really?" she said. "Not even the clinic has AC."

I laughed. "And I think the bar has one of the few refrigerators in the town," I said. "Stocked with beer, of course."

"Of course," Maria laughed, too. "They do like their alcohol here. We have one small fridge in the clinic," she added. "And it rarely works."

We continued laughing together until her break was over. It felt good to relax.

The next day, Sunday, as I prepared to return to Boda to ready for Monday classes, Maria and I sat together in a small bar just a few blocks from the clinic. Located at the convergence of three dirt roads, one of which was the town's main thoroughfare, it was a perfect location to people-watch. Across the street was an open-air market with the smells of meat and fish wafting through the air. People from all across the small town came there to sell their wares or to trade for whatever they needed to get through the day. This was mostly the work of women. And they did it with babies strapped across their chests and heavy loads atop their heads.

Conversely, the bar was filled with mostly men. In a male-dominated culture, it was clear who did the heavy lifting.

Maria and I watched as children ran freely about, often without parental supervision. It reflected the tribal mentality of the people, who believed that children should be raised by the entire village.

One mother caught our attention as she struggled to balance a load of wood on her head while keeping track of her three small children who were running amok along the edge of the road, dangerously close to an open ditch through which flowed a rancid mix of raw sewage and runoff from a nearby river that snaked through the town. These were scenes that had become familiar to us during our time in central Africa. Yet, they continued to fascinate us.

We both focused on the mother.

"Do you remember our conversation in Bangui before coming here?" asked Maria, as we watched the mother yelling at her children to stay away from the ditch. "You never really answered my question."

I knew exactly what Maria was talking about but tried to deny it. "About the street riots?"

She looked away, shaking her head. "Why is it so hard for you to open up, John?" she asked. 'You came to see me this weekend, so you must want a relationship. But you don't share."

"What does that mean?" I asked, still trying to stall. "I don't *share*?"

"You don't share yourself," replied Maria, now turning back to look at me. "You don't talk about your past. Your family. Past relationships. Nothing. We talk about Africa. Our jobs. Why we're both here. But nothing about *you*," Maria scolded. "I've told you about me. About my family. My parents. But when I ask you about *you*, you always try to change the subject. It was the same in Bukavu. Then Bujumbura. Bangui. And now here."

As Maria spoke, I sensed this was a pivotal moment in our relationship. But still I couldn't find the right words.

As I hesitated, she continued. "I'm not stupid, you know. It's not difficult to guess. But I need to hear it from you. I need you to share. Yourself." She continued, gesturing to the family as they passed by the bar. "I see that woman, and I think of *my* mother. I also think of all the women who come into the clinic each day or that I visit in their homes. We don't have the proper equipment to diagnose them. But I know how sick many of them are. And what they're sick with. And it makes me think," said Maria, nodding toward the mother, who had now passed, but continued to yell at her children. "What if she dies? What will happen to her children? How will they grow-up without their mother? What kind of people will they become?"

I knew it was my moment to open up about my mother, about my insecurities. But I let the moment pass. I just didn't have the courage.

Later in the day, despite Maria's obvious disappointment with me, she had still walked with me the short distance to the little bus station where different types of vehicles—most in various states of disrepair—waited for enough passengers to disembark. I found a small pickup bound for Boda that had a few passengers sitting in the open bed, squeezed in among some cargo. There was just enough space for me.

I hesitantly said goodbye to Maria, both of us choosing not to mention anything about our awkward conversation. We hugged, but I understood that I'd some real soul-searching to do if I expected our relationship to move forward in any kind of meaningful way.

I rode in the back of the pickup, bouncing up and down as it slowly made its way along the rugged road between Mbaiki and Boda, sat beside a man and his two young sons, both barefoot, who were also returning to Boda. They appeared to be similar in age to the children who Maria and I'd been watching just a few hours earlier.

But the interaction between the boys and their father was so different.

While the children in Mbaiki had been rambunctious and clearly happy alongside their mother, these two boys sat quietly, almost apathetically, with their father in the pickup. I was old enough to understand that children always reacted differently with their mother. But I'd never given much thought as to *why*. Why did kids often feel more comfortable expressing themselves with their mother? Why was the father's role so different?

Why was *my* father's role so different.

CHAPTER TWENTY-ONE

In the fall of 1982, my sister moved away from home to begin college in Rhode Island while I remained with my father to begin high school.

The summer had been a tough one.

Dad had tried his best to maintain the daily routine, but my sister and I were lost. We expressed it in different ways. But the root of our emotions was the same. To deal with it all, she moved closer to her friends, and ultimately was excited to get a fresh start away from our little town of Gardner.

I, on the other hand, moved deeper within myself, where I would remain for many decades.

Should our father have recognized our pain? Perhaps.

But he was a product of the Great Depression and World War II. His generation didn't believe in talking about their feelings. If someone was hurting, you dealt with it quietly. Tucked it away, and used your self-discipline to keep it there.

But children lack that self-discipline. They need to talk. They need a way to release their pain. They need to mourn.

The closest my Dad and I came to sharing our pain during that summer and fall of '82 was during long walks together near the water's edge at Crystal Lake. Before my sister departed for college, she joined us once. I could tell she was uncomfortable. It wasn't a place she wanted to be. As for me, I still associated the lake with my childhood. A place where I would ride my bike and play catch with my father, as the cool, fall breezes swept across the water, blowing the oak and maple leaves about.

But during that summer and fall, there was no bicycle. No game of catch. Just long stretches of silence as we sat side by side on my dad's favorite bench and looked out together across the calm waters of the lake.

One brief conversation would stick with me through the years.

As a child, I didn't really appreciate the depth of my father's words, how he was letting down his guard and allowing his son to see the man behind the façade that his generation so often erected in the name of stoicism.

"I have loved three women in my life," began my father. "Each as different as could be. One a young French girl from Normandy. One a southern girl from Kentucky. And one, of course, your mother. When you're young, love is most pure. And also most uncontrollable. It makes you do things you would never do as an older, hopefully wiser, man. But it's from the consequences of such recklessness that you learn the value of stability. You and your sister see me now as a fifty-five year old man who has lived the past twenty years in the same house, following the same routine nearly every day. But when I was just a bit older than your sister, I was a very different person. It was also a different time. A time of war. I survived it. I'm not really sure why. But I did. And when I returned, all I wanted to do was to find a quiet place where I could live out my life with someone for whom I cared. That quest took me from Boston to Montana, and back again. For a while, I thought I'd found what I was looking for. But it wasn't until I was nearly forty years old that I finally found the person who I believed I would spend the rest of my life with. Your mother. But fate intervened once again. So now, all I have is you and your sister. You both are my legacy, and I love you both more than you could ever know. I'll now spend the rest of my life watching you both grow into the kind of people who I always tried to be."

My father then turned to me. "No matter where your lives take you and your sister, Johnny, I'll always be there for you. I may not always have the right answer, or the answer you want to hear, but I'll always support you the best I can. That is now my role. And many years from now, when I'm on my deathbed and looking back over my life, I want to be able to tell your mother, in the life that follows this one, that I did the best I could as a father."

And that was it. There was nothing left to be said. We both rose from that bench and walked up the gentle slope from the lake's edge, stepping gently over the gravestones that dotted the hillside. We then came to a row of simple stones, the one on the end engraved simply: *My dearest Kathleen*.

My father put his hand on my shoulder before kneeling down at my mother's side.

CHAPTER TWENTY-TWO

George, Yvette, and Luc remained in the basement of the bank until morning, until they were sure that the American recon unit had given up the search and returned to the northern perimeter of the Lorient Atlantic Pocket. In truth, the unit had not tried very hard to find George, having received orders to abandon the search less than an hour after he had disappeared. George was puzzled by the short search, but Yvette and Luc understood.

"They were just using you, George," said Yvette, as they brushed the dust from their clothes and ascended the stairs that led out of the basement. "They're hoping that you'll convince me and Luc to continue communicating with the other Resistance fighters, and send back locations for the Army to bomb."

"Which we will," added Luc. "We don't need any convincing to do that. The sooner the Germans are driven out of Lorient, the easier our search for our parents will become."

It'd been their plan all along.

Yvette and Luc realized that the Army would probably send George to find them and to encourage their continued cooperation with the Allies. So, from a nearby vantage point they had watched as the recon unit approached, before moving to grab George and pull him down into the basement.

It'd all worked perfectly.

"But you didn't find your parents," said George, as they made their way south along the river's edge, still under cover of darkness.

"No, but now we're sure they made it this far," said Yvette.

"Your uncle saw them?" asked George, remembering their family connection in the region.

"We never talked to him," replied Luc. "He was killed in July during one of the Allied bombing raids."

"I'm so sorry," said George, stopping to take Yvette's arm. But she continued walking.

"Ironic, isn't it," she said. "Killed by friendly fire."

"But one of his neighbors told us the story," continued Luc, understanding his sister's anger. "They had seen our parents with our uncle just days before the raid."

"That's great news," said George. "But where did they go after that?"

"We don't know," said Luc. "But at least we know they made it out of Normandy. They're here, somewhere" he said, his tone confident. "We'll find them."

"But now what?" asked George hesitantly, as they stopped for a moment by the river's edge, kneeling down to splash some of the cold water on their faces to help stave off their exhaustion. "If I don't return to the perimeter, they might consider me AWOL."

"We took a huge risk in bringing you here," said Luc. "You'd rather return to your unit?"

"Of course not," said George. "That's not what I meant. But eventually I'll have to return, and the longer I'm gone the more likely it becomes that I'll be charged by the Army."

"You don't understand, do you?" said Yvette. "They don't care about you. With everything going on in this crazy world, why would they care about one soldier?"

"I'm talking about when this war is over," said George. "If they charge me, then we'd be separated for a long time. Perhaps years."

"If we survive the war, that is," replied Yvette.

Luc shot his sister a stern look. "Don't think like that, Yvette," he said. "We'll survive. We'll find our parents."

"Luc's right," added George. "We must live day by day, but still find hope in thoughts of the future?" He paused, almost surprised at his own words. "In fact . . ." His voice trailed off, as he rose from the water's edge.

Yvette looked at him. "What is it, George?"

A big grin appeared on Luc's face.

"I was just thinking . . ." said George, searching for the right words.

Luc's grin widened even more. "I think he's asking you to marry him. And if you want my opinion, about time."

Yvette was dumbfounded. "What? Are you crazy! Take a look around," she said, waving her hand at the ruins that surrounded them.

"I love you, Yvette," said George, taking her hand. "Amid all this horror, why can't there be love?" He dropped to his knees. "I have little to offer you. I have no ring. I have no promises that we'll survive this war. But I do have my unconditional love to offer. Will you have me?"

Yvette broke into tears and lifted George to his feet. "Yes," she said without hesitation. "I love you. And I'll marry you."

Luc looked on, still grinning, and wiping tears of joy from his eyes. "Now all we have to do is to find a priest."

The three of them laughed, and then embraced before turning to watch the fireworks display downriver. The American bombers had returned and were hitting the German positions near Keroman. The war was entering its final six months.

CHAPTER TWENTY-THREE

Upon my return to Boda following that first visit with Maria, I decided to make some changes. Looking back, it was probably a mistake to go to such extremes, as I was unprepared for what I would see. But it was my attempt to answer Maria's criticisms of me. Did I do it strictly to please her or to truly address my own shortcomings?

All of these years later, I still don't have a good answer.

Nevertheless, each afternoon following class, I walked across the schoolyard to the nearby mission to volunteer in their little clinic. Operated by four Catholic nuns with limited training and supplies, it was different from Maria's clinic in that it wasn't trying to save people, but rather make them as comfortable as possible in their final days, as they succumbed to the complications of full-blown AIDS.

The mother superior was Sister Agnes, a nun from the Brittany region of France—the irony of which I didn't fully appreciate at the time—who had also spent many years in America at various AIDS hospices.

By the time I arrived in Africa, AIDS had already swept across the continent, and the intervention of American pharmaceutical companies was still more than a decade away. With little to stop the scourge from continuing its spread, missionaries were often on the frontlines of hospice care, filling a need in a culture that typically shunned those with the disease.

On my first visit to the clinic, Sister Agnes made it clear that her priority was serving the patients not the resident priests.

"These priests are sent here from France," she began, speaking good English from her years in the States. "Sent as punishment for some sin committed at home. They stay a few years, complete their penance and then return home. While here, they have little interest in the people they're supposed to serve." She then looked hard at me and asked, "What about you? Are you here to serve these people or to serve yourself?"

I'd given her the same answer that I'd been giving to people ever since first deciding to join the Peace Corps. I wanted to help people.

I have no doubt that Sister Agnes saw through me much in the same way as I knew Jafari had seen through me. "I think you're doing it to impress your girlfriend," he said upon hearing of my new volunteer activity. "I'm surprised Sister Agnes would allow you in the clinic."

"You know her?" I asked.

"Everybody knows her, and most are either afraid of her, or respect her, or both." he replied, as we sat together with Lisa at one of the bars in Boda. "She comes into town each Wednesday to purchase supplies, and then returns to the clinic. But while she's out, the children surround her like some rock star. She draws more attention than either of you," said Jafari.

"Why?" asked Lisa. "I wouldn't think that a nun would be so popular."

"She's genuine, and the people know it. The children sense it. She really is touched by God."

I looked at Jafari and smiled. "I didn't take you for a religious man."

"Oh, make no mistake, my friend, I never go to church. I understand the hypocrisy. The priests talk about peace at their weekly sermons, but they never leave the confines of the mission. Sister Agnes interacts with the people. She's a true messenger of hope. And when this town explodes—which it will," he added. "She may be the only person capable of putting it back together again. Unless she becomes a target herself."

It wouldn't take long for Jafari's premonitions to become reality. But until then, I continued with my routine of teaching mornings, volunteering at the clinic afternoons, and visiting Maria on weekends. On a few occasions, she came to Boda and spent time at the clinic with me. At first, I think she doubted my sincerity. But as time passed, she grew to appreciate my daily effort to support the work of Sister Agnes.

Like me, Maria had grown-up in the Catholic Church, but had remained more connected to the Church than I ever had. So she respected Sister Agnes's work on a different level. But above all, I think she saw that the Boda clinic represented what happened when clinics like hers failed in their task to educate the people about the importance of birth control, particularly the use of condoms.

While the AIDS epidemic in the United States in the 1980s and early 1990s was partially a result of drug addicts sharing needles, in Africa, it was almost entirely the result of unprotected sex. And once diagnosed with the disease, there was little to be done except to make the patients as comfortable as possible, and wait for the end to come.

What made my work both unbearable and rewarding, was the number of small children in the clinic. Abandoned by their families upon being diagnosed with the disease, Sister Agnes had made it her life's work to give them love and dignity in their final days. During my very first visit to the clinic, I'd watched her hold an infant in her arms as he struggled to breathe before passing away. She had then lain the baby in his crib, covered him with a blanket, and said a prayer over his lifeless body.

"They cry uncontrollably from the pain," she had told me that day, seeing how distraught I'd become watching the scene unfold. "But as they continue to struggle to catch their breath, they become quiet. I know at that moment God has reached down to take away their pain and give them peace in their final moment. And in those final moments, I want them to be held and loved, as they pass into the hands of our Lord and Savior. That is the work we do here, my son. Do you have the strength to accept this calling from our Lord?'

I didn't answer Sister Agnes that day, but by returning to the clinic the next day, and the day after that, I gave the best answer I could.

And I think Sister respected that.

When Maria visited the clinic to see me, I think she respected it, too. Strangely enough, her approval wasn't as meaningful as I'd thought it would be. For over those few months in the fall and winter of 1990, I'd begun to deal with life and death in a way that I'd been unable to do eight years earlier.

When my mother passed away.

CHAPTER TWENTY-FOUR

I was watching my favorite James Bond film with my father when the call came. I was only fourteen, but knew exactly who was calling. My sister had been in the other room watching *Dynasty* and had rushed into the room when the phone rang.

She also knew.

"She died, didn't she?" said my sister, who was just a few months away from her high school graduation.

"Yes," replied my father. "That was Dr. Hogan. Your mother passed away just a few minutes ago."

Following a ten-year long battle with cancer, our mother was gone. It'd been one hell of a fight, one that changed the lives of nearly everyone who knew her, even the doctors who cared for her.

But it was always a battle that was going to be lost.

In his own way, our father had been preparing my sister and I for many years. But despite his best efforts, we were left with an emptiness that would remain unfilled for many years.

It was the summer of 1975 when the diagnosis had first come. I was only seven, my sister eleven. We'd been vacationing in Cape Cod, staying as we did each summer in condos near the lighthouse in Chatham. We'd just returned from a beautiful day of flying kites on the beach.

My sister and I shared one bedroom, while our parents used the other. There was a common living area, kitchen, and one bathroom. I was in our bedroom preparing to take a shower to wash the beach sand from my body when I heard our mother crying. I told my sister, and we peeked through the door of the bedroom to see that our mother and father were together in the bathroom. The door was slightly ajar, and we could see our mother standing in front of the mirror, her shirt off, back turned to us, her right arm lifted above her head, telling our father, "I can feel it, George. I can feel the lump."

A month later, my father would tell my sister and I that mom had breast cancer and would begin a treatment that might allow her to live a long life. But he also told us that it was possible that the treatment would not work. With that, my sister broke down, sobbing uncontrollably.

But I did not.

In many ways, it was the beginning of my own form of stoicism.

"I was lucky to survive the war," our father said to us that day. "But I want both of you to be prepared for the possibility that your mother might not be as lucky."

As I listened to my father, I didn't really understand the connection between his experiences in the war and our mother's sickness. I'm not even sure if my sister understood. But to our father, it was all connected. It was all a part of the same story of tragedy and loss that had defined much of his life.

CHAPTER TWENTY-FIVE

In late December of 1944, heavy snow blanketed Western Europe. Allied forces were trying desperately to hold-on to Bastogne on the edge of the Ardennes Forest in Belgium following a surprise German offensive of nearly a quarter million men that history would come to know as the Battle of the Bulge.

General Patton had swung his 3rd Army northward and pushed his troops day and night to relieve the weary warriors of the 101st Airborne that were fighting valiantly to deny the Germans their path to Antwerp and Hitler's last hope of a negotiated end to the war.

Heavy snow also blanketed much of Brittany in western France causing both German and Allied forces to hunker down and wait out the storm. It was the opportunity that George, Yvette, and Luc had needed to move freely through the northeastern districts of Lorient in search of a priest.

They had found one willing to conduct the ceremony near the shelled-out remains of Église Saint-Joseph-du-Plessis, only a few blocks from where Yvette and Luc's parents had last been seen. The plan was to marry secretly without informing George's commander. Despite Yvette and Luc's belief that the Army wouldn't care about their union, George was unconvinced and didn't see any reason to risk charges and forced separation from Yvette. They would marry, and then go their separate ways, with George returning to the Allied lines while Yvette and Luc continued the search for their parents. Despite the heavy fighting underway in Belgium, many believed the war would be over by the late spring or early summer, at which point George and Yvette would reunite and find a quiet place to settle in Brittany, or even return together to America.

They found shelter from the storm in a house near the remains of the church. In the simple, stone house's front room, George and Yvette received their vows from Fr. Rene, with Luc as the sole witness. As he stood there watching his sister prepare for her life after the war, he couldn't help but think back on the past six months since their return to France following nearly four years of exile in Britain.

It felt like they had lived a lifetime in the span of those few months. From Utah Beach near their childhood home of Sainte Marie du Mont to the Allied victory at Cherbourg where George and Yvette had nearly been killed. From a few weeks of relative quiet at Granville through their march with Allied forces into Brittany, and finally to Lorient.

It was hard to believe they had survived it all. Hard to believe their country was still standing after five years of war. But one could sense that the dark cloud that had enveloped Europe was beginning to dissipate, and that freedom would once again radiate from the shores of France as a signal to the world that liberty was humanity's rite of passage.

Luc had become hardened by the agony of war, but even he had to smile and wipe a few tears of joy as he watched his sister take George's hand. Later that afternoon, he stepped outside to give the newlyweds a few hours of privacy.

The snowstorm had ended and the skies were beginning to clear. Almost on cue, the Allies resumed their bombing of the German U-boat base in southern Lorient. Luc stood atop the ruins of the nearby church and watched as flashes of light spread across the horizon, evidence that there were still battles to be fought. He was anxious to resume the search for his parents, but as he looked over his shoulder at the small house where his sister and George were sharing a few intimate moments, he knew it could wait until morning.

CHAPTER TWENTY-SIX

Living by myself in my own little hut on the edge of Boda, I wasn't privy to most of the conversations that took place between the members of the teaching staff. Living among them, Lisa was able to pick up some of it, as her Sangho had gradually improved. But the teachers still didn't include her in most of their business.

We remained outsiders.

So it came as a complete surprise when I arrived at school one day in early January of 1991 to find the students milling about. Not even the customary soccer game was underway.

I tried to speak with some of the students who were turning-around and making their way back into town. "Où allez-vous?" I asked. "Pourquoi tu n'es pas en classe?"

"Il n'y a pas d'enseignants, monsieur," replied one of my students. "Ils ne viennent pas."

Just then, I heard Jafari's voice.

"Par ici, John. Viens par ici," he said.

I saw him standing near one of the small vendor's stalls that lined the dirt road leading to the school. On a regular day, students would line-up in front of their favorite one, getting something to eat before classes began. But on that strange day, the students walked right past them.

"What's going on, Jafari?" I asked, stepping out of the way of the wave of students who were retreating from the school. "Where are all the teachers?

"On strike, John. The whole country."

"What are you talking about?" I said, not understanding what was happening. "How can the teachers just not show up?"

"I shouldn't even be here," he said. "And neither should you. The other teachers will take it as an insult. I told Lisa to stay at her apartment. I tried to get word to you, but you'd already left your house."

I was so confused. "Why are they on strike?"

"They haven't been paid in two months," answered Jafari. "No government worker has. There are already reports of rioting in the capital. It has begun."

"What has?" I asked incredulously. "What has begun?"

Jafari put his hand on my shoulder. "What I've been telling you and Lisa about since you first arrived. This place is ready to explode. These strikes will be the trigger."

I shook my head and watched the students continue to stream by. "But why haven't I heard anything about any of this?"

"Maybe because you've been so busy with Sister Agnes," he replied, not accusingly, but simply as a matter of fact. "We used to meet almost every day for a beer after class, but for the past few months, you've been at the clinic."

"What about Lisa?" I asked. "She didn't know this was coming?"

"Nobody knew when it would start. Word just came late last night from Bangui that everyone should stay home, not report to work."

"What about the students," I asked. "What happens to them?"

Jafari shrugged. "What happens now to this entire country?" he replied. "It's anybody's guess."

"So what should I do now?"

"Wait," said my friend. "We wait. And hope for the best."

In the days and weeks that followed, I continued volunteering at Sister Agnes's clinic and continued visiting Maria each weekend in Mbaiki. I also did my best to remain informed about the political chaos in the capital, believing that Jafari was correct in his assumption that the unrest would eventually spread across the country.

He had explained that after achieving independence from French colonial rule in 1960, the Central African Republic had been rocked by a series of military coups, culminating with the overthrow of President Dacko by General Andre Kolingba in the early 1980s. Upon gaining control, Kolingba outlawed labor unions and political parties while cementing his power by drafting a new constitution and forming a national assembly. By the late 1980s, under increasing pressure from France, Kolingba lifted the ban on union activity, permitting workers to organize and strike. Almost immediately, students and unemployed civil workers united to strike for economic and government reform.

But Kolingba publicly rejected their demands and had many of their leaders arrested, resulting in a series of riots which had just begun to subside when Maria and I'd arrived in the country. Although the riots had begun primarily in response to Kolingba's economic policies and power-grab, there was also an ethnic and religious element to them that was even more pronounced outside the capital of Bangui. This element of the unrest particularly concerned Jafari—and many others—who understood that religious tensions were not far beneath the surface of everyday life throughout the nation.

The period of relative calm that had held during my first half-year in the country was then challenged once again when teachers, health workers, and other civil servants—who had not been paid in months—decided to strike. With the country teetering on the edge of bankruptcy, Kolingba had prioritized the salaries of the police and military, realizing that he needed their support if he expected to remain in power.

But this time around, he had been unable to quell the uprising.

Within weeks, finance officials and transportation workers had joined the strike. Then, as the strike continued, students took to the streets of Bangui demanding the government pay their teachers and allow them to resume their education. It was a demand that was left unheeded by Kolingba. Instead, he ordered his police to respond to the protests with tear gas. Students responded by building barricades to block the major Bangui roads, further hurting the country's already damaged infrastructure.

To make matters even worse, the student demonstrations had been infiltrated by members of a Muslim extremist group that had been operating in the northeastern region of the country, on the border with the Muslim-dominated countries of Chad and Sudan.

Rumors of executions and rape then began to circulate around the capital. Blaming the students, Kolingba unleashed his police force, which responded to the rumors with illegal detentions and torture of their own. It was only a matter of time until the unrest spread beyond the capital to smaller towns like Boda and Mbaiki.

In early February, the Peace Corps' assistant country director in CAR arrived in Boda as part of a country-wide trip to determine security risks to the volunteers. Lisa and I met with him at the local Gendarmes headquarters. We'd also asked Jafari to join us.

"You need to evacuate them," said Jafari to the AD, after we'd listened to him insist that it was safe for the volunteers to remain. "You've already shut down operations in Bangui. Why not throughout the country?"

"Bangui is dangerous now," admitted the AD. "But the violence has yet to spread. And we don't believe it'll."

"Foolishness!" barked Javari. "In the best of times, these small towns beyond the capital are not safe for Westerners."

"I appreciate your concern for their well-being, sir," replied the AD. "But we always have the best interests of our volunteers in mind when making any decision."

"Bullshit," snapped Javari. "Lisa and John have been here for more than six months, and not once have you sent someone to check on them."

Others in the room stared at us.

"It's okay, Javari," I said, trying to calm him down. "We're okay here." I looked at Lisa to confirm, but she said nothing.

"It's especially unsafe for women," added Jafari, seeing Lisa's reaction. "Don't you remember what happened in Mbaiki just last year?"

The AD looked at Jafari blankly. "I'm sorry, sir. I only arrived in-country last June."

I was equally surprised. "What do you mean, Jafari?" I asked. "You know something about Maria's predecessor?"

"She was attacked and raped," said Jafari without hesitation. "And the Peace Corps tried to cover it up."

I was flabbergasted. Could that have really happened?

"With all due respect," said the AD. "The Peace Corps would not do that. We protect our own."

"You're either very misinformed, naive, or both," said Jafari. "When it happened, the Peace Corps didn't even issue a protest with the regional authorities. You sent someone to investigate for a few days, sent the girl home, and that was it. And worst of all, you continued to send young kids into these towns telling them they could somehow make a difference. What needs to happen before you realize it's unsafe? Does someone need to get killed?"

Just then, we heard a commotion at the entrance of the police head-quarters. We all turned as the door to our meeting room swung open, and in walked Sister Agnes.

"Sister?" I said, surprised. "Comment saviez-vous que nous étions ici?"

"Jafari told me," replied Sister, nodding toward Jafari and addressing the AD. "It's not safe here, sir, for John or Lisa. I know you've had the volunteers in Bangui relocated inside the ambassador' compound during the protests. You should do the same with all of these children across the country. It's your responsibility."

The AD hesitated. "You're well-informed, Sister," he then admitted. "But we still feel that towns like Boda and Mbaiki are safe. If we feel otherwise, or if the situation changes, then all volunteers will be promptly evacuated."

"You know, sir," continued Sister. "I have lived here for many years. I have seen your Peace Corps volunteers come and go. They all mean well. But they all come here without any comprehension of what they're getting themselves into."

"I disagree," said the AD. "They're well trained before arriving in-country."

Sister waved her hand dismissively. "No one can be trained for this. You're foolish to think otherwise. If you'll not protect them, then I'll allow them to stay with me inside the mission. At least they will have the protection of our walls and gates."

"Thank you, Sister," replied the AD. "That is very generous of you. We don't believe it's necessary. But it's certainly your right to do so. So, I thank you for watching over them."

"The Lord shall watch over them," replied Sister, rising to leave the room. She then motioned for Lisa and I to follow. We did so without hesitation.

You didn't say 'no' to Sister Agnes.

Over the weeks that followed, Sister Agnes did indeed watch over Lisa and me.

It was admittedly a bit odd living in quarters designed for priests and sisters. But it was an absolute pleasure to start each day with a hot shower, not to mention having access to a working toilet. I'd admittedly grown tired of cold bucket showers and shitting into a hole.

Lisa and I'd separate rooms in different wings of the expansive stone mission, probably built in the early twentieth century. But we could tell from the looks we received from the two residing priests that they didn't approve of our presence.

But even they were unable to say 'no' to Sister Agnes.

She ran that mission with an iron fist . . . and a heart of gold. From the moment she arose each morning at 5 am, to the moment she laid her head to rest at nearly midnight, she was a nonstop example of the power of religious faith, exuding a holiness that could cause even an agnostic such as myself to rethink his position.

Each morning, Lisa and I met in the kitchen for Sister's special breakfast. The mission had its own cook and maid, but there was nothing quite like Sister's pancakes, eggs, and coffee. But mostly we enjoyed the conversation that would always take place among the nuns and the priests.

My French was improving, and I was able to follow more of the conversation than I'd been able to do even a few months earlier. Occasionally, they would speak in English, and sometimes even use some Sangho. They would speak of their homes in France and Belgium. But mostly they talked about the current political strife in the country. Sister has clearly lived through some hard times in her life, but she seemed particularly worried about the present situation in CAR.

"I fear that even new elections will not bring peace to this country," she said one morning as we were helping her to clear the table and wash the dishes. "When I first arrived in this country, there was a certain degree of hope, even amid the poverty and sickness. But now, I don't see that same hope in the eyes of the people."

"What do you see?" asked Lisa.

"Inevitability," she replied, simply. "I see inevitability."

We waited for her to explain what she meant, but she had finished with the dishes and was now on to the chapel for morning prayers before going to the clinic.

As the teachers' strike persisted, I continued my work in the clinic alongside Sister Agnes. Lisa would join me some days, but she often struggled to control her emotions when holding one of the sick infants. On one particular day, she had become especially distraught, putting one of the infants back in his crib before running outside.

"I don't know how you do that, John," she said, wiping tears from her eyes as she sat on the doorstep of the clinic, overlooking a small vegetable garden that Sister Agnes had created and that Lisa enjoyed tending. "I just can't bear to think of those children being in so much pain . . . and being so alone."

"They're not alone. We're with them." I tried to console her, but she pushed me away. I noticed that her hands were actually shaking and that she had become quite pale.

"But they need their family," she insisted. "How could their parents just abandon them like that?"

"I don't know," I replied. "Sister Agnes once said that some burdens are simply too much to bear," I recalled. "Maybe the parents just don't know what to do."

Lisa shook her head, clearly unmoved. But then began rubbing her temples. Something else seemed to be wrong.

"Are you okay?" I asked. "You don't look well."

"Just a bad headache. I'll be fine. I'll stay out here for a while to get some air," she said, still sitting on the doorstep. "It's okay. You can go back inside."

Less than ten minutes later, I was startled to hear one of the nuns yelling. "Viens vite au jardin. Lisa s'est évanouie!"

We all rushed outside to see what had happened. When I arrived, Lisa was on the ground and Sister Agnes was holding her head in her lap. Her face was even paler than before and sweat was streaming down her forehead.

"What's wrong with her?" I asked frantically. "Is she breathing?"

As always, Sister Agnes was calm and reassuring. "Yes, her breathing is all right. She must have fainted. Go get some wet clothes from the clinic so we can wipe her brow."

When I returned a few minutes later, Lisa had awoken and was sitting-up.

"What happened?" she asked, clearly disoriented.

"C'est bien ma chère," comforted Sister Agnes. "But you're burning-up. Let's get you inside and into a cold bath."

As Lisa lay in the tub waiting for her temperature to come down, Sister Agnes called for a doctor to come from the town's hospital. Within less than an hour he was there and checking Lisa who was now resting in her room.

"She has the symptoms of malaria," said the doctor, who Sister frequently called upon to assist in the clinic. "I'll bring some medicine, but she's going to have a rough couple of days."

I was stunned. "But how can that be?" I asked. "We all took antimalarial medicine before leaving the States."

"No antimalarial drug is a hundred percent protective," said the doctor in French. "It must be combined with other protective measures, such as mosquito netting around the bed."

I looked at Sister. "Both of our rooms here at the mission have netting," I said.

"After being bitten by a mosquito, most people show symptoms within four weeks. But for some, it can be many months later," explained the doctor. "Was she always using netting?"

Neither of us had it in our own accommodations.

Sister saw my expression and realized what I was thinking. "C'est bien, John. It's not your fault." she said. "Lisa will be okay. Like the doctor said, the next few days will be tough, but once the medicine takes effect, she'll recover quickly."

"Can I stay with her?"

"Of course," said Sister. "It's not contagious. She'll have headaches, body aches, and a general malaise. A familiar face by her bedside will definitely help to lift her spirits."

As Sister Agnes and the doctor had predicted, the first few nights were the worst. Lisa could barely tolerate the migraine-like headaches, and she sweated so much that we must have changed her bedsheets nearly every hour. When a few of the teachers visited, she barely recognized them. At times, I wasn't even sure she recognized me. It was scary. But by the third day, the drugs had kicked-in and she was more like herself.

"You really scared us," I told her, sitting at her bedside, holding her hand.

"Can't get rid of me that easily," she replied with a smile. "Who's going to keep you out of trouble?"

We both shared a good laugh.

"Any news about the strike?" she asked.

"Nothing new," I answered. "Jafari thinks it could go on for months. The students are still protesting in Bangui and demanding that the president step down."

"That's not going to happen," replied Lisa. "He'll never give up power until he's forced out."

"Same way he gained power originally," I added.

"Yup. I think it's the same throughout Africa," agreed Lisa.

"You're probably right," I responded. "Any regrets?"

"Regrets?"

"About coming here," I said.

"It's been quite an adventure," she said. "Quite an adventure, indeed. But no regrets."

We sat quietly for a few moments, reflecting on it all.

"What about you and Maria?" she then asked. "Still going okay?"

"I guess so," was my best response. "Now that you're feeling better, I'll probably go to Mbaiki this weekend."

"That's good," she replied, before looking away and gazing out the window at the garden for a while.

I could tell that she wanted to say something. "What is it?" I asked. "You're feeling okay?"

"Oh, I'm fine," answered Lisa. "Believe me, it's great to sit up in bed and start thinking about eating some food."

"But?" I knew there was more.

She finally looked at me. "I've been wanting to tell you this for some time, but could never find the right moment. But now that we're alone . . ."

"What is it?" I pressed.

"It's about Maria." She hesitated

"I don't understand."

"When she was here a few weekends ago, do you remember when she and I met for lunch, while you were in the clinic?"

"Yes. You went to Jafari's parents' bar. Right?"

"Yes." Again, a hesitation.

"Did she tell you something? Something about us?"

"No, nothing about your relationship. But she did tell me something and then made me promise not to say anything to anyone, including you."

I was beginning to get apprehensive. "What?"

Another long pause as Lisa searched for the right words. And when they came, they hit me like a ton of bricks.

"She told me that she was assaulted in college, and that it almost happened again during her first week in Mbaiki. If it'd not been for one of the clinic's security guards . . ."

I nearly fell out of my chair, undoubtedly agape, as I flashed back to all of those conversations with Maria, including the time when she accused me of not opening up. "I can't believe she never told me!" I said finally. My voice was surely too loud.

"I think, that's why she didn't tell you," Lisa said. "She thought that you would react angrily."

"How should I react?" I snapped. "She didn't trust me enough to tell me!"

"It's not about *you*," said Lisa, a tinge of disappointment in her voice. "This happened to *her*, and for whatever reason, she didn't want to tell you." She then put her hand upon mine. "Can I give you some advice?"

I nodded.

"Just because she didn't tell you, doesn't mean that she doesn't care about you. But I think she was worried that you'd react in the wrong way." Lisa was choosing her words carefully. "And maybe make things worse."

"So what should I do?" I asked, trying to remain calm. "If she's in danger . . ."

"She has to make that decision. Whether to stay or leave. We can't make it for her."

I could only shake my head. "Jafari was right," I said. "He kept telling us it wasn't safe here. And that things would get even worse."

"Maybe so," replied Lisa. "But even if we wanted to leave, where would we go? The capital? It's worse there. We just have to trust that the Peace Corps will evacuate us if things get any worse."

"Any worse?" I scoffed. "How can things get any worse?"

"Believe me, they can."

She was probably right.

"So why did you tell me?" I asked. "Why now?"

"Because if things do get worse, the three of us are going to need each other. And we can't afford any surprises," said Lisa.

I nodded.

Lisa had become a good friend.

CHAPTER TWENTY-SEVEN

When my mother was first diagnosed with breast cancer, she had chosen a mastectomy over chemotherapy. For nearly five years, it appeared that she had beat the disease. But it was simply lying dormant, waiting to pounce again.

When it did, it struck her lungs.

This time around, there was no choice but to undergo chemo. She and my father had been warned by the doctors about the side-effects, but had decided to wage the battle with the goal of seeing my sister graduate from high school.

She fell short of that goal by only a few months.

The final year had proven the worst.

Mom was in and out of the hospital nearly every month, in many ways suffering more from the treatment than from the disease. It'd robbed her of a certain quality of life—a dignity—that we all deserve, and perhaps saddest of all, it'd caused her to question her own faith.

Raised in an Irish Catholic household in Boston, she had been taught that bad things happen to bad people. I was really too young to understand her torment, but it was something that my father would speak about for the remainder of his life.

"I never forgave the Church for that," he said to my sister and I many times in the years and decades following her passing. "The Church should give people comfort and peace of mind in their final years. But they couldn't even give her that. Their teachings made her feel that she had done something wrong. Imagine that! For your entire life you commit yourself to the Church, and when you need them most, they're not there for you."

Instead, it was our mother's friends who were there for her, visiting nearly every day.

Her best friend was Mrs. Cormier, who had experienced her own struggles in life, but who was always a calming influence on mom. There was Mrs. Frie who lived up the street and was the wife of a doctor who had often provided advice and support as my mother and father struggled to rationalize everything. They had two children, one with whom my sister remained close over the years.

Mrs. Healy lived across the street from Mrs. Frie. Her husband could fix almost anything, and my father often called on him to help repair things around our house. There was also Mrs. Atter whose husband owned a small grocery store in town. They had three sons of their own, all of whom were my childhood friends. Mrs. Atter would knock on our door nearly every day in the weeks before and after my mother's passing, bringing all kinds of food for us to eat.

And then there was Dr. Rosenthal.

He lived on our street and had become my mother's doctor in the final year of her life. He would visit her almost every evening while walking his dog, which he would tie to a tree in our front-yard before ringing our bell. My mom's passing hit him especially hard. Less than a year later, he left his medical practice and moved away with his family.

Our mother had touched so many lives. None of us really understood the breadth of her impact until her funeral at Holy Spirit Church. It was the day after one of New England's worst Nor'easters. We didn't really think anyone would be able to get to the church.

But we were wrong.

I can still remember walking down the aisle with my father and sister to take our seats in the front pew of the church. There were so many people packed inside that some were standing along both sides of the church and in the rear. I saw my teachers, my coaches, and my neighbors. People who I'd known for my entire life, and people who I'd never seen before.

There were nurses and doctors who had cared for my mom, come to pay their final respects for a battle well fought. And, of course, there were my mother's best friends, including Mrs. Cormier, Mrs. Atter, Mrs. Frie, and Mrs. Healy. I remember my father touching my mother's coffin as she left her favorite church for the final time, and I remember all those people who came to our house afterward.

But I remained upstairs in my bedroom, unable to interact with anyone. Mrs. Atter found me sitting on the edge of my bed looking out the window at our backyard, unable to cry or scream. She put her arm around me and pulled me close, saying "If you need anything, John, if you just need to talk, you can always come to our house."

But I never did that.

I never talked to anyone. Not even my own sister. I kept it all inside, unwilling to let anyone get too close. It would limit my friendships, cause relationships to fail, and keep me isolated for much of my life.

I have often thought about how it could have been different. Maybe if I'd been able to properly say goodbye to my mother? I don't know.

I remember the last time my father took my mother to the hospital. Dr. Rosenthal had said it was time. I watched from my second floor bedroom window as he and my father helped my mother in the front seat of our car, fastening her seatbelt and squeezing the oxygen tank into the back seat.

Over the years, our father told us many times about that final drive to the hospital and how our mother didn't want our last memory of her to be of a woman lying in her hospital bed waiting for death to come. As a result, my sister and I didn't visit our mother during those final days of her life.

If we had, would things have been different?

"A part of me never forgave Dad for that," my sister said to me years later. "I can understand why he did it. But it wasn't his decision to make."

"Dad always said it's what mom wanted," I reminded.

"Maybe. But I was old enough to decide for myself."

Nearly ten years later I was volunteering for Sister Agnes and holding infants in my arms as they took their final breaths, not wanting them to be alone as my mother had been alone in those final hours of her life.

That experience was part of my grieving process. My sister took a different route, absorbing herself with friends and her career. Is there a correct way to grieve? Probably not. But it needs to be done if you're going to move forward. And that was something our father always preached. Keep moving forward.

CHAPTER TWENTY-EIGHT

During the First World War, there had been a Christmas truce in 1914. Thousands of British, French, and German soldiers, exhausted by the unprecedented slaughter of the previous five months, had left their trenches and met the enemy in No Man's Land, exchanging gifts, food, and stories.

In World War Two, there was no such large-scale truce. But history would record a smaller, more intimate event that occurred on Christmas Day in 1944 near the village of Aachen, Germany, as the Battle of the Bulge raged just across the border in Belgium.

Three American soldiers, one badly wounded, had become lost in the snow-covered Ardennes Forest as they tried to find the American lines. They had been walking for three days while the sounds of battle echoed across the hills and valleys, until they had come upon a small cabin in the woods.

Inside, dwelled Elisabeth Vincken and her sixteen-year-old son, Fritz. She had been hoping that her husband, a German soldier, would arrive to spend Christmas with them.

But he never came.

Instead, on Christmas eve there was a knock on the door. Elisabeth blew out the candles and opened the door to find two enemy American soldiers standing at the door and a third lying in the snow. Despite their rough appearance, they seemed hardly much older than her son. They were armed and could have simply burst in.

But they didn't.

Elizabeth invited them inside and even helped to carry their wounded comrade into the warm cabin. She didn't speak English and the three Americans spoke no German, but they managed to communicate in broken French.

As Elisabeth prepared a meal to share with her three guests, there was another knock on the door. Expecting to find more Americans looking for food, Fritz went to open it, but instead found four armed German soldiers. Elisabeth came to the door and said that they were welcome to come in, but that they would have to leave their weapons outside because there were three Americans inside. One of the German soldiers stared at her long and hard, but then put down his weapon, saying "Es ist Heiligabend und hier wird nicht geschossen."

It's the Holy Night and there will be no shooting here.

Sadly, there was no such truce in Lorient.

On Christmas eve, George, Yvette, and Luc had joined many other French Resistance fighters sitting atop a hill in the eastern district of Lorient, sharing a bottle of wine and watching the Allied bombs continue to fall on the German positions near the port. It was hard to believe that anybody could have survived such a pummeling, but the Germans were well dug-in and appeared prepared to wait out the Allies through the winter and spring.

"If we just collapse their perimeter," said one of the fighters to Luc, "we could surround those Nazi bastards in a matter of days, and it would be over."

"That's not going to happen," replied Luc, as George and Yvette nodded. "You said yourself that you're receiving reports that an entire American division may be moved north toward Belgium to deal with the German push toward Antwerp. That's the priority now, not what happens here."

"Maybe so, but it wouldn't take a large force to take that sub-base. Probably a few hundred special forces could do the job."

"Why risk them?" said Yvette, sitting beside George with her head on his shoulder and watching the fireworks in the distance. "Keep bombing them, and maybe they'll give up."

"That's unlikely, too," said Luc. "They've held out this long. They're not going anywhere."

"I wonder if they want this war to be over as much as we do," said George, stroking Yvette's long, dark hair which she rarely let down. "They must have families they want to see again, too."

"Remember," said Luc, "your family is safe back in the United States. But all across Europe, families have been driven from their homes. I'm sure it's even worse in Germany, considering how many bombs have been dropped on them. There may not be much for them to go back to."

George nodded, and for a moment he thought about his mother who he had not seen in more than a year, wondering if she would accept his union with Yvette. But his thoughts were fleeting, as more bombs exploded in the distance.

Home still seemed so far away.

He and Yvette had already decided to stay together through New Year's, and then split up. He would return to the Allied perimeter of the Atlantic pocket and do his best to explain his absence to his commanders, without saying anything about their marriage. If they were lucky, the Army would allow him to return to Yvette in Lorient under the guise of collaborating with the Resistance. If not, he'd find another way.

But in the few days they had left together, they would move farther south and hopefully contact people who had seen Yvette and Luc's parents in recent months. It was a risk, as the bombing was less than a mile away. Luc had wanted to push ahead on his own, but Yvette refused to be left behind. George understood his wife's need for answers, so didn't hesitate to join the search.

Their plan was to follow the Scorff River southward to where it flowed into the Le Blavet River at the Point de L'Esperance, before flowing into the sea. It was a partially elevated, largely agricultural area under the control of the Resistance who used the vantage point to call in Allied bombing raids whenever they saw significant German movement. However, they often came under sporadic artillery fire from the Germans who knew what they were doing but lacked sufficient ammunition to do much about it.

By all reports, the Germans were barely hanging on, unable to be resupplied by land or sea. But their commander was a stubborn son of a bitch who was unwilling to surrender, pledging to fight to the last man. Eventually that battle would come, but Luc and the other Resistance fighters didn't expect any major offensive by either side until spring arrived. The hope, of course, was that Germany would surrender by then. But as reports continued to come-in from Belgium, it seemed increasingly likely that the war would continue at least until summer.

And so, on December 26, 1944, George, Luc, and Yvette left the relative safety of the northeastern sector of Lorient and began to move south along the riverbank. Within a matter of hours, they had moved farther south than they ever had before.

They were being guided by two seasoned Resistance fighters, Robert and Victor, who had been with Luc and Yvette off and on since their arrival in Lorient weeks earlier. It was also these two experienced fighters who had brought them into contact with the people who had last seen their uncle. And now they were trying to pick up the trail once again, following the path that many civilians had followed in search of food and water.

But as their group continued to walk along the river's edge, George couldn't shake the feeling that they were headed into trouble.

By the middle of the next day, they had left the rubble of the city behind and entered the wide-open spaces of Le Cosquer, a series of farmhouses and hamlets within a stone's throw of the bustle of the city, yet still a world apart. In good times, it grew much of the food that fed the city, while also providing a quiet retreat where the city-dwellers could escape the fast pace of the city that lay just across the river. Since the war began, it'd become a lifeline and a refuge to the citizens of Lorient.

Following the Allied landings in Normandy and their subsequent push into Brittany the previous summer, the Nazis had put a stranglehold on the city, trying desperately to hold on to their sub-base at Keroman, one of their few remaining outlets to the Atlantic in Europe. For practical purposes, they had held the civilian population of Lorient hostage, believing that the Allies would be less likely to bomb certain locations with civilians nearby. American forces had indeed taken great care to avoid most civilian targets, instead focusing their attention on the sub-base in the southern quadrant. Nevertheless, the entire infrastructure of the city had been destroyed.

There was no electricity or running water. The petrol stations had long since run dry. And grocery stores hadn't been restocked in months. As a result, both the German and civilian populations had abandoned most neighborhoods in the northern half of the city and moved south. The Germans to reinforce their sub-base for the inevitable Allied attack, and the civilians to Le Cosquer, where they could farm and retrieve water from the two nearby rivers and collection of small lakes. Some had decided to make a break for freedom by following the seashore to the east. But they ran the risk of being targeted by the German E-boats that patrolled the rivers and shoreline for a few miles in each direction.

It was into this environment that George, Yvette, Luc and their two guides were now walking.

On one hand, it was a relief to move away from the ruins of the city and the constant threat of German snipers. But on the other hand, they were now well within range of German artillery positions just across the river. As Luc paused to look west through his binoculars, he could clearly discern German troop movement. Despite everything they had been through over the past six months, it was one of the few times he had actually *seen* Germans.

And it was disconcerting.

He handed the binoculars to George and pointed out the enemy locations. As George adjusted the focus and saw the same German troops, that uneasy feeling in George's gut worsened yet again. Something was telling him that the next few days were going to be hard.

CHAPTER TWENTY-NINE

When Lisa had made a full recovery from her bout with malaria, I traveled to Mbaiki to see Maria, not quite sure of what I was going to say to her about the revelations that Lisa had shared. A part of me was angry for being shut out. But I also understood that Maria didn't completely trust me, or at least didn't think I was mature enough to handle the truth.

When I arrived in Mbaiki, we never got the chance to talk about it. News from the capital was that the riots were spreading to the nearby towns of Bimo and Pissa, which were on the road to Mbaiki. If the violence continued to spread westward, Mbaiki would be next. It was happening so quickly that we suspected that the Peace Corps was undoubtedly unprepared. For now, we were on our own.

"I want to stay here," said Maria, as we sat together in her accommodation near the clinic. "We're so short-staffed as it is."

"I understand that," was my reply, knowing that it wasn't going to be easy to convince her to leave. "But if you come to the mission for just a few days, it'll be safer while we wait for the rioting to stop."

Maria shook her head. "You know that's not going to happen. Not until there's a new government."

"And the current government is not going to leave quietly," I understood.

"Exactly," replied Maria. "So why not just continue our work and wait for the Peace Corps to make up their minds?"

"I'm not sure that will happen soon enough," I said, remembering the meeting with the assistant director. "They were convinced that the riots were not going to spread. You know their bureaucracy better than me. By the time they receive instructions from Washington, it may be too late."

"I have people who I trust here. Just like you do in Boda. I think it's safer to just stay here, rather than trying to evacuate," argued Maria. "Anyways, where would we go? You heard the radio reports. The rioting has reached Pissa along the road from Bangui. There's no way for the Peace Corps to get us back to the capital, even if they wanted to."

"That's why I'm saying we should stay at the mission for a few days," I said. "If the riots approach Boda, then we can head west toward Berberati. There are a lot of volunteers posted there, and there's an airport."

I could see that Maria was considering this option. But she remained torn. "I just hate to leave the clinic. It's not fair to the others."

"I know. But you know better than I that we'll become targets if the riots spread here or to Boda. You have to trust me on this."

Maria looked at me and I could tell that she wanted to say something. Perhaps she somehow knew that Lisa had already told me her secret. If she couldn't trust me enough to share that secret, how could she trust me with her own safety? But she never said it. Instead she just nodded. "Okay, let's go back to Boda."

Later that afternoon, as we were waiting for a ride back to the mission, I began feeling dizzy. This is all we need right now, I thought. Could I be getting sick like Lisa? But when I started feeling a sharp pain in my lower back, I realized something else was wrong.

"Are you okay?" asked Maria as I sat down on the curb near the bus station. "You're white as a ghost."

"I'm not sure," I replied, now struggling to breathe. "Something really hurts."

"Malaria isn't airborne, so you couldn't have gotten sick from Lisa," replied Maria, putting her hand to my forehead. "But you're burning up. Let's get you back to my clinic." She started to help me up.

"No," I replied vehemently. "We need to get back to Boda. I'll be okay. Just see if you can find someone who is leaving now."

Maria reluctantly agreed, but before she had taken more than a few steps, we heard the honking of a horn. A large pick-up approached us. Maria stepped back from the dirt road, unsure of who was driving. The wheels were huge, with custom rims. The windows were all tinted. And the engine roared with a power unlike anything else we'd heard in the small towns of Mbaiki or Boda. As it pulled alongside us, the window on the passenger's side rolled down.

It was Jafari.

"Get in, both of you," he commanded. "We'll take you back to Boda. The riots are coming this way."

I struggled to my feet and peered inside the vehicle to see who was driving. It was Eric, the French diamond merchant from Boda.

"Come on," repeated Jafari. "You can't stay here any longer. It's too dangerous."

Maria had never met Eric, and I'd only spoken to him a few times at Jafari's parents' bar. I knew he had been gone from Boda for a few months, presumably having returned to France to sell the diamonds that he had bought from the locals. Maybe, I thought, he had returned upon hearing the news of the unrest in the capital. But whatever the reason for his presence, he was our ticket back to Boda.

"You don't look well," said Jafari, as I climbed into the back cabin with Maria. "We need to get you back to the mission. Maybe you got the same as Lisa."

"I don't think so," answered Maria. "He says he has a sharp pain in his back."

Eric looked over his shoulder as he continued to drive through the streets. "C'est peut-être une appendicite?" he said. "L'hôpital de Boda ne peut pas gérer cela. Il a besoin d'un hôpital à Bangui."

"Ce n'est pas possible," replied Jafari, and then changed to English. "There's no way to get to Bangui. The main road has already been closed. Our best option is the mission. And if necessary, Berberati."

I have learned over the years that certain things happen purely out of luck. Sometimes bad luck. Sometimes good. Either way, it's always hard to rationalize. Why did it happen that way? Why me?

There is just no way to explain why Eric and Jafari happened to be driving through Mbaiki at that particular moment on that particular day. If they had been fifteen minutes earlier . . . or later . . . we would've missed them. But, for whatever reason, luck was on our side that day.

Maybe it was my mother watching over me.

A few hours later we were back in Boda. The pain in my lower back had somewhat subsided, but I felt so weak that I could barely walk. Eric, Jafari, and Maria helped me into the mission where Sr. Agnes had prepared a bed for me, the same bed where Lisa had laid only a few days earlier. The doctor arrived shortly thereafter and began applying pressure to different areas on my lower back, sides, and lower abdomen.

He looked at Sister and shook his head. "Je ne pense pas que ce soit une appendicite," he said, but added that he needed a urine and a blood sample from me to be sure.

"Paludisme?" asked Sister. Malaria.

"Peut être," replied the doctor. Maybe. "Mais la douleur dans son dos est plus préoccupante pour moi," he added, expressing is concern for the pain in my back.

"If it's not appendicitis," asked Maria. "Then what?"

"Je ne sais pas," answered the doctor. "Mais nous avons besoin de ces résultats le plus rapidement possible."

"But how quickly can the hospital test his blood and urine?" asked Maria, thinking that they were probably preoccupied preparing for the possible onset of violence in the town.

"Aujourd'hui," promised the doctor. "Aujourd'hui."

He was correct. Only a few hours after taking my blood and urine samples to the hospital, the doctor telephoned Sr. Agnes with the results.

It was both good and bad news.

CHAPTER THIRTY

George, Yvette, Luc, and the two Resistance fighters spent their first night in Le Cosquer in a farmhouse near the estuary of the Ruisseau du Plessis, well beyond the range of German artillery.

But still, George struggled to sleep.

It'd been many months since he had enjoyed a proper night's sleep, but he could usually nod off long enough to regain some strength. Yet, for the past few nights, he had probably slept less than a few hours total.

At one point, he rose from bed, moved quietly out of the room so as not to disturb Yvette, and wandered outside. He must have walked around the grounds of the farm for hours, even venturing inside the barn where the owners of the farm kept their pigs and poultry to protect them against the brutal cold of the winter.

"Couldn't sleep, huh?" said a voice, startling George. He turned to see Luc standing by the barn's side door smoking a cigarette with a half empty bottle of whiskey in his hand.

"No, can't seem to shake this feeling," said George.

"What feeling? That we're not going to make it out of here alive?" replied Luc, half-joking, yet serious enough that George didn't laugh.

"I don't know. I feel like something is coming."

Luc laughed, taking a swig from his whiskey bottle. "I've felt that for the past four years!" he said. "Hell, let it come!"

"I don't know about you, Luc," shot back George. "But I want to get out of here alive."

Luc walked closer to George. "Honestly, do you think we'll actually get through this war alive?"

George stared at Luc, surprised by his words. "It's not like you to be negative. What's wrong?"

"How often have you and I been alone together?"

"Not often, I suppose."

"So I guess I can tell you what I'm really thinking now," said Luc.

"Okay."

"I'm glad you and my sister got together and decided to marry. Glad a few people can find some kind of happiness in all of this chaos."

"But you don't think that our relationship will last, do you?" said George.

"Oh, I think it'll last, all right," replied Luc. "If we survive, that is," he added without hesitation. "I didn't think we'd make it this far, to be honest."

"Then why can't we make it a little bit further?"

Luc took another drag of his cigarette. "I stopped thinking about tomorrow. Doesn't seem to make much sense."

"Since I married Yvette, tomorrow is *all* I think about," said George. "We all need hope." The two men stood beside each other near the pig pen. "Without it, what's the point."

"Hope is a dangerous thing. It can distract you. Get you killed."

"Maybe," said George, not much liking the tone of the conversation. "What about your parents? You still *hope* to find them, don't you?"

Luc paused, and threw the nearly empty whiskey bottle to the ground. "Our father is dead. He was killed by a Vichy police officer months ago."

The Vichy was the puppet government under French General Petain set up by the occupying German forces throughout France to oppose the Free French Resistance that was led by General Degaulle from his exile in England.

"What?" said George, incredulously. "Why didn't you tell me? Does Yvette know?"

"No. It'll devastate her."

"You have to tell her, Luc," said George.

"He was hanged," said Luc, his voice cracking. "Captured and hanged. Made an example of, no less. How can I tell her that?"

It didn't make any sense. "But why?" replied George. "Why would they care about him?"

"He was recruiting more Resistance fighters to oppose the local Vichy government, which was barely holding on to power as the Allies entered Brittany after D-Day. They rounded up as many Resistance fighters as they could, and executed them."

"My God," said George. "It's unbelievable. What about your mother?"

"As far as I know, she's still alive. Hiding somewhere in this area. Robert is going out first thing tomorrow to contact someone who may have more information."

"I don't know what to say. I'm so very sorry," consoled George. "But I think you need to tell Yvette. She has a right to know."

"I know. But I just don't know how," said Luc, his voice cracking.

CHAPTER THIRTY-ONE

The hospital in Douala overlooks the six-thousand-foot-long Wouri Bridge that joins downtown Douala with the port of Bonabéri, one of the largest and busiest ports in the Gulf of Guinea on Africa's west coast. During my week-long stay in the hospital, there wasn't much else to do except gaze out the window at the busy streets of Cameroon's second largest city. With its mixture of traditional, colonial, and modern architecture, Douala appeared different from the other African cities I'd visited over the past year. I could even see the edge of a Western-style residential area with a mixture of apartment buildings and single family homes. One of the many nurses who visited my room during the day said that her family lived in that gated community, which had become popular with the city's growing middle class. She was also eager to share her country's rich history, or perhaps she just thought it would help keep my mind off of everything else. Either way, I enjoyed our daily chats.

"We don't get many Americans staying in the hospital," she said on one occasion in near perfect English. "Sometimes we get French expats, but that's about it."

"You're English is so good," I told her, happy to have the small talk. "Where did you study?"

She smiled. "Right here in Douala. But I grew up in the UK."

"Your parents worked there?'

"Yes," she replied. "My father was a diplomat and my mother a professor. I got to see a lot of amazing places growing up."

"Why did you come back here?"

She shrugged. "This is my home. No matter where I go, I'll always think of Douala as home."

I nodded.

"What about you?" she asked. "Where is home?"

"Massachusetts."

"I went to Boston once," the nurse replied. "You have family there?"

"Yes," I replied. "My father and sister."

"You must miss them," she said, as she continued to take a blood sample. "Do they know you're here?"

I looked away. "No, I haven't called them."

"You should. I'm sure they'd want to know what has happened to you."

In truth, I was still trying to understand everything that had happened to me over the past few weeks.

As I lay in the mission waiting for the doctor to inform us of the results of my blood and urine tests, the streets of Boda began to erupt with violence. The riots that had plagued the capital continued to spread across the country. Students in Mbaiki had joined the street protests only hours after Eric and Jafari had evacuated Maria and me.

Then, like a wave moving west, it was Boda's turn.

It began with students taking to the streets and chanting their desire to return to school, but just as had happened in the capital, the student protests were then infiltrated by Muslim extremists. It was just as Jafari had long feared. Boda was a powder keg waiting for a spark.

In a town where many of the shops and stores had been taken over by Arabs, thereby disenfranchising many of the locals, racial animosity was already simmering near the surface, ready to spill over. And in such an environment, extremists thrived, pitting one ethnic group against another.

"I think we need to get the three of you out of here now," said Jafari, sitting at my bedside along with Lisa, Maria, Sister Agnes, and Eric. "Can he be moved, Sister?"

"Yes," she replied. "But I think we need to wait as long as possible to get the test results. If you leave here now and the phone lines go down, there'll be no way of getting the results to you."

"Redo the tests in Berberati," suggested Eric. "We could probably get there in four to five hours."

"Without knowing exactly what's wrong, I would advise against it," cautioned Sister. "If he needs medication, four or five hours might be too long. I'll call the hospital now to see if they can expedite the results. But with everything happening on the streets . . ." Her voice trailed off as she left the room to make the call.

Everyone was quiet for a few minutes.

Eric spoke first. "We can probably wait an hour, but no longer. These protests are going to continue spreading and getting more intense. We need to somehow stay ahead of them"

"But won't they also spread to Berberati," said Maria. "Is that really a better option than Bangui?'

"There's no way we could get to Bangui now," replied Jafari. "Eric and I were coming from that direction when we saw you in Mbaiki. The main road from Bangui was already closed behind us. We were lucky to get through."

"And if the road to Berberati is closed?" persisted Maria.

"The French have a military base near Berberati," said Eric. "And I have contacts there. If the situation gets worse, we can go there for protection."

"What about the Peace Corps?" asked Lisa, who was continuing to regain her strength following her bout with malaria. "Surely they'll come get us. I already called them to say that John is sick."

"And what did they say?" questioned Jafari.

Lisa looked down. "They said to wait."

"Exactly," replied Jafari. "Like it or not, you're on your own."

CHAPTER THIRTY-TWO

On the evening of December 29, 1944, George, Yvette, Luc, Victor, and Robert set out from the farmhouse in the eastern region of Le Cosquer under cover of darkness with the intent of reaching Port Louis on the very southern tip of Lorient. It was a route which would bring them even closer to the German positions than they had been the day before. But they had little choice. Robert had a contact in the port area with possible information about the location of Yvette and Luc's parents.

They began their journey by following the small Ruisseau du Plessis southward until it flowed into Le Blavet. From there, they used the ruins of the Pont du Bonhomme to cross over to the eastern side of Le Blavet, giving them a clear line to Port Louis. Their goal was to reach the small village of Locmiquelic before sunrise, lay low for the day in the farmhouse of a Resistance fighter who Victor trusted, before making the final push to Port Louis the following night.

They walked single-file along narrow, snow covered, country roads, beneath a starless sky, passing through the small villages of Saint Sterlin, Kergatamignan, and Stervil. They would occasionally see people watching them from their windows, but no one dared emerge. At times, the war seemed so far away. But then they were snapped back to reality by the sound of explosions coming from the direction of Keroman U-boat base to the southwest.

The Allied bombers were hitting it again.

Tracer fire would temporarily light-up the sky as the Germans attempted to target the bombers. But it was pointless. They flew too high and were relentless. Nevertheless, the Germans refused to surrender despite the constant pummeling by the B-17s.

When does a person finally admit defeat, wondered Luc. Would *he* have been able to admit it? Never. But many French had.

Luc had been born after the end of the Great War, but his father had told him stories of the great battles fought at the Somme and Verdun. Nearly an entire generation of men had been lost. France had won the war, of course. But for practical purposes, that was the end of them as a world power. When the Germans invaded again in 1940, the French army was in no mood for a fight. They quickly capitulated, much to the chagrin of Winston Churchill who had wanted them to fight on to the bitter end, or until the New World came to the rescue of the Old World, as he often said.

Everything would be different when the war was finally over, understood Luc. A new world order would arise from the ruins of Europe. And George represented that new order. A daughter of the Old World marrying a son of the New World. It was enough to bring a smile to Luc's war-beaten face.

But first he had to find a way to tell Yvette about their father.

It was nearly five in the morning when they reached the outskirts of Locmiquelic. They slowly made their way down the Rue de L'eglise toward the farmhouse where they would stay. It was near what remained of the Eglise Saint Michel. Constructed in the eighteenth century, the church had survived the first four years of the war, but had finally succumbed to Allied bombs that had fallen well short of their target across the harbor. It was a setting that reminded George and Yvette of where they had been married and spent their first night together near the Église Saint-Joseph-du-Plessis, just north of the Le Cosquer.

Victor's friend, Gabriel, was waiting for them as they approached his farmhouse. "Viens, dépêchons-nous à l'intérieur. Le soleil se lève vite!" he said, worried that they would be seen by the Germans who always maintained careful surveillance of the area, on the lookout for Allied incursions or Resistance movements.

George, Yvette, and Luc could see that Gabriel's house had been recently rebuilt—or at least patched together. "Tu vis seul ici?" asked Luc, not seeing anyone else in the house.

"Oui," replied Gabriel. "I sent my wife to England when the war began." He paused. "And my two sons were killed last summer as the Allies arrived in Brittany."

"They fought bravely," injected Victor. "Trying to deny the Nazi's access to L'île Saint-Michel, a special place for the inhabitants of Locmiquélic."

Just off the coast of their village, between them and the base at Keroman, the island of Saint-Michel had served many purposes over the centuries. A thousand years earlier, her lights had guided ships through the dangers of the rocky harbor. Then a small chapel was erected, dedicated to Saint Michel. The abbots soon arrived and established the Priory of Saint-Michel-des-Montagnes.

But now, it was occupied by the Germans.

"L'île est un lieu saint pour nous," said Gabriel. "And before this war is over, we'll drive those German bastards from it!" He then saw that the others were staring at him. "But tonight, we lay low."

"Je vous remercie pour votre hospitalité," said Luc. "We will take leave of you once the sun sets."

"Vous êtes le bienvenu chez moi aussi longtemps que vous le souhaitez," replied Gabriel. "But I pray that you'll find what you're looking for in Port Louis."

Gabriel then invited his guests to join him at his simple wooden table near the fireplace for breakfast. As they ate, Luc made eye contact with George and seemed ready to tell Yvette about their father. Once the meal was done, he took Yvette into an adjoining room while George remained at the table and listened as the others planned their next move toward Port Louis.

"My contact will be waiting for us here," said Robert, spreading out a map and pointing at the Le Pivain Michel church. "Luc says that he knows the area well. It's near the Fort de L'aigle where he and Yvette used to visit as children."

"Do you really believe that we'll find their mother there?" asked George.

"Oui," replied Robert. "It's a secure area. Our Resistance brothers and sisters have fought bravely to keep it out of the hands of the Germans. It has been a refuge for many civilians escaping the center of the city."

George nodded, and looked over this shoulder toward the room where Luc was breaking the horrible news to Yvette. He wanted to be there for her, but understood that it was between brother and sister.

"Si tragique ce qui est arrivée à leur père," said Gabriel, seeing George's anguish. "Those Vichy scum are as evil as the Germans, if not more." He pounded the table. "We'll get our revenge. In time."

Just then, Yvette came running out of the room, past where they were all sitting, and out the door.

"Yvette!" yelled George. "Don't go outside. It's not safe."

But she was gone.

CHAPTER THIRTY-THREE

Believing we couldn't wait any longer to leave Boda, Eric and Jafari helped Lisa and Maria get me into Eric's truck. Just as we were preparing to pull-away, Sister Agnes appeared from inside the mission. She had just heard from the hospital.

She looked at me, smiled slightly, and nodded her head before speaking quickly to Eric and Jafari. I leaned forward to listen, but couldn't discern what they were saying. Eric then started pulling away. I tried to protest, but was still too weak to mount much of a fight. All I could do was to turn around in the backseat and look out the rear window. I saw Sister Agnes standing there, stoic as always. I raised my hand to wave goodbye, and she did the same, before making the sign of the cross.

And that was it.

Eric pulled out of the mission's front-gate, turned the corner, and Sister disappeared from my view.

At that moment, something told me that I would never see her again.

"What did she say to you?" I asked Eric and Jafari. "Was it about the test results?"

"Yes," replied Jafari, speaking as he looked out the truck's passenger window at the scenes of violence beginning to envelop the streets. "They showed that you have Dengue fever."

"Dengue fever," I repeated incredulously. "How did I get that?"

"Ce n'est pas inhabituel ici," said Eric, adding in heavily accented English, "not usually dangerous."

"He's right," said Maria. "We had a lot of cases of it at the clinic in Mbaiki."

"How did I get it?"

"Probably from a mosquito," she replied.

"So it's the same as malaria?" asked Lisa, sitting to my right in the rear cab of the truck, with Maria to my left.

"The fever can last longer," answered Maria. "But, yes, it's mostly the same. Except . . ." Her voice trailed off.

"Except what?" I repeated, suddenly fearing the worst.

"It can lead to hemorrhagic fever, which can be fatal," replied Jafari, turning around to look at the three of us. "We need to be upfront about all of this," he added. "There's no point in hiding anything."

Maria and Lisa both nodded. "But it's rare," added Maria, putting her hand on my leg.

"And there's something else," said Jafari, turning back around to look out again at the streets of his town. "Sister Agnes also said that you have kidney stones."

That didn't surprise me. In my last year of college, I'd had stones. They were the most painful thing I'd ever experienced.

Until now.

"That explains the pain in my side and back," I said. "So what do we do now?"

"We get you to Berberati," said Jafari. "As quickly as possible. Once there, we can get you to a private hospital or the French military base. Sister said that you may need fluids intravenously. Or, at worst, a blood transfusion, if the fever worsens."

"Blood transfusion," I reiterated. "Jesus."

"It'll be okay," comforted Maria. "At least we know what's wrong."

"I suppose so," was my meek reply. But it didn't make me feel much better.

As we drove down Boda's main street, I watched as the student protests began to turn ugly. A few shops had already been burned, and Jafari said that there were reports of gunshots near the police station. I could even see a few of the students from the school running down the street throwing rocks and bottles.

I thought again about Sister Agnes, and worried for her safety. Eric had heard that one of the local mosques had been attacked, which would undoubtedly cause retaliation against the Christian churches, perhaps Sister's mission. It was all so difficult to process. And as we continued to drive out the town, something told me that I would never return to Boda again.

A few hours later, we arrived in Carnot, the halfway point to Berberati. The town had been named after nineteenth century French President Marie François Sadi Carnot, who had advocated for the exploration of central Africa before his assassination in Lorient, France, in 1894. It was the second time that my travels in Africa had led to a connection with that little French town in Brittany where my father had been stationed during the war, some fifty years earlier. The irony of it all didn't escape me, but as Eric pulled into the local hospital, it was admittedly the last thing on my mind.

During the ride to Carnot, the pain in my back had returned, even more acute than before. It was hard to believe that such a small thing could cause so much pain. But it was debilitating to the point that the hospital needed to put me on a gurney to get me from Eric's truck to the emergency room upon our arrival. I did my best to slow my breathing and speak as little as possible, as even the most minimal exertion resulted in severe pain. Maria pleaded with the doctor and nurses to give me pain medication, which eventually they did following an explanation of my condition by Jafari.

"How long do I need to stay here?" I asked about an hour later after the pain had again subsided.

"I'd like to get back on the road as quickly as possible," answered Jafari. "But they want to take another blood sample first."

Maria was shaking her head. "Look at this place," she said, gesturing to the dilapidated conditions of the emergency room. "We have no way of knowing if the needles are even sterile. For all we know, they could have been used with AIDS patients."

That was a scary thought. "So let's get out of here, now," I replied. "Get the doctor to give me more pain meds. Enough to get us to Berberati."

"What if the hospital there's not any better?" said Maria. "If the riots have already reached them, the hospitals could already have been overwhelmed."

"Eric already called ahead to his contact at the French base there," said Jafari. "They have started airlifting non-essential personnel out of the country."

"Going where?" asked Lisa.

"Douala," answered Jafari.

"Cameroon?" I asked, surprised.

"The French also have a base there," replied Jafari. "Right now, any place is better than here."

The final leg of our exodus from the Central African Republic was anything but smooth. In an effort to stop the spread of the riots, the government had established checkpoints between Carnot and Berberati. We passed through the first few without any problem, but then came the third, just before we entered the city. Having passed through many such checkpoints since my arrival in Africa more than a year earlier, I'd become accustomed to the bribes that were always part of the process.

So when I saw Eric reach into his pocket and retrieve a wad of bills, I wasn't surprised. But when they were rejected by the guards in a loud commotion, I realized that something was different. I watched from the backseat of the truck as Eric was escorted to a tent that had been erected by the side of the road to serve as a command post. Maria grabbed my arm and squeezed, clearly shaken by the turn of events, as Lisa leaned forward to speak with Jafari who remained in the front seat.

"Let's wait a few minutes," he said. "No reason to overreact."

But just as he said that, I saw him reach into the glove compartment and retrieve Eric's handgun. I'd known it was there, but also knew that most foreigners carried weapons in their cars in the event of an attack. But knowing it was there, and seeing it pulled out, were two completely different things.

"If they see you with that . . ." I started to say to Jafari, but then realized that Maria and Lisa had not seen the gun.

But it was too late.

The situation went from bad to worse as both girls began screaming at Jafari to put the weapon back in the compartment. He attempted to calm them, but to no avail. Two of the guards heard the commotion and began to approach our truck, while Eric remained in the tent with another guard.

Seeing the guards approaching, Jafari quickly slipped the gun under his seat, raised his hands in view of the guards, and stepped out of the vehicle. He addressed the guards in Sangho, which Eric didn't speak.

"We're taking these three Americans to the French military base," he explained. "The boy is sick."

The guards peered into the truck.

As Jafari continued talking with them, I could see them beginning to relax. I then watched as Jafari carefully reached into this back pocket to retrieve his wallet, quickly slipping the guards some money. They looked over his shoulder to see if their partner had seen the transaction.

He had.

The guards then began arguing among themselves. Eric used the distraction to return to the truck. We all waited there for a few minutes, and then drove off, leaving the guards to fight over their bribe.

"You could have gotten us killed, Jafari!" said Lisa, after we'd passed through the checkpoint.

Jafari turned around, clearly not happy with the girls' outburst. "If either of you react like that again, we will surely not reach the base. You have to trust me, or we don't have any chance of making it."

He was right, of course. Without Jafari and Eric, we never would've made it out of Boda. We probably owed them our lives. But neither could I blame the girls for reacting like they had. This was certainly not the situation we expected to find ourselves in when we signed-up for the Peace Corps. Instead of helping the locals, we were running from them.

"We trust you, Jafari," I said, trying to calm the situation. "And you too, Eric. When we all get to Douala, I'm sure it'll be a relief."

"I won't be coming with you," Jafari replied. "My place is here."

I was stunned.

"You can't stay here," I pleaded. "This is only going to get worse."

"It's my country. I'll be all right." The tone of his voice wasn't reassuring.

I wanted to protest, but knew it was pointless. Deep inside, I probably always knew that Jafari would not be traveling with us, and that we would never see him again. Like Sister Agnes, he had entered our lives for reasons that I didn't yet understand. But they had saved us, in more ways than one.

We did indeed make it to the French military base on the western outskirts of Berberati later that same day. As promised, Eric's contact was waiting for us. He turned out to be a sergeant with the necessary pull to get me placed in the base's infirmary where I received fluids intravenously while waiting for our airlift.

"We'll part ways here," said Eric. "I have a flight to Zaire later today."

"I thought you were coming with us to Douala," said Maria. "What's in Zaire?"

He looked at us and smiled. "Diamonds, of course. I'll be meeting an old friend of mine. I think you know him."

"Who?" I asked.

"Gaspard, the merchant from Bukavu."

"You're kidding, right?" I said. "You never told us you knew him."

"All the merchants know each other," he replied. "We compete for the diamonds, but we know that we're in a place where we're welcomed and hated at the same time. We need each other. After all, this is Africa."

TIA, I thought. Gaspard had said the same thing. TIA.

"Does he know you're with us?" asked Maria.

"Of course. The sergeant is actually his contact, not mine. He wanted me to look out for you. Thought that you'd get yourselves into some trouble, and was clearly right" said Eric, smiling. "Take care of yourselves," he then said, his duffle bag in hand. He shook Jafari's hand and then mine before hugging the girls. "And don't come back here. Ever. The rest of the world is waiting for you. But this continent doesn't deserve your help. It never did."

With that, he was gone.

Less than an hour later, Jafari and two soldiers helped us onto the C-160. He made sure we were strapped in safely, and then departed, with barely a word. Maria, Lisa, and I looked out the window and saw him standing with the sergeant as the plane's engines roared to life. We waved at him, but he didn't see us. Moments later, the plane lifted off, and we were on our way to Douala.

CHAPTER THIRTY-FOUR

Yvette ran out of the farmhouse and into the snow covered field. George followed close behind, all the while yelling at her to come back inside. It was daylight, and the Germans across the river were likely to see the movement.

"Please, Yvette," he screamed. "Come back."

But she kept running through the snow until she came to the next property, delineated by a low stone wall. George finally caught up, and grabbed her arm. "We need to go back," he pleaded, looking in the direction of the river.

She pushed him away. "You knew, didn't you!" she said. "You knew, and kept it from me." She was hysterical.

"Luc needed to tell you himself, Yvette," he replied. "He was just waiting for the right time."

She dropped to her knees. "How can this be, George? We've come all this way, and for what?"

"Your mother, Yvette. Luc believes she's here. Nearby."

She shook her head, and pounded the ground. "Too many lies."

"He wasn't lying to you, Yvette," said George. "Luc just wanted us to have a few days of peace together."

She laughed. "Peace! I haven't seen peace in nearly four years."

"But if we *can* find your mother . . ."

She cut him off. "No! They killed my father! And for what? He just wanted this country to be free. To go back to the way it was before."

"It'll never be like it was before," said George, kneeling beside her in the mixture of snow and dirt. "But in time, maybe we can make it better. And your mother can see that happen."

She hesitantly reached for him, and they embraced. As they did, explosions could be heard from across the river. The Allies were bombing again.

"We really need to get back. It's not safe out here."

"I just want to stay here for a few minutes," she answered. "I'm not ready to see my brother yet."

"You can't blame him. He thought he was doing the right thing."

She hugged George tighter. "I don't blame him. I blame those bastards who killed him. I want revenge."

"Someday soon, justice will find them," said George.

"Not if Luc and I find them first."

George grabbed Yvette's shoulders and shook her. "Don't talk like that, Yvette. When this is all over, crimes will be punished. Properly."

"You don't understand!" she protested, now pushing him away. "It's not *your* father who was killed!"

"No, Yvette. You're right. But I do know the pain of losing a parent."

George had told her that his father had died from cancer before the war began. "But it's not the same. My father was taken from me for no reason!"

"And he'd want you to live a good life. He wouldn't want you to risk everything to avenge his death."

"His murder!"

"Yes, his murder," George agreed. "But we're already here, so let's find your mother."

She looked him in the eyes. Intensely. "Are we going to make it? Are we going to survive this war? Or end up like my father?"

He pulled her close. "Yes, Yvette. We're going to survive this war and live a long life together."

"Here?"

"I don't know," replied George honestly. "I just know we'll be together, somewhere. But right now, we need to get back to the farmhouse and wait there until dark."

She nodded and they both stood up and began walking back toward the house, climbing over the nearby stone wall. But before they had gone very far, George heard the unmistakable whistle of an incoming mortar shell.

"Incoming!" he screamed.

He pushed Yvette so hard that she nearly left her feet, falling over the stone wall in a heap. George tried to dive over the wall too, but lost his balance and fell back, remaining on the other side of the wall from Yvette. He yelled out her name as the shell came in. "Yvette!"

Luc had been watching from the farmhouse window and came running out when he saw the explosion. Robert, Victor, and Gabriel followed close behind.

"Yvette," he screamed, repeating his sister's name over and over again as he ran to her location through the snow.

He saw George first, lying on the ground, writhing in pain, reaching for his leg, the snow around him soaked in blood. Luc knelt beside him and immediately put pressure on the gruesome gash just above George's left knee. "Yvette?" Luc said, frantically. "Where is Yvette?"

George looked behind him toward the stone wall. "There," he said, pointing. "I pushed her over there. Behind the wall. She's safe."

But she wasn't safe.

As Luc climbed over the stone rubble, he saw his sister.

"No!" It was a blood curdling scream.

Yvette was gone.

EPILOGUE: PART 1

It was nearly summer when Lisa, Maria, and I arrived in Paris. We'd been in Douala together for nearly three weeks, waiting for the Peace Corps to send us home. We'd been told numerous times that we'd be leaving the next day. Sometimes it was supposed to be on a direct flight to the United States. Other times to Belgium, or even Egypt.

The Peace Corps still moved slowly.

Finally, they sent us to Paris.

The riots had spread so quickly that the Peace Corps had clearly been caught flat-footed. Some days we were angry and blamed our government. Other days we were more relaxed and understanding, realizing the logistical nightmare of relocating hundreds of volunteers who were in crisis.

In the end, the Corps decided to pull out their volunteers from all of equatorial Africa. Things had gotten so bad that the French army was considering sending reinforcements to the region to restore order. But ultimately, they never did. Instead, most of the French bases throughout the region were abandoned. Five years later, though, they would return in response to the genocide in Rwanda, some of which occurred in and around Bukavu on Lake Kivu.

And so the cycle of violence in Africa would continue unabated.

TIA.

Sometimes, I think we were sent to Paris as some sort of an apology for the way the entire mess was handled by our government. The official reason was that they wanted me to undergo more tests in a Western hospital, and the most direct flights were between Douala and Paris. But whatever the reason, we took advantage of the opportunity.

I was supposed to stay at the Bretonneau Hospital near Le Cimetière de Montmartre for the duration of my stay in the City of Lights. But on two consecutive nights, Lisa and Maria left their nearby hotel to meet me in my room. We then slipped away into the Paris night, visiting such amazing locales as Notre Dame, Montmartre, and the Eiffel Tower. All the while, we knew that we would only be together for a few more days before returning Stateside, where we would likely go our separate ways. At least for a time.

And then the next adventure would begin.

Nearly thirty years later, I took my family to Europe. Two of my five children would soon be starting college and I knew it would probably be our last chance to travel as a family. It was also the 75th anniversary of D-Day and I wanted them to see the places where their grandfather had been so they could someday pass on his story to their own children. My sister had also joined us for the trip.

We explored Devonshire in western England where my father and Yvette had first met. We then took a ferry from Southampton to Calais, before renting a car and driving down the west coast of France to Normandy. There, we visited the small town of Saint Marie du Mont where Yvette had been born, and walked along Utah Beach. We then continued south into Brittany, and to Lorient. And we made it all the way to Port Louis, which had been George, Yvette, and Luc's destination in that winter of 1944.

After burying his sister, Luc had indeed found his mother in Port Louis. They both survived the war and were able to return to their home in Saint Marie du Mont. Luc's mother passed-away not long after. But Luc remained and helped rebuild his hometown as part of the Marshall Plan, America's plan to rebuild Europe. He spent the remainder of his life in Normandy, occasionally visiting Lorient. He succumbed to cancer in 2005 at the age of 85, and was buried beside his sister in a cemetery near the farmhouse in Locmiquelic where she had been killed by the mortar shell.

My family and I visited that cemetery and placed flowers atop the simple gravestones, along with a photograph of my father, taken by his mother on the day he had left for the war in 1943. He was so young, and his entire life lay ahead.

My sister and I embraced, understanding that a part of our father had never left Locmiquelic, and his beloved Yvette.

PART TWO

SECOND CHANCES: *FROM HONDURAS*
TO BIG SKY COUNTRY

CHAPTER ONE

Built in the years following the First World War, the Biltmore Hotel in Coral Gables near Miami Beach was a dreamlike setting complete with hand-painted frescoes on vaulted ceilings, brilliant travertine floors, fine marble columns, carved mahogany furnishings, and lavish gardens.

During the Roaring Twenties—and even into the Great Depression— the Biltmore was one of the most fashionable resorts in the entire country, hosting European royalty and Hollywood stars. President Roosevelt was a frequent guest. As was Al Capone. Everyone who was anyone stayed at the Biltmore, enjoying fashion shows, gala balls, aquatic shows in the grand pool, elaborate weddings, and world-class golf tournaments.

Then it all changed with the onset of the Second World War.

It's nearly impossible to comprehend the carnage of the war. By the time the Allies launched Operation Overlord in June 1944, America was already losing more than two hundred of its soldiers each day in combat, more than six thousand every month. Nearly double that amount were injured, later brought home in need of varying degrees of care and con-valescence. To accommodate the sheer numbers, the military took the extraordinary step of converting some of the largest and best known hotels in the country into military hospitals.

One such hotel was the Biltmore.

Adapting the building to its new use, the Army sealed many of the luxury hotel's windows with concrete and covered the travertine floors with layers of government-issue linoleum. It was then renamed Pratt General Hospital providing more than one thousand beds for injured sol-diers returning from the European and Asian theatres of war.

In early March of 1945, George arrived at Pratt.

"I don't remember too much of what happened following Yvette's death," said my father, as we sat side by side on his favorite bench overlooking Crystal Lake. I'd just returned home from Washington, DC, where I'd stayed at George Washington General Hospital for three days following my departure from Africa and a short stay at the hospital in Paris.

"I was told later that Yvette's brother had somehow gotten me back to the American lines where they operated on my leg in a field hospital before sending me to England. For practical purposes, my war experience in Europe ended right where it began, in Devonshire, where I'd first met Yvette before the D-Day landings."

"How long were you there?" I asked.

"Months," my father replied. "They did the best they could. The alternative would've been to lose the leg. As it was, they had to take a few inches off this leg," said my father, tapping his left leg.

"How did you get from England to Florida?" I asked.

"Of course, that was before flights across the Atlantic were commonplace," answered my Dad. "So I returned in the same way I'd gone. On board the *Queen Elizabeth*."

Built by the British in the 1920s, the *Queen Mary* and her sister ship, *Queen Elizabeth*, were handed over to America by Winston Churchill in 1942 to serve as "GI shuttles," transporting American soldiers back and forth across the Atlantic. Their ability to carry upward of fifteen thousand men—an entire division—made them the workhorses of the US Army throughout the war, bringing fresh soldiers into battle and injured ones home.

"Do you remember anything about the voyage?" I asked, taking full advantage of my father's rare openness about the war.

"Nothing," he said flatly. "I suspect I slept most of the six days it took to cross the Atlantic. Once we arrived in New York, I was probably transported by train to Florida. But even that, I don't remember very well." My father then paused, before asking, "Do you remember much about your flight from Africa to Paris?"

It was a good point. I remembered very little. When Maria, Lisa, and I'd finally left Douala, the Dengue was gone, but I was still struggling with the kidney stones. To make matters worse, I'd developed an infection. The Peace Corps' medical staff had considered removing the stones with surgery in Paris, but instead waited until I arrived in Washington.

"How about the hospital in Florida," I continued. "Do you remember much about it?"

"Very little about the first few weeks," he answered. "But then I met Ruth." My father hesitated. "But that's another story altogether."

"I'd like to hear it, actually," I said. "I know a little about her, but not too much. Was it hard to forget about Yvette?"

The moment I said it, I regretted my choice of words.

My dad looked at me, and I thought he'd reply angrily. But his reaction was quite different.

"No matter what happens between you and Maria, Johnny," said my father. "You'll never forget her. Like Yvette and I, you shared something powerful for a short period of time under extraordinary circumstances. The real challenge will come when those circumstances are different. Will the same feelings persist?"

"You don't think they will?" I asked.

"I've often thought of what Yvette and I would've done had she lived," considered my father. "Would we have remained in France or returned here?"

"What do you think?" I asked. "Do you think she would've been happy here?"

My father smiled, fifty years of reflection clearly coming to fruition. "Probably not. But I doubt I would've been happy in her little town in Normandy, either."

"So you don't think it would've worked?"

"As I said, when the circumstances change, the feelings often change, too."

"But why, Dad?" I asked. "Why do the feelings have to change? If they're real, they should remain."

"Yvette and I were drawn together for reasons that are difficult to explain. We were completely different people. Different backgrounds. Different beliefs. But we did have one thing in common."

"What?" I asked.

"Hope," replied my father simply. "We both needed *hope*. The hope that we'd be alive the next day. The hope that the war would end and we could see our families again. In each other, we found that hope. In many ways, our love for each other was born of the need for that hope."

"And Maria and me?'

"Only you can answer that," said my Dad. "You both found a sense of strength and security in each other's company. When the need for that security is no longer there, will the emotions be the same? Only time will tell."

"But do you think I should go to Puerto Rico to see her?" I asked my father, genuinely seeking his guidance. "Or should I just . . . let it go."

My father put his hand on my leg. Physical contact wasn't his way, so his touch always meant a lot to me. "If you don't go, you'll likely regret it for the rest of your life as you wonder *what might have been*."

I nodded. I'd already made up my mind about my next move. But my father's affirmation of that decision was important for me to hear.

CHAPTER TWO

When Christopher Columbus discovered the island of Puerto Rico in the fifteenth century, he named it *San Juan Bautista*, after St. John the Baptist. The city where he landed became known as Puerto Rico (meaning rich port). Then, in the early sixteenth century, the names were accidentally reversed by an unknown cartographer . . . and were never corrected.

By the middle of the century, the Spanish had walled-in the city and built two huge forts to fend-off attacks by the French, Dutch, and English, all wanting to control the island for its ideal location to launch expeditions to explore the New World. Nearly three hundred years later, the island was attacked by the United States during the Spanish-American War, becoming a commonwealth, which it remains to this day.

The night I arrived in Puerto Rico to be reunited with Maria, she took me to the Old City where we walked together along the cobblestone streets with their blue hue, passed buildings painted a myriad of pastel colors, and through the Plaza de Armas where the youth of the city would gather each night to frequent the cafes that encircled a large, central fountain.

We continued, hand in hand, along Calle San Francisco, passing by the Cathedral de San Juan Bautista, with its elegant Gothic facade, before coming to the Paseo del Morro, a narrow path that hugged the shoreline, wrapping around the city's northwest corner. We arrived finally at the Castillo San Felipe del Morro San Juan, the monumental sixteenth-century Spanish fortification resting atop a cliffside promontory, its rusted cannons still pointing seaward.

"This is such a beautiful place," I said, as we reached the Punta Del Morro and sat side by side on the stone wall, the fortress walls rising behind us, the Caribbean waters lapping at the rocky shoreline in front of us.

"To me, the most romantic place there can be in the world," said Maria, as the warm breeze lifted her hair.

I nodded. "Certainly a long, long way from Boda and Bangui."

Maria and I'd flown together from Paris to Washington, DC, along with Lisa. Although my time with the Peace Corps officially ended due to my illness, Maria and Lisa were given the choice of returning overseas to a different post. Maria had quickly declined, choosing instead to return to Puerto Rico where she would decide her next steps. Lisa, somewhat to our surprise, had decided to return overseas to a posting in the Philippines, a place that would later play a significant role in my own life's journey.

But that's another story altogether.

"So, now what?" I asked Maria, as we watched the waves crashing against the rocks near the old Spanish fort. "You'll look for a job here?"

"I know that I want to do something with medicine," replied Maria, without hesitation. "I've been thinking a lot about epidemiology. Maybe even going back to school to get my master's."

"Is epidemiology similar to what you were doing in Mbaiki?"

"Kind of," she answered. "It looks for the causes of diseases in populations."

"Like AIDS."

"Exactly," she replied. "But not only AIDS. Any disease really. Like how the flu is more common in poor areas where access to vaccinations are not as common."

"But you want to stay in Puerto Rico?"

"Not necessarily," responded Maria, as a young couple strolled by, the man's arm tightly around the slender waist of his girl. "I'll probably apply to schools on the mainland."

"Have you thought about where?"

"Tulane has a great program in epidemiology. I was actually accepted there for my undergraduate studies, but chose to remain in Puerto Rico to be closer to my mother."

I thought for a moment. "Isn't Tulane in New Orleans?'

"Yes. I visited the city once, and loved it."

We sat quietly for a few moments until I finally found the courage to ask the one question that I'd traveled to Puerto Rico to get answered. "What about us, Maria? What do you think will happen between us?"

At first, Maria didn't reply, as she stared out across the beautiful aqua blue waters of the Caribbean, before finally asking, "What about you? What are your plans?"

I wanted to say, *my plan is to be with you.* But I understood that she was looking for something different. "Believe it or not, I actually liked teaching in Boda," I said. "So I'm thinking of continuing as a teacher."

"Really?" she said, lifting her brow in surprise. "I didn't really think teaching was that . . . important to you."

Something about her tone hurt my feelings. I was still so insecure.

"I don't know if I'll spend the rest of my life as a teacher," I replied defensively. "I'm definitely not as certain about my path as you seem to be about yours. But I liked teaching, and I actually think I was pretty good at it while in Boda. Who knows, maybe I'll also go back to school to get my master's. Maybe even in New Orleans. But please don't sell me short and assume that I can't also do important work."

I surprised even myself with my outburst, and had expected Maria to push back. But her reaction was quite different.

"Wow," she said. "I never heard you speak like that before. With that kind of passion and certainty!" She jumped down from the wall and positioned herself right in front of me, staring right into my eyes, and putting both her hands on my knees. "I never meant to sell you short. I'm sorry if

I gave you that impression. I want you to find your path, just as I want to find my own path."

"But your path is not better or more important than mine."

"I never said it was," replied Maria, still facing me. "But I want us to make the right decision about our careers. That decision is more important than our relationship. At least for now."

"Meaning?"

"Meaning just that," said Maria, now turning away from me and looking toward the ocean. "I made some bad choices in college, and I don't want to repeat those same mistakes again."

"Mistakes with relationships?" I asked, remembering the secret that Lisa had told me in Africa.

"I put other people's needs and wants ahead of my own. I won't do that again. Esta vez me pondré primera a mí."

"I'm not asking you to put our relationship before your career," I replied, putting my hand on Maria's shoulder and turning her around. "Why can't we have both?"

"It never works that way," she replied defiantly. "The guy always thinks he's more important."

And there it was. I finally understood.

"I don't know everything that happened to you in college. But I'm not those guys. I would never disrespect you. Never."

And for one of the few times since I'd first met Maria in that little clinic at the base of the Nyungwe National Forest in Rwanda, she began to cry. "I was so stupid. I thought he cared about me. I trusted him."

I wanted to ask more, but knew it wasn't the right time. "It's okay, Maria," I said instead, pulling her close. "We'll figure this all out. It'll be okay."

CHAPTER THREE

Lying in his hospital bed in the Pratt military hospital in Coral Gables, there was little for George to do each day except stare out his window. If he sat up straight in his bed, he was able to look down on the golf course that lay just beyond his window. Occasionally, a group of officers would play the course. But for the most part, it lay unused for the duration of the war. So for most of each day, George simply lay in bed, listening to the radio. He preferred the classical music that his mother and father had raised him on. But most stations played a mix of big band music whose popularity was starting to wane in favor of the new crooners of the time, such as Frank Sinatra and Bing Crosby.

And occasionally, George would listen to news reports about the war.

By March of 1945, American and British forces had entered Germany, crossing the Rhine River near Oppenheim, just as Russian forces had entered Austria. Squeezed from the East and from the West, Germany began to contemplate surrender.

But in Asia, there was no end in sight.

Douglas MacArthur had led the liberation of Manila in the Philippines, leaving much of the city in ruins, while American warplanes dropped incendiary bombs on Tokyo, causing a firestorm that enveloped much of the city, killing tens of thousands of civilians. The battle for Okinawa was already underway, the first step toward the eventual invasion of mainland Japan, an undertaking that Allied leaders feared could lead to more than a million American casualties.

Yet, what George most wanted to hear was news from Lorient.

History would record that the German garrison inside the city would hold out until early May, refusing to relinquish control of their sub-base at Keroman. But in the spring of 1945, the world was no longer focused on

Normandy and Brittany. Instead, humanity was looking intently toward Berlin and Tokyo for the beginning of the endgame.

But the end to George's war had already come. As he lay in bed, he wondered what the future held in store for him.

The nights were often the worst.

Unable to sleep on his side or stomach because of the brace around his leg, George was forced to lay on his back, alone in the darkness, staring at the ceiling. Occasionally, lights from outside his window would cast shadows on that ceiling, playing tricks with his mind, sometimes morphing into battlefield scenes or landscapes from near Lorient. When he was finally able to fall asleep, he most often experienced the worst of nightmares, awaking suddenly to find himself drenched in sweat and shaking. On one particular occasion, he had screamed so loud that the nurse on duty ran into his room.

"George!" said the nurse, grabbing his shoulders and shaking him. "You have to wake up. You're having a bad dream."

George opened his eyes, disoriented.

"It's okay," continued the nurse, trying her best to calm him. "Would you like some water?"

George shook his head, still trying to focus his thoughts.

The nurse reached for the clipboard that hung from the foot of the bed, and quickly scanned George's medical history. "I see that you've already been here for a while. Leg injury suffered in the European theatre. Purple Heart. Translator for Army intelligence."

That last piece of information surprised George. He was certainly never a member of an Army intelligence unit. But he figured it probably didn't matter much, anyways.

"What's your name," he asked finally. "I've seen you for the past few nights."

The young nurse smiled. "Well, my name is Ruth. I was transferred here earlier this week."

"Transferred from where?" George asked, his mind clearing.

"Jacksonville," Ruth replied. "But I definitely prefer it here."

"Do I detect a Southern accent?" asked George. "Maybe Tennessee?"

Ruth's smile widened. "Close. Kentucky," she replied. "Ever been there?"

"Can't say that I have. Besides Georgia, where I did my basic training, I have only seen a few states. Massachusetts and New York."

"Ummm. Well, since I don't detect a New York accent, you must be from Massachusetts," replied Ruth.

"Correct," said George, impressed. "Not too far from Boston."

"Really?" said Ruth, her voice notably excited. "I'm hoping to go to school in Boston when this war is finished."

"What school?"

"Radcliffe."

"Near Harvard," said George. "I know that area. Harvard Square in Cambridge. It's one of my favorite places in the city."

"When was the last time you were there?"

George looked away from Ruth, toward the window. "It seems like such a very long time ago." In truth, it'd only been a few years. Before his father died, he had taken George to see Harvard, his alma mater. It'd made an impression. "I'm hoping to see it again soon."

"Well, who knows. Maybe I'll see you there someday." Ruth returned George's chart-notes to the hook on the bed. "But I better get back to my desk. I'll check on you again in a few hours."

"Thank you, nurse," replied George, enjoying the conversation they had shared.

"Please, call me Ruth."

George smiled. It felt good. It'd been many months.

CHAPTER FOUR

When people think of the Caribbean, they most commonly imagine powdery white sandy beaches meeting aqua blue waters so clear you can see the coral reefs lurking beneath the surface, as schools of tropical fish swim past. But the reality of the Caribbean is quite different. Those pristine beaches are rare. Many of the reefs are dying. And unregulated fishing has pushed many species of tropical fish to the edge of extinction.

But there's one island that does live-up to vivid imagination.

Culebra.

The charming archipelago, with a calypso-like vibe, is less than twenty miles from Puerto Rico's mainland. It has no major hotel chains, stores, or restaurants, and her waters teem with sea turtles and tropical fish swimming freely among mesmerizingly beautiful—and healthy—coral reefs. Mostly a natural refuge, it remains spared from the overdevelopment that has destroyed the natural beauty of much of the Caribbean, instead providing opportunities for beach combing, kayaking, hiking, and, of course, snorkeling in a serene, uncrowded setting. On top of all that, it has one of the world's most beautiful beaches, Playa Flamenco.

It was here that Maria took me on the second day of my visit.

After taking a ferry from Fajardo on the eastern coast of the Puerto Rican mainland, we arrived at the terminal in the Bajia de Sardinas on the southwest side of Culebra where we rented two motor scooters and made our way across the island along a narrow two-lane road that abruptly ended, blocked by rising sand dunes. We chained our scooters to one of the palm trees that lined the road, kicked off our sandals, and began the half-mile hike over the dunes. It was midday and the sun was high and bright, but a light breeze kept us reasonably comfortable as we struggled through the powdery sand.

But the struggle was soon rewarded . . . ten-fold.

Maria reached the top of the dunes first, removing her jean-shorts and loose-fitting white blouse to reveal her bikini. I took one last swig of water in order to reach the top, cognizant that Maria was laughing at me.

"Come on, old man," she said. "Paradise awaits."

She was correct.

As I finally reached the top of the dune and looked down upon the beach, I was in awe. Without question, it was one of the most stunning views I'd ever seen.

"How often do you come here," I asked, sitting down on the sand to take it all in.

"Incredible, isn't it?" said Maria, joining me on the sand.

"An understatement."

Maria nodded. "Actually, I haven't come here since high school."

"You came here with a boyfriend?" I asked, sheepishly.

She smiled. "No. A school field trip."

"Fieldtrip? Why weren't *my* field trips like this?"

A few hours later, as we raced to beat the setting sun, we set up our tent and prepared for our one night on the island. We'd brought some canned foods and a small camping stove, which Maria would use to prepare our meal. Surprisingly, there were only a few other campers on the beach, which stretched for perhaps a mile, in the shape of a crescent-moon, wrapping around the lagoon.

It was like our own private paradise.

After dinner, we took a long walk along the shoreline as the sun set below the horizon.

"Were you serious about going to New Orleans," I asked her.

"Probably," Maria replied. "I know I want a master's degree, and Tulane has a good program."

"A friend of mine from college lives there," I said. "Maybe I could stay with him while I find a job."

Maria stopped, turned, and looked at me. "I want to be honest with you. Nothing is more important to me than getting my degree."

It seemed like a good time to push a bit harder. "Why?" I asked. "Why is it so important to you? You can do a lot with just your undergrad degree."

She seemed to anticipate my question. "Because I didn't do my best in college, and I want to make up for it."

"You're a lot smarter than me," I admitted without pause. "Why didn't you do better? What happened?"

"I prioritized a relationship," she replied, the regret clear in her voice. "And I didn't have the strength to walk away from it when he began . . ." Her voice trailed off.

"You know I'd never hurt you, right?" I said, not really sure what to say. We both looked down at the warm water as it washed over our feet.

"You're different. I know that very well," replied Maria. "But still, I don't want to make any mistakes that I'll regret later. When I have my master's, I'll probably see things differently. But until then . . ."

"So you're saying that I shouldn't go to New Orleans?"

She looked out across the lagoon, and then waded farther into the waters. "I'm saying we should enjoy this night together, and worry about everything else tomorrow." She waded farther still, until it'd reached her shoulders. She then removed her bikini top. "Come on," she said. "Let's take a swim."

I'll admit, it was a very effective way to change the subject.

CHAPTER FIVE

As summer approached, George couldn't wait to get out of the military hospital. The humidity of southern Florida was already settling-in, and even though his room was in the air-conditioned wing of the hotel-turned-hospital, he was made to spend upward of two hours every day in the outdoor swimming pool as part of his rehabilitation. Ordinarily, using a resort's pool would be a great way to pass time and start to put the horrors of war behind you. But adjusting to his injury was taking both a physical and emotional toll.

When the artillery shell had exploded, killing Yvette, the shrapnel had torn through George's thigh, ripping most of the muscle and shattering his femur. Metal plates and screws were used to repair the bone, but it caused the leg to actually shorten by a few inches. The Army said that he'd eventually be fitted with special shoes that he'd have to use for the remainder of his life. But until then, he'd need to adjust to using crutches as he moved around the hospital.

Some days were harder than others. On one particularly bad one, George could be heard cursing and arguing in the pool with his physical therapist, a young man not much older than he was.

"You should feel lucky to be alive," said the man, trying his best to remain patient. "A lot of guys never made it back."

But there were times when George wished he hadn't made it back, instead dying alongside his wife. The guilt was nearly unbearable, all-consuming.

Why had he been spared? Why not her?

It didn't make any sense. He wanted to yell at the therapist some more. Anything to release his pain.

And then he heard her voice.

Ruth.

"How long have you been standing there," he asked, seeing her at the other end of the pool.

"Long enough to hear your tirade," she replied, arms folded. "What's that all about?"

George was embarrassed. "Sorry you had to hear that. I didn't mean . . ."

"Don't apologize," she scolded. "Apologize to Eddy. He's your therapist."

George looked at Eddy, who shrugged his shoulders. "Don't worry about it," he said. "Believe me, I get a lot worse."

"You shouldn't get anything, Eddy," said Ruth, "except respect."

"Sorry," said George. "I didn't mean any disrespect. I appreciate what you're doing for me."

"Don't worry. Let's get you out of the pool. Your session is over."

Ruth came over to the edge of the pool and assisted Eddy to lift George out of the pool. Once he was sitting on the edge, Ruth helped him to get up on his crutches. It wasn't an easy process.

"Take your time, George," said Ruth, sensing his frustration. "It'll take time to get used to everything."

George bit his lip, trying his best to refrain from any further outbursts. But it was hard.

Ruth watched him. "Do you need help?" she asked. "Or can you do it yourself?"

"I can do it," replied George, although he wasn't so sure. "It's just . . ."

"Just what?"

"Different," finished George.

Ruth smiled. "Like I said, it'll take time. But I think you're making good progress."

George finally found his balance. "Why do you care?" he snapped, immediately wanting to take it back. But his frustration was always near the surface.

But Ruth just laughed. "I care about all of you."

"I'm no different?"

Another giggle. "Well, I'm still hoping that you'll show me around Boston."

"Radcliffe."

"You remembered!" replied Ruth. "If you go to Harvard like your father did, then maybe I'll see you there."

George was surprised that she had remembered their conversation from a few weeks earlier. "I doubt I'll be going to Harvard."

"Why not. It's a good goal. And I hear that GIs can go to college for free."

"Really?" responded George.

"You should look into it," said Ruth, as they walked slowly together toward the hospital's rear entrance from the pool area. "It'll help to take your mind off things."

Maybe she was right, he thought. If nothing else, he needed to stop being so negative about everything. He *was* lucky to be alive. Even if tortured by the guilt of it.

"Yes, I'll do that."

"Good for you," said Ruth, as they entered the building. "Keep the faith."

Ruth then touched George's arm ever so slightly. "See you around, then?"

The contact surprised George. But he wasn't complaining. He was nice to have that human touch again. "Doesn't appear I'm going anywhere."

Ruth giggled as she walked away down the long corridor.

George watched her until she disappeared around the corner, and then continued in the other direction toward his room. But halfway there, he stopped, and decided to make a detour to the small library that was maintained for the patients. Once there, he would request information on Harvard University's admissions process.

But as he slowly made his way down the east corridor of the hospital, he heard a commotion coming from the patients' lounge. Curious, he turned the corner at the nurse's station and was immediately met by dozens of soldiers in different degrees of rehabilitation, doing their best to celebrate.

"What's happening?" asked George.

"It's over," screamed one young man, hopping up and down on his one-leg. "The war in Europe is over!"

Germany had surrendered.

On April 30, with the Battle of Berlin raging above him, the Soviets surrounding the city, the Americans having cut-off any avenue of escape, and his dream of a thousand year Reich all but dead, Adolf Hitler killed himself in his Fuhrerbunker beneath the city, along with his wife of forty days, Eva Braun. In his will, he named Admiral Donitz as his successor, believing that he would carry on the fight to the last man.

But he didn't.

A few days later, Berlin fell to the Russians and Donitz ordered all German forces to lay down their arms. The unconditional surrender of Germany was signed on May 7 in Reims, France. Later that same day, German forces that still occupied the southern quadrant of Lorient, surrendered as well.

As George absorbed the news, he felt anything but elation. *Just five months,* he kept saying to himself. *Just five months.* If Yvette had survived for five more months, she would've seen her beloved country finally at peace.

CHAPTER SIX

Following our moonlight swim in the lagoon of Culebra, Maria and I returned to our tent and sat down together on the sand, staring up at the night sky, in awe of its beauty.

"Do you remember the sky at that resort in Bujumbura," she asked, transfixed by the multitude of stars hanging above.

"It was the most beautiful sky I'd ever seen . . . until now." And then I added, "I also remember one of our conversations at the resort, and a similar one in Mbaiki a few months later."

She looked at me quizzically.

"You asked me about my mother."

"Yes, of course," she replied. "And I think I owe you an apology for that. I kept a secret from you, so I'd no right to expect you to be completely honest with me."

I put my arm around her. "It's okay. I guess we all have our secrets."

We sat quietly for a few moments before Maria continued. "I do have one question for you, though."

"Oh, oh," I said, jokingly. "Here it comes."

Maria chuckled too. "I've wondered why exactly you did volunteer for Sister Agnes's mission in Boda. Was it for me?"

Fair question. "In part," I replied. "I wanted to impress you. But I think Sister Agnes saw through that motivation and would have none of it. In the end, I think I came to understand that I needed to do it to put something to rest."

"Really?"

"I've come to understand that I never properly mourned my mother's death. I think a part of me always regretted not being with her when she died."

"They didn't want you or your sister to see her that way."

"That's true. But it doesn't change that feeling that I've kept bottled-up for many years. I guess I thought that caring for those children in Boda in their last hours of life would somehow release that regret."

"And did it?"

Another good question. "In all honesty, not really. But what that clinic did give me was more self-confidence." I stopped. "I bet that sounds selfish."

"No. I think it was you who said that we needed to be in Africa for *ourselves* first. If others benefited, all the better."

I remembered that it was Jafari who had told me that. And even my father had once said something similar. "So I guess the question is, did we benefit from the experience?"

I was surprised by how quickly Maria answered. "I know I did. Without that experience, I doubt I'd be so sure of my path."

I nodded. "I wish I was as sure as you."

"About teaching?"

"Yes. Don't get me wrong. I know it's what I want to do with my life. But I'm definitely not thrilled about going back to school to get my master's. I never cared much for school."

"You don't really need a master's to teach, do you?"

"I was never planning to be a teacher in college," I said, "So I never took any education courses. So if I'm going to get my teaching credential, I need more classes. I might as well get my master's at the same time."

"You sure you want to do that in New Orleans?" asked Maria, studying me intently. "Knowing that we might not be able to spend much time together?"

"I might not be that easy to get rid of," I said, smiling slyly. "We'd find time to be together, I'm sure."

I could see that Maria wanted to say something in response, but resisted. If I'd been smarter, or at least more perceptive, I would've taken her reaction more seriously. But I didn't. Instead, I simply changed the subject.

"When will I get to meet your mother?" I asked.

Maria hesitated. "I don't want to rush things with her," she said finally. "I've only taken one guy home to meet her, and it was a mistake." Maria put her hand on my leg.

Again, if I'd been more perceptive, I would've taken the delay as a sign that perhaps Maria had some doubts about our relationship.

But I didn't pursue it. Maybe I was afraid to consider the truth. Maybe my father had been right when he told me, "You both found a sense of strength and security in each other's company while in Africa. When the need for that security is no longer there, will the emotions be the same? Only time will tell."

"No problem," I replied instead. "So what's the next stop on my Puerto Rican tour?"

"Our next stop?" Maria repeated, gazing at me for a moment, almost as if she was looking inside me. And then suddenly, her expression became flirtatious. "How about inside the tent?"

CHAPTER SEVEN

By the end of the Second World War, more than sixteen million men and women had served in uniform. Wanting to avoid some of the problems which arose following the First World War when the government failed to properly support veterans, President Roosevelt began preparing for the soldiers' return well in advance. His plan became known as the GI Bill and was signed into law in June of 1944, not long after D-Day.

The Bill allowed servicemen and women to attend college, tuition-free, while also receiving a cost of living stipend. As a result, nearly half of all college admissions in 1947 were veterans. As Roosevelt had hoped, the GI Bill opened the door of higher education to the working class in a way unheard of before. In a sense, the war resulted in a more educated society.

In addition to education, the government guaranteed loans for veterans who borrowed money to purchase a home. This enabled hundreds of thousands of people to abandon city life and move to mass-produced homes in the suburbs, completely changing the landscape of the nation forever.

Medical care for veterans was also provided in the bill and resulted in the establishment of dozens of hospitals across the country, including Pratt Hospital in Coral Gables, with the sole purpose of providing care for veterans.

By 1956, almost 10 million veterans had received GI Bill benefits, including George, who had enrolled at Harvard University to begin the spring semester in 1946.

"It was life-changing," said my father, sitting between my sister and I on his favorite bench overlooking Crystal Lake. I'd just returned from

Puerto Rico and had informed them of my decision to get my master's degree in New Orleans. It was also an opportunity for the three of us to visit Mom's grave.

"Without that GI Bill, everything would've been different," Dad added.

"But why did you choose Harvard?" my sister asked. "Whenever you've talked about it, it always sounded like a bad experience."

"It wasn't the right place for me, that's for sure," Dad replied without hesitation. "I wanted to be an architect, but didn't have the proper math skills. Yet, the school kept allowing me to register for classes which I'd no chance of passing."

"But you still stayed and graduated," I confirmed.

"Yes. I made it through, but only after I changed my major to economics," said my father. "And that change was *my* decision, without any help from the university," he added. "If I'd changed schools, I would've lost the benefits from the GI Bill. But that wasn't my main reason for wanting to stay."

"What was your reason?" I asked, curious.

"The same reason you're going to New Orleans," said my dad. "I wanted to be near a girl."

"Ruth," said my sister.

"Yes, Andrea" replied my father. "When I left the hospital in Florida in the fall of 1945, I'd no idea of what I wanted to do with my life. So it seemed to make sense to follow her to Boston."

"She went to Radcliffe, right?" recalled my sister. In many ways she knew more about that part of our father's life than I did.

"That's correct. But she did it the hard way, working part-time to cover her expenses. I was given everything I needed by the government. All I'd to do was to study and pass my classes. But even that proved difficult."

"Your father had also gone to Harvard," I remembered.

"He did," confirmed my father. "He also went to Columbia to get a philosophy degree. I guess he was what you could call a *professional student*."

"That's definitely not what I want to be."

My sister laughed, nodding her head in agreement. She had recently completed her master's in communications and was working at Simmons College in Boston as an assistant to the president, coming home most weekends to visit our father.

"But at least you realize you need that master's degree, Johnny," said my dad as we sat on the bench beneath one of the many maple trees in the cemetery which had gravestones dating all the way back to before the Civil War.

"And the fact that I'm doing it in New Orleans?" I asked, wanting to know my father's opinion about my decision.

"I can probably predict what will happen," answered my father honestly. "But you have to figure that out for yourself by living through it. What's most important is that you get that degree."

And that's exactly what I intended to do.

In the summer of 1991, I moved to New Orleans to begin my master's degree at the University of New Orleans. I found a little apartment in an old Victorian house on Felicity Street in the Garden District. It was just a few blocks off St. Charles Street along which ran the famous New Orleans streetcar, which I used each weekend to visit Maria in her dorm at Tulane University, across the street from Audubon Park.

After working for a few weeks at a Walgreen's on St. Charles just down the street from the Trolley Stop Cafe, I was able to land a teaching job at a little Catholic School in Metairie, a sprawling suburb of the Big Easy.

It was a long commute each morning, taking the streetcar down to Canal Street near the French Quarter, then transferring to a bus that took me to City Park, where I would change busses again to get to the school in Metairie. My colleagues kept encouraging me to find an apartment closer to the school. But I refused. I wanted to be near Maria.

Not to mention the fact that the French Quarter was within easy walking distance of my apartment. For a twenty-four-year-old kid trying to find his way in the world, the city was seductive, seemingly without rules. My neighbor in the old Victorian house was a stripper in a club on Toulouse Street in the French Quarter, a few blocks from Bourbon Street. We never talked much, although I went to see her show one night, without Maria, of course. It was my first time in a strip club. And also my last. There was a desperation I saw in the faces of the patrons as they ogled the girls, who themselves wore a permanent expression of hopelessness and inevitability. It was a scene I wanted no part of.

What I did like about the French Quarter was the music.

My favorite place to go, either alone or with Maria, was Fritzel's Jazz Pub on Bourbon. I never listened to jazz before going to New Orleans. But there was something about the improvisation that thrilled me. How the musicians were able to create music on the spot, seemingly never playing the same song in the same way twice. There was a certain freedom to it that I envied.

And of course, there was the food.

My favorite Creole dishes were jambalaya and crawfish étouffée which were available in nearly all restaurants, but never prepared like they were at Mother's, a cafeteria-style eatery on Poydras Street.

My ideal night-out was dinner at Mother's with Maria, followed by jazz at Fritzel's, and ending with beignets and coffee at the Cafe du Monde near the Riverwalk along the Mississippi. When Maria and I were together, we'd often take long walks along the river, always being sure to return to the Canal Street trolley station by 1 am to catch the last streetcar uptown.

Riding the streetcar along St. Charles Street in the early hours of the morning was especially magical. Even more so with Maria sitting by my side on the wooden benches. Together we'd admire the grandeur of the Victorian mansions that lay behind the giant oak trees that lined St. Charles. We'd often try to guess the life story of the passengers who boarded the streetcar in various states of drunkenness at the different stops along the line.

Young. Old. Black. White. Rich. Poor.

All different kinds of people.

My experiences in Africa helped me to appreciate the diversity of the city.

And it also helped me to recognize its ubiquitous racism.

Even though nearly two-thirds of the city's population was African American, few of them lived in the Garden District. When an African American boarded the streetcar west of Louisiana Avenue, they inevitably drew wary looks from the white passengers who were heading home to their upscale neighborhoods near Tulane. Of course, the same was true in cities across the country. But there was something different about it in New Orleans. Something more sinister. More in-your-face.

Such as David Duke.

During my first few months in the city, the former leader of the Ku Klux Klan was running for governor of the state. It was surreal, to say the least. Almost daily protests, particularly in the African American neighborhoods, disrupted the city's daily routine and pulled police away from crime prevention, which was always a challenge in the city anyways. A few of the protests even turned violent.

On one particular occasion, while trying to get home from work, my bus was caught in the middle of a protest near City Park. Nothing bad happened, but as I sat in my seat looking out the window at the scene unfolding around me, I couldn't help but remember the riots in Bukavu and Boda. I thought about Jean Pierre and Ron. Gaspard and Eric. Lisa and Jafari.

And Sister Agnes.

During those months that I volunteered in Sister's mission, we'd frequently talked about the Catholic Church, and faith in general. I told her that my mother had been a devout Catholic all her life, but in her final months when she had needed the Church most of all, it'd not been there for her. Sister Agnes would do her best to explain the difference between the Church as an institution and the church as the house of God.

But to me, there was little difference.

The Church claimed to care for its "flock," but would often turn its back on those most in need if they didn't meet the Church's stringent criteria for membership and obedience. Sister would counter with the argument that the rules of the Church didn't always reflect God's will, that many of those rules had been developed in a time when the Church's role in maintaining social order was very different. But to me, it was an empty argument.

The Church needed to enter the modern world.

It was with these feelings that I began teaching at a Catholic school in Metairie . . . and riding that bus back and forth every day. I taught math and science, and—believe it or not—religion. Remarkably, the same person who doubted the integrity of the Church was being tasked with teaching its doctrine to Middle School students.

Needless to say, it wasn't a smooth start to my Stateside teaching career.

The principal of the school was Mr. Genco, an experienced educator who had no doubt seen dozens of new teachers like me, who thought they knew everything, but in reality, knew nothing. During my first week at the school he observed one of my religion classes, and called me into his office the next day to discuss what he had seen.

"What did you think of your lesson?" he began, taking notes without looking up from his desk.

"Definitely could have been better," I replied meekly, expecting a good tongue-lashing from my new boss.

The lesson that Mr. Genco observed was meant to be a discussion about Jesus's Sermon on the Mount where He had said, "Blessed are the meek, for they will inherit the earth." Not really knowing what to say to the students, I'd used my experiences in the Peace Corps to compare the *meek* to the people of Bukavu and Boda and their struggles to take back the land from their colonial rulers. Although the kids seemed captivated by my stories, I doubted it was what Mr. Genco was looking for.

But I was wrong.

"Lessons can always be better," he said, now putting down his pen and looking at me. "But I thought that you took an interesting approach."

"Was it okay to use my own experiences?" I asked.

Mr. Genco nodded. "Sometimes I think it's okay. Especially if your own experiences somehow mirror what the lesson is about. And I think you did a pretty good job of explaining the Beatitudes . . . with a modern twist."

"Thank you," I replied, not really sure of what else to say.

Mr. Genco smiled. "You know, I hired you for this job because of your Peace Corps experience. The Church needs more of that kind of idealism, I think."

"I'm not really sure I understand," I admitted. "I actually thought you wouldn't like the lesson."

"Don't get me wrong," responded Mr. Genco firmly. "There is a lot you need to improve. You didn't ask any questions. You didn't move around the classroom. You didn't check the students understanding of the lesson. You just talked for nearly thirty minutes. The students listened because they were interested in the story. But teaching has to be more than just storytelling."

"Yes, sir. I guess I just wasn't sure how to teach the lesson. I admit that religion is not my strong suit."

And then Mr. Genco really surprised me. "I disagree. I think it can actually be one of your strongest."

"Really?'

Mr. Genco stood up and walked around from behind his desk to sit beside me. "What these children need most of all, John, is empathy. An awareness of the feelings and emotions of other people. Some get that at home. But most don't. As a Catholic school, I see that as our most important mission."

I'd no idea what to say.

Mr. Genco continued. "You may know that I lost my son last year. He was killed in the Gulf War in Kuwait."

"Yes, sir. One of the other teachers told me. I'm very sorry."

"He joined the military because he wanted to make a difference." He paused, biting his lower lip and trying to collect himself. "And I think he did . . . make a difference. And maybe you joined the Peace Corps for the same reason."

I hadn't, but it certainly wasn't the appropriate time to correct Mr. Genco.

"We want our students to look beyond themselves," continued Mr. Genco. "To see the world as it is, but also as it could be. To me, that's the core of good, moral teaching. Not just Catholic teaching, but moral teaching that encourages children to seek a better world."

Mr. Genco retired just a few months later, clearly unable to come to terms with his son's death. But I have always remembered what he said to me that day in his office. He had not only affirmed my teaching, but had told me that good teaching must aspire to lift up children to a higher level of awareness and responsibility. It wasn't merely about teaching facts. It was about using that information to make a better world.

CHAPTER EIGHT

George arrived in Cambridge in the winter of 1946 to begin his studies at Harvard University. Using the allowance provided by the GI Bill, he rented a room from a widower who owned a large colonial home on Brattle Street, just a few blocks from Harvard Yard. The home had been in the lady's family for generations. When her husband had not returned from the war, she found herself and her two small children living alone in the sprawling home, built just decades following the American Revolution. In need of additional income, she opened her home to boarders.

At the time of the Revolution, Cambridge was primarily rural, with no easy access to Boston, which lay across the Charles River. With Harvard as its centerpiece, the area became the hub of the literary revolution, home to such famous poets as Henry Wadsworth Longfellow, James Russell Lowell, and Oliver Wendell Holmes, all drawn there by Harvard's intellectualism.

The construction of multiple bridges across the river, along with the onset of the Industrial Revolution in the late nineteenth century, the town underwent a transformation, soon becoming one of New England's main industrial cities with such huge employers as the New England Glass Company, Carter's Ink Company, and the Kennedy Biscuit Factory, which would later become Nabisco.

Then came the Great Depression and the war, causing the town to transform yet again.

As George arrived to begin his studies, the town's population was shrinking, with working-class families—who had made their living in the factories—replaced by single people and young couples. Harvard University stepped forth yet again to play a dominant role in the city's life and culture. But it was now joined by Radcliffe College and the Massachusetts Institute of Technology, making Cambridge the intellectual center of the United States once again.

On any given night, Harvard Square—located directly outside of Harvard's gates—was crowded with young people. They came from across the country—and indeed from around the world—to partake in the intellectual life that had returned to Cambridge. These were the young people who had been shaped by the Great Depression, who had freed Europe and Asia from tyranny, and who were now poised to take America to even greater heights as a world power. Many decades later, they would become known as the Greatest Generation. But in the winter of 1946, they were young adults, old enough to understand the world as it was, and still young enough to dream of what it could become.

George never considered himself part of that intellectual elite. His father, he knew, would've fit right in. But he had been at Harvard at the beginning of the Industrial Revolution when the town of Cambridge had a very different vibe and the world was a very different place.

At that time, America was still recovering from the Civil War, and the country was by no means a world power. But more than a half-century later, George found himself mixing with some of the greatest minds of the mid-twentieth century, including future Chief Justice William Rehnquist ('49), future attorney general and presidential candidate Robert Kennedy ('47), and future secretary of state and Nobel Prize winner Henry Kissinger ('50).

Yet, George had come to Harvard with no intention of trying to change the world and with no interest in the intellectualism that oozed from Harvard Yard. He had come to Harvard because of a girl.

When they had first started talking to each other at the hospital in Florida, George was torn. A part of him felt guilty about talking to another woman so soon after Yvette's death. But another part of him knew he needed to move on, to put the war behind him, and to find his own way in the world. In the beginning, it was her gentle kindness that pulled him in. While the other nurses and orderlies were doing their jobs as expected, she seemed to genuinely care. But beneath the surface, he had detected her strength, her feistiness.

George and Ruth had little in common.

He from the North. Massachusetts.

She from the South. Kentucky.

Even though the Civil War was nearly a century in the past, there remained more than just a geographical difference between the two parts of the country. There were distinct cultural and social differences as well, almost as if the two regions were separate countries. These differences were often at the forefront of George and Ruth's conversations, sometimes causing their discussions to become more like debates, as each stood up for their region's customs and traditions. But they could always fall back on what they had in common.

Both were only children, and both were the products of strict parents.

Ruth's father was a school principal who expected the household to run like a classroom. Her mother—as with most women of the time—was expected to remain at home, caring for Ruth, cleaning the house, and making sure that supper was on the table by six. But from a very young age, Ruth didn't like what she saw. She loved her mother dearly, but never understood why she was always so deferential to her father. When the war began, Ruth saw her opportunity to get out.

By the early 1940s, many women were working in factories, building the weapons that would be sent overseas and used by their husbands, boyfriends, and brothers to fight the war. Indeed, many of Ruth's high school friends went to work in the textile mills of Lexington, Kentucky which were turning out tens of thousands of military uniforms every month.

But Ruth didn't see herself in those surroundings.

She wanted to see new places and meet new people with different perspectives. She saw how military service was taking men and women from small towns and large cities across America and transporting them around the world. She wanted to be a part of that, and nursing seemed to be her best option.

So after graduating high school in 1944, Ruth announced to her shocked parents that she had enlisted in the Army Nurse Corps and was being sent to Florida for training. By then, the sheer number of casualties returning from the war was overwhelming the existing infrastructure of medical care across the country. Nurse trainees were being fast-tracked through their programs and sent to the largest military hospitals to support the existing, short-handed staff. After a few months there, they might be sent overseas to Europe or Asia to work in the field hospitals near the frontlines.

That was what Ruth was hoping for when she met George in the spring of 1945. When the war in Europe ended in May, it seemed as though she wouldn't have her chance. But throughout the summer of 1945, as the public was being prepared for the invasion of Japan and the human slaughter that would undoubtedly ensue, Ruth and her colleagues were readying themselves to receive the orders that would send them to Asia.

But those orders never came.

In early August of 1945, patients and staff gathered around the television to watch President Truman announce the dropping of the world's first atomic bomb on Hiroshima. Three days later, a second bomb exploded over Nagasaki, and the war ended.

As the hospital erupted in jubilation, Ruth had mixed emotions. Despite the dangers, she had wanted to go overseas. It was going to be her opportunity to see the world. But that opportunity was now suddenly gone.

Yet, since the very day that she had enlisted, Ruth had been preparing for her next move once the war was over. There was no way that she was going to go back home. She wanted to make her own way in the world, without interference from her parents. Since early 1945, she had been applying to colleges, mostly on the East Coast. One school in particular had caught her interest for its renowned liberal arts curriculum.

Radcliffe College.

And now she was there, with George nearby.

CHAPTER NINE

Established in the late nineteenth-century and occupying more than one hundred acres filled with oak trees and lined with historic buildings constructed from white limestone and orange brick, Tulane University has long been one of the country's most beautiful campuses.

If arriving by streetcar from St. Charles Avenue, you face Gibson Hall, housing the school's admissions offices. Behind the hall is an expansive lawn known as Gibson Quad, sided by such buildings as the School of Architecture, the Department of History, the Collins Diboll Art Gallery, and Carrollton Hall, one of the school's many dorms. During warm days— of which there are many in New Orleans—the quad is filled with students sitting on the stone benches along the lawn's perimeter or laying on blankets spread-out on the grass. Some are studying. Some sleeping. But all, in their own way, are basking in the glory of the Tulane experience.

Maria and I often met on Gibson Quad on a Saturday or Sunday afternoon, as it was near her dorm room in Carrollton Hall, and not far from the Howard-Tilton Library where she often studied. We'd usually spend an hour or so talking on the quad before walking across St. Charles Avenue to stroll through Audubon Park.

Sometimes we'd take the streetcar downtown to the French Quarter or River Walk. But as the fall semester stretched toward Thanksgiving and her workload increased, our visits grew shorter, typically limited to a few hours near her dorm. I treasured whatever time I'd with her, but I knew I was definitely playing second-fiddle to her studies.

Nevertheless, my male ego hurt, and I often struggled to hold it in check.

"I think it's important to have some kind of balance," I said to her one time, as we sat on the edge of Gumbel Fountain near St. Charles Avenue, at the entrance to Audubon Park. "You can't study twenty-four hours a day. You need some fun, too."

She shrugged. "I didn't come here to have fun. I could have stayed in San Juan for that. I thought you understood."

I could feel the tension. "I do understand. My studies are important to me, as well," I replied. "But I probably don't like it as much as you do." I smiled, trying to lighten the mood.

Another shrug. "You're right. I like my program. A lot. And I like the people in it. I'm making a lot of new friends. I don't see anything wrong with that."

Which I was beginning to understand meant that *our* relationship was becoming less relevant.

"There's absolutely nothing wrong with that. I'm so proud of you and genuinely happy that you're doing something that means so much to you. I can only hope that I'll feel the same about my career choice at some point. But . . ."

Maria cut me off. "Look. I want both things. I really want to spend time with you, but I want to be successful in my program. If you can't accept that, then . . ."

It was my turn to cut her off. "Then what?"

I could see her take a deep breath. "I'm going to be honest with you, and I don't want to hurt you. So, please, just hear me out. Okay?"

Now it was my turn to shrug. "Okay."

"In Africa, we needed each other. We relied on each other. We gave each other strength. If we didn't have each other, I hate to think what would've happened. But it's different here. We can rely on other people. And I don't think there's anything wrong with that. But it makes our relationship . . . different."

"Different, in what way?"

"We're less dependent on each other."

Maria kept talking, but my mind was again wandering back to what my father had said to me before I'd left for New Orleans. "I can probably predict what'll happen, John," he had said of my intention to meet Maria in New Orleans. "But you have to live through it yourself. You shared something powerful with her for a short period of time in extraordinary circumstances. The real challenge will come when those circumstances are different."

When I realized that Maria had finished talking, I asked her, "Do you feel differently about me now, Maria, than you did when we were in Africa,"

"Differently?"

"Yes. Do you feel differently?" I repeated. "When we were in Douala, waiting to be told what would happen next, do you remember what we said to each other?"

There was a slight pause in Maria's response, which spoke volumes.

"We said we loved each other and wanted to spend our lives together."

"We were scared," she replied. "Unsure of what would happen."

"So you didn't mean it?" I asked, my heart sinking.

"I did mean it," she said. But then her tone changed as she jumped down from the ledge of the fountain. "But this is exactly what I didn't want to happen. You're making me feel like I have to choose between my studies and our relationship. It's not fair!" The increasing volume of our discussion was starting to attract the attention of passersby.

"I'm not making you choose. I want you—"

Maria cut me off. "Are you really that insecure, that you can't accept the fact that I'm finding my own way."

"What?" I was dumbfounded.

"Why can't you be happy for me!"

"Maria! I *am* happy for you. I already said that I'm so proud."

"I won't feel guilty about focusing on my studies."

"Slow down, I'm not trying to make you feel guilty. I just want to understand how you feel about me."

"Why is it always about *you*," she replied, her anger continuing to grow. "And why can't you just be satisfied with what we have." She was pacing back and forth in front of me.

"That's exactly what I'm trying to understand."

She threw up her arms. "I just can't do this right now," she said. "I have exams tomorrow."

And with that, she crossed the street and walked back toward her dorm.

Should I have followed her? Perhaps. But in retrospect, I think I made the right decision in not doing so. I'd a lot to think about, particularly her comment that I was insecure. It hurt, but in many ways, she was right.

CHAPTER TEN

Radcliffe College for women was founded in Cambridge in the late nineteenth-century, just down the street from Harvard yard. From the beginning, the two schools maintained a close—if not odd—relationship whereby professors from Harvard duplicated lectures, providing them first for the men of Harvard and then crossing the Cambridge Common to provide the same lectures for the women at Radcliffe. Many of the professors resented the relationship, contending that they were wasting their time by teaching young women.

Despite such opposition, Radcliffe began expanding their campus in the first few decades of the twentieth century, adding a gymnasium, a library, and two dormitories, Briggs Hall and Cabot Hall, which faced each other from opposite ends of the Radcliffe Quadrangle.

By the time Ruth moved into Cabot Hall in 1947, the majority of Harvard courses were coeducational, allowing the women of Radcliff to share classrooms with Harvard men. Although she and George were not in any of the same classes, it was quite a step forward for women.

"Are you getting a lot of flak from the men?" asked George, as he and Ruth sat on a bench on the edge of Cambridge Common, a small triangular park bordered by Massachusetts Avenue, Garden Street, and Waterhouse Street.

"My stats class is the toughest," replied Ruth, dressed warmly to endure the cold March weather. "I always raise my hand, but the professor never calls on me."

"It'll just take some time," comforted George, himself dressed warmly, his crutches resting against the bench.

"I know. But it's frustrating, especially when I know the answer and the boys don't." She paused to reflect. "But I guess I can't complain too much."

Like the male soldiers, the female nurses who served during the war were entitled to benefits from the GI Bill. The amounts were significantly less, with more restrictions, and Ruth still needed to hold a part-time job to cover all of her expenses, but she was using her benefits to open doors at Harvard University, which had previously been closed to women.

"You *earned* the right to be here," corrected George. "And you're paving the way for other women to follow."

Ruth laughed. "That's too much pressure for me. I just want to pass my stats class, and maybe get called on once or twice."

George laughed.

As they began their studies in Cambridge, George was pursuing a degree in architecture, Ruth in liberal arts. George had seen the Old World of Europe, much of it destroyed by war. While in the hospital in Florida, he had become fascinated with the Marshall Plan, America's ambitious plan to rebuild the continent following the war. He had read articles about how the plan endeavored to rebuild the cities in an architectural style that mimicked their original appearance. Similar plans were being drawn-up for the rebuilding of much of Asia, including Japan, which had been reduced to rubble following more than three years of relentless bombing by American warplanes.

At times, George considered what would've happened if Yvette had survived and if he had not injured his leg. Would he have remained in France and participated in its rebuilding? He now had no intention of returning to Europe, but his fascination with architecture was unquestionable. If he could get through the program at Harvard—considered one of the best architectural programs in the country—perhaps he could put his skills to work in helping to build the United States into a world power.

Ruth, though, was unsure of her direction.

Many of her colleagues from the hospital in Florida had continued in the nursing field once the war ended. But she wasn't sure if that was the right path for her. Meanwhile, her parents—who had reluctantly supported her decision to enroll at Radcliffe—still wanted her to pursue teaching. But she wasn't sure about that either. So liberal arts seemed like her best option, providing a breadth of study that would perhaps help her to choose a career path.

The environment at Radcliffe and Harvard was nothing short of inspiring. She could feel it in the air. The country was changing and higher education was leading the way, with the Ivy League colleges of the East Coast at the forefront of the social revolution.

"How about you?" asked Ruth. "How are your classes going?"

George sighed. "They're tough, especially calculus. I wish I'd taken more math in high school."

"I'm sure you can find a tutor," suggested Ruth. "Why don't you meet with your advisor."

"I should," agreed George. "But it's just so damn difficult to get around with these crutches, especially in the snow and ice."

"Aren't people patient with you?"

"Oh, they're SO patient. The other day I'd trouble getting down the stairs into the subway. These two men came over and actually carried me down the stairs, saying, 'Thank you for your service,' as if I were some superhero."

"Wow," said Ruth. "That must have made you feel good."

"Of course. But I just can't wait until I can get rid of these crutches and move around like everyone else."

"It'll just take some time," said Ruth, repeating what George had said to her only a few minutes earlier.

They both laughed.

But neither had any delusions about the struggles that lay ahead.

America was changing. Radically. And they were right in the middle of the social tidal wave. In the decades to come, veterans of the war would become the country's movers and shakers, and women would begin to take their rightful place in the workforce. America had emerged from the darkness of war as the new light of the world. Although the world had not seen the end of war, it'd perhaps seen the end of world wars. But as George and Ruth settled into their new lives in Cambridge, none of that really mattered to them. They cared about their studies. And they were beginning to care deeply for each other.

One of their favorite weekend activities was to take the subway into Boston, getting off at the Tremont Street Station near the Commons, and walking a few blocks down to Washington Street and into the Theatre District. Top among the nearly fifty theatres in the district was the Paramount, showing such popular productions such as *Oklahoma*, *Carousel*, and *Kiss Me, Kate*, which was Ruth's favorite. George preferred the opera, his favorite being Puccini's *Tosca*, which often showed at the Shubert and Wilbur theatres.

Whenever they had a little extra money, they took an early train into the city and enjoyed a pre-theatre dinner at the Parker House, located not far from the State House in the nineteenth century Omni Parker House Hotel on School Street, frequented over the decades by such literary giants as Ralph Waldo Emerson, Nathaniel Hawthorne, Henry Wadsworth Longfellow, and Henry David Thoreau. George's father had actually been a contemporary of Hawthorne's, having briefly lived down the street from him in Concord in the late nineteenth century, and proudly displaying a signed copy of the *Scarlet Letter* in his Study at the family home in Gardner.

In the spring of 1947, George took Ruth to that family home to meet his mother. It was a two-hour train ride from Boston, a ride that George had been taking each month since he had returned from the hospital in Florida. The train would pass by Fort Devens in Aire where George had first been sent for indoctrination upon joining the military in 1943. It was always hard to believe that it'd been nearly four years since he had arrived there as a skinny, naive, nineteen-year-old kid, without any idea of what lay ahead.

Would he have done it all over again, knowing what lay ahead?

Yes, but not necessarily for his country, because he wasn't particularly patriotic. Not because of duty and honor. Because he wasn't particularly motivated by either. Not because of a purpose higher than himself. Because he rarely saw the world in that way. He would do it all over again because of Yvette.

And now, Ruth

He had actually told his mother about Ruth before he had told her about Yvette. It was an easier conversation. But when he finally had shared his experiences in France with his mother, he was relieved to finally be able to release some of the anxiety that he had been holding inside for many months. His mother had held him tightly as the words poured out.

"It's all right, Jimmy," said Elizabeth, using her son's middle name, as she almost always did. "All that matters is that you came back to me. Now you have your entire life ahead of you."

"With Ruth?" asked George, as he sat beside his mother in the parlor of their home.

"Perhaps. But be patient. Don't rush things," advised Elizabeth. "Finish your studies, and you'll find the right path. Perhaps Ruth will walk that same path with you. Perhaps not. But enjoy each other's company. Treasure each day."

"How did you feel when Dad died?" asked George. "How long did it take you to get over it?"

"I don't think anyone ever *gets over it*, Jimmy. I'll carry it with me for the rest of my life. Your father was an important part of my life, just as Yvette was an important part of yours."

"Sometimes I think that I'm disrespecting her memory, Mom, by being with Ruth. Am I doing the right thing?" George was trying to fight back some tears.

"Nonsense," replied George's mom. "You respect her memory by living your life the best you can. By being the best person you can be. She will always have a place in your heart. Remember, the human heart is far deeper than we often give it credit for. It has the capacity for happiness *and* sorrow. Love *and* loss. It may sometimes feel like it's breaking. But it always endures."

George studied his mother and looked around the room. "Do you ever wish you had left Gardner after Dad died?" asked George. "Maybe returned to Boston or even New York?"

Elizabeth smiled. "The human heart is also restless, especially when you're young. As it gets older, it finds peace in simple ways. This house for example. I can still feel your father's presence here. Especially in his study."

"Do you visit him at the cemetery?"

"I do, almost every Sunday. I often take one of his favorite books and read a passage aloud."

George shook his head, and his mother saw it.

"It's all right, Jimmy. I know that living with your father was difficult, at times. But someday you'll see him differently. Someday, when you're more secure."

"More *secure*?"

"I know you left home because you needed to break out on your own. Every boy feels that same urge. Your father had a big personality. It was easy to be overwhelmed by it. But in time, you'll come to appreciate his memory in different ways. When you do, perhaps you'll find yourself at his gravesite, too. But for now, you must find your own path. Prove to yourself that you can be successful."

"Do you think I will be, mom?" wondered George. "Successful?"

"Of course. You can do anything you put your mind to."

"Thanks, Mom."

They embraced again.

He had respected his father. Probably even feared him. But he had also been in awe of him. Especially as a young boy. He always seemed to have the right answer to any question. But as George grew older, he felt distance from him. So many times he had wished they could have had conversations similar to what he had just experienced with his mother. But his father seemed to exist on a different level, never able to come down to the level of a teenager trying to find his own path.

His relationship with his mother had also been strained, particularly in those final few years of his father's life, when caring for him had taken up nearly all of her time and energy. He often felt that she had little time left for him. So being able to talk so frankly with her now, meant a lot to him.

And so did her warm greeting of Ruth.

"I'm so glad that you and George have each other," she said to Ruth, as the three of them sat on the front porch of the house, from which you could see Crystal Lake in the distance. "Life is not meant to be lived alone when you're young."

"Thank you so much for inviting me," said Ruth. "George always talks a lot about you."

Elizabeth laughed. "Probably not always in the best way."

"Mom!" said George, embarrassed.

"It's all right, my dear. When I was your age, I'm sure I thought I knew more than my parents. We all share many of the same struggles when we're young. And when we're old, for that matter."

"It must be lonely to live in this big house all by yourself," said Ruth. "You should come to Boston more often to visit us."

Elizabeth waved her hand dismissively. "The big city is for young people. This is my home. And my husband is nearby." She motioned toward the lake, and nearby cemetery.

"He sounds like a remarkable man," said Ruth. "George said that he also went to Harvard."

"Yes, but that was a very, very long time ago. In a different time."

"Do you think it has changed for the better?" asked Ruth. "Or do you think things were better before?"

Elizabeth thought for a moment. "I'm sure your parents, Ruth, are much younger than me, and probably have a very different viewpoint. But things have become so . . . *fast*. Everybody seems to be in a rush. It's what I like best about Gardner. It moves more slowly."

"Actually, my parents also struggle with the recent changes in the country. Especially the role of women."

Elizabeth tilted her head slightly. "Yet, their daughter is attending a school which was once men-only."

Ruth wasn't quite sure how to take the comment. "Yes, it was hard for them to accept it. But they're supportive now."

"As they should be," replied Elizabeth. "I certainly didn't agree with Jimmy's decision to join the Army. But I supported him as best I could. Sometimes parents just have to swallow hard and hope their children find their way in this world."

"You must be so relieved that he came back to you."

"He's all that I have left in this world," said Elizabeth, reaching for her walker to help herself stand-up. "Now, let's get going or we'll be late for church."

Ruth looked at George, mouthing *church*?

It was pointless to resist. They were on his mother's turf, now.

CHAPTER ELEVEN

The city of Gardner was first settled in 1764, around the same time as the Methodist movement began in New England. In the beginning, Methodist services were held in homes by circuit rider clergy who traveled from town to town throughout northeastern cities and towns, including Gardner. By the middle of the nineteenth century, Gardner had grown quickly into a lumber and furniture-making center in Massachusetts. By the end of the Civil War, the first Methodist congregation had been established in the town, which had seen its population grow to nearly ten thousand. In 1877, a new Methodist Church was erected on Chestnut Street, not far from downtown Gardner, which was less than a mile from Crystal Lake . . . and Elizabeth's home.

Throughout the first few decades of the twentieth century, as Gardner continued to grow as an industrial hub, membership in the church grew steadily. When Elizabeth first began attending services at the Chestnut Street location, the church had more than two hundred members and enough funds to support growing social and youth needs.

To support such needs, a gymnasium, bowling alley, kitchen, and classrooms were added in 1929, not long before the stock market crash and the beginning of the Great Depression. During those difficult years, Elizabeth could always be found volunteering at the church's soup kitchen. George often accompanied his mother, and was sometimes given the task of peeling the potatoes to make the soup.

"What church do your parents attend?" asked Elizabeth of Ruth, as they walked with George along Central Street, past Monument Park which remembered the fallen of the First World War.

"My mother still goes to the Baptist Church every Sunday," said Ruth. "When I was young, I would always go with her."

"Jimmy used to come with me, too. But I don't think he has gone in many years. Maybe the two of you'll find your way to a good Bible-based church in Boston."

Ruth glanced at George, who just shook his head, trying to stay out of the conversation.

"Have you ever gone to a Baptist church?" asked Ruth of Elizabeth.

"Oh my goodness, no," replied Elizabeth, without hesitation. "There is nothing wrong with it, of course," she added. "I know many fine people here in Gardner who attend the local Baptist church."

"I remember how much I loved the music," said Ruth. "After church, I would sing the songs as I walked home with my mother."

"That's very nice, my dear," responded Ruth. "But, of course, it's the Bible passages that matter most."

"Of course," replied Ruth, looking to George for help.

Elizabeth continued. "We need to get back to the Bible. We've moved away from it. Especially the young people. You used to see families going to church together. But not so much anymore."

"Maybe people want to go," reasoned Ruth. "But they don't have the time. Especially with more women now working."

George smiled at that comment.

Elizabeth sighed. "Yes, you're right about that. I fear the American family is at risk."

"So you don't agree with women working?" questioned Ruth, careful with her tone.

"It was certainly necessary during the war. But now you see so many young couples having children. Who will care for them?"

Finally, George spoke up. "Women have the right to pursue a career, too, Mom. Not all of them want to stay home."

"I understand that. But what about the children? If both parents are working, who will raise them?"

"Maybe the wife stays at home for a few years after the child is born, and then begins working when the child is old enough," offered George.

"And how old would that be, Jimmy? Three? Four? Five?"

"Maybe when the child begins school," suggested George.

"And when the school day is over, who will be home to let the child in?"

George was becoming frustrated. "I don't know, Mom. People will figure it out."

"And while they figure it out," said Elizabeth, "what will become of the children?"

Ruth took George's hand and tried to diffuse the situation. "Your mom has a point, George. There is a lot to figure out."

When World War Two began, there were one hundred and thirty million people in the United States. By 1960, it'd increased to one hundred and eighty million, a nearly forty percent increase. The Baby Boomers had arrived, and they would change the country in ways which were unimaginable in 1947 when George and Ruth were beginning college. Education. Religion. American values. It would all change. And within twenty years, the country would be nearly unrecognizable. There was indeed a lot to figure out.

CHAPTER TWELVE

As Maria and I considered the future of our relationship, we gave each other the necessary distance, and immersed ourselves in our respective schools. While nowhere near as historic as Tulane, the University of New Orleans had an attractive campus located on the shore of Lake Pontchartrain. More importantly to me, it was affordable and located near my teaching job in Metairie, allowing me to take the city bus to class each evening.

Dr. Busby was my educational psychology professor during my second semester at UNO and seemed genuinely fascinated by my experiences in Africa, which I sometimes shared during open discussions in the classroom. She was also aware of my day job as a Catholic school teacher, and once commented that it was a far cry from the mission school in Boda.

"Would you ever consider returning overseas," she asked one time when I was meeting with her to discuss my thesis topic.

"I haven't really given it a lot of thought," I replied, honestly. "I guess I'm waiting to see what happens here in New Orleans."

She studied me and seemed to sense my restlessness. "You know, a few years ago I visited a school in Honduras as part of an accreditation team. I've kept in touch with the owner of the school, and they're often looking for new teachers, particularly from this country. If you wanted, I could send her your name."

The offer took me off-guard. "Thank you, Dr. Busby. I'll give it some thought."

As the weeks passed without any contact with Maria, the offer became more and more intriguing. But with a few more semesters still remaining to earn my master's degree— which I'd promised my father I would complete—I did my best to remain focused on the tasks at-hand, which included the daily challenge of teaching young teenagers.

As I undertook that challenge, I always did my best to remember the words of Mr. Genco, the school's principal during my first few months on the job.

"We want our students to look beyond themselves," he had said. "To see the world as it is, but also as it could be. To me, that's the core of good, moral teaching."

His words seemed to align with my own experiences and what I'd seen of the world. But there was also a disconnect between the idealism of those words and the reality of the Catholic Church, with its emphasis on structure and conformity. The more I tried to reconcile the two, the more disillusioned I became with religion.

Of course, there had been exceptions.

Sister Agnes.

She understood that the Church's main role—at least in the Third World—was to help lift people out of poverty and to comfort them in their time of greatest need. She had remained singularly focused on that mission, despite the disinterest of the clergy who shared the same Mission with her.

But in the Western World, the Church had a different role to play, and one that Mr. Genco was well aware of: to encourage people to look beyond themselves and to inspire them to become better, more caring, people. But that role demands the teaching—and, indeed, the modeling—of tolerance. Tolerance for all lifestyle choices, not just those that align with the Church's medieval doctrine.

I didn't feel that the Catholic Church in my country was generally tolerant. Unfortunately, those feelings came to the attention of my superiors and jeopardized my job as a teacher at the little Catholic school.

Following one of my religion classes in which the topic of homosexuality arose, I was summoned to the pastor's office. I'd only spoken with him a few times in the nearly eight months that I'd been at the school. He had never visited classrooms or offered to teach any religion classes. He never joined students on field-trips or attended school events. We only saw him each Friday during the school's weekly liturgy, dressed in his robes, and looking down at us from his perch upon the altar. The students were not inspired by him. They were afraid. His words didn't lift young spirits. He tore them down, only able to criticize them for whispering in their seats during his homily.

In short, it was all about *him*.

"A few parents contacted me about your recent religion lesson," he said to me as we sat in his office. "They were not pleased about your position on homosexuality."

"My position?" I replied, genuinely confused.

"You were condoning such behavior?"

His hard stare was disconcerting, to say the least.

"With respect, Father, I wasn't condoning it or condemning it. I was simply discussing it. Trying to answer the children's questions."

"Once you open the conversation, you're giving the impression that there's validity on both sides," he said. "Don't you agree?"

Are you kidding me? I thought.

"I'm sorry, but I don't understand," I said instead. "It's not an appropriate topic?" I was trying hard to remain calm.

"You respond to questions about it by simply giving the Church's position."

"And what is the Church's position, Father?"

With that, he became visibly irritated. "You're teaching religion in the school, and you don't know the Church's position on this topic? How can that be?"

"I thought my role was to encourage the students to explore their faith."

"Your job is to teach Church doctrine. Period."

And with that, the meeting abruptly ended.

Was he representative of the Catholic Church as a whole?

Although I hoped not, I suspected otherwise.

Sister Agnes had taught me the difference between faith and religion. Religion, man-made, the product of institutions. Faith, more personal, a relationship between the believer and his or her God. Yet, in my short life, I'd observed the two to be inexorably mixed. A mixture that seemed to have brought more harm than good to the world.

As I left the pastor's office, I thought about Mr. Genco, and wondered if his retirement was due to factors other than the death of his son.

Perhaps he had become disillusioned about the Church, like me.

CHAPTER THIRTEEN

By the summer of 1949, George and Ruth were preparing for their final year at Harvard and Radcliffe. She continued to live on-campus, while he continued to rent the same room in the widower's house. Following some difficult semesters, both had discovered their respective career paths. Ruth's liberal arts studies had led her to conclude that teaching was her passion, a realization that greatly pleased her parents. George had reluctantly given-up on his dream to be an architect—unable to manage the advanced math classes—and had settled instead upon a degree in economics.

But during that last summer of perhaps the century's most consequential decade, George and Ruth had discovered something else: the depth of their love.

Their first three years in college had been like mastering rough seas, as both institutions found themselves caught in the headwinds of change that were pulling the country in new directions.

Every class that Ruth took seemed solely focused on preparing future teachers for the social and cultural changes imminent. While she was hoping to learn the best way to teach multiplication facts to third graders, she instead was forced to listen to one lecture after another on the changing role of educators, one that placed them in the role of parent as well as teacher. With so many women entering the workforce, and so many children recently born, schools understood the gap that was forming. Ruth often wondered how her father, a school principal in Kentucky, would adjust to the change. Would he accept it, or fight its inevitability?

For George, every class he took seemed solely focused on preparing future economists for a global economy. Everything was becoming intertwined. Yet, America seemed to stand above it all.

Much of the world had become dependent on American dollars to drive their economies, and as Europe and Asia continued to rebuild following the devastation of war, much of the world was looking to the "shining city on the hill" to provide hope for a better world.

Indeed, many of George's classmates yearned to stand upon that hill, yelling at the top of their lungs, proclaiming that America was fulfilling its destiny. One of George's classmates that perhaps yelled the loudest was named Henry Kissinger. Everyone suspected that he would become a person of significance, but few in the class liked his braggadocious persona.

On one particular occasion, as the class was discussing new economic policies in Europe, Henry became especially animated, refusing to allow anyone else the opportunity to chime in. George, having reached his limits of tolerance, confronted him.

"Why don't you sit down and shut up, Henry, and give someone else a chance."

The entire class erupted in applause.

Afterward, Henry approached George in the hallway outside of the class. "I'll run this country someday," said Henry. "What will you do?"

George smiled and said simply, "I think I've already done enough." He then tapped his leg with his cane, and walked off.

But America was far from perfect, beginning to experience its own internal strife. The Red Scare was sweeping the country, infecting private as well as governmental institutions. Despite losing more than twenty million of its citizens during the war, the Soviet Union was now flexing its newfound muscle. It controlled nearly all of Eastern Europe and was making inroads throughout Asia. America had found a new enemy and had begun to grow fearful of that enemy's entrance into their own backyard.

But the more liberal institutions of higher learning, such as Harvard and Radcliffe, were becoming a check on its own government's tendency to see communism where it didn't exist. Good men and women were being unfairly accused of heinous crimes. The rule of law seemed to be slipping away.

Students had begun speaking up—often taking to the streets outside Harvard Yard—understanding that it wasn't the vision of America that many of them had fought so bravely to defend. Yet, despite such protests, it wasn't enough to keep the witch hunts from reaching inside the university's prestigious halls.

One of their own professors of physics had fallen under investigation for possible ties to the Soviet Union, and there were rumors that the university's own president would soon resign amid the board of trustees' displeasure with his reluctance to choose a side. He had called for a ban on hiring teachers who were communists, but had resisted calls to dismiss those who had already been hired.

Although no one realized it at the time, what was occurring on campuses across the country was a precursor to an even wider student rebellion that would occur nearly twenty years later, one that would be led by the children of the Greatest Generation—Ruth and George's generation—who were now just starting to take their place at the reigns of history's most powerful nation.

But neither of them were comfortable amid such social upheaval.

Although not threatened by it, they felt overwhelmed. That somehow they were being forced down a road not of their choosing. So they had retreated into the calm and familiarity of each other's arms.

"I wish we were graduating now," said Ruth to George, as they sat together on the quad outside of her dorm watching a group of students making protest signs. One of the signs read: *America is not a Police State, YET!* "This is all getting so scary."

"Yes," replied George with a sigh. "It's definitely not what I'd expected. But I guess we don't have much choice but to see it through."

"And then what?" asked Ruth. "Stay here?"

George had been giving that question a great deal of thought, and this seemed like his opportunity to float the idea with Ruth.

"I always wondered what it was like out west," he said, carefully watching Ruth for her reaction.

"Out west?" repeated Ruth. "Like California?"

"No, like Montana and Wyoming."

Ruth stared at George. "What? Really? What's out there?"

"Well, none of this," said George, motioning to the growing crowd. "A quiet place where we can live-out our lives . . . together."

Ruth turned to George. "Do you really see us spending our lives together?"

"Don't you?"

"Of course, I do," said Ruth. "It's what we've talked about. But in Montana? That's definitely a place I've never considered."

Since the end of their second year at Harvard and Radcliffe, George and Ruth had begun seriously considering a life together. George had sensed that Ruth would've committed earlier, but something held him back. Maybe it was the memory of Yvette, or the nightmares that he still endured nearly every night.

But as time passed, he found ways to bury the pain.

At times, he worried that it would somehow find its way to the surface, revealing itself in ways that could hurt Ruth. And that was the last thing he wanted. She didn't deserve that. In his darkest hours, she had been there for him. She had helped him through those difficult months in the hospital, and had stood by his side during those first few years of college as he adjusted to his lack of mobility. And now, as they looked to the future, she seemed willing to follow him across the country.

"I think it was that movie we saw a few months ago," said George. "The one with Errol Flynn."

"*Montana*," said Ruth, remembering the name. "I didn't realize you liked it that much."

"Not so much the movie," admitted George. "But there was something about the scenery. It seemed so peaceful. I guess that's what I really want. To find some quiet place where the people are genuine and the pace of life is slow."

Someplace like Brittany in France, he thought.

Ruth nodded. "A lot different from this," she said, watching the students continue to make their protest signs. "Is there work out there for us?"

"I'm sure there are schools where you could work."

"And you?"

"I'd find something," said George. "Perhaps at a bank."

"If that's what you really want," said Ruth. It didn't seem it was what *she* wanted.

"I want to go there with you, Ruth," said George. "But only if you want to."

She shrugged. "So I guess there's only one question remaining," said Ruth, with a sly smile.

"What's that?"

"Do we go there as boyfriend and girlfriend . . . or something more." She continued smiling.

He knew exactly what she meant.

CHAPTER FOURTEEN

"So you decided to get married?" I asked my father, as we sat together once again on our favorite bench overlooking Crystal Lake, admiring the particularly spectacular autumn foliage that had arrived in New England earlier than usual.

"Yes, but we wouldn't actually marry for another year, in Kentucky, on our way to Wyoming."

"Did you really choose that part of the country because of a movie?" I asked.

My dad laughed. "Sometimes I wish I'd never seen that movie."

"Why?"

"We both liked Boston, especially the theatre. But I couldn't see myself living that close to my mother, and a part of me really wanted to live in an agricultural area."

"Because of what you saw in France?"

My father considered that for a moment before answering. "In part," he said finally. "Despite the death and destruction, there was something about the people that struck me. They had a unique combination of dependence upon each other, and independence from the larger society. I guess I was looking for a real sense of community, and I thought I would find it out west."

"And did you?" I asked.

"That's another story," answered my father. "What about you?" he then asked. "What's your next move?"

It was Thanksgiving when I returned to see my father. The leaves had mostly all fallen from the trees, and a chilly breeze was sweeping across the lake. But I didn't care. I'd come home seeking my Dad's guidance. The following June I would finish my master's degree and would then have to decide where to go. Would I stay in New Orleans? Return to Massachusetts? Or perhaps follow the advice of Professor Busby and go to Honduras.

Most especially on my mind: *what about Maria?*

"My decision to go west was a selfish one," said my father. "Oh, I asked Ruth if she really wanted to go. When she agreed, I left it there. But I should have tried to see it from her perspective. I should have been more empathetic. But I wasn't."

I remembered what Maria had said to me that day in Audubon Park. "Are you really that insecure that you can't accept the fact that I'm finding my own way," she had said. "You think it's always about *you*."

"So you think I should let it go?" I asked my father. "And move on."

"Relationships have a better chance of success if both people are more or less on the same path. If one has to sacrifice his or her dreams for the other, the relationship probably won't work."

"I don't have to go to Honduras," I said. "I could just as well stay in New Orleans, if that's what she wants to do."

"But what *does* she want to do?" asked my father. "Do you even know?"

Good point, I thought. I'd never really asked her. "I know her career is important to her."

"You can each have your own career," replied Dad. "But *where* you pursue that career is often just as important as the career itself. Is it some-place where both people can be happy? If you go to Honduras, she may not be happy there. Conversely, if she goes back to Puerto Rico, you may not be happy there."

"Then we compromise," I offered. "We go someplace else."

"You may be getting ahead of yourself, son," said my dad. "You clearly want a long-term relationship with her, but does she want one with you?"

My father was always blunt.

"When we were in Africa, we talked about it." As soon as I said it, I realized how foolish it sounded. "But I guess that was different."

"Yes," replied my father. "Very different. In some ways, I don't think you've moved on from that experience. Perhaps she has."

"She sees me as a part of her past, but not her future?"

"Maybe," said my father, nodding.

"So what should I do now?" I sighed, confused.

"You're going back to New Orleans for another six months. I guess that's your timeline to determine what she really wants. But don't force it. If you do, she'll come to resent you. Go with an open mind, but be realistic."

I could tell by my father's tone of voice that he didn't think it would work, probably because he had lived through something similar, had made the wrong choice, and didn't want me to make the same mistake. But to his credit, he didn't say it directly. He knew it'd to be my decision.

CHAPTER FIFTEEN

Mardi Gras is believed to have first been celebrated in North America in 1699 when the French explorer Pierre Le Moyne d'Iberville made camp downriver from the future site of New Orleans and decided to hold a small gala, knowing it was *Fat Tuesday* back home in France. A few years later, French soldiers and settlers followed Iberville's lead by feasting and wearing masks as part of Mardi Gras festivities in the newly founded city of Mobile, which still claims to have the oldest annual Mardi Gras celebration in the United States.

La Nouvelle-Orléans was founded in 1718 by the French Mississippi Company, under the direction of Jean-Baptiste Le Moyne de Bienville. Mardi Gras celebrations started shortly thereafter. The Spanish, who ruled the city with a strict form of Catholicism in the late eighteenth century, tried to limit the celebration by banning masquerade balls and public disguises. But they soon realized that it was impossible to regulate.

The celebrations simply went underground.

By the mid-nineteenth century, New Orleans had transformed from a small backwater town into a major metropolis and seaport. To revitalize interest in Mardi Gras, a secret society calling themselves the *Mistick Krewe of Comus* organized a parade with the theme of "The Demon Actors in Milton's Paradise Lost." Along with a lavish grand ball, Comus reversed the declining popularity of Mardi Gras and helped establish New Orleans as its clear epicenter for generations to come.

But in those early days, original societies such as Comus, and new ones such as Momus and Proteus, were exclusively male and white. Women and blacks formed their own groups, with such names as Les Mysterieuses and the Pleasure Club. Amazingly, it wasn't until 1993 that the New Orleans City Council passed an ordinance that prohibited these societies—often called Krewes—from discriminating on the basis of race, religion, sexual orientation or national origin.

Needless to say, not everyone agreed with the new ordinance.

The year before, I'd enjoyed my first Mardi Gras with Maria. We'd spent most of our time along the main parade route which passed just down the street from my apartment before continuing downtown, along Canal Street, and then turning onto Bourbon Street and winding its way through the French Quarter. We both did our best to catch as many strings of beads as we could with one hand, while balancing our Hurricane drinks with the other.

But with the new ordinance of 1993, our second Mardi Gras experience was quite different. Since returning to the city following my Thanksgiving visit with my father, Maria and I'd been spending more time together. I did my best not to be pushy and to be more accepting of her singular focus on her studies. We never spoke about the confrontation that had occurred months earlier near Tulane, and never directly addressed our future together. But with a weeklong vacation for Mardi Gras, I thought we would've such an opportunity to talk things through.

But we never did.

On the last day of the weeklong festivities, Maria and I found ourselves near the Riverwalk, just a few blocks from the French Quarter. The final parade of Fat Tuesday was about to pass by, and we'd found a prime location from which to watch the hedonic spectacle.

Unbeknownst to most of the onlookers who surrounded us, however, those unhappy with the new ordinance had planned a spectacle of their own, taking advantage of the media cameras which were always present along the final stages of the parade.

Shortly after 8 pm, the first sign of trouble arose.

The parade could be seen turning the corner from St. Charles onto Canal, about four blocks from our location, when a large group of people emerged from nearby LaFayette Square and poured onto Canal, breaking through the police lines along the sidewalk. At first, they seemed to be mostly drunk teenagers taking a shortcut into the French Quarter. But when they decided to sit down in the middle of the street forming a blockade of the approaching floats, the police quickly descended upon them.

Then, from behind the nearby Riverwalk Mall—which extended along the Mississippi River—another large group appeared and began making their way toward the sit-in. Police tried to cut them off, but were overwhelmed by the sheer number of protesters. Maria and I, along with others around us, became caught in the human wave rolling down Canal Street.

By then, it was complete chaos.

Many of the protesters were in costume, some in blackface, and all chanting, "Mardi Gras for Whites! Mardi Gras for Whites!"

At one point, Maria fell to the ground. I tried to lift her up, but was pushed down myself. We somehow managed to get to the sidewalk and hold onto one of the lamp-posts that lined the street. From there, we made our way into a little cigar bar at the corner of Canal and Magazine. Inside, people were pressed against the window, watching the melee grow larger.

And then, we heard the gunshots.

At first, nobody inside the bar moved. But once people realized what the sound was, it became bedlam. Tables and chairs were overturned as people scrambled toward the back of the bar, and out the rear door that led into an alleyway. Maria and I became swept up in the exodus. We somehow found ourselves near a smelly dumpster behind the bar, huddled against the wall with a group of strangers.

"Where do we go now?" asked one woman, her face white with fear.

"What's happening?" said another, looking in both directions. "Were those gunshots?"

"I think so," said her boyfriend, or perhaps husband, wiping his bloodied hand across his shirt. "We should get out of here!"

"No," I said. "It's best to stay here. Whatever's happening is on Canal Street. It's safer back here."

"But this place stinks," said another girl, realizing that she was squatting in a pool of urine. "I need to get out of here." She got up and began to run down the alley.

Others followed.

"Come back," I yelled. "It's not safe out there."

But they were gone.

Maria and I watched as they reached the end of the alley, looked both ways, and then sprinted out onto Carrollton Avenue. As they did, a massive crowd passed-by, sweeping down the street toward Lee Circle, swallowing them up.

"What should we do, John?" asked Maria.

"Feels like Africa, doesn't it?" I said to her, with a slight grin on my face, and my eyes wide.

She was clearly taken aback by my comment. "Is that a good memory for you?"

I saw the disappointment in her eyes. "No, of course not," I assured her. "But here we are again. Together. In the middle of the excitement."

"Excitement?" repeated Maria. "You're still back there, aren't you? Still in Africa."

I saw the other people staring at us. "I'm sorry, Maria. I didn't mean it that way. I just meant that we were *together* in Africa."

"We're together now," she shot back, cutting me off. "But you're looking back. Living in the past."

"I didn't mean it in that way," I repeated, almost pleading. "Let's just get out of here."

But she didn't say anything as I took her arm and pulled her down the alley, the opposite way from which the others had run. "Let's just try to get near the river, and then we can make our way uptown."

But as we walked with the crowds through the Warehouse District, I'd a sinking feeling, realizing that the relationship had taken a bad turn.

She had been right, of course. I'd never really put Africa behind me. Something inside still yearned for the emotional high that came with unknown, even dangerous, situations. I'd yet to fully admit to myself that our relationship had been built upon those highs. I still wanted them. But she didn't. She wanted to move on to a more hopeful future.

An hour later, we arrived at Tulane, tired and bruised from our run-in with the riotous crowd. For a few moments, we stood outside of her dorm in silence, until finally she spoke. "I'm sorry. I just don't think I can do this anymore. I care for you so much, but . . ." She wiped a tear from her eye. "This isn't what I want."

"I shouldn't have reacted the way I did," I replied, unconvincingly. "I'm so sorry."

She waited for me to say more. But when I didn't, she pulled away. "I think we need to take a break. I need some time to figure things out."

But Maria had already figured it out. She no longer wanted to be with me. I'd failed her.

"Let's be sure to stay in touch," was the last thing she would say to me, as she walked away.

I stood outside her dorm for a few minutes as others returning from the parade pushed past me. I then dropped my head, turned, and walked to St. Charles Street, where I waited alone for the next streetcar to take me back down into the Garden District. As it rattled along its tracks, I sat alone, staring out the window, watching the houses of grandeur pass by. A deep feeling of loneliness and sorrow began to overtake me.

In the days that followed, I waited for her to call, not having the guts to reach out first. But I knew it was over. Our journey together had ended abruptly . . . because of me.

I never went back to the Tulane campus again.

A few weeks later I graduated from the University of New Orleans with my master's degree in education. I fulfilled my promise to my father. And a few months after that I was on a plane to Honduras.

CHAPTER SIXTEEN

As the fifth largest in the country, the Crow Indian Reservation lies in southern Montana, just north of the Wyoming state line, within parts of the Big Horn, Yellowstone, and Treasure counties, massive territories with very small populations.

The land is flat, covered mostly in grasslands, allowing the Bighorn, Wolf, and Pryor Mountains to the southwest to be seen from nearly any vantage point on the reservation. The Little Bighorn River meanders through the small towns that dot the countryside, at one point passing by the sight of General Custer's Last Stand, where he was killed by Sitting Bull in 1876, toward the end of the Indian Wars.

Despite its reputation as cattle-country, beneath the ground lurks one of the country's largest supplies of coal. Yet, the Crow people have been among the poorest in the country for the past hundred years.

At the southern end of the reservation lies the little town of Wyola, and just a bit farther north is Lodge Grass. Both towns support populations of little more than a few thousand, a mix of old-guard cattle ranchers and Crow, somehow able to maintain a peaceful—if uneasy— coexistence.

Each town's main street is dirt, lined with a few bars, a bank, a post office, and a small schoolhouse. Summers are hot, with only a dry breeze passing over the prairie to make it bearable. The winters are nearly *unbear-able*, with constant below-zero temperatures and relentless winds whipping across the landscape. It's an unforgiving land, scattered with people who maintain a fierce independence from institutional order, yet who are completely dependent upon the land to make or break their existence.

It was onto this land that George and Ruth came in the fall of 1950.

Ruth had found a job teaching a combination fourth-fifth grade class at the four-room schoolhouse in Lodge Grass, while George had landed a job at the bank in Wyola as a teller and loan officer.

They'd found a little apartment just down the street from Ruth's school, behind the town's only market. In such a conservative place, living together had only become possible following their marriage a few weeks earlier in Ruth's hometown in Kentucky, where they had stopped on their way to Montana from Boston.

Neither of Ruth's parents had been particularly enthusiastic about the union, but both respected George's service to the country, so had swallowed hard and given their blessing. George's mother had been extremely displeased that the marriage had not occurred in *her* church. Yet, even she found it difficult to protest, seeing how happy her son was with Ruth. As much as she hated to see him leave again, she knew that this time was different. If he had been able to return home to her from war, she had no doubt that he'd be able to return from the American west.

"Do you think you'll stay out there long?" she had asked George before he left, as they sat together on the porch, with Crystal Lake in view.

"I don't know, Mom," he replied. "I'm not sure if working in a bank is for me. But we'll give it a shot."

His mother nodded. "Just be sure that you do your best to adjust to the surroundings. If you don't, your marriage will suffer."

George looked at his mother curiously. "Is that what happened to you and Dad?"

"It was certainly difficult for me to come to Gardner. I didn't know anyone here, and I'd been used to the city. But your father wanted to come here. To come back to his hometown."

"So you didn't like it in the beginning?"

Elizabeth laughed. "Oh, God no! It seemed like the end of the earth to me. But I found my church and made some friends, and it became home. But those first few years were tough."

"I hope Ruth likes it out there."

"I think she'll be okay," said Elizabeth. "It's you I'm worried about."

As George helped Ruth decorate their new apartment in Lodge Grass, he thought a lot about his mother's words. She was right. He didn't do well with change. Yet, he had dragged his wife clear across the country.

Was it a mistake?

Was he being selfish?

Time would tell.

CHAPTER SEVENTEEN

"Satan himself lives in San Pedro," a local mortician once said. "People here kill people like they're nothing more than chickens."

After my experiences in Africa, I thought I was well prepared. I thought I knew what I was getting myself into. But the more I learned about Honduras, the more unsure I became.

This was going to be something entirely different, I quickly realized.

In a country of less than ten million people, an average of twenty were being murdered every day, nearly all the result of an endless drug war started during the revolutions of the 1980s and continuing into the nineties. Drugs were pouring in from such nations as Colombia on their way to the US border with Mexico, and ultimately onto the streets of America to satisfy the nation's insatiable appetite for illegal substances.

As those drugs made their way north through Honduras, San Pedro Sula was a known way-station, bringing violence and death to the streets of a once beautiful Latin American city.

Unfortunately, that city was the location of my new school.

Located on the country's north coast, just south of the Guatemalan border and within driving distance of many Mayan ruins, San Pedro had long been the country's manufacturing and commercial hub. Dozens of *maquiladoras*—export assembly plant—churned out garments that were sold for bargain prices at some of the best known department stores in the United States.

The average hourly wage in these sweatshops was less than one dollar.

My school was located in one of the city's more upscale neighborhoods called the Colonia Los Laureles, at the foot of the forested Merendon Mountains, just across the Rio De Piedras, which meandered through the city's northernmost neighborhoods. It was a picturesque location, and far enough from the mean streets of the city's violent, southern barrios that a person could walk along the neighborhood's main bulevar and feel *reasonably* assured of returning home safely.

The school had been the dream of Doña Olga, a native German, whose family had moved to Honduras following the Second World War to try their luck in the garment business.

Now, well into her seventies, her parents having long ago passed away, Olga was a force to be reckoned with, respected throughout the city, at least by those who remembered far more peaceful times. The violence that was tearing her city apart was also breaking her heart, and she saw education as one way of putting it back together again.

But it was a tall order.

Although the country's literacy rate was surprisingly high for a Third World nation, it was largely the result of the numerous private schools across the country. Public schools were little more than recruiting grounds for drug dealers, searching for young, naive teenagers who could be easily manipulated to do their bidding. Although Olga's school was private, it was largely tuition-free, operating with donations from other prominent citizens who shared Olga's vision.

Additionally, the K-12 school's graduation rate was nearly one hundred percent, unheard of in the country, even among private schools. Upon graduation, many students left the country to attend universities in America. Sadly, most never returned. But some did. Some of my colleagues in the school were alumni who had gone overseas to complete their education and had then returned to teach at Olga's school. In many ways, it was the best sign of the impact she was making.

"I'm glad you decided to join us, John," she said to me in heavily accented English on my first day as I arrived by taxi from the airport to meet with her at the school. "Dr. Busby spoke highly of you," she added, referring to my former professor at the University of New Orleans who had suggested that I consider the job.

"Thank you, Doña Olga. I'm looking forward to the experience."

She nodded, studying me carefully, no doubt trying to determine my sincerity. Almost immediately, she reminded me of Sister Agnes. "I have you teaching fifth grade," she said. "Is that acceptable to you?"

"Any grade level is fine," I said, hesitant to say that I preferred high school. "Will all of the classes be taught in English?"

She smiled. "Yes, unless you're confident with your Spanish."

I smiled back. "I'm afraid it's pretty poor. But I'll do my best to learn some."

"I see here that you taught in Africa," said Doña Olga, looking at the resume that I'd sent to her months earlier. "A French-speaking country?"

"Yes," I replied. "I was in central Africa, teaching math . . . in French."

"Impressive."

"I'm afraid my French was never very good either, Doña Olga." I admitted sheepishly.

"But it'll make it easier to learn some Spanish."

I nodded. "Hopefully."

"Don't worry too much about it here at the school. Most of the teachers speak English. It's around the city that you'll find it useful to speak some Spanish."

"Any suggestions about apartments?" I asked.

"There are certainly many available," said Doña Olga. "But you need to be careful of the area. Some are very dangerous. Until you find something you like, you're welcome to stay in the staff-housing we provide on-campus. It's not very luxurious, but will suffice for a while."

"Gracias," I said. "Eso es muy amable de tu parte."

Olga's eyes widened. "So you do speak some Spanish."

"Just a little," I said, choosing not to tell her about my short stay in Puerto Rico.

During my first few weeks in San Pedro Sula I did my best to familiarize myself with my new surroundings, always being careful to avoid certain parts of town. Upon Doña Olga's recommendation, my most frequent excursion was downtown to the Gran Hotel Sula located along the Boulevard Morazan, and across from the Parque Central, a popular hangout for the city's young population. With a nice bar, cafe serving American food, and a swimming pool, I felt comfortable . . . and safe . . . at the hotel.

I found many other Americans there, as well.

During those first few weeks, I didn't ask too many questions of my fellow expats. But I would later discover that many of them were US government *contractors* who were in the country to assist the Honduran government in various capacities. It was a relationship which dated back to the late nineteenth century, and one that continued to impact both countries in profound ways, particularly with respect to immigration policy.

When the United Fruit Company arrived in the country at the end of the nineteenth century, the fruit industry was decentralized and primarily in the hands of individual landowners who sold their crops locally. But that changed quickly as United Fruit built railroads, established their own banking systems, bribed government officials, and systematically swung the whole of Honduras into a one-crop economy: bananas. By the start of the First World War, United Fruit owned almost one million acres of Honduras' best land. Consequently, Hondurans who had long relied on subsistence farming for their livelihood became completely dependent upon the company for their survival.

Toward the end of the twentieth century, President Reagan had expanded that dependence by increasing military aid and arms sales to Honduras while using the country to train neighboring Nicaraguan contra-rebels in their effort to overthrow the Sandinista government, which Reagan was convinced had communist leanings. But such moves hastened—and strengthened—the militarization of Honduran society, inevitably leading to political repression.

American influence also served to restructure the Honduran economy by pushing for internal economic reforms that prioritized the exportation of manufactured goods, especially in the garment industry. While families such as Doña Olga's benefited, average Hondurans greatly suffered, unable to earn enough money to support even their simple lifestyles. As a result, many turned to the drug trade for additional income, while others headed north in hopes of making it to the US border . . . and the dream of a better life on the other side.

I'd seen the devastating effects of European colonialism first-hand while in Africa, and was about to experience the same in Latin America. While America never presented itself as a colonial power, it'd been exactly that for more than a century, with equally devastating consequences.

Occasionally, such consequences would reach all the way to our southern border, as caravans of migrants, escaping the violence in Honduras, arrived with hopes of a new beginning. Rarely did the American public have any understanding that it was our own policies that had driven those migrants to risk everything for the chance at a better life.

CHAPTER EIGHTEEN

While Ruth settled nicely into her role as a teacher in the small schoolhouse in Lodge Grass, George struggled at the bank in Wyola. The manager was Crow, having worked his way up through the ranks over many years to become one of the few Native Americans who held a prominent position in the small community. But he wasn't exactly enamored with whites, unable to forget the stories his father and grandfather had told him of life on the reservation in those early years. Much to George's chagrin, he felt that he had become the target of the manager's wrath.

"I feel like you're treating me differently," George once told him.

The middle-aged man stared hard at George. He never smiled. "I expect the same of all my employees."

"Yes, but I get the feeling you expect more from me."

"And why not?" shot back the manager. "You're not even *from* here. Not only are you taking a potential job away from my people, you're also taking one away from your own people. Locals. All because you're from . . . Harvard."

What a bastard, thought George. "Then why did you hire me?"

"I didn't," replied the manager, his voice rising. "This bank is privately owned. Its largest investors wanted you. Guess they thought it would improve the bank's image or something."

"Who're the investors?"

"White cattle ranchers," replied the manager.

On the surface, relations between the cattle ranchers and Crow appeared amicable. They often drank together in the same bars, attended the same rodeos, and spent the weekends in Sheridan, just across the border in Wyoming. But as George was learning, deep mistrust lurked not far beneath the surface.

For good reason, of course.

The Crow had first arrived in southern Montana and northern Wyoming in the late seventeenth century, attracted by the nearby river, mountain beauty, and open grasslands that favored their horses. But as white settlers began traversing their lands in the eighteenth century, threatening their way of life, they watched as other tribes chose to fight back.

The Crow, however, took a different path, seeing an opportunity to rid themselves of two of their fiercest rivals: the Lakota and Nez Perce.

By the nineteenth century they had agreed to assist the United States military as scouts against their rivals. This led the government to grant the Crow nearly four million acres of prime land in the Yellowstone region, in an agreement known as the Laramie Treaty. But as was so often the case, the government later reneged on the agreement.

By the 1880s, the Crow were forced to cede more than half of their land, nearly all along the Bighorn River. That land later became prime cattle country and made millionaires out of a select group of ranchers, a few of which went on to own the Wyola bank.

"The Crow are good people," said Ruth one night and she and George sat on their porch enjoying the evening breeze. "And they've been through a lot. So much was promised, given, and then taken back. You can't really blame them for being bitter."

"I don't," replied George. "But I think we have the right to be here."

"Maybe. But they don't see it that way. I'm sure the manager simply wants more opportunities for his people."

George was surprised by Ruth's words. "Whose side are you on, anyways?"

Ruth reached out to touch George's arm. "You can't look at it as two sides. We both need to be on the same side. Otherwise we haven't learned anything from history."

"Then what should I do? Just put up with the manager's attitude?"

Ruth hesitated for a moment.

"What is it?"

"Well, my school is looking for a high school business teacher," said Ruth. "Maybe that's an option."

"Teaching? Are you serious?"

"Why not," replied Ruth. "You're certainly qualified, and I'm sure the school would love to have a Harvard grad." She smiled.

"The bank manager certainly didn't appreciate my degree."

Ruth shook her head. "There's no shame in changing careers. When I started at Radcliffe I certainly never thought I'd become a teacher. But here I am. It's rewarding, and I'm enjoying getting to know the kids. Especially the Crow. They're such proud people, and I think we can learn a lot from them."

"I thought they were supposed to learn from you," said George.

"Believe me, I learn something new every day."

CHAPTER NINETEEN

By the early fall of 1993, I'd settled-in nicely to my new school on the outskirts of San Pedro Sula, enjoying the interaction with my students and the rest of the staff. Living in the staff accommodation on-campus certainly made everything much easier, allowing me to get up each morning just before classes began, and return there for lunch.

But living alone was hard.

Evenings were probably the hardest. Some nights I hung out with the other teachers who lived in the accommodations. But most of them were married and had their own lives to lead. So, with little else to do, I began going to the bar at the Gran Hotel Sula most nights. It was the beginning of a long struggle with alcohol which—while never affecting my work performance—was a clear indication that I was far from at peace with myself.

My insecurities and lack of self-confidence would dissipate with a bottle of beer in my hand. There had been a few occasions in New Orleans when Maria had told me to *slow down*. But in San Pedro, nobody whispered in my ear.

I was certainly not alone in my love for the bottle, as nearly all of the expats in the bar were equally inebriated nearly every night, at which time many of them would speak freely about their roles as government *contractors*. The stories were fascinating, although undoubtedly exaggerated. They also enjoyed my tales of adventure in Africa, which I didn't need to greatly exaggerate.

When the bar closed, I often walked back to the school, which was probably not a smart thing to do, given the city's crime rate. But during those late-night hours, I did my best thinking. Almost always, my mind wandered back to comments that Maria had made to me over the few years I'd known her. She had always recognized my insecurities, and in the end, it was probably one of the main reasons why I found myself alone, rather than with her. She was always the confident one. Always the one with a clear plan for the future. But I was still lost, something that I only seemed to recognize following a long night of drinking.

Then by morning, the whole cycle would start again.

It was during such a cycle that I first met Gabriela.

She was a manager in the hotel, in charge of event-planning, often passing through the bar on her way to one of the hotel's ballrooms where the largest events were held. We'd made brief eye contact a few times, but nothing more. She seemed disinterested in bar culture. Nearly all the patrons were men, and their crudeness worsened as the hour grew later. I wasn't always comfortable with the tone, so it begs the question: *Why did I keep going back?*

It was just that very question that Gabriela alluded to one night as I sat alone in the hotel's cafe, having abandoned the regalia of the bar for quieter surroundings and a late night snack.

"You're better off here," she said, approaching me as I sat at the counter. "They don't seem like your crowd."

"Really?" I replied. "And what kind of crowd would be my crowd?" It was the first time I'd seen her up-close, and she was stunningly attractive.

"You know who most of them are, right?" she said, her shoulder-length hair just touching the top of her white dress that conservatively hugged the contours of her body, falling just above her knees and highlighting her mocha skin.

"I suppose," I replied. In truth, I didn't really know. I'd assumed that most were the so-called government contractors, somehow tied to America's complicated involvement in the nation's affairs dating back to the eighties. But I wasn't completely sure what a *contractor* was.

"You should hang out with teachers from your school."

I was startled. "How do you know I work at a school?"

"I asked around."

"Really?" That was encouraging, I thought. "My name's John, by the way. Your English is really good."

She extended her hand. "I'm Gabriela. Take my advice, John, spend less time in that bar."

"I'm not sure I understand."

"Some of those guys have been coming here for many years, and their line of work might not be what you think."

"Government contractors?"

"A few, maybe," she replied. "But most have . . . multiple lines of work."

I still didn't understand, but figured it didn't really matter. "Thanks, Gabriela. I think you're right. I need to spend less time in that bar."

She nodded, and then changed the subject. "Where are you from in the States?"

"Massachusetts," I answered, still sitting at the counter as she stood beside me. "Have you lived in the States?"

"California, with my mom."

"Really? I guess that explains your English. You barely have an accent,"

She smiled. "Thanks. It's definitely an advantage here at the hotel."

Just then, another manager approached and whispered something in Gabriela's ear. She nodded to the manager, before turning back to me. "Guess I need to get going."

"Okay. Maybe I'll see you around?"

"Maybe. But don't let me see you in that bar again," she said. "Okay?"

"Okay."

I watched her walk away toward the hotel's lobby. Before turning the corner and disappearing, she turned back, and smiled.

Maybe there was hope for me after all

CHAPTER TWENTY

George's first day of teaching had been memorable.

It was shortly after seven in the morning when he had first heard the sound. *Clip-clippity-clop. Clip-clippity-clop.*

What the hell is that, he thought. He rushed over to the open window in the classroom and looked eastward across the open plain. At first, all he could see was a cloud of dust rising from the dry ground. And then they appeared, just over the small hill behind the school.

His students arriving.

On horseback.

It was quite a site, and one that he would never tire of seeing. Ahote ("the restless one"), was the oldest, and would always lead the way. He was always followed by Ahiga ("he fights") and his girlfriend, Algoma ("valley of flowers"). Bringing-up the rear on most days was Abukcheech ("mouse"), by far the smallest of the pack.

They ranged in ages from fourteen to seventeen, and came from various small villages around Lodge Grass. They rode bareback to the edge of the school's property, jumped off their horses nearly in unison, tied them to a nearby fence, brushed the dust off their clothes, and then walked to class.

On that first day, they entered the classroom, acknowledged George with a subtle nod, and took their seats. And there they remained throughout the day, barely making a noise. George did his best to engage them in his English and history classes, but they refused to speak. When the final bell of the day rang, they waited for George to dismiss them. When he did, they quietly left the room and made their way outside to their horses.

And then they were gone.

"I couldn't get them to say a single word," said George to Ruth that night.

She laughed. "Yes, they never do. It's not their way."

"What do you mean?"

"It's disrespectful for them to speak in the presence of elders. Even if they're white."

"Then how do they learn?"

"They're listening," said Ruth. "And observing."

"So they'll never speak?"

"Eventually a few will, probably the older ones like Ahote" replied Ruth. "But it took me weeks. Alina gave me some useful suggestions, and they worked."

"Alina?

"Alina Stevenson. The teacher across the hall. She's been at the school for five years. Talk to her, you'll learn a lot.'

That's exactly what George did, and in doing so, Alina became his mentor, and his friend.

She had come with her family from South Dakota just before the war. Now in her early thirties, she had recently married the owner of the local market, Sam Stevenson. His family had been prominent in Lodge Grass for generations, earning the respect of both the ranchers and the Crow. As a teacher, Alina had become equally as respected.

Her secret? She didn't try to turn the Crow children into model white students. She met them on their own terms. And over time, they revealed themselves to her.

"Earn their trust, George," she had said to him one afternoon after class, as Ruth listened, nodding in agreement. "It'll take time, but they will eventually speak in your class."

"And how do I do that?" asked George. "How do I earn their trust?'

"By not trying to change them. By accepting their culture. By respecting them."

"But what about the white kids in the class?" George asked. "I need to treat both groups differently?"

"Absolutely!" was Alina's answer, without hesitation. "Kids learn differently, so we must teach them differently."

George nodded. This was a new concept to him.

Alina saw his confusion. "You're from a small town, correct?" she said.

George nodded.

"When you were growing up, all the kids in your class were the same, right? White."

George nodded again.

"So your teachers taught you as a group, because you shared more in common than not. But it's different here." Alina paused, and looked out the window. "In fact, it's changing across the country. Especially in the cities. As we become more diverse, we're going to have to learn new ways of teaching kids." She turned back to George. "This little school is a microcosm of that."

In the months that followed, Ruth, George, Alina, and Sam became good friends. Some nights they enjoyed a game of cards at Sam and Alina's house. Other evenings at George and Ruth's. Occasionally, they ventured into Lodge Grass's little downtown, which consisted of little more than a few churches, a few bars, a post office, and Sam's market which lay just across from the railroad tracks that ran through the town.

None of them were drinkers. So when they went to the saloon, it was mostly to people-watch. And there was always something to watch. On one particular night, a drunk young Crow and an equally drunk ranch-hand had gotten into an argument over a game of poker. The argument was taken outside at the bartender's insistence, at which point they both drew knives. From inside the bar, George watched through the window as the town's sheriff approached the men from across the street where he had been camped waiting for just such an altercation.

The sheriff was a big man, half Crow, half black, something that was common on reservations throughout the Midwest, a result of the black migration westward following the Civil War, and the intermarriages that resulted. This sheriff ran the town like it was still the frontier at the end of the nineteenth century.

But he had no choice.

With hatred simmering just beneath the surface, alcohol was often the catalyst to bring it to the surface, over a woman or a game of cards. But the sheriff understood his people, and preferred to teach them a lesson rather than put them in jail, since he knew they needed to return to work the next day to provide for their families.

George watched as the sheriff approached the two men, grabbed both by the collar, lifted them up on their toes, and smashed their heads together. Both men crumpled to the dirt street in a heap, and the sheriff walked off. When the men rose to their feet, they stared at each other for a moment, and then went their separate ways. George smiled. Now that was justice, he thought.

But it was a long, long way from Boston, and George struggled to adjust.

He enjoyed spending time with Alina and Sam, but he often longed for the city. He missed the theatre, and mostly the opera. And there were times—although he didn't like to admit it—that he missed his mother. He knew that Ruth also missed her family in Kentucky, but she was always able to remain positive. Never complaining.

Some nights he'd lay awake in bed—while Ruth was sound asleep beside him—and think about everything that had happened to him since he had left home for the war in '43. It seemed like lifetimes ago. Yet, he was still in his twenties, with so much ahead of him. But mostly he lay awake because he was afraid to sleep. For it was in the darkness that the demons came.

He would dream of the war. Of Normandy and Cherbourg. Of Lorient. And, of course, of Yvette. He would relive her death over and over and over again, each time waking up screaming, his body drenched in sweat, with Ruth gazing down at him with a petrified look. He had thought it would all go away in time. But it'd only been getting worse.

"Maybe you should see someone," Ruth said one time, as they sat on the edge of the bed together following a particularly bad nightmare.

"See someone? Like a shrink?"

George was too proud for that. It wasn't his generation's way.

"There are thousands—maybe millions—of men just like you. They're struggling with everything they saw during the war. There is no shame in asking for help."

But he never would.

Few of his generation did.

They had returned from the horrors of war and attempted to live ordinary lives. But many didn't have the emotional means to do so. In some ways, it was the Army's fault. They had focused so much on the men's physical health, that they had neglected their mental health.

But these were men and women who had grown up during the Great Depression, who had known hard times even before the war. They had fought with pride, and had returned with that pride. And it was that pride that often isolated them. They married and had children, often in an effort to find normalcy. But many had remained isolated. Lost in their memories of war. And no matter what they did to block those memories, they always returned to the surface, especially in the deep of the night.

Ruth watched as George rose from the edge of the bed and walked over to the window. He remained there for a while, staring into the night.

To make their situation even more challenging, she was pregnant.

CHAPTER TWENTY-ONE

Born in San Pedro Sula, Gabriela was an only child, brought to America at a young age by her mother who was escaping an abusive husband. With the help of relatives in Los Angeles, they had settled in Beverly Hills, living in the small pool house of a Hollywood agent for whom Gabriela's mom worked as a housekeeper.

On the surface, it was a good life. Certainly not *Beverly Hills 90120*, but still comfortable. Yet, Gabriela never brought her friends home while in elementary school. Not because she was ashamed of her simple living conditions, but because she and her mother rarely got along. All she really wanted was to be loved by her mother. But instead, she felt like a burden.

"You remind me of your father," her mother had said to her following a particularly bad spat. Gabriela was in high school, and from her mother's perspective, was becoming more and more rebellious.

"You never loved him anyways, did you?" Gabriela replied. "You always said that he abused you, but I never saw that."

"You were just a young child. You didn't understand what you were seeing."

"Maybe. But I know that my Dad loved me."

"Then you should go back to him," blurted Gabriela's mother. As soon as she said it, she regretted it. But it was too late.

Gabriela stared at her mom, and left the room. A few months later, she was back in Honduras and caring for her father who was dying from liver cancer, the result of a lifetime of alcoholism.

"Why didn't you go back to California after he died?" I asked Gabriela one night, as we sat in the hotel lobby enjoying each other's company during her break.

"I couldn't stand my mother. I thought she was manipulative. I still do."

"You don't think she was abused by your father?"

"I asked my father that one time, not long before he died. He told me that he had never abused her, but admitted that he was often drunk."

"So maybe that's the reason your mother left him," I suggested. "His alcoholism."

"Then she should have told me that. Why lie?"

"Would you want to live with someone who was always drunk?" I asked.

Gabriela smiled. "Like you?"

Ouch. "I'm not *always* drunk."

"No, you're not. Anyways, I think my mother would've left even if my father had been a perfect man. She always wanted to go to America."

"Maybe she just wanted a better life for you."

"She wanted a better life for *herself*. She didn't care about me."

"I doubt that, Gabriela. I'm sure she loved you."

Gabriela shrugged her shoulders. "It doesn't matter now, anyways. This is my life now." She gestured to her surroundings. "I just want a good life for my two sons."

Gabriela had first told me about her two children, Andres and Fernando, just a few weeks after our initial meeting in the cafe. When she did, I knew she was watching my reaction very carefully.

And I guess I passed that initial test.

Nevertheless, I'd yet to meet them. In fact, I'd never even seen where Gabriela lived. She always insisted that we meet at the hotel. I didn't find anything necessarily odd about that, but was certainly curious about a lot of things, including the story of the boys' father. I'd received little snippets here and there, but it often left me with more questions than answers.

"When my father died, I was only seventeen," said Gabriela one night as we sat on the couch in the second floor lounge of the hotel, near the window that looked down upon the Parque Central. "I thought about going back to California, but then I met the boys' father. If *my* father had lived, I'm sure he would not have approved, but I didn't have anyone telling me what I should or shouldn't do. And I was lonely."

"It's tough being alone."

She nodded. "And in the beginning, he treated me well. He was well-connected in the community, and even helped me get this job at the hotel."

"What kind of work did he do?" I asked.

There was a slight pause. "Different things," Gabriela said. "Some of it I didn't like, but . . ." Her voice trailed off.

"What kind of things?" I pressed.

Another pause. "This is a hard place to live, and people do what they have to in order to survive. But whatever his mistakes, he was a good father. At least in the beginning."

"What changed?"

"We had only been together for a few months when I became pregnant. When Andres was born, we lived those first four years with his parents. They owned a small mercado here in the city, and he would sometimes help out. But when Fernando was born, it changed."

"How?"

"I wanted to get married," said Gabriela. "And I think his parents wanted the same. But he didn't. And that's when it began to fall apart."

"Why didn't he want to get married?"

Gabriela smiled. "Lots of questions, huh?"

"I'm sorry. I didn't mean to push. But you just seem so . . . smart."

Gabriela laughed. "So why did I have a child so young, you mean?"

I nodded sheepishly. "I'm not judging you, but . . ."

"It's okay, fair question. And I guess I don't have a really good answer. Maybe if my father had lived, it would've been different. Maybe if I'd gone to college. Maybe if I'd gone back to California. Maybe if I hadn't felt so alone. Maybe. But I don't regret any of it, since two beautiful children were the result."

"Do the children live with you?"

"They're mostly at his parents," answered Gabriela. "He's in the capital, Tegucigalpa, most of the time."

"So you live by yourself?" I asked.

"Right now, I'm staying with friends until I can save enough money to get my own place. Then the boys will be with me full-time."

"Maybe I can visit you sometime."

Gabriela shook her head. "Oh no. It's not a safe area for you. But it's cheap."

"Not safe for *me*?"

"Well, let's face it. You stand out. *El gringo*."

We both laughed.

"Yeah, heard that before."

"But when I find my own place, it'll be in a good area. A safe area," said Gabriela, almost defiantly. She seemed to have something to prove.

I tried to absorb it all, still feeling that I was missing some important pieces. But I didn't feel it was my place to push anymore. "Is there anything I can do to help?"

"Right now, I could just use a good friend," she replied. "Is that okay with you?"

CHAPTER TWENTY-TWO

In the nineteenth century, the Great Plains, including the area near Lodge Grass in southern Montana, was the last Native American holdout in America. As settlers headed west to join the gold rush of the mid-century, few had put down roots in the plains, mostly due to its dry weather and large Native American population, including the Crow, Lakota, and Nez Perce.

But after the Civil War, that all changed.

The post-Lincoln governments granted large swaths of the plains to settlers and the railroads, and a confrontation between the Plains Indians and government forces became inevitable. By the late 1860s, most Native Americans in other regions of the growing nation had been forced onto reservations . . . or killed outright. Vowing to avoid the same fate, the Plains Indians—including the Lakota and Nez Perce—settled in for a long and fierce fight.

In the hopes of destroying the tribes' livelihood and shortening their holdout, the government allowed the railroads to kill scores of buffalo herds as they lay mile after mile of track. The more the buffalo were needlessly slaughtered, the angrier the tribes became . To them, the railroad represented an end to their livelihood, one they had relied upon for a millennia.

It was into the center of this chaos that Armstrong Custer rode in the summer of 1873 when he arrived to take control of the Army's 7th Cavalry, and to do battle with the Plains Indians. But he quickly found them elusive. They were expert horsemen, rode fast, and knew the terrain better than he did. They were ferocious and resolute, fighting for their individual lives and, indeed, for their entire culture.

Of all the Plains tribes, the Lakota were considered the fiercest, led by Sitting Bull and Crazy Horse. Custer first clashed with them near modern-day Yellowstone in 1873. It was a short and indecisive battle, but served to lay the groundwork for the battle that would take place a few years later on the banks of the Little Bighorn River.

"I still don't think I need to drive," said Ruth, sitting beside George as he drove through the small town of Garryowen on their way to the Little Bighorn Battlefield National Park, near the Little Bighorn River. "I can just walk from our apartment to the school."

"You can walk *now*," replied George. "But what about three or four months from now? By then, you'll be in your eighth month."

"Then you can drive me," said Ruth, clearly not relishing the thought of driving.

"What if I have drama rehearsal after school? You'll just wait?" asked George. "Why not take the car home and pick me up later."

Ruth remained unconvinced. "I don't know. It just seems unnecessary."

George turned to Ruth. "You're scared," he said, with a smile.

"Of course not," she replied, and then added, "Well, maybe a little."

They both laughed.

"The park will be a good place to learn," said George, as he turned onto the dirt road that led up the hill toward the monument that stood just beyond the park's entrance. "Not many people will be here this time of day."

George continued driving up the hill, past the National Cemetery that had first been established in 1886, and included the remains of soldiers from many of America's wars. In 1940, the site was transferred from the US Department of War to the National Park Service and renamed the Custer Battlefield National Monument.

It was a desolate location.

As George and Ruth stepped out of their Hudson Commodore to change places so Ruth could begin driving, the air was cold and the wind was brisk, lifting Ruth's hair and causing her to raise her collar. Winter was nearly over, but snow still remained around the monument and beside the narrow road that ran atop the ridgeline that stretched southward, running parallel to the Little Bighorn River below. Before getting back into their car, they paused to watch the construction of the new highway nearby. From their perch atop the hill, they got a good view of its expanse.

"It'll change everything around here," said George. "While I was still at the bank, customers would always talk about it."

"The teachers, too," added Ruth. "People are really scared it'll cause these little towns to die."

"But at least it'll make it a lot easier to get down to Sheridan," said George, referring to the good-sized town just across the state-line in Wyoming. He and Ruth enjoyed going there, as it was one of the few places in the region that maintained a small playhouse, showing some of the year's most popular stage productions.

"People will go to Sheridan and Billings to do all their shopping, and little markets like Alina's husband's will suffer," said Ruth.

George nodded. "They're building these new highways every-where. It seems as though no matter where you go in this country, things are changing."

Before getting into the car, Ruth glanced at the nearby monument and read the plaque that was posted nearby. *The remains of 220 soldiers, scouts, and civilians are buried around the base of this memorial, forever a reminder of the events of June 26, 1874.*

Following the Civil War, the US government had signed a treaty rec-ognizing South Dakota's Black Hills as part of the Great Sioux Reservation. But after gold was discovered there, the government decided to break the treaty and take over the land.

The tribes didn't take the betrayal lying down.

Those who could, left their reservations and traveled to Montana to join forces with Sitting Bull and Crazy Horse at their fast-growing camp along the banks of the Little Bighorn River. And there, they prepared for battle.

It was early June of 1874.

In response, the Army dispatched three columns of soldiers, including Custer's 7th Cavalry, to round up the Native Americans and return them to their reservations. The plan was for Custer's cavalry and Brigadier General Alfred Terry's infantry to rendezvous with troops under the command of Colonel John Gibbon and Brigadier General George Crook. They'd then find the Indians, surround them, and force their surrender.

But the plan quickly fell apart.

Crook was delayed, significantly reducing the size of the government's forces. Nevertheless, Terry, Custer, and Gibbon continued forward toward Little Big Horn Valley. Once there, it was decided that Custer should move in alone, surround the tribes, and await reinforcements.

Around midday on June 25, Custer's scouts—which included Crow—located Sitting Bull's camp. But instead of waiting for reinforcements as had been planned, Custer prepared a surprise attack for the next day. He then divided his more than six hundred men into four groups. One group was to stay with the supply wagons while another two would attack from the south. Custer would lead the final group—more than two hundred men strong—attacking from the north.

As June 26 dawned, the two groups that were supposed to attack from the south never arrived to join Custer, even though they heard heavy gunfire coming from Custer's position, north of the Little Bighorn River. Consequently, almost as soon as Custer began his attack, he found himself on the defensive, realizing that he was in trouble.

Some stories later recounted that his men panicked, broke ranks, dismounted their horses, and scattered. Other stories said that they came together to form a final defensive perimeter . . . before being overrun.

Regardless of which version, Custer and his men had nowhere to hide and nowhere to run. Their final minutes were undoubtedly horrific, as they realized they were at their end, soon to succumb to the bloodlust of the tribal warriors.

All 210 men under Custer's command were killed. Most were scalped. Custer's body was found near what would come to be called Custer Hill, sometimes known as Last Stand Hill, alongside the bodies of his men, including his brother and nephew, and dozens of dead horses.

The tribes reveled in their victory for a time, but their celebration was short-lived . . . as was their freedom.

When word of Custer's death reached Americans proudly celebrating their nation's centennial, they demanded retribution. Within a year, most of the tribes involved in the Battle of the Little Bighorn had been rounded up . . . or killed. In May of 1877, Crazy Horse surrendered at Fort Robinson, Nebraska. He was later bayoneted and killed after an altercation with an Army officer. After fleeing to Canada, Sitting Bull eventually surrendered in 1881. He was later killed by policemen during a conflict at his house in 1890.

The age of the Great Plains horse culture was over.

Ruth was driving slowly along the dirt road a few miles south of the Battle of Little Bighorn Monument when she abruptly braked, causing George to lurch forward.

"What?" he asked, surprised. "Why did you stop?"

"Look over there," Ruth said, pointing off to their left. "You see them?"

George did. And what a magnificent site it was.

A small herd of wild horses were grazing just down the slope from the road. One of the creatures looked up and stared straight at George and Ruth's car, before turning and slowly moving away. "Incredible," said George. "You don't see them much anymore, especially this close to the park."

"You can almost imagine the soldiers riding them into battle."

"Yes, there's certainly a lot of history here," said George, still in awe.

"And many ghosts," added Ruth.

CHAPTER TWENTY-THREE

Shortly before Christmas in 1993, I went to the Grand Sula Hotel to pick up Gabriela for dinner. It was going to be one of the few times that we ate away from the hotel, having heard good things about the El Portal de las Carnes, located a few kilometers from the hotel in one of the more upscale neighborhoods in the city.

But after waiting in the hotel lobby for nearly thirty minutes, I became concerned, knowing that she was rarely late. Finally, one of her colleagues from the front desk saw me and walked over to my location near the concierge's desk.

"She left a few hours ago before her shift was finished," said Maria, dressed in the formal attire of the front-desk staff. Her English was nearly as good as Gabriela's.

"Was she sick?" I asked. "We were supposed to meet for dinner."

"I'm honestly not sure what happened. She left very quickly."

"Really?" I said, starting to get even more concerned. "She didn't let me know anything."

"I'm sorry," said Maria. "I really don't know."

Then someone called my name from the nearby bar. I turned to see David waving at me. "Come on over here, stranger," he yelled across the lobby. "Long time, no see."

David was one of the regular customers at the bar, and one of the loudest. Well into his fifties and seemingly in a perpetual state of inebriation, he could talk nonstop for hours, regaling the bar's patrons with endless stories of his exploits as a government *contractor*. I was in no mood for him, but also realized that he knew just about everything that happened in the hotel, and perhaps knew something about Gabriela.

"We haven't seen you for weeks," he said, slapping me on the back as I stood beside him near the bar. "What happened? You're too good for us? Or is it that pretty lady of yours?"

"Have you seen her today, Dave?" I asked, not interested in getting into a long conversation with the guy. "Maria said that she left in a hurry a few hours ago."

"Sure," he replied, taking a drink from his glass, undoubtedly a rum and coke. "She was here earlier. But can't say that I saw her leave."

"Okay, then," I said, turning to walk away, knowing that Dave would offer me a drink, which was the last thing I needed. Over the past month, I'd been able to really slow-down my intake . . . entirely because of Gabriela's influence.

"Hey," said Dave, "before you disappear again, maybe you'd like to know a little bit more about your girlfriend. Wouldn't want you to get blindsided or anything."

I was so tempted to keep walking, but for some reason I turned around. "What would that be, Dave?"

"Have a seat, and I'll tell you." He tapped the barstool beside him. "But you may not like what I have to say."

A few hours later, I was taking a taxi into the southeastern suburbs of the city, past the Aeropuerto Internacional Ramón Villeda Morales, and toward La Lima, where Chiquita Banana once maintained offices during the heyday of the city. But that was long ago. What remained were some of the most dangerous neighborhoods in the city, including Colonia Rivera Hernandez, my destination.

When I told the taxi to drop me off on the street corner across from a dilapidated market, the driver turned to me and said, "Cuidado, mi amigo. Esta es una zona muy peligrosa."

I really had no understanding of just how dangerous it was.

It wasn't a place where Americans were supposed to go, never mind an American who spoke little Spanish. But I'd seen worse. In Africa. As I walked through the streets of Colonia Rivera Hernandez, it felt like I was back in Zaire, in the slums where I'd met Jean Pierre. But I had no choice but to keep moving forward. I needed to see if Gabriela was all right.

As I walked, I thought about my conversation with Dave. He had been right. I didn't like what he had to say. But for some reason, I wasn't particularly surprised. I'd seen it before. Gabriela had been reluctant to talk much about her children's father, and now I knew why.

She'd been a victim of abuse.

In the States, such victims had options. Places they could go. People they could talk to. Help they could get. For the most part.

But in much of Latin America—and throughout most of the developing world—there are few such places. Women are very much on their own, at the mercy of male-dominated societies who perceive women as second-class citizens. I'd seen it in Africa, too.

Gabriela had somehow garnered the strength to walk away from it. But with no place else to go, she found herself living with a friend in the slums of Colonia Rivera Hernandez. Thankfully, she had a good job at the hotel and was trying to lift herself back up and make a better life for herself and her two children.

But did I have the strength? Was I secure enough with myself to put the needs of two small children ahead of my own selfish wants and needs? If Maria had been around, she would undoubtedly have said, *no*. Even my father and sister may have said the same. But I was on my own, lonely, and desperate to be loved. So I kept walking that night in search of Gabriela.

As I walked, I thought more about what Dave had told me.

"You know, John," he had said. "Most of the guys in this bar are running from something. Child support. Back taxes. Who knows what else? Or maybe they just think they have a better shot at bedding a young girl here."

"What about you?" I'd asked. "Why are you here?"

"Simple," replied Dave. "My military pension goes a lot farther down here than it does Stateside."

"You were in the military?"

Dave laughed. "Hard to believe, right? I always have a drink in my hand."

"I just assumed that most of you were CIA or something."

Another laugh, this time louder. "Well, maybe a few. But most of us are ex-military guys who served in countries like this, around the world. When we got out, some of us went to work for private contractors."

"I keep hearing that phrase," I said. "But I never really knew what it meant, and was afraid to ask, I guess."

Dave nodded. "You have to understand that the American military outsources much of its nastiest work. The big guys don't like getting their hands dirty, afraid that it'll become public and jeopardize their funding. So they hire private firms."

"You mean mercenaries."

"Sort of. But they're not fighting wars. Mostly they're providing security. I first came down here to work for United Fruit, providing security for their corporate members as they traveled around the country. Then I hooked up with some of these other guys you see in this bar to start-up our own . . . businesses."

"You mean drugs."

Dave took a sip from his glass. "I'm not proud of it. But, yes. I've made some good money. Not selling it. But providing security for those who transport it."

"I don't understand," I said. "Why would a Honduran drug dealer hire an American to provide security?"

"It's complicated," said Dave. "But it began in the mid-eighties when the US government was trying to get weapons into the hands of the Contras who were fighting the Sandinistas in Nicaragua. It was illegal to sell the weapons to them, so they used private contractors to bring the weapons down here from the States. But some of those contractors were then hired by the cartels to use their empty planes to bring drugs back into the States. Our government knew what was happening, but turned a blind eye because they were so intent upon fighting communism."

"So you brought drugs into the States?"

"No," said Dave adamantly. "But me and some of the guys in this bar provided security for those who did."

"You're telling me that Americans were transporting illegal drugs into America using the same planes that were being used to bring weapons illegally into Honduras and Nicaragua?"

"That's exactly what I'm telling you. Big business. And everyone was happy. America got their little war in Central America. The cartels got their product into the States. And a bunch of us got rich serving two masters."

"And it still happens?'

"Yes, but not as blatantly anymore. When the whole Iran-Contra thing hit the press in the States, everything went underground, no longer sanctioned by the government. That's when the security business came about. Before, it was the US government providing security by simply looking the other way. When they got out, the weapons continued coming down here, but through third-parties who needed security. The planes were still coming in with weapons and leaving with drugs."

"Who were the third parties?"

Dave looked at me. "You once told us a story about the wars in Africa being funded by diamonds, right?"

I nodded.

"It's the same here. Just drugs instead of diamonds. America gets its wars. The drug dealers get rich. And the poor people of this country are caught in the middle."

"And people like you're getting rich, too," I added.

"No question about it," agreed Dave. "But I never pretended to be a moral man. You would think, however, that our own government would have some semblance of it."

"So, why tell me all of this? Maybe I'll tell the wrong people."

Dave laughed, a loud, bellowing laugh. "Who would you tell? Everything is connected down here. Everyone is on the take. It's a nasty business and its tentacles reach everywhere. Including into the pockets of friends of Gabriela's boyfriend. Or ex-boyfriend. Or whatever he is."

I was blindsided by that. "What do you mean? He was involved in all of this?

"I can't say that *he* was, but he'd sometimes come into the hotel with his friends, some of whom we knew were in the *business*."

"Gabriela knew that?" I asked.

"I told her one night, yes. And when her boyfriend came to pick her up, she confronted him. Right over there," Dave pointed toward the lobby. "I saw him hit her. Not long after that she moved in with a friend in Colonia Rivera Hernandez. Which was probably the worst place to go since those neighborhoods are controlled by various gangs working for the cartels."

"Jesus," I said.

"John," said Dave, taking a big swig from his drink. "Jesus Christ gave up on this part of the world a long time ago."

CHAPTER TWENTY-FOUR

On some occasions, when they had a little extra money, George and Ruth ventured down to Sheridan, just across the state line in Wyoming. It was a bustling town, with plenty of restaurants and one recently remodeled theatre that helped to satisfy George's love for stage productions.

On special occasions, they would even stay at the Sheridan Inn for a night.

Located just off Main Street, across from the train depot, it'd been built in 1894 and was definitely showing its age. But it still retained that feeling of the Old West, complete with photos in the lobby of Buffalo Bill and Sitting Bull standing side-by-side during one of their famous Wild West shows.

William F. Cody—aka Buffalo Bill—had already done a lot by the time he came to be one of the influential figures in the inn's early days. As a young rider for the Pony Express, he had earned distinction for one of the fastest rides in the history of the Express. By the early 1880s, he was dazzling audiences with what would soon become his Wild West show, gaining him international prominence.

Among his fans were some of Europe's most powerful leaders, including Queen Victoria, whose photo also adorned the inn's lobby. Although Bill never owned the building, he did purchase the interior furnishings and lived at the inn whenever he was in town for one of his shows, often holding auditions from the inn's massive front porch.

"I love sitting here," said Ruth, as she rocked back and forth in one of the chairs on the porch while watching a train pull-out of the depot across the street on its way north toward Billings. "It's so relaxing."

"Considering how much we're paying for the room, you should love it," joked George. "But you're right. Everything seems so calm here."

Ruth had given birth a few months earlier to a beautiful baby girl who they had named Elizabeth, after George's mother. But feeling almost immediately overwhelmed with their new lives as parents, they had decided to get away for the weekend, grateful that their good friends Alina and Sam had offered to babysit Elizabeth in their absence.

"All new parents struggle," Alina had said. "But you learn to adjust. I did, and so will you."

Ruth wasn't so sure. "It's just difficult not working," she replied. "I miss the classroom."

It'd been a difficult decision, but Ruth and George had decided that Ruth should stay at home with Beth for the remainder of the school year. The school's principal had agreed, provided that George took over some of her teaching duties. Which he did.

But the first few months had been far more challenging than they had anticipated. Their income had been cut in half. Things were cheap in Lodge Grass, but they had become accustomed to a certain degree of flexibility that two incomes provided. Now it was different. Before, they didn't have to think twice about spending a weekend in Sheridan. Now, it was a struggle.

"You were right about teaching me to drive," said Ruth, sipping her coffee as they continued to sit together on the porch of the inn. "It does give me at least a small sense of independence during the day."

George nodded. "You just have to give it some time, Ruth. I know everything is different now, but . . ."

"I know it's only temporary, George. But what's really bothering me . . ." She hesitated.

"What is it?" George pressed, leaning forward.

"Well, to be honest," she said slowly. "*You've* changed."

"Me?" answered George, surprised. "How so?"

"I know there's more pressure now. Money is tight. We're sleeping less. But . . ."

"But what?" snapped George, starting to feel attacked.

Ruth dropped her head. "That's what I mean."

George shook his head. "I don't understand."

"You're always angry," said Ruth. "Like now."

"I'm not angry. I'm just trying to understand what you mean." George was becoming more frustrated.

"But your tone of voice . . ."

"Just tell me what you mean. What am I doing wrong?"

"You're not *doing* anything wrong, George," said Ruth. "In fact, you're doing all the right things. You're teaching more classes. Doing more after-school activities to earn more money. You help me with Beth in the evening."

"Then what?"

"You never have any patience. You're always snapping at me. You even did it with Alina before we left."

"I didn't snap at her," contested George. "She just kept asking the same question over and over."

"She was asking questions about Beth. She was just trying to understand our routine with her."

George kept shaking his head. "I don't know."

"Look, we both knew that things would be stressful for a while. But we need to stay as positive as possible while we adjust. Just like Alina said, it takes time."

George thought for a moment about the conversation he had had with Alina just a few days earlier while he was waiting for Ruth to pick him up at the school following his drama-club class.

"Is everything okay, George?" she had asked him, as they sat in her classroom waiting for Ruth to arrive. "I thought I heard you yelling at the students today."

"It wasn't anything," replied George. "One of them was cheating on a test."

"Then give them a zero. No need to yell."

"I *have* given a zero before. But they still do it." George stood up and began pacing back and forth.

"Then send them to the principal," suggested Alina, watching George with a worried look. "He'll take care of it."

George nodded, but kept pacing.

"Maybe you should drop a few classes," suggested Alina. "I'm sure the principal would understand."

George stopped. "Why would I do that?" he snapped again.

Alina stood up and walked toward George. "Because you're on edge. And it's affecting your students . . . and Ruth."

George stopped pacing. "Ruth? She said something to you?"

"No, but I can tell that something has been bothering her. I even suggested that the two of you get away for a few days. Sam and I can take care of Beth."

"We can't afford that."

"George," said Alina, grabbing his arm. "Listen to me. You need to calm down. Everything will be okay. It's not easy being new parents."

George finally sat down in one of the student's desks. "I don't know, Alina. It's just so hard. Maybe it was a mistake to come out here."

"*Out here?*"

"Out west. Maybe we should have stayed in Boston."

"What would be different?" asked Alina. "You probably would still have had Beth. Ruth would probably still have stayed home with her. And you would still have had financial pressure."

"Yes, but maybe I would've found a better job."

"You don't like teaching?" asked Alina. "You know, you're getting pretty good at it."

"Thanks to you," admitted George. "Without your help, I don't know where I'd be."

It was true. During his first few months at the school, he had no idea what he was doing. But Alina had been there for him, giving suggestions. Even teaching a few of his lessons while he watched. And outside of school, the two couples had become close friends. Their weekly card games at each other's homes—and occasionally at a local bar—had been a great way to unwind. But with the arrival of Beth, they could no longer do it as regularly.

"When I told my mother that Ruth was pregnant," said George. "She wanted me to come home. She was sure that she could help find me a teaching job in Gardner, and she would then help with Beth."

"Why didn't you go?"

"Pride, I suppose," said George, in a moment of honesty. "I want to make this work."

"But if you're not happy?"

"I just want Ruth to be happy. And I don't think she is." George was beginning to tear up.

"Ruth is fine here, George. I'm sure she misses her family in Kentucky. And probably even misses the big city. But she'll be happy if *you're* happy."

"I don't think things are that simple," said George.

"Actually, George," said Alina. "They are sometimes."

Just then, George felt Ruth touching his shoulder.

"Where did you go?" asked Ruth, still rocking in her chair on the porch of the inn.

"Nowhere," said George. "I was just thinking about something that Alina told me."

"What did she say?" asked Ruth.

George turned to look at Ruth. "Are you happy here? I mean, really happy?'

"Here at the inn?" asked Ruth. "Of course. I love coming to Sheridan."

"Because you miss living in a big city?"

"Sure," admitted Ruth. "Sometimes I miss it. But I like Lodge Grass. The people are very nice. Especially Alina and Sam."

"But . . ."

"Is that what's bothering you?" asked Ruth. "You don't like it here?'

"I'm worried that *you* don't. That you followed me all the way across the country and regret it."

Ruth stopped rocking and reached for George's knee. "Listen to me. I just want us to be happy *together*. We have a beautiful girl who needs our love, and needs to see us love each other. You've seen students who don't come from loving homes. They never turn out well. I want Beth to grow up in a household where she feels safe and able to express herself. I don't want her to grow up feeling tension and anxiety."

"I do want the best for you . . . and Beth."

"I know you do, George. But the best thing you can do for us is to be happy yourself. It'll make our house a better place . . . for the *three* of us."

George nodded.

CHAPTER TWENTY-FIVE

For the most part, I enjoyed a good childhood. It changed, of course, when my mother died. But even after her passing, it was probably still better than most. Our house was modest, yet located on one of the more affluent streets in the town, with plenty of other children with whom I could play. The Atters. The Fries. The Gazettas. All good families, with parents who were doctors, lawyers, and small business owners, who wanted the best for their children.

But unlike many of my friends, I was never a particularly good student in school. Neither was I very popular, especially in high school. The older I got, the fewer friends I had. But most everyone knew who I was because of my place on the baseball team. The sport gave me confidence and a sense of purpose. And I think my father understood that. He would almost always attend my games, often standing behind the backstop when I was pitching so he could let me know after the game how I'd done. He was never critical. Always encouraging.

But he could also be strict with my sister and me. Probably too strict.

Years later, I would come to understand why he was that way. Partly it was generational. Partly it was his relationship with his own father and mother. And partly, of course, his experiences in the war and in Montana. That understanding helped me to rationalize everything. I never blamed him for anything. Was never angry with him. But I came to understand that many of my own struggles in life, along with my long search for personal worth, could all be traced back to those so-called formative years as a child.

Would it have all been different had my mother lived?

Perhaps.

As mothers so often do, she provided balance in the house. She allowed my sister and I to express ourselves in ways that our father would not . . . or could not. When she passed, that outlet was lost. She also understood the importance of relationships, and always encouraged me to have friends. I think I'd always been shy, somewhat of a loner, even before her passing. But she would always encourage me to invite friends over the house, or walk me over the Atter's house to play with her best friend's three children. Then, after her passing, as I began high school, that all ended. Without her encouragement to do otherwise, I spent more and more time alone.

"How do you feel about kids, John?" asked Gabriela, as we sat together in her two-room apartment in Colonia Rivera Hernandez that she shared with a friend. They both had two children, and when everyone was together, it was tight quarters, to say the least.

"To be honest, Gabriela," I said. "I never gave it a lot of thought. I was never around many small children growing up. Neither my father nor my mother had any siblings, so there weren't any cousins. Mostly, it was just my sister and me."

"Yeah, it was the same with me," replied Gabriela. "As an only child, it was mostly just my mother and me. But when I came back here to be with my father, I saw something very different."

"Big families," I said.

"Exactly. Here, everything is about family. It's really the reason why I stayed after my father died, rather than going back to California to be with my mother."

"You liked it."

"I did," said Gabriela, pausing for a moment to reflect, before continuing. "Despite it all, I have no regrets."

Hours earlier, after I had been dropped off by the taxi driver on the edge of the neighborhood, I'd wandered for nearly an hour trying to find Gabriela's house. I had the address, but there were no street signs and few of the houses had any numbers. As I walked, I attracted much attention.

At one point, a group of teenagers approached me, and then encircled me, shouting in Spanish. One came up from behind and touched my back pocket where I had my wallet. And I could see that another had a bulge beneath his shirt, near his waist. He kept tapping it, and I could only assume it was a gun. As the situation became untenable, two adults suddenly emerged from a dark alley and began shouting at the kids, who quickly scattered. One of the adults spoke broken English and encouraged me to leave the neighborhood immediately. When I tried to explain my purpose for being there, they just shook their heads and walked away, leaving me alone again.

I was just about to give up and return to the school when a young woman approached me. It didn't take any street smarts to realize that she was a prostitute. Disappointed that I wasn't looking for her services, she began to walk away, but then stopped, and turned-around.

"¿Por qué estás aquí, gringo?" she had asked. "Es peligroso aquí."

I showed her Gabriela's address and tried to explain my purpose. She stared at me for a moment, but then motioned for me to follow her. Less than five minutes later, I was at Gabriela's house. I thanked the girl the best I could and then watched as she disappeared into the night, no doubt in search of clients.

"I remember you telling me about your experiences in Africa at the mission with the children," recalled Gabriela, as we continued to talk inside her simple house. Her two children were always close by, playing with a few toys on the concrete floor. Fernando was barely one. Andres almost five. They were spending a few days with Gabriela before returning to their grandparents' house.

"Yes," I replied. "With Sister Agnes. It was so hard to see all of those sick children. But I also have no regrets. It was an important experience for me."

Gabriela was studying me as she now held Fernando in her arms. "But did it change the way you looked at children?"

"Change?"

"Well, your first experience with small children was . . . watching them die. It must have stuck with you."

She was right about that.

For a moment, I had no response. So Gabriela continued. "Mira, by coming here, you've entered *my* world. My reality. And I just want to be sure you won't make that world any more difficult than it already is."

"I would never hurt you," I said.

"It's not *me* I'm worried about."

"I know, the children," I said, looking at Andres and Fernando. "Maybe I can help you to find a better place where you can live with them."

"Why would you do that?"

I was surprised by the comment. "Because we're friends," I shrugged.

"That's all you want? Friendship?" Her tone was disconcerting. But in retrospect, it was understandable. She had been hurt. Badly hurt. And didn't want to get hurt again.

"You can trust me," I said. "I just want to help."

"You don't need to feel sorry for me, John. I'm fine here." She looked at the boys. "*We're* fine here."

Realizing that things were starting to go sideways, I changed the subject in an effort to lighten the mood. It worked. An hour later, the four of us were taking a taxi back to the hotel to have a late dinner together.

I wanted so much to ask more questions about the children's father, but knew the time wasn't right. Instead, we enjoyed each other's company for a few hours.

I have no doubt that Gabriela was testing me and my reaction to the boys that night. I guess I passed the test, because in the weeks and months that followed, my relationship with her began to evolve into something much deeper than friendship.

CHAPTER TWENTY-SIX

As was true across the United States in the early 1950s, Montana was experiencing some major cultural and economic changes. Before the war, many rural towns across the state still didn't have electricity or indoor plumbing. By the early 1950s, nearly all did. Servicemen who had fought in the war returned home from battle to find Montana and the rest of the country in the midst of the greatest economic prosperity they had ever known. Many used the benefits of the GI Bill to secure low-interest mortgages, allowing them to buy homes, start families, and open their own businesses.

America was truly on the rise.

But there were consequences.

With a growing middle class, Montanans could buy more food, creating a higher demand for farming and ranching. To keep up with the demand, farms and ranches became increasingly mechanized. Suddenly, fewer people were needed to operate larger farms and ranches. Many rural families—who had long depended upon agriculture for employment—began moving to the larger cities seeking work. As urban populations increased, cities like Great Falls, Bozeman, and Missoula needed to build more houses and factories. This demand for building supplies gave rise to the state's lumber, aluminum, and oil industries. The discovery of oil near Billings in 1951 helped to satisfy the demand, but dramatically changed the city, practically overnight.

Transportation was changing, as well. As the new highway between Sheridan and Billings neared completion, people like George and Ruth could choose between the two cities for their weekly shopping and occasional weekend getaways. Consequently, they spent less and less time—and money—in small towns like Lodge Grass.

Slowly, those towns began to die.

The new highways also impacted the railroads, which saw a major decline in the early 1950s. Thousands were laid off, and many small towns—which were not near enough to the new highways—lost their main source of transportation, further isolating them and all but ensuring the towns' collapse.

Those who struggled financially during the 1950s were often those who suffered social hardships as well. This was especially true of Native Americans, including the Crow. As it'd done so many times before, Congress decided to change its policy toward the tribes following the Second World War by terminating most federal support for schools and health clinics on the reservations. With no place else to go for their education, many Crow families sent their children to "white" schools, such as the one where George and Ruth taught in Lodge Grass.

George was now into his third year of teaching, and Ruth had recently returned to the classroom following a year off to remain at home with Beth. But as the new school year began, they saw their classes nearly double in size. Making matters even more challenging, the white students and their families were becoming resentful of the influx of so many Native American students into *their* school.

Everyone felt the tension and realized the situation wasn't sustainable. On top of that, one of Ruth and George's good friends, a rancher, had caught his arm in the blades of one of his new harvesting machines. He was lucky to be alive. But unable to work his land, and unable to find any laborers, he had turned to his friends for help.

"Do you think you can help me out, George," said Stan. "Just for a few weeks."

George was hesitant. "I'm not sure if I can. I never worked on a farm before."

"It's not difficult work," replied Stan, a burly man in his fifties who had inherited the land from his father. He was primarily a rancher, maintaining a sizable herd of cattle, but also grew wheat and flax. "But the work is best done early in the morning."

George thought for a moment. "Well, we do have a short vacation coming up at the school. I could probably help for a few days. But with this leg," George tapped his leg with the cane that he continued to use every day, "I'm not sure how much I could really do."

"Don't worry," said Stan. "Once you're up on the horse, it won't matter."

George swallowed hard, unable to admit he had never ridden a horse.

"Who knows," continued Stan. "Maybe you'll prefer the farm and decide to leave the classroom. I'm sure you won't miss them Injuns."

George wanted to respond to Stan's slur, but thought better of it, knowing his friend was having a tough time. Anyways, he knew that most of the ranchers didn't care for the Crow, or more accurately, downright hated them. He never fully understood it, but realized it was a feeling so ingrained in the ranchers' psyche that it would probably never change.

George and Ruth had met Stan and his wife, Louise, about a year earlier at a card game hosted by one of the teachers. During their few years in Montana, poker had become one of their favorite pastimes, with games held at different friends' houses each Friday evening.

Ruth was actually a pretty formidable player, while George just enjoyed the conversation. During the game, some smoked. Some drank. But everyone enjoyed each other's company. It was always a welcome relief from the toils of the work week.

Occasionally, George and Stan would step away from a game to talk about the war. Stan's son had been killed at Iwo Jima, and he himself was a World War I veteran of the Battle of the Somme. He was one of the few people that George felt comfortable sharing his experiences in France.

"You still have nightmares?" he had asked Stan one night.

George nodded. "Some are worse than others. But I just can't seem to get through the night. I always wake up tired."

"You talk to Ruth about it?"

"Not really," replied George, looking down. "I'm not sure she understands."

"Wasn't she a nurse?"

George nodded.

"Then I'm sure she'd understand. Probably better than most."

"I guess so. It's just hard to open up. I wish I could just forget it all."

Stan put his hand on George's shoulder. "That will never happen. It's been more than thirty years, and I still think about it nearly every day."

"You have nightmares, too?"

"Not every night," answered Stan. "But sometimes, sure. You learn to live with them, I suppose."

"Does it make you feel angry?"

"Angry?" repeated Stan. "Not particularly. It wasn't anyone's fault. Just war."

Just war, repeated George to himself. He wished it would *just* all go away.

"You're not drinking are you?" asked Stan. "I see a lot of that with the veterans who have worked for me."

"No," said George. "Maybe just a glass of whiskey on a Friday night. That's about it."

"Good for you," said Stan, slapping George on his shoulder. "Stay away from it. It caught me for a while, but I was able to give it up. Now I do my best thinking when on horseback. Helps me to clear my mind."

George fulfilled his promise and helped Stan and his wife for a few days on their farm. But it wasn't easy.

On his first morning, as he tried to get-up on Stan's horse, he struggled, unable to use his injured leg for leverage. Stan and another ranch hand tried to help, but George resisted, too prideful to receive a lift-up from the two men. Eventually, he made it, but not before wounding his ego more than his leg. He knew that Louise and Ruth had been watching. But neither woman was laughing. They were just worried about George's state of mind.

"He gets frustrated easily," observed Louise. "Is he like that at home?"

"Sometimes," replied Ruth. "And I don't always know how to respond."

"A lot of the veterans are that way. Had our son survived, I'm sure he would've been, too."

"How did you and Stan get through that?" asked Ruth, as the two women watched George and the ranch-hand slowly move away across the plains, preparing to herd some cattle together. "It must have been heartbreaking."

"There is nothing harder. But it probably brought Stan and I closer."

"Really? I would think it would push most couples apart," said Ruth, as they both began walking toward the barn to begin cleaning the horse stalls.

"No doubt. And I'm honestly not sure why it was different for us. But we leaned on each other, maybe because we had no one else. Neither of us have family nearby."

"You have a sister, don't you?" recalled Ruth. "Where did she move?"

"Chicago. And Stan's brothers moved back East, too. One to Detroit. The other New York. More jobs there, I guess."

"Have you and Stan ever thought about moving away?" asked Ruth, as the two women entered the barn.

"I think about it, but I don't talk with Stan about it. I know how important this farm is to him. It would break him if we had to move."

"But if it were up to *you*?"

"Then, yes," replied Louise, without hesitation. "I'd rather live in the city. This may be God's country, but it's a hard place. A lonely place. But I suspect this is where we'll spend the rest of our lives." Louise took Ruth's hand. "But it doesn't have to be that way for you, my dear. You're still young. Maybe you and George would be better off going back to Boston."

Ruth nodded. "We've talked about it. But I think it's hard for him to admit that things haven't worked out here as he had planned."

"Yes, the male ego," said Louise, with a sigh. "It does get in the way of things, doesn't it?"

A few hours later George and the ranch hand returned from the pastures. Stan was waiting for him, with a stepstool.

"Here, George," said Stan. "Use the stool. It'll be easier to get down."

George wanted to protest, but thought better of it. His leg was aching. "Thanks," he said, swinging his leg over the horse and stepping down, brushing the dust from his clothes. "I don't know how you do that every day. It's hard work."

Stan smiled. "Every day for the past forty years, including when I was a child." He turned to his ranch hand. "How did George do?"

The young black man shrugged his shoulders. "Could have done it myself." And he walked away.

George heard the comment.

"Ignore him, George," said Stan. "I appreciate what you're doing. And he could not have done it himself. It's always a two-man job."

"You're being kind," said George. "But I think I would've actually enjoyed it . . . if I didn't have this damn pain in my leg. There's a certain peacefulness about it. The land is beautiful."

Stan slapped George on his back. "Good for you. Now let's get to the barn to help the women."

By the end of the weekend, George had done just about every job imaginable on Stan's farm, from herding cattle to hooving the horses to toting water back and forth from the well to the drinking troughs. While he felt good about helping his friend, he was frustrated by his inability to do even the most menial tasks without significant struggle.

He had tried it *with* his cane, but couldn't get much done with his one free hand. And he had tried it *without* his cane, only to find his leg just wasn't stable enough to maintain his balance. As he sat with Ruth in their house preparing to return to school the next day, he seemed to have reached his breaking point, one of the few times that Ruth remembered him crying.

"You should be thankful that you can do the work *at all*," said Ruth, as they sat side by side on the couch, with their lesson plans spread-out on the coffee table, and Beth playing with her toys on the floor. "So many veterans can't even walk."

"I know," said George, trying to hold back his tears in front of Beth. "But I just want to be . . . normal."

"What's *normal*?" returned Ruth. "Is it physical? Emotional? Intellectual? You're one of the smartest men I know. You went to Harvard, for God's sake. Focus more on that, and less on your physical limitations."

"What about when Beth gets older and learns to ride a bike? I couldn't even chase after her to be sure she didn't fall."

"What about when she needs help with her homework," countered Ruth. "Maybe her French. How many parents can help with that? You can."

For a moment, George thought back to his own childhood, sitting in his father's study, completing his French and Latin lessons. He didn't want that for his daughter. He hadn't even wanted it for himself. How much would've been different if he had never had those lessons. Maybe the Army would never have selected him to be a translator. Maybe he would never have met Yvette. Maybe he would never have been injured.

Maybe.

It was all just too much to contemplate. Too overwhelming. And it was holding George back. Keeping him from moving forward and finding a more positive path.

Ruth knew it.

But she didn't know how to help.

And something inside was telling her that time was somehow running out to find a solution. As Beth grew older, she would begin to understand her father's struggles. Was that the kind of childhood that Ruth wanted for her daughter? Would she have to make a choice between her daughter and her husband? It was almost unthinkable.

CHAPTER TWENTY-SEVEN

About a two-hour drive from San Pedro Sula, along the north coast of the country, is Miami, a small village that is seemingly little more than the jumping off point to the Jeanette Kawas National Park. But as I arrived there with Gabriela, Andres, and Fernando for a weekend getaway, it became quickly apparent that we'd found something much more.

A paradise.

Since visiting Gabriela at her house in Colonia Rivera Hernandez, a lot had changed. We'd become nearly inseparable. I'd settled into a predictable routine at my school, and was actually enjoying the teaching. I'd become friends with Doña Olga's son, Jackie, who—for practical purposes—ran the school from a business perspective.

At school, he was professional and reliable. Outside of school, he was a party boy and a philanderer. But he spoke near perfect English, having attended college in the States, and was my guide to San Pedro. In my first few months at the school, I'd explored very little of the city and the surrounding communities. With Jackie, and his best friend, Miguel, I'd seen sides of the city that I would not have otherwise experienced.

On one particular evening at Doña Olga's house—where I was often invited for dinner—I sat with Jackie on his mother's porch after she had gone to bed with her husband.

"What do you think of Honduras, so far," he asked, as we both drank from our bottles of Cerveza Salva Vida. "Is it what you expected?"

"To be honest," I began. "It's like two different worlds. The difference between the rich and poor is extreme."

Jackie laughed. "Isn't that true just about anywhere?"

"Not like this," I persisted. "Even Africa didn't have these extremes."

"It probably did during their colonial era. The rich whites and poor blacks. But when the whites pulled-out and went back to Europe, they left behind a broken society."

"And here?"

"It was America that pulled out," said Jackie. "They built much of this country back in the day when they ran the fruit companies. And then their involvement in the civil war in Nicaragua changed the country yet again. And definitely not for the better."

"You mean drugs?"

Jackie nodded, and took another swig of his beer. "Not just the drugs themselves, but all the businesses it spawned. Along with all the corruption."

I thought about the guys at the bar of the Grand Hotel Sula. And about Gabriela's ex-boyfriend. "There was corruption in Africa," I said. "But not always the extreme violence."

"Drugs are big business. But if it continues unchecked, this place will become nearly unlivable."

"Why do you stay here, then?" I asked. "Don't you worry about your family?"

"Of course. But our lifestyle is better here than it would be any-where else," admitted Jackie. "Here, I can live a good life. If we moved to the States, who would I be? Just an ordinary guy." Jackie wasn't shy about speaking the truth.

"But don't you get tired of living in this city?" I asked. "It's not exactly a beautiful place anymore."

Jackie reached for another bottle of beer. "Let's be honest," he said. "It's a dump. But there *are* some beautiful places not too far away."

"Such as?"

"Miami," said Jackie, without hesitation. "Near Tela. You should take Gabriela and her two boys there for some camping. The beaches are amazing."

And so I did.

Arriving on the Jeanette Kawas National Park's shoreline felt almost like washing-up on a deserted island.

As Gabriela, Fernando, Andres, and I stepped out of my jeep and walked a few hundred feet along a dirt road toward the beach, we were surrounded by the shouts of howler monkeys. Their outlines were visible swinging through the thick jungle of vines, banana plants, and giant ferns that extended all the way to the beach. Surprisingly, the two boys were not scared of their surroundings. Gabriela, on the other hand, was spooked.

"What's the matter?" I asked, laughing. "No monkeys in San Pedro?"

"Very funny," she replied, constantly looking over her shoulder. "Is this where we're camping?"

I laughed. "No. Don't worry. We'll camp on the beach."

"Is that safe? I don't see anyone else around."

"There is a Garifuna village just down the beach, and some of the resorts of Tela are about a mile beyond that."

Gabriela nodded, but seemed unconvinced.

Tela, which means "land of hills and craggy mountains" in the native language of the Garifunas, had seen a long and turbulent history, dating as far back as the sixteenth century when English privateers and pirates operated in the area, looking for ways to attack the Spanish schooners that hauled fortunes in precious metals and stones.

By the late nineteenth century, the economy of Tela—and the other small towns, such as Miami, that dotted the northern coast of Honduras— had become primarily dependent upon the cultivation and production of bananas. In the early twentieth century, the local municipalities started giving land grants to foreigners who, at first, wanted to promote the local economy, but later became more focused on their own profits. It was an inauspicious beginning to the so-called golden age of banana production in the country.

Within a decade, Tela had become an important port and head-quarters of the Tela Railroad Company, a subsidiary of the United Fruit Company. The company brought in many laborers, first to build the rail-road, and then to work the banana plantations as it continued to expand its footprint across the country.

Many of those workers were African-descended people from the English-speaking Caribbean, especially Jamaica and Belize. While not slaves, their lifestyle wasn't much better.

As profits flowed in, United Fruit built a new town for its employees called Tela Nueva, just outside of the older town. It was carefully planned, yet segregated by race, with the best housing located in the "White Zone"—later called the "American Zone"—in which only Euro-American employ-ees lived. It included a hospital, schools, and even a golf course. But the laborers from Jamaica and Belize were forced to live in barracks outside the White Zone.

When the golden age of banana production faded into history and most of the Euro-Americans departed, the White Zone was transformed into resorts for the wealthy. Located just down the beach from Miami, these resorts enjoyed unobstructed views of the emerald cliffs that extended down into the bay of bright, turquoise blue water.

"Thanks so much for bringing us here," said Gabriela. "It means a lot to me that the boys have this opportunity. It's rare that they get out of the city."

"Of course," I said, as the four of us sat together on the sand. "I'm glad you could come. Jackie said it was beautiful here. And he was definitely right." We all looked around at the natural splendor that surrounded us.

"You don't mind being with the boys?" she asked.

I knew she was watching me closely, awaiting my reply. "I just want the best for the three of you. But there *is* something I wanted to ask you." Something that I'd been working-up the nerve to ask for hours.

"What's that?'

"Well, before we left, I overheard you talking on the phone," I began slowly. "I don't understand much Spanish, but enough to know that you were talking with the boys' father, and that you mentioned Tela."

I could tell Gabriela was surprised, and struggled to find the right response. "I'm sorry. I don't want to keep anything from you, but I also don't want you to get involved in . . . that. It's a bad situation."

"I can take care of myself."

"I know you can. But you don't know these people. I'm not even sure if *I* know them that well."

"You can tell me, it's okay."

Gabriela thought for a moment before answering. "Well, I know what Dave must have told you," she said.

"He's an ass," I replied. "I don't believe much of what he says."

Gabriela looked at me. "But what he said about Jorge is mostly true."

"Jorge being the boys' father?"

"Yes," answered Gabriela. "He's not a good man. Or at least he isn't anymore."

"What changed?"

"Bad friends, mostly. I still believe he's a good person at heart. But he was pulled in the wrong direction."

"And he hurt you," I said.

"He was around guys who treated their women poorly. Eventually, he did the same."

I stared at Gabriela. "I'm sorry, but it almost sounds like you're making excuses for him."

"No," replied Gabriela immediately. "No excuses. Not anymore. But for a while, I did." She watched the boys getting too close to the water and ran after them. When she returned, she was less apologetic.

"I've made some bad decisions. No question about it. And I can't forgive what he did to me. But he will always be the children's father."

"Is that why you called him?" I asked.

A moment of awkward silence. "He knows that you and I have been spending time together, and he doesn't like it. Doesn't want you near the boys. So I called him to explain."

That seemed odd to me. "But what did you need to explain?"

"That he needs to accept it. That you and I are . . . together."

"Are we?" I smiled.

Gabriela smiled back. "I think so."

We shared a laugh that helped to lighten the mood.

"But we need to be careful," continued Gabriela. "If he was capable of hurting me in public, there's no knowing what he might do to you. He's still influenced by some bad people."

"Oh, I wouldn't worry about that, Gabriela. There isn't much he can do," I said dismissively, although I was less confident on the inside.

"It's not that simple," said Gabriela. "Jealousy is a powerful thing. Especially in the hands of someone who has a lot of negative influences in their life. That's why it's so important to me that the boys have positive influences."

She then looked at me, waiting for my reply.

"I think I can do that. Be a positive influence."

I'm sure I wasn't as convincing as Gabriela had hoped, but it seemed to satisfy her. At least for the moment.

The next day, I emerged from our tent to the beauty of the early morning. The beach was quiet, save for a few Gurufinas heading out onto the bay, presumably to fish. Andres, Fernando, and Gabriela were still asleep, giving me some time to walk down the beach toward one of the nearby resorts in search of a place to bring them later for breakfast.

Camping was definitely not my thing, and it was something that I'd rarely done as a child. But the two boys were clearly enjoying themselves, having stayed up late playing in the sand and looking up at the stars, unobstructed by the distant lights of Tela. But I was now in need of a hearty breakfast, as the bread and water we'd brought along weren't doing the trick.

About a mile down the beach I came to the nearest resort, still mostly quiet in the early hours of the morning, save for a few workers combing the sand and setting up the beach chairs for the day. Upon closer observation, it was clearly a resort whose heyday had already passed.

The pool was empty.

Some of the windows were boarded-over.

And most of the beachfront facade needed some new paint. But its location on the beach, with the emerald cliffs in the background, was spectacular nonetheless.

I headed into the main lobby in search of the hotel's restaurant, and was pleased to discover that it did indeed serve breakfast. Only a few guests were present, choosing to sit outside beneath some palm trees, on the patio that extended toward the empty pool. Before returning to Gabriela and the boys to share the good news, I decided to get myself a cup of coffee and read the newspaper for a bit, so they had some more time to sleep.

Less than ten minutes later, and well into my second cup of coffee, I was doing my best to read the Spanish sports section when I was approached by one of the guests who had been sitting outside at a nearby table. He was a young guy, probably in his early thirties, well built, and wearing a T-shirt, shorts, and sandals. I was startled when he promptly sat down opposite me, crossed his legs, and slapped down his own newspaper on the table in front of me.

I stared at him for a few seconds before finally saying, "¿Puedo ayudarte, senor?"

He smiled at me. "¿Cómo está Gabriela? ¿Dormistes bien?"

I was taken aback. "¿Perdóneme? ¿Quién eres tú?" *Who was this guy? How did he know Gabriela?*

"No deberías estar con los niños. No son tuyos," he said, his smile now disappearing, as he leaned forward.

"¿Qué?" I said, my voice rising. "¿Quién te envió aquí?" But then I remembered what Gabriela had told me about the children's father. "¿Jorge?"

The guy's smile returned. He nodded slightly, stood up, grabbed his paper from the table, and walked away without saying another word.

Feeling an intense combination of fear and anger, I left a few pesos on the table to pay for my coffee and then hastily retreated down the beach toward Gabriela's tent, repeatedly looking over my shoulder.

I couldn't believe what had just happened. I'd clearly been threatened, but to what end?

It felt like something out of a movie.

When I arrived at the tent, I found Gabriela and the boys outside playing in the sand. I motioned for her to step around the tent so we could talk. When I told her what had happened, she didn't seem the least bit surprised.

"I'm so sorry," she said. "I knew this was a mistake. I think we should go back to San Pedro."

"Now?" I replied, incredulously. "Run away, just like that?"

"It's not worth the risk. Let's just go."

"No!" I said, undoubtedly too loudly. "We can't run away! Let's take the boys to get some breakfast and talk about it."

Gabriela took my hand. "It's okay, John. Calm down. Believe me, it's better if we just return to San Pedro and let things quiet down for a few days. We can then decide what to do next."

Reluctantly, I took her advice.

Following my junior year at college in Kansas, I'd returned home for a few weeks to spend time with my father, something I would do nearly every summer for the next thirty years. Sometimes my sister would join us. But on this particular occasion, it was just my father and I. As would become our routine, we found ourselves sitting side by side, overlooking Crystal Lake.

It'd been a particularly hot and humid summer—my father's least favorite—so the breeze that swept across the lake that afternoon was especially refreshing. I noticed that the water was unusually high, nearly spilling onto the narrow road that ran along the shoreline just down the hill from my mother's grave.

"Do you still visit Mom every month?" I asked. It'd been more than six years since her passing.

"Yes," Dad replied. "But it certainly means more when you or your sister can join me."

My sister had graduated from college the same year as I'd started, and was now working in Boston. Her apartment in Brookline was only a few hours from my father, so she was able to visit a few weekends each month. I suspect that she didn't always want to spend that weekend in the little town of Gardner. But she understood it meant a lot to our father.

Over the years, I often asked my sister why she stayed in Boston. Why she didn't have that urge to move-away, like I did.

"My friends are here," she would always say. "And I like the city. Anyways, somebody has to spend time with Dad. He can't always be alone."

She always felt a certain obligation to our father. Maybe it was that father-daughter dynamic which so often determines a woman's sense of worth as a woman, and as a person. A dynamic which can produce both positive and negative consequences. Whatever the reason, despite my annual pilgrimages to Crystal Lake to reconnect with my father, her bond with him was undoubtedly tighter.

"Your mother would be proud of you both," my father said to me. "But it would've been difficult for her to accept you going so far from home to attend college, even though it was very important to her that you and your sister finished college. She never had that opportunity. Her family just never had the money."

I asked my father's advice that afternoon about a girl I was dating at college. In my early twenties, I often had too much pride to seek his advice. But our conversation that day would stick with me for many years.

"Based on my own experiences with Ruth while attending Harvard, I'd always thought that college was a good place to meet someone, perhaps even marry them someday. But your sister's experience in college was different. But probably more typical. She struggled to balance studying and dating. At that age, you'll almost always prioritize the relationship. And that can lead to a lot of bad decisions with long-term consequences."

"In what way?" I asked.

"Well, you're likely to choose a path based upon the relationship rather than a career. There is nothing necessarily wrong with that. But if you choose the wrong career path as a result, then later in life you can easily become resentful of the relationship that pushed you down that path."

"Is that what happened to you and Ruth?"

"In some ways," Dad replied. "But my main mistake wasn't taking advantage of the resources that Harvard had to offer. I spent most of my free time with Ruth, instead of making connections at the school that could have helped me to start my career. On top of that, I chose to start my career in a part of the country that intrigued me. The job itself was secondary. But when my job at the bank failed, and as I struggled to adjust to the rural lifestyle, it affected my marriage to Ruth."

My father then paused for a moment before continuing. "And there's no doubt that my experiences in the war were still . . . lingering."

"Lingering how?" I asked.

It remained a difficult topic for my father to discuss.

"I've always thought that people should resolve their own problems without turning to others for help," he said. "But some problems are not easily resolved alone. Especially deep-seeded ones."

"Like trauma from war?"

My Dad nodded. "I eventually overcame it. But it was, in many ways, too late."

My father turned to look at me. "So you want to be careful, Johnny, that you're really ready for a relationship before you dive in too deep. Are you ready to commit to it a hundred percent? Are you ready to put the needs of your partner ahead of your own? Are you able to compromise? Able to sacrifice? Able to communicate? Are you able to share your feelings? If the answer to any of those questions is *no,* then it's better to take a step back. Otherwise, you're being unfair to the other person. And almost inevitably, the relationship will fail."

I thought about that conservation with my father as I drove back to San Pedro from Tela with Gabriela and her two children.

Was I ready to fully commit to her *and* the children? Was I ready to put *their* needs ahead of my own?

Or should I take a step back?

I wished my father was there to offer some advice.

CHAPTER TWENTY-EIGHT

George walked hand in hand with Yvette down the dirt road behind their little house that continued for a few miles, all the way to the beach. It was a beautiful summer day, as most were on the Cotentin peninsula. The birds were chirping and the flowers blooming. Men worked around their houses, continuing to rebuild from the Battle of Normandy that had devastated their neighborhoods nearly two years earlier. Women tended to the children who ran freely from one yard to another, jumping over fences and stone walls, and darting in between the rubble that was gradually being carried away with each passing day. But there was still a lot of work to be done. Later in the day, George would join the rebuilding efforts, preferring to work the afternoon and evening shifts, giving him time each morning to enjoy the beach with Yvette.

As they arrived near the sandy shoreline, they found a spot atop a nearby dune and looked out across the beach, still filled with wrecks of military vehicles left behind by the Americans from their landings in June 1944. For a few moments, George and Yvette sat in silence, both remembering that first day they had arrived from England as part of the Great Crusade to set Europe free from Nazi tyranny.

But most of Europe was still living a nightmare of the war's aftermath. Millions of displaced people throughout Western Europe were trying to find their way home, while millions more were trying to escape the Soviet rule in Eastern Europe. The Americans, British, and Soviets had carved up Germany and were now preparing for the long game, which would become the Cold War.

But all of that seemed so far away.

George and Yvette had survived the war, deciding to settle in her hometown of St. Marie du Mont. Her parents had accepted George into their little family, particularly Yvette's brother, Luc, who had grown to think of George like a true brother. The three of them had endured horrors seemingly unimaginable. But it'd all been very real, especially their nearly six-month ordeal in Lorient. The Germans had finally surrendered the city to the Allies in May of 1945, in the same month that all of Germany had capitulated.

"Sometimes I still can't believe we survived it all," said Yvette. "There were so many times that I really didn't think we were going to make it."

"I know," agreed George, leaning back on his elbows as Yvette rested her head on his chest. "But there's still so much to do."

Yvette nodded. "What will happen to all of this equipment?" she asked, motioning toward the beach. "Will it just be left to rust?"

"Vehicles that haven't already been sold will probably be melted down and used to form new steel. There's such a shortage."

"America must be rich to leave so much behind," joked Yvette.

"I'm sure it's just cheaper to leave it behind than transport it all back to the States. It'll all be gone eventually, and then the beach will be for tourists once again."

"Hard to believe," conceded Yvette. "So much has happened here. We must never forget."

"Somehow I don't think the world will forget. This whole place will probably become a tourist attraction where people will come for generations to remember the landings."

Yvette shook her head. "And to think that ten years ago this was a place that most people had never heard of."

"Now, it belongs to history."

George and Yvette lay quietly atop a sand dune, trying to make sense of it all. He stroked her hair as a gentle breeze passed over the beach, seemingly unwilling to blow too hard, so as not to disturb what had become hallowed ground. Soon, they both found themselves drifting toward sleep, succumbing to the calm of the morning.

Just then, George was pulled back to consciousness by the concussion of bombs exploding just feet away. He felt a sudden, excruciating burning sensation in his leg. He tried to jerk Yvette awake. But she lay motionless, her head still upon his chest. He shook her again, and this time felt the wetness on his hands. Blood. Yvette's blood. He pushed her limp body off of his, and reached down to grab his leg. But there was nothing there. His leg was gone.

"George!" said Ruth. "Wake up." She was shaking him. "You're having a nightmare. It's okay. I'm here with you."

George bolted up in bed, sweat pouring down his face, his heart pounding.

It'd happened again.

Seven years had passed, but George was still struggling to cope with the memories of war. He did everything possible to redirect his thoughts. He was working longer hours at the school and had recently started a weekend job at the train yard in Sheridan. Ruth was doing her best to cope, but she needed her husband to be a father. Yet, he was rarely home. But even when he was, he remained distant, often sitting alone on the porch. Feeling that she was near the end of her rope, she paid a visit to Alina one evening, carrying Beth in her arms.

"I don't know how much longer I can take this, Alina," said Ruth. "With each passing day, he seems to be slipping farther from me."

"How is he with Beth?" asked Alina, as they sat in her kitchen. "Does he spend time with her?"

"I feel that he wants to be present for her, but almost doesn't know how. I can see it in his eyes. He's fighting inner demons, Alina, and I don't know how to help him anymore." She wiped tears from her eyes.

"He won't seek help?"

"A counselor? No," answered Ruth, shaking her head. "I've stopped asking, just makes him more upset." Ruth lifted Beth from her lap and put her on the kitchen floor. "But without help, I don't know how he can be the father that Beth needs."

"Has he talked to you about what happened in the war?"

Ruth shrugged. "A little. But whenever I bring it up, he just changes the subject or becomes irritated, saying that I could never understand."

"That's probably true, but still," said Alina. "Listen, it's unimaginable what he must have seen. Wasn't he in Normandy in '44?"

"Yes. He's mentioned a few of the towns that he passed through, but that's about it."

Alina thought for a moment. "What about his mother? Have you reached out to her?"

Ruth shook her head. "She doesn't like me very much. Never did. I remember the first time I met her at her house. She made me feel so unwelcome."

Alina smiled. "It's understandable, isn't it? War had taken her son away. And then you were taking him away again."

"It wasn't my decision to come here. I followed George. *He* wanted to come here."

Alina studied Ruth. "Could that be part of the problem? *You're* not happy here."

"I'm not happy here because I don't have the family I want," said Ruth, her voice rising. "I don't care where I live, so long as the three of us are at peace."

Alina reached out to take Ruth's hand. "I know, my dear. I know. You're in a difficult position. But remember how many women are going through the same problems. So many men are struggling. It's a tragedy that our society is unable or unwilling to give them the help they need."

"So what should I do then? Just put up with it and hope it gets better?" said Ruth. "I'm honestly not sure I'm that strong."

"Then reach out to the one person who might be able to get him to listen."

"His mother," said Ruth knowingly, with a sigh.

What did she have to lose?

CHAPTER TWENTY-NINE

"What do you remember most about your mother?" Gabriela asked me, as we sat across from each other at a little restaurant near the town square of Santa Rita, a few miles from the Mayan ruins of Copan. We'd decided to spend the weekend together to talk through everything, the boys had returned to be with their grandparents.

"I remember her being sick, of course," I said. "But I also remember the good times before that. Our family trips to Maine and Cape Cod during the summer. Those were always fun times."

"Where would you go in Maine?"

"There was this little town called Wells that we would visit each July for a few days, always staying at the same motel near the beach. We'd spend the day together on the beach – my sister and I often flying kites - and then have dinner at this fish restaurant just down the street from the motel. Those were perfect days."

Gabriela smiled. "It's a nice memory. I wish I'd similar memories with my mother and father."

"At least you were with him when he died," I said. "I wasn't with my mother, and it still haunts me." The loss of a parent was something that Gabriela and I had in common, and one that had undoubtedly drawn us closer together.

"But you still had your father and sister," said Gabriela. "I didn't have anyone."

"Do you regret not going back to California to live with your mom after your dad died?" I asked as the waitress brought our food.

"It would be easy to say *yes*, but then the boys would never have been born."

I nodded. "I guess there are never any easy answers to these things. Life always seems to be such a labyrinth."

Gabriela nodded in agreement. "What about us?" she asked. "Do you have any regrets?"

"Of course not," I replied honestly. "I admit that the incident in Tela was hurtful, scary, even. But it wasn't your fault. I'm just not sure where we go from here. I can see the same situation occurring again and again."

"Yes," agreed Gabriela. "I guess we have some decisions to make."

And Copan seemed like the ideal place to make those decisions. It was quiet, quaint, and picturesque, with cobbled streets, old churches, and a certain charm that was most definitely absent from San Pedro. It was also another place recommended by Jackie.

"Go there," he had said. "It's a good place to think things through, and you'll learn something too. There's lots of history there. The glory days for this part of the world."

Located in the mountains of western Honduras, the Mayan ruins at Copan were spectacular. Before dinner, Gabriela and I'd explored the ancient city with a guide who had explained the periods of its development before the city was abandoned in the early ninth century, not to be rediscovered for nearly five hundred years, and not to be studied in detail until the mid-twentieth century.

The centerpiece of the tour was seeing the *Plaza of the Hieroglyphic Staircase*, with its ten-meter-wide steps, and more than a thousand individual glyphs. The guide explained that the Maya were actually multiple groups of indigenous people whose common culture reached its height more than a thousand years ago, and whose ancestors still inhabited parts of Mexico and Central America.

Like other great civilizations, the Mayans formalized their language into a codified writing system. Their glyphs were used—much like those of Ancient Egypt—to represent words, sounds, and syllables through the use of pictures and other symbols. Historians believe that the Mayans used more than seven hundred glyphs. Like most civilizations, they were keen to record their history and achievements and went so far as to record notable events on pillars, walls and large stone slabs like the Ancient Egyptians and Romans.

But our guide was careful to point out that the most famous Mayan invention was undoubtedly their calendar, which recorded repetitive cycles of time based on the movements of the sun, moon, and planets. They made very careful recordings and objective conclusions about those heavenly bodies which led to their calculation of a year to be 365 days and a lunar month to be thirty days. Their level of accuracy, given their lack of modern tools, was incredible.

As I listened to the guide share the Mayan's incredible history, it made me consider my own place in time. How would I be remembered when I was gone? Would I leave behind anything of value? Would I discover my role in this life? My purpose? My destiny? Was I meant to remain in Honduras with Gabriela or go someplace else?

"What about your father?" asked Gabriela as we continued to enjoy our meal at that little restaurant near the town square of Santa Rita. "Was he your inspiration?"

"He was a teacher for much of his career," I answered. "But he never encouraged me to become one, but didn't discourage it either. I guess he felt that I needed to find my own path."

"What about your sense of justice?" asked Gabriela. "Your values? Do you think you get them from your father?"

"My sense of justice?" I repeated, not really sure how to respond to that question.

"Yes. Right from wrong. Good from bad. Did you learn that from your father?"

I shifted in my seat. Gabriela was really probing. "I think we all learn some of that from our parents. But I think we also learn it through observation. I certainly saw a lot of bad things in Africa, and I hope I learned something from it."

"Did you?" asked Gabriela, leaning forward. "Learn something?"

"I suppose I learned that people generally do the best they can to survive, and it's not always possible—or fair—to judge another's action solely from your own perspective. You remember my stories about Jean Pierre?" I asked.

Gabriela nodded.

"It would be easy to say that he was doing something wrong by selling those diamonds. But he was doing it to support his family. If he hadn't done it, what would've become of his younger siblings? Would they have survived?"

"You know," said Gabriela, "the boys' father would probably say something similar about his actions. That he was doing it to give us a better life."

"I don't judge him for that. But the way he treated you can't be excused. And if the boys grow up seeing that, don't you think they're more likely to do the same to their own girlfriends or wives someday?"

"So you think that a father's most important purpose is to be a good role model?"

"Yes," I replied simply. "My father may have been too strict, but he was always a good role model. Always treated my mother properly. And always tried to do the right thing for my sister and me."

"I want Andres and Fernando to grow up with a father like that," said Gabriela.

"I agree that every child deserves *at least* that. But I also think there's more to it. Good schools. Nice neighborhood. The opportunity to attend college. It all matters."

"But in the end," said Gabriela. "What matters most is the family. How much they love each other."

"True."

Gabriela looked down at her food. "And do you think it's different with step-parents?"

"Different?" I asked.

"Do you think step-parents love their children differently?"

We'd finally arrived at the question that would determine everything. The question that Gabriela had really wanted to ask all along.

"Well, I suppose the *feeling* is not exactly the same," I said cautiously. "But I think step-parents should certainly do everything possible to give their step-children the best life possible."

"But why wouldn't the feeling be the same?" asked Gabriela, shifting in her seat, clearly not satisfied.

"Maybe it is *sometimes*," I conceded. "But I suppose there's not always the same connection as between a child and a biological father."

"But won't the child feel that?" pressed Gabriela. "Won't they feel that the love is not the same?"

I thought about that for a moment, searching for an answer that would satisfy her. "I'm sure there are times when a closer bond forms over time," I said. "I suppose it's really up to the stepparent."

Gabriela nodded. "Yes, it is."

CHAPTER THIRTY

Doña Olga's health had been deteriorating for months. She was overweight and had long suffered from diabetes. But a bout with pneumonia had landed her in the hospital for weeks. Only recently had she returned home. When Gabriela and I returned from Copan, I went to visit her. She was in good spirits but visibly weak.

"Copan has always been one of my favorite places to visit," said Doña Olga as she sat up in her bed sipping coffee. "I wish I could go there again, but it's probably no longer possible."

"Do you think you'll be able to return to school soon?" I asked. "I know how much everyone misses you."

"I'm afraid it's going to be awhile," she responded. "The doctors tell me that I need to rest." She groaned. "It's difficult being old."

"I'm very sorry, Doña Olga," I said. "I know how important the school is to you."

"It's okay," she said, unconvincingly. "If I can't return, then my children will run the school. It'll always carry on."

This inspired me.

"But enough about me," she said. "How is Gabriela and her two boys?"

I was surprised. "How do you know about them?" I asked.

"I have my sources." She smiled. "But seriously, I've heard some disturbing things about the boys' father. Are these true?"

She was very well informed.

"To be honest, Doña Olga, I don't know what's true and what's not. It's all very confusing. But what seems painfully clear is that this is not the place for them. They need a fresh start, someplace else."

"And you're going to provide that opportunity?"

It's what I respected about Doña Olga most of all. Her directness.

"It's a big responsibility," she continued. "Are you up for it?"

I dropped my head and looked at the floor. "I believe it's the right thing to do."

"But are you up for it?" she repeated. "You're talking about taking three people out of familiar surroundings and moving them to a new place. Not a simple task. A lot could go wrong."

"I know," I conceded. "But it can't continue the way it is now."

"Do you love her?"

"I do, Doña Olga. Very much," I replied without any hesitation. "But I just can't see how our relationship can succeed here."

"Because of the boys' father, you mean."

"Yes. I don't think he'd ever accept it."

Doña Olga considered my words for a moment. "But they're *his* children. Shouldn't he have a say?"

I was a little taken aback. "Even if he abused Gabriela?"

Doña Olga put down her coffee on the nightstand beside her bed. "I didn't realize that. I'm so very sorry for Gabriela. It's unforgivable. But as the father, he can make it very difficult for you. It's not like the States, you know. Women have very few rights here."

"That's why we're thinking it might be best to leave the country."

Doña Olga's eyes widened. "My, my," she said. "That's certainly a big decision. You haven't been with her very long, have you?"

"A few months," I replied. "But long enough to know that I want to be with her."

"And the children, too?" added Doña Olga, studying me carefully.

"Yes, of course," I replied, probably unconvincingly. "The boys, too."

When she didn't say anything, I continued. "I respect your advice, Doña Olga. I always have. I really would like to know what you think. Are we making the right decision?"

There was another long sigh from the lady who reminded me so much of Sister Agnes. "Well, I'm afraid you're not going to like what I have to say."

Doña Olga was right. I didn't like what she had to say. But I'd listened to every word. I respected her too much. When she finished, I thanked her, and then went to see Gabriela.

"What did she say?"

"She gave us her blessing," I replied without hesitation.

I should not have lied to Gabriela, and I'm not completely sure why I did, other than I wanted things to keep moving in a particular direction.

The truth was that Doña Olga had *not* given us her blessing. In fact, she had strongly expressed the contrary. She felt the likelihood of getting the father to allow the children to leave the country was remote. And even if it were possible, was I really ready to be a father? I hadn't known Doña Olga long, but long enough for her to get a sense of me. She intuited I wasn't ready for such a responsibility.

But the simple fact was, I didn't want to be alone any longer. Maria's rejection had been difficult to handle, and I'd never fully recovered. In Gabriela, I'd found someone who really seemed to *need* me. It provided a feeling of self-worth that I'd been missing for much of my life. So, I barreled ahead without considering the long-term consequences.

CHAPTER THIRTY-ONE

"Are you sure you want to do this?" asked Gabriela, as we drove to Tegucigalpa, the capital city of Honduras. "It's not too late to change our minds, you know."

"I'm absolutely sure, Gabriela. I want this more than I've ever wanted anything before. It's not going to be easy, but we'll make it through," I said, so confidently that I'd nearly convinced myself.

"I love you, John," she said, putting her hand on my lap as we drove the winding roads through Tigra National Park in the country's central region.

"And I love you, Gabriela. Everything is going to be okay. Don't worry."

But as we arrived in Tegucigalpa, there *was* plenty to worry about.

With a dark and turbulent history of corruption and poverty, the city had long been considered one of Central America's most dangerous places. Many poor Hondurans living in the countryside migrated to the city in search of work, only to find little available. Consequently, many turned to illegal means to survive.

But two things were different about *Tegus*, as the locals called it. First, as the country's capital, political corruption was rampant, and it'd seeped down into the law enforcement ranks who often looked the other way as drug-related crimes grew exponentially. Second, with nearly a million residents, Tegus was double the size of San Pedro, and consequently, suffered from nearly double the crime.

Crime and corruption are a bad combination anywhere, whether it be in Central America or Africa. But the violence surrounding the drug-trade in Honduras seemed significantly worse than that which surrounded the diamond trade in Africa, even as both supported civil wars. Although I was only in my mid-twenties, in three short years I'd learned an important reality about the world: crime and poverty were inextricably mixed, with devastating consequences.

But despite the dangers of Tegucigalpa, sections of the city had retained a certain old world charm. As Gabriela and I entered the city, we drove along winding streets that meandered down the hillside and into the downtown area, where the Central Park, the Metropolitan Cathedral, and most of the old buildings were located.

We were headed to the Paseo Liquidambar, a bustling pedestrian street that connected the park with the Bonilla Theatre about five blocks away. In between were many shops and restaurants, along with the Museo de Identidad Nacional and the National Art Gallery. And adjacent to that was the National Congress building, behind which was the city's Town Hall, our final destination. We found a parking spot near the gallery, crossed the street, and walked up the steps to head inside.

Before entering, I noticed Gabriela glance over her shoulder. I turned as well, and followed her line of sight toward a man who was leaning against the stone wall that sided the steps. Once inside, I asked Gabriela if she had known him. She shook her head and said simply, "Forget about it."

But it wasn't that simple.

"It's him, isn't it?" I asked. "The boys' father," remembering that he often worked in the city.

"He can't stop us," she said. "So let's not worry about it."

But I remembered the incident at the hotel in Tela and what Doña Olga had said to me about trying to leave the country with the children. "Sooner or later we're going to have to deal with him, Gabriela," I said. "You realize that, right?"

Gabriela stopped in the middle of the lobby and took my hand. "Yes, but not today. Today is about you and me."

I nodded.

"So, last chance to back out," said Gabriela, smiling.

"Never," I replied, although I suspected my voice quivered a bit.

We approached the front reception desk.

"¿Cómo puedo ayudarte?" asked the young receptionist.

Gabriela looked at me one more time. I nodded. I was ready.

"Nos gustaría casarnos," said Gabriela, after taking a deep breath.

We were getting married.

Was I rushing in without thinking about the long-term consequences, just as Doña Olga had warned?

Unquestionably.

Was I naive, and even foolhardy?

Probably.

Did I properly understand the responsibility of caring for two young children?

Definitely not. In truth, they were rarely at the forefront of my thoughts.

I hadn't even informed my father and sister of my intention to marry Gabriella, knowing they would have tried to talk me out of it. That realization alone should have been a red flag. But I was blinded by love. Or perhaps more honestly, blinded by the need to no longer be alone, and by the need to simply be needed.

So, just as my father had always preached, I kept moving forward.

But towards a very uncertain future.

CHAPTER THIRTY-TWO

George sat with his mother on a bench overlooking Crystal Lake, about a hundred feet from where his father was buried. He hadn't been to the cemetery since the funeral, shortly before he had joined the Army and was sent to France. And despite everything that had happened over the ten years that followed, George didn't regret leaving Gardner . . . or his mother. He had needed to get out. There had been no doubt about that. Even his mother had come to understand that.

But her long life had also taught her an important lesson. You can't keep running for a whole lifetime. Sometimes you have to stop and take stock of it all. If you don't, your life will have no direction, no purpose.

Her sense of purpose had always come from her faith. No matter what obstacles life had put in her way, she had always been able to fall back on that.

"You should come to church with me, George," she said. "The prayers will do you well."

George stared straight ahead, across the lake. "I'm not sure they'd do me any good. I think my problems are much deeper."

"The Lord knows your heart better than anyone. He's always there for you. Waiting."

"I know you believe that, Mom," said George, clenching his fist, yet trying to speak respectfully to his mother. "But as I've said many times, I don't share those same beliefs."

Elizabeth had promised herself that she wouldn't get into an argument over religion with her son, so she reluctantly changed the subject. "How is Beth? She must be getting so much bigger."

George turned to look at his mother and smiled, thankful that she had chosen to avoid the confrontation. He had not come home to fight. In fact, it wasn't even his idea to come home. Ruth had pushed him to do so. He had resisted at first.

"She's doing well," replied George.

"And you and Ruth? How are you doing together?"

George knew that Ruth had been in touch with his mother. At first, he'd been angry about it. But he was genuinely tired of always being angry, so had decided not to make a big fuss.

Anyways, maybe the visit would do him some good.

"It's been tough, Mom," he said. "I know it's mostly my fault. But no matter what I try, I can't seem to let go of the past to focus on the present."

"Have you tried speaking with someone? Maybe a priest or a counselor? I'm sure there are many veterans who are seeking help, too. There's nothing wrong with that, you know."

"Ruth has asked me to, many times. But I've always resisted. I guess I want to find my own way."

"But if you haven't found that way yet, Jimmy, then perhaps it's time to try something different."

"Maybe," replied George. He had to try something different, he knew, or he was going to lose Ruth. And Beth.

"Maybe you should think about coming back here to Gardner," suggested Elizabeth, cautiously. "I know it's not what you want, but for a short time it might be the best thing for you. I'm sure you could find a teaching job here."

For a moment George didn't answer. He continued to look out across the calm springtime waters of the Crystal Lake.

"It doesn't have to be permanent," continued Elizabeth, sensing her son's hesitation. "Just long enough to get yourself to a better place in your head and heart. The three of you could stay with me, or find your own place."

"I don't know, Mom," said George, finally. "Sometimes I just feel like such a failure."

Elizabeth put her arm around her son. "You're not a failure. But you've been through an ordeal which would break most men. You're still coping. You just need a little help."

"Sometimes I wonder what my life would've been like if Dad had lived," pondered George aloud. "If I'd never joined the Army. Never gone to France. Never met Yvette."

"You can't hold on to those regrets. They'll tear you apart."

"In my heart, I know that," said George, wiping a tear from his eye. "But my head doesn't seem to want to let go. It keeps putting these horrible images in front of me."

"You're still having nightmares?"

George nodded. "I've tried everything to distract myself. Drinking. Smoking. Working longer hours at the school. Even working a weekend job on the railroad. But no matter what I try, I'm always feeling anxious or angry. Or both."

"Have you ever thought that those feelings may have been there *before* you went to war?" suggested George's mother.

"Before?" repeated George, looking at his mother.

"Yes. Maybe your father made you feel anxious growing up and you've been carrying that inside of yourself for all of these years. He was a hard man to live with. Believe me, I know."

George was surprised to hear his mother talk like that. "I never knew you felt that way about Dad?"

"I loved your father dearly. And in ways which you probably can't understand. But he was a man who demanded attention, and wanted things to be done a certain way. His way. He was often tough on you, but he believed it was the best way to prepare you for everything that was to come."

"The war?"

"Yes, including the war. When it began in '41, he was already quite sick, but he understood what was coming. He knew that you'd eventually be called. He was scared for you. For all of your generation. But he often said that all of you would find greatness. That your generation would change the world." Elizabeth put her hand on her son's knee. "He was right, you know. All of you *have* changed the world. A thousand years from now, students around the world will still be studying about the war. About Normandy. The battle for Berlin. The bomb dropped on Japan. All of it. Everything is different now. And it's because of your generation."

Elizabeth turned to her son and lifted his chin. "No matter what you do for the rest of your life, nobody can take that away from you. You must understand how it defines you, and then do your best to move on. Forgive your father, but understand he did what he did so you'd be tough enough to survive that ordeal. Which you did. And now it's time to finally come home from the war. It's time to move on with the rest of your life."

George embraced his mother and began sobbing uncontrollably.

"But how? How do I do that? How do I move on?"

"You begin again. A fresh start."

George lifted his head from his mother's shoulder, and looked toward his father's grave. Maybe it was time to finally come home.

CHAPTER THIRTY-THREE

For a short time, I found a *home* on Green Forest Drive in Silver Spring, Maryland. I was at peace. But my demons always lurked just beneath the surface of my facade, waiting to rise up and steal away my happiness. For nearly ten years they had been held at bay. But they were becoming restless yet again.

Following our shotgun wedding in Tegucigalpa, Gabriela and I had traveled to Florida to live on Anna Maria Island, staying in Doña Olga's vacation home which she had so generously allowed us to use for a few months as we adjusted to our new lives. Although she had not agreed with our decision to leave Honduras, she had wanted us to start the next leg of our journey in safe surroundings.

Sadly, while we were staying at her place, she passed away at her home in Honduras, with her husband and children by her side. Following her bout with pneumonia, she had been diagnosed with pancreatic cancer. The end had come quickly. Many of San Pedro's most notable residents attended her funeral to pay their final respects to a truly remarkable lady. I'd been fortunate to have known her, if only for a brief time.

While Gabriela and I stayed at her place on Anna Maria, we were waiting for the visas of the boys to be processed. It'd been a complicated process, made even more so by the initial unwillingness of the boys' father to give his consent to their departure from the country. Ultimately, Gabriela and I contacted my former bar-mates at the Grand Hotel Sula, including Dave, who had agreed to pay the father a visit and present him with an ultimatum.

I never knew exactly what they had said to him. But it worked. Not long after, he agreed to allow the visas to be processed.

A few weeks later, Gabriela and I received a postcard from Honduras. On the front was a photo of the Grand Hotel Sula. On the back was written: *Best of luck with your new life. Glad we could help. Probably best if you don't return here again. Dave.*

The question of where to settle in the United States had been another challenge for Gabriela and me. As beautiful as Anna Maria Island was, it offered few employment opportunities for either of us. That left either Massachusetts near my family, or California near Gabriela's mother. We literally flipped a coin one day on the beach . . . and soon found ourselves driving from Florida to California to settle—albeit temporarily—in Long Beach.

Known primarily for the Port of Los Angeles, Long Beach is not a particularly attractive city, despite its proximity to Los Angeles and Orange County. Yet, it's far more affordable and provides easy access to the other beach towns of southern California, such as Newport Beach, Seal Beach, and Laguna Beach. And for two young adults hoping to restart their lives, it provided many opportunities.

Within a few weeks of our arrival in the late summer of 1995, Gabriela's mother agreed to go to Honduras to get the boys, since Dave had advised against either of us showing-up in San Pedro.

It was undoubtedly a difficult trip for Gabriela's mother since it was the first time she had been to Honduras since leaving more than twenty years earlier when Gabriela was still a small child. But she had clearly wanted to reconcile with her daughter and believed the trip to Honduras was one way to do that.

Gabriela and I met them at LAX a week later.

The boys embraced their mother and the three of them shared a good cry. They were together again. Not surprisingly, their reaction to me was more tentative, undoubtedly torn between their father and their mother's new husband. But I made little effort to comfort them, instead focusing on Gabriella.

It would become a common occurrence.

Within a few weeks, the boys began school. Andres was starting third grade, while Fernando was in kindergarten. Gabriela also went back to school, enrolling in a vocational nursing program at a nearby community college to become a home healthcare provider, something she had been wanting to do for years, undoubtedly the result of the time she had spent caring for her ailing father years earlier. I began teaching eighth grade at a little Catholic school in nearby La Mirada, and quickly began enjoying the job.

Yet, my home life was far less successful.

Although things began reasonably well, it didn't take long for things to go sideways. Time and time again it became clear that I didn't have what it took to be a good father, something which Doña Olga had predicted. Although I attended the boys' school events and soccer games, took them to the park most evenings, and to dinner and a movie nearly every Saturday, Gabriela often felt that I was doing it out of a sense of obligation rather than love. This sometimes led to arguments. The more we argued, the more I retreated within myself. It was a vicious cycle.

Upon occasion, outsiders would pick up on our little family's malfunctions.

"Andres seems distant in class," said his teacher during a parent-teacher conference. "He's a smart boy. But he struggles to focus."

"He's still adjusting to his new surroundings," replied Gabriella. "I'm sure it will take time."

The teacher glanced at her notes. "Yes, I know he recently came from Honduras with his younger brother. Maybe he is missing his extended family. They all stayed behind in Honduras?"

"Yes," said Gabriella. "John and I thought it was better to bring them here for a fresh start. Things were hard there."

"I see," replied the teacher, flatly. She was an older lady, clearly with years of teaching experience. "We have to remember that children perceive hardship very differently. What's hard for the adults is not necessarily so for the children. And vice versa. Have you considered counseling?"

"Counseling?" repeated Gabriella. "You think there is something wrong with my son?"

"Of course not. But depression is not something to be ignored."

"You really think he's depressed?" I finally chimed in.

"To be honest with you, he has all the telltale signs. But it's certainly not uncommon with children who have recently been uprooted. A happy home life can make all the difference."

"The boys are happy at home," I replied, almost defensively. "We do a lot of things together."

"I'm sure you do," said the teacher calmly, sensing my agitation. "There is no substitute for the quality time that parents spend with their children."

Quality time.

As the meeting ended, I could tell that Gabriella had become upset.

"She seemed out of line," I said as we drove home.

"Maybe. But maybe she was right."

"What do you mean?"

"I'm grateful for everything you're doing for me and boys, John."

"But?"

"But your interaction with them is … limited."

My agitation was returning. "What do you mean? The four of us do a lot together."

"But it's not really quality time. Is it?"

I didn't reply.

"The teacher was right. The boys left behind a large, extended family that gave them a sense of security and belonging. Now that security has to come from just you and me."

"I'm doing my best, Gabriella. I really am."

She reached across and touched my leg, not wanting to argue. "I know you are."

But was I really?

As I struggled at home, I searched for ways to spend more time at school where I felt more comfortable and self-assured. Over time, this led to my interest in school leadership, particularly due to the encouragement of my school's principal, Sister Bridget, who reminded me of Doña Olga from Honduras and Sister Agnes from Africa. And of my mother.

"Have you ever considered an administrative position?" she once asked.

"I'm not sure I could do that, Sister," I said. "I think I need some more experience."

It was then that she had closed the door to her office and sat down in the chair across from me. "Nonsense," she said. "It's time for old people like me to get out of the way and let young leaders step up. The students like you. The parents like you. You're organized. Speak well. And you have a vision for how you want things to be. In education, those are some of the key components of leadership. You should think about it."

Like my mother, Sister Bridget was an Irish Catholic, having retained some of her old country brogue despite living in America for most of her life. And like Sister Agnes, she believed strongly in social justice, and thought the Church's main purpose was to advocate for the less fortunate. And like Doña Olga, she commanded your attention and demanded the best work ethic. You never wanted to let her down.

To further encourage me to become a school principal, Sister Bridget allowed me to run the school during her absences, which became more frequent as the months went by. She was battling cancer, just like my mother.

Knowing that Sister Bridget was planning to soon retire, I considered applying for her job. But instead I focused on leadership positions on the East Coast, if for no other reason than I thought a fresh start would be good for myself, Gabriela, the boys.

I was wrong, and Sister Bridget seemed to know that.

"I don't know too much about your personal life," she said one day when I visited her in the hospital. "But you've moved around a lot in a short period of time. Africa, New Orleans, Honduras, and now here. That sometimes indicates that a person is searching for something and has yet to find it."

"I suppose you're right," I replied one day, sitting on the edge of her hospital bed. "I've always done okay professionally, but I can't seem to make things work in my personal life."

"It's hard being a stepfather. In nearly fifty years of working with children and their parents, I can't say that I've seen it work very well too many times."

I nodded. "Yes. I'm afraid I'm not doing very well with it. I know what I need to do, but I just can't seem to do it."

"Do you really think that moving to a different state will help you *do it*? You haven't been here very long at all."

I shrugged. "Probably not. But I don't know what else to do."

"Obviously, I've never been married, so I'm probably not the best person to talk to about this." We both laughed. "But, again, I've observed a lot over the years, and the families that seem to be the closest are those who are able to communicate openly. Able to share their feelings with one another. In the absence of that, people tend to create their own narratives. That usually creates even more problems."

It was ironic that I could communicate so effectively at work, but was unable to do so at home. I didn't share my feelings with Gabriela about much of anything, especially the boys. So she did create her own narrative as to why I wasn't more affectionate or communicative with them. At times, her assumptions were right. But when they were wrong, I would become irritated and then more withdrawn, which made the situation worse. But as Sister had said, in the absence of communication, we all make our assumptions.

Even our pending relocation to the East Coast was something that we didn't talk much about. But perhaps Gabriela also thought that a fresh start would do us all good.

Yet, the boys – at least Andres - didn't seem to agree.

"I wish we could stay here," said Andres to me one day as we sat side by side on a bench in a neighborhood park. Fernando was enjoying the swings. "My best friends are here."

"You'll make new friends," I replied, almost certainly too dismissively. "What matters most is that the four of us will be together."

Andres looked at me, clearly wanting to say something. But he remained quiet.

If he had spoken that day, he would undoubtedly have told me that we were not really *together*. That there was no emotional connection. No expression of love.

He was retreating within himself, just as I had done as a child following my mother's death. And for very much the same reason. In his mind, he had lost a parent. And I was proving to be an inadequate substitute.

After only a few years on the west coast, our little family of four loaded-up a U-Haul with our few belongings and headed across America to start the next chapter of our lives in Silver Spring, Maryland, in a little house on Green Forest Drive.

Before leaving, Gabriela and her mother had finally made peace with one another, laying to rest a nearly two-decade-long spat that had pushed them farther and farther apart.

"I've always wanted what's best for you," said her mother, as we all sat in the living room of her modest Long Beach home. "I wish you had never gone back to Honduras, but I always respected you for doing so. You were always the strong one."

"I'm just glad that I was with Dad for his final few years. Nobody should die alone."

As I listened to them, I couldn't help but think of my own mother who had died alone in her hospital room. She was incoherent, often drifting back and forth between the past and the present. Our father didn't want that to be our last memory of our mother. But it'd deprived us of being able to say goodbye. Andres and Fernando had also been deprived of saying a proper goodbye to their father, instead being swept away from him in our rush to bring them to this country.

"Wherever life takes you, my daughter," continued Gabriela's mother, "know that I'm with you, and that I'm proud of you. I wish you only happiness."

CHAPTER THIRTY-FOUR

The train trip from Massachusetts to Montana is a long one, nearly sixty hours, passing through Cleveland, Chicago, and Minneapolis, and then running along the Canadian border before finally turning south at Great Falls in Montana for the final leg into Billings. George enjoyed the ride. The scenery was beautiful, particularly as the train passed over the Canadian Rockies. But mostly he enjoyed the solitude.

Once it left Minneapolis, the train was less than half-full. He knew it was a sign that the country was changing, moving away from train travel in favor of flying or driving. He didn't particularly like the change, but knew it was unstoppable. Regardless, his focus was on Ruth and Beth. And as he sat in his chair looking out the window at the passing landscape, he was nearing a decision.

His mother had been right.

He had never really come home from the war or moved past his father's harsh parenting. It remained hard to believe that his dad's approach had somehow been in his best interest, that it'd somehow helped him to survive the war, as his mother had inferred. The only thing that he seemed to have gotten from his father was a bitter taste in his mouth.

Why couldn't he have been more nurturing? More affectionate? More loving?

But what really bothered George most of all was that his approach with Beth was becoming more and more similar to how his father had treated him. It was a cycle, and somehow it needed to end.

"I'd like you and Beth to return to Boston with me," said George to Ruth, as they walked along the Bighorn River near downtown Hardin, about thirty miles north of Lodge Grass. "It'll be a fresh start for all of us."

"But what would really change, George," challenged Ruth, who had been giving a great deal of thought to everything while George was visiting his mother. "Different location, but the same problems."

"Well, I know for sure that things are less likely to change if we stay here. At least by going home it gives us a chance."

"*Home*?" repeated Ruth. "*Your* home. Not mine. My home is in Kentucky. Why don't we go there?"

"Because I know I can find a teaching job in Gardner. What if I couldn't find something in Kentucky?"

Ruth shook her head. "It's always about *you*, George. What's best for *you*. What about Beth and me? Why aren't we the main consideration?'

George stopped walking and grabbed Ruth's arm. "You *are* my main consideration. I want to make this move for the two of you."

Ruth pulled her arm away. "That's simply not true. You're doing it for yourself. I repeat, why would anything be different if we moved to be near your mother?"

"It's not about being near my mother. It's about going somewhere where we can have a fresh start, but where I'm guaranteed to find a job."

Ruth kept walking along the river.

"I want to stay *here*, George," she said, almost angrily. "I like it here. I like the school. The community. I like our friends. It's a good place for Beth to grow up. If you want to leave, then leave. But Beth and I won't be coming with you."

"But if we stay here . . ."

Ruth cut him off again. "If we stay here, then perhaps you can get some help. Find a way to deal with what you're feeling." Ruth stopped walking, turned, and looked at George. "Look, I want this to work. I want you to stay here with us. But if you're not willing to get that help, then I don't see how it can work. It'll just be the same cycle over and over again."

"She's right, you know," said Alina to George. He had gone to see his good friend, valuing her judgment.

"Whether you remain here or go back to Massachusetts or Kentucky, what're you able and willing to change?" she said. "What Ruth wants most of all is a kind and loving father for Beth. We both know you're capable of that, but Ruth needs to see some evidence of it."

"Evidence?"

"Let's be honest," continued Alina as they sat together on her porch, rocking back and forth on two chairs that looked out over her front yard, with the town's main street less than thirty feet away. It was a Friday night, and many people were on their way to the bar.

"You have two modes of behavior. Either you're lost in thought and unwilling to speak with anyone, or you're angry and frustrated. Ruth understands why you're that way, but she needs to see an effort to change."

"I believe I can change," said George. "But I also think that new surroundings will help."

"Then perhaps the best thing to do is to return to your hometown, find a job and a place to live, and work on *yourself*. Then, maybe in time, Ruth and Beth can join you."

"You mean separate? But for how long?"

"Only you'll know the answer to that, George . . . if you're honest with yourself."

George nodded. Maybe Alina was right, he thought.

CHAPTER THIRTY-FIVE

In my journeys, I had been lucky to meet some incredible people who could easily be described as mentors. Sister Agnes. Mr. Genco. Doña Olga. Sister Bridget. And in Maryland I was fortunate to find yet another.

Father Lawrence.

Although the relationship started with a traumatic event, it would continue for many years. I'm not sure how much he benefited from the relationship. But I certainly benefited immensely.

The world changed on December 7, 1941, with the Japanese attack on Pearl Harbor. Two years later, my father was in the Army and headed to France.

The world changed again on September 11, 2001, with the terrorist attacks on New York and Washington. Although it didn't directly impact my life the way that Pearl Harbor had forever changed my father's, it was nevertheless a day which I would always remember.

It was my second year as principal of my new school in Maryland, located along one of the main roads leading into Washington, DC. Both Andres and Fernando were at my school. Gabriela had recently started an office job at a community-based law firm in nearby Takoma Park, having abandoned the idea of home healthcare because it reminded her too much of her father's final few months.

Following breakfast that morning, we said our goodbyes, got into our respective cars, and went our different ways, the boys riding with me. Our house was less than ten minutes from the school, perhaps fifteen from Takoma Park.

The boys and I had arrived at the school—as we usually did—around 7:30, which gave me plenty of time to get the school ready for another day, including the selection of a prayer for the daily assembly, held in the cafeteria for all of the students following the 8 am bell.

Every time I selected a prayer, I couldn't help but remember my mother, Sister Agnes, Sr. Bridget, and Mr. Genco. Despite my own mixed feelings about the Church, so many of the major influences in my life had been associated with the institution. Not to mention the fact that I credited my career in education to that same institution.

After the assembly each day, I would usually walk around the school and visit a few classrooms, including first grade which was taught by Mrs. Page, whose husband worked at the Pentagon. By the time I arrived at her classroom on that particular morning it was nearly 9 am. I greeted the children and spent a few minutes walking around the room, looking at the work they were completing before going on to the next class.

As I walked down the hallway, the school's counselor stepped out of the staff lounge and motioned for me to come inside. When I did, everyone was huddled around the TV, visibly upset as they watched the images of the burning north tower. As we stood there trying to understand what we were seeing, the second plane crashed into the south tower. At that point, many of the teachers began crying, one nearly collapsing to the floor. We later learned that her son worked in New York's financial district, not far from the towers.

As word spread and more teachers entered the room, we began discussing what to tell the students. Despite my mixed feelings about religion in general, and the Catholic Church specifically, I understood that there were times when religion played an important role in people's lives.

September 11 was definitely one of those times.

I called the parish pastor, Father Lawrence, and asked him to immediately come over to the school for a prayer assembly. In the short time that it took him to walk across the parking lot, another plane had struck, this time at the Pentagon.

I immediately thought of Mrs. Page.

I rushed to her classroom to find her on the floor, with her students gathered around.

She had fainted.

As the paramedics arrived, Father Lawrence prepared the assembly. We heard fighter jets roaring over the school, heading into the city, probably from nearby Andrews Air Force Base.

Parents were also starting to arrive, wanting to pick up their children and take them as far away as possible from DC, which was now being shut down and government buildings evacuated. We convinced most of them to stay for the prayer assembly. But just before Father Lawrence began, the south Tower collapsed. Murmurs began to spread through the assembled crowd of students, parents, and teachers. Then gasps. Then screams and wails.

Father Lawrence, nevertheless, began.

A Harvard graduate who had entered the priesthood late in life, Father Lawrence was the right person at the right time to guide our little community through the tragedy. He was calm by nature and always able to find just the right words to reassure those in need.

By the time he had finished the prayer assembly that day, I could see in the faces of those in attendance that his words had had a calming effect. Eyes were still red and watery, but hearts had been filled with a positive message of hope and resilience. It was the Catholic church at its best.

In the months following the attacks, everyone was trying to make sense of a newly complicated world. Andres and Fernando were old enough to understand what had happened and, like everybody, had lots of questions. Gabriela did her best to provide answers, but was herself rattled by the events. It was my opportunity to step up and help.

But I was unable.

Or unwilling.

At home, I felt unsure of myself. Less confident. More vulnerable.

At work, I was in charge. I had confidence. Purpose. And direction.

In short, I was happier at work than at home.

Just like I'd been in California.

It wasn't because of Gabriela, or Andres, or Fernando. They were doing all the right things, waiting for me to reveal myself. Waiting for me to finally reach out to them, instead of always needing to come toward me.

Maybe it was just easier at work. Maybe there was less need for compromise. Less need for all of those things that my father had once told me were necessary for a relationship to succeed.

But I didn't want to hurt Gabriela and the boys.

Yet, that was exactly what I was doing.

"This isn't working, John," Gabriella said one day when we were alone in the house, the boys spending the night at a friend's house. "You leave early in the morning. Come home in the evening. You even work some weekends. And when you are here, you seem to purposely avoid the boys. It hurts me."

A familiar argument was brewing.

"I'm tired when I come home, Gabriella. I just want to rest."

She was shaking her head. "You know that's not the reason. You refuse to emotionally engage with the boys. It's like you're intimidated by them."

"Intimidated? Definitely not."

"Then what? Whenever I complain, you make an effort for a few days. But then it returns to the same routine. It's been years, and nothing ever really changes. Can't you see how much the boys need you? They'll soon become young men. They need a father figure more than ever."

"I do my best to provide a good life for the three of you. Doesn't that count?"

"Of course it counts. We live in a nice house, in a nice neighborhood. Your school is a good place for Andres and Fernando."

"Then what do you want from me?" I asked, my voice rising.

"I want what I've always wanted. A father for my children." She began to cry. "Maybe we should try counseling. We have to try something before it's too late."

"Too late?"

"This is not the life I want, John. Not the life I want for the boys."

For months, Gabriella persisted about the counseling, believing that it would get me to open up and discuss my feelings, maybe even become more affectionate with the boys.

I eventually agreed, knowing that I couldn't continue having two different personas: one at work, one at home.

And for a while, therapy actually seemed to help.

The counselor got us both talking about our childhoods and the influence of our parents. I talked about my mother's death in ways I never had to anyone. Gabriela talked about her father's passing. I would talk about how my father was too strict. Gabriela about how her mother was never present. I would talk about Africa and Maria. Gabriela about the children's father.

But the thing about counseling is that it forces you to take a hard look at yourself. Often, you don't like what you see.

So while therapy helped our relationship in the short term, I didn't have the courage to keep up the fight in the long term. It was just easier to go back to the way I'd always been. To erect the walls that had always kept others at a distance. The walls that had always kept me safe.

But despite the growing wedge between us, neither Gabriela or I were willing to give up. She still wanted a father for her children. And I still wanted that person who I could come home to every evening. That person who would always say *I love you*.

Silver Spring, Maryland, a northern residential suburb of Washington D.C., has long been one of the most ethnically diverse cities in America. While nowhere near as attractive as its neighbor, Bethesda, a revitalized downtown and more affordable housing make it an attractive location for people working in D.C., providing easy access into the capital via the beltway or major thoroughfares such as Georgia and New Hampshire Avenues. The nearby campus of the University of Maryland also gives the city a young vibe.

One of our favorite weekend activities was to visit the Smithsonian museums in DC. The boys understandably liked the Air & Space Museum most, while I enjoyed the Natural History Museum. Gabriela's favorite was the Native American Museum, which had just recently opened. Each time we went there, I couldn't help but think of my father and his experiences near the Crow reservation in Montana.

As we'd walk along the Mall, between the Washington Monument and the Capitol, any passerby would've assumed we were a happy family. At certain moments, we were. But they were just too infrequent.

To make matters even more complicated, Gabriela had turned to the evangelical church for the kind of support that she wasn't receiving from me. The boys also found some degree of solace there, immersing themselves in the various youth activities.

"They like going," said Gabriella one Sunday while getting dressed. "Most of their friends go, too."

"Their friends from my school go to an evangelical church?" I said, almost laughing. "As far as I know, most of them go to the Catholic church."

"They're getting new friends. Better ones."

"Kids who go to your church are *better*? You really believe that, Gabriella?"

"They feel like they belong there. That's what matters. A sense of belonging."

"It's the same for you?"

"I suppose. Sometimes I feel lost. My church gives me a sense of direction. Meaning."

"Our marriage doesn't provide that?"

She didn't answer.

As Gabriela became more and more shaped by the beliefs of the church, I became even more distant, uninterested in listening to her constant evangelization. I tried a few times to attend. But it was always a disaster. I felt uncomfortable. When Gabriela would see my reaction, it further drove that wedge between us.

"You have to be willing to give in to it. Let yourself go. Surrender to Him."

"It's not that easy for me," I said as we drove home one Sunday afternoon. "The message is okay. But ..."

"It's not about the message," said Gabriella, as the boys listened in the back seat. "It's about our relationship with Christ. If you can open-up to Him, maybe you can open up to us."

Was her church that different from the Catholic church where I worked? In truth, there were more similarities than differences. But to Gabriela, the differences were profound, and she wasn't afraid to constantly remind me of them. In my mind, those constant reminders crossed a red line. A line that separated my successes at work from my failures at home.

Ironically, in a last-ditch effort to save the marriage, I crossed that line myself by reaching out to Father Lawrence for guidance. He agreed to help, but only if Gabriela would participate. Despite her feelings about the Catholic Church, she agreed.

"Although I appreciate everything you're doing for the school," said Father Lawrence, as the three of us sat in his office in the parish rectory. "You need to balance your time at school with the time you spend with your family."

"I think we spend a lot of time together, Father," I said. "But I admit that it's not necessarily quality time."

Gabriela nodded her head in agreement.

"And what *is* quality time to you, Gabriela?" asked Father.

"It's not that John ignores the boys, but they feel that they're some-how . . . in the way. Not a priority. I can see how it affects their self-esteem, especially Andres," answered Gabriela, her arms crossed as she sat in the chair beside me.

"How about that, John?" asked Father Lawrence. "Do you feel the boys are in the way, somehow a hindrance to your relationship with Gabriela?"

"Of course I'd like Gabriela and I to do more things together, Father. But we can't always afford babysitters."

Gabriela sat quietly.

"I'm not really talking about it from a financial perspective, John. More from an emotional one," said Father. "Do you consider the boys to be some sort of competition for Gabriela's affection?"

"Competition?" I repeated.

Father turned toward Gabriela. "You said that John spends most evenings alone in the bedroom watching TV and is then upset when you're late coming to bed because you're spending time with the boys."

Gabriela shifted in her seat. "Yes. Sometimes I feel pulled in two directions, like I have to choose between being with John or the boys."

"Is that something you agree with, John?" asked Father, now turning toward me.

It was my turn to shift uncomfortably in my chair. "We always have dinner together and then sometimes watch TV together for a while. But then, yes. I guess I do go to bed early while Gabriela and the boys are still together."

"And do you ever feel jealous about the time they spend together?" Father Lawrence asked me.

"Not really *jealous*, Father," I said. "But I certainly wish Gabriela and I had more time for just us."

Father nodded, and then turned back to Gabriela. "It seems that the four of you do a lot of *things* together, but that it's not done with the kind of emotional commitment that you're expecting from John. Is that accurate?"

"I don't think I'm asking too much," said Gabriela, her voice revealing some irritation. "I just want him to be a father to my two boys."

Father Larry sat back in his chair, clearly considering Gabriela's response. "You said *my* boys. Do you also consider them to be *John's* children?"

At that point, Gabriela became even more agitated. "It's *John* that doesn't consider them his children. That's the problem," she said, her voice rising. "We've all been together for many years and they still don't call him *dad*. What does that tell you?" Then she began crying. "All I ever wanted was a father for them. Is that so much to ask?"

"Of course it's not too much to ask," said Father Larry, his tone consoling. "Every mother wants what's best for her children. But you have to balance what you want with what's realistically possible," continued Father. "If John hasn't met your expectations so far, is it realistic to think that he will now?"

Gabriela's eyes widened. "So, I should just accept less than what the boys need?"

"Not less than what *they* need, Gabriela," said Father Larry. "But perhaps less than what *you* are expecting."

Gabriela was becoming more and more exasperated. "I knew this was a mistake! Of course you're going to side with him!" she said, motioning toward me.

"I'm not taking sides," countered Father, his voice always calm and even. "I want what's best for *both* of you . . . and the boys. From what I can see at school, they're great kids. And that's a testament to you . . . *and* John," continued Father Lawrence. "And you know something else?"

"What?" said Gabriela, wiping her eyes and nose, and trying to catch her breath.

"I've seen all sorts of parents during my time as a pastor, and to be honest with you, many of them are far less involved with their children than either you or John," began Father. "Most don't have the time, or the means, or the interest. But you and John seem to have made the time, and you have the means. You can argue that your level of interest is not the same, but it rarely is. Children get their cues not only from how they're treated by their parents, but by how they see their parents interacting with each other," explained Father Lawrence, turning toward Gabriela. "You say that the boys don't consider John to be their dad, right? But what do they hear from *you*? Do you tell them that John is their dad? Do they hear you telling John that he's a good father?"

And then Father Larry turned to me.

"Is there something more you can do, John? Maybe spend more of the evening with Gabriela and the boys? Maybe tell the boys how much it means to be their *dad*?"

I nodded. "Yes, I can do that, Father."

"And what about you, Gabriela?" continued Father. "Can you maybe acknowledge the things that John *is* doing well, and focus less on those things you *wish* he was doing. It may never be exactly the way you want it to be. But let's face it, when is life ever *exactly* the way we want it to be?"

In the weeks and months that followed, things did get better. But as was so often the case, it was fleeting.

Was it mostly my fault?

Probably.

No matter what I tried, I always felt that Gabriela wasn't satisfied. A more self-assured person may have been able to withstand that.

Father Lawrence had been right. I *was* jealous of the boys. Not just for the time they spent with Gabriela, but for the bond the three of them shared. I often felt like I was on the outside looking in, like I wasn't needed. And what I really wanted, more than nearly anything else, was to be *needed*. It's what gave me purpose and direction.

And as things continued to deteriorate, Gabriela began telling me that I was *damaging* the boys emotionally, that I was somehow hindering their development. She would often say that in front of them, making things even more drastic and present for everyone.

But a part of me knew she was right. It was a cycle, and it needed to end. My father had been treated a certain way by his father, and as a result had treated my sister and I the same way. And now I was doing the same with Andres and Fernando. How many generations of children would have to endure the sins of their fathers? Where would it end?

In the winter of 2005—with no clear answer available—I moved out.

CHAPTER THIRTY-SIX

The older I became, the closer I felt to my father, despite the fact that we lived so far apart for so many years, seeing each other only during the summers. Would I have felt differently if the visits had been more frequent or if we'd lived closer? Remembering the old adage, *distance makes the heart grow fonder*. Perhaps.

There was no denying the fact that our lives had remarkable similarities and parallels.

His experiences in Europe during the war with Yvette. Mine in Africa, Puerto Rico, and New Orleans with Maria.

His relationship in Boston and Montana with Ruth. Mine in Honduras and America with Gabriela.

How he joined the Army to get away from home. How I joined the Peace Corps to do the same.

Even our personalities were shaped largely by similar events. The loss of a parent. An overbearing parent. Insecurity.

In the spring of 2006, I returned home during my school's spring break to visit my father and seek his advice. I knew that I was at a crossroads with Gabriela, but wasn't sure of what should come next. Should I move back into the house and try again to make it work? Should I give up on the relationship but stay nearby? Or should I move away and start all over again?

"It was unquestionably one of the most difficult decisions I ever made in my life," said my father. "But I'd failed with Ruth and needed to admit it. I'd struggled to move on from the war, and in many ways I never really did. I just learned to cope. There is really no good way of doing it. Of moving on. You just need to take that first step, and the rest will follow."

"So it was *your* idea to get divorced from Ruth?"

"I'd wanted her and Beth to come back here with me," answered my father. "I thought a fresh start was what we needed. But she saw through that. She knew it wouldn't be any different. So we separated. For a while I stayed nearby. But it was too difficult working together at the same school. In the end, it was her who asked for a divorce. I couldn't blame her."

"So you left immediately?"

"Soon after, yes," replied Dad. "I thought it would just make it harder for everyone if I stayed. Harder for everyone to move on."

"What about Beth?" I asked, as I considered how my own decision to stay or leave would affect Andres and Fernando.

"Before I met your mother, I'd go back to Montana each summer to spend a few weeks with her. Of course, I sent Ruth money each month to help with expenses. But within a few years of our divorce, she remarried."

"Did you ever meet her new husband?" I asked.

"Once," answered Dad. "Awkward, of course. But he was clearly a good man and was willing to be a good father to Beth. Better than I ever was. I was happy for them both."

I considered what my father had said. "So you think it's better to just move away and let everyone start over?"

"I do, yes. Others would disagree with that, I'm sure. But in the end, you have to do what you think is best for yourself, Gabriela, and the boys. You just have to make the decision."

"Should I give it one more try?" I asked.

"Again, you have to make that decision yourself, Johnny. But if you don't feel that you or Gabriela are willing to make some significant changes, then it's time to step away and start again. There is no use lying to yourself about it. Deep inside, you know the answer."

I did. But it still wasn't easy to admit that I'd failed so miserably. Yet, my father seemed to clarify things for me. He reinforced what I already knew.

I was nearing forty and seemed to have made little *real* progress in my life. I'd found some success professionally. But it was all overshadowed by my personal failures, first with Maria, then with Gabriela.

What made it most frustrating was that I knew *why* the relationships failed. But I could never make the necessary corrections. As I sat beside my father on our favorite bench, watching the water lap against the stone barrier just below the nearby lane, I realized that he had faced many of the same failures in his life. He had been unable to open up to his daughter, Beth, just as I had failed to open up to Andres and Fernando. We had both erected walls that were built too strongly to easily tear down.

"There is always someone else, Johnny," he said, sensing my turmoil. "It's often the reason people stay in relationships longer than they should, because they're afraid of being alone. Since your mother passed, I've been alone . . . and it's not easy. But I'm old and coming to the end of things. You're still young, with much of your life yet to be lived, and lived well. You don't need to worry about being alone. If you and Gabriela decide to go your separate ways, both of you will find someone else."

"When mom died, you went back to see Ruth, right?" I recalled.

"I did," said my father. "And it was foolish. You were in high school and your sister was in college. It'd been more than thirty years since our divorce, and both of us had recently lost our spouses. But it quickly became clear that it was wrong to try to rekindle a flame which had long ago been extinguished. That was more than twenty years ago now. I've lived alone since, but I've enjoyed watching you and your sister find your own way in life."

"Life isn't easy, is it, Dad?" I said. "It keeps pushing back."

"It does," agreed my father, putting his arm around me. That physical contact was rare for him. It felt good.

"But you can't give up," he continued. "You have to keep moving forward. Someday, you'll look back on it all—with the perspective of time and experience—and you'll know if your choices were right or wrong. But when you're in the middle of it, you just have to make a decision . . . and move on." My father tightened his arm around me. "You'll be all right, Johnny. Just lift yourself up, and find a new adventure. The rest will take care of itself."

And that's exactly what I did.

I returned to Maryland to finish-out the school year, but never went back to Gabriela and the boys, instead choosing to live in the old nun's quarters above the school's cafeteria. I'd asked Father Lawrence for permission, and he had agreed, not surprised that things had not worked between Gabriela and me.

"I'm sorry, John," he said. "But you're both unable—or unwilling—to meet each other in the middle, so it might be the best decision to go your separate ways, peacefully."

I looked at Father Larry, surprised by his comment.

He seemed to know what I was thinking. "I know," he said, chuckling. "The priest is supposed to counsel couples to stay together and never divorce."

"Something like that," I said.

"Well, I've worked with a lot of couples over the years, and believe me, some of them never should have married. Maybe they were too young or too naive. Whatever the reason, if it's clear they're incompatible, do you still encourage them to stay together? I never thought so."

"So you think Gabriela and I were too young when we got married?"

"I think *you* were too young," said Father Larry, directly. "It takes a tremendous amount of maturity for a man to accept a woman's children as their own. Somebody who is very self-assured and without much jealousy perhaps has a chance. But most men are unable to make it work because every time they look at the children, they're reminded that their wife was with another man. To be able to set aside that emotion takes a certain kind of person."

I nodded. "I guess I'm not that kind of person."

"Maybe if you'd been older when you married. But if it doesn't get off to a good start, it's very hard to play catch-up, especially if your partner has high expectations."

"I still feel like a failure," I admitted.

"It's a failure. There is no getting around that. But both of you're still young and will likely remarry. And it'll probably have a good chance of succeeding, because you'll both be older and wiser, having learned a lot from your relationship."

Funny, it was very similar to what my father had said.

A part of me wished I could remain at Father Lawrence's school. He had been good to me. But another part believed it was best to move away. Far away. So when the end of the school year arrived, I began applying for jobs in other states . . . and other countries. I was again feeling that urge for an adventure.

Perhaps one like Africa or Honduras.

I came close to accepting a job at a school in Kurdistan, in northern Iraq, at the height of the insurgency, which had made the country one of the most violent places on Earth. But I came to my senses in time, realizing how difficult it would've been for my father and sister.

Eventually, the right opportunity came along. The timing seemed especially right, as my divorce from Gabriela was going to finalize that July, and the school wanted me to start in August. But those final few months were hard, much harder than I'd expected. Despite everything, Gabriela and I remained close on some level. We both cried the day I told her about my new job, and cried again as we left the courthouse in Rockville following the signing of the divorce papers.

"I'm so sorry it has come to this, Gabriella. It's not what I wanted."

"It's not I wanted either. But we both know it's the right thing to do."

"Do you regret any of it?" I asked, as we sat on the retaining wall just outside the courthouse.

"Strangely enough, I don't. The boys and I certainly could not have stayed in Honduras. There was little opportunity there. Here, we'll be ok."

"It's all my fault, isn't it?" I was trying so hard not to completely break down, still refusing to fully reveal myself.

"If it had been just you and me, then maybe it would have worked. But the boys were always my anchor, in more ways than one, I suppose."

"Somebody will make you happy, Gabriella. I believe that. I just wish it could have been me."

"Me too." She wiped the tears from her eyes.

A few days later it was time to say goodbye to the boys.

My sister was visiting that day, having come down from Boston to support us all, particularly the boys with whom she had grown very close. She and Gabriela stayed upstairs as I went downstairs to see the boys and say my goodbyes. But despite my own tears, the boys didn't cry.

They had never felt loved by me, and had never been able to express themselves confidently in my presence.

As I climbed the stairs, I looked back and saw that they had restarted their Nintendo game. It hurt, but it was appropriate. I'd let them down, and they were as indifferent to my departure as I'd been to their presence.

That night, I returned to my little room above the cafeteria in the school, packed my bags, and took the bus down Georgia Avenue to Union

Station in DC. I'd decided to take the train home to Boston where I would spend a few weeks with my father before departing for my new job.

As I rode the Acela through Philadelphia and then New York, heading through Connecticut and Western Massachusetts before arriving in Boston where my father was waiting to pick me up, I'd lots of time to sit in the darkness, watch the lights of the cities pass by, and think about the past ten years.

In many ways, it was similar to that trip my father had taken to Montana fifty years earlier following his visit with his mother in 1955. You could even say that my father and I had been on that train for much of our early lives, getting off occasionally at stations along the way, but always getting back on as we traveled to the next destination, always in search of something very elusive: contentment.

Dad would finally get off his *train* permanently when he met my mother in the early 1960s. He was nearly forty.

I, too, would be nearly forty when I finally stepped off my *train*, having met someone new . . . just as my father had predicted.

Where did we meet?

The most unlikely of train depots.

Dubai.

The next adventure was about to begin . . . and what an adventure it would be.

PART 2: EPILOGUE

A few years ago, I took my family to Montana and Wyoming to see where my father had spent the five years of his life that seemed to have impacted him most of all. After my mother's passing, he spoke most frequently about "going west," as he always called it. He told only a few stories about his time in Europe during the war, but many about Montana and Wyoming. There had clearly been something about the experience that had changed him, and I wanted to better understand it. And like our trip to France a year earlier, I wanted my children to experience their grandfather's journey. One day, I hoped they would pass on the tales of that journey to their own children, and in that way, my father's legacy would live on.

By then, I was back in California with my new family, living in a suburb of Los Angeles. I was the principal of a little private school, my wife worked from home, and our five children were all growing up too quickly. The oldest, Ryan, had just graduated from college. His brother, Daniel, had a few more years to go, while the youngest three—Nadine, Liza, and Nathan—were all in high school. Like all families, we had our struggles. But to think of how far we had all come, what we'd all endured— especially the children—it always brought a smile to my face. I'd become a blessed man.

I'd finally stepped-off the *train*.

The seven of us flew into Denver, rented a car, and drove north along highway 25, stopping for lunch in Casper, Wyoming, before arriving in Sheridan in the late afternoon where we met my sister who had flown in from Boston. We all checked into the Sheridan Inn that my father had frequently visited with Ruth, and settled-in for a good night's rest . . . although the kids stayed awake most of the night, swearing they had heard ghosts. They had probably been right.

The next morning, we piled into our minivan and drove north through the prairie-land, with the Little Bighorn Mountains rising up to our west, until we arrived in Lodge Grass. As we crossed-over the railroad tracks, we passed by the market that had long ago been owned by Alina Stevenson's husband. We turned down Main Street on our way to the school where Dad and Ruth had taught. I felt I knew the place from his stories.

As we drove slowly with the windows rolled down, it was apparent that the town had all but died. Most of the stores and even the bars were gone. A few kids rode their bicycles in the street, and a few old men sat on their porches. But that was about it.

Much of the town had been abandoned.

We continued along Main Street as it wound its way up the side of a small hill, atop which was the school. As we pulled into the parking lot, we were greeted with stares from many of the students who were on their lunch break. Most were clearly Crow, coming from nearby towns to attend one of the few schools that remained open on or near the reservation.

Walking inside, the school secretary greeted us. We told her our story, and she proceeded to tell us that she had worked at the school for more than forty years. Before that, she had been a student in the school. She showed us the pictures along the wall of the main hallway, organized by year.

She pointed to the year 1952.

And there they were.

My father. Ruth. And Alina.

"I remember your father and his wife," said the secretary. "I never had them as teachers, but I did have Mrs. Stevenson. She was my music teacher."

"When did she leave the school?" my sister asked.

The old lady thought for a moment. "I remember that your father left first. Then his wife—or ex-wife—a few years later. And finally Mrs.

Stevenson. I believe she went to Billings, and then Seattle. She died a few years ago, we heard."

"Do you remember anything about my father's ex-wife, Ruth?" I asked.

"I remember her remarrying. She seemed happy. For a few years the little girl came to school here, but then they moved to Sheridan." The woman paused. "Just about everyone moved either to Sheridan or Billings. Guess you can't blame them. Not much left here, really."

"Why did you stay?" asked my sister.

The woman shrugged. "No reason to leave, really. I have a good job here. A house. My family is nearby. Everything I need. But this place is not for everyone. It's a hard and desolate life. Not much to do except think about everything you've done . . . or failed to do. It can play tricks with your mind."

"Indeed," I replied, recalling my father's many struggles.

Later that afternoon we drove a bit farther north, following the Little Bighorn River, to the site of Custer's Last Stand, where my father had taught Ruth to drive. A cold wind pushed across the open land as the seven of us stood at Custer's memorial. Whenever our father talked about the location, he inevitably mentioned the wild horses that would often graze along the single-lane road that ran atop the ridgeline where the memorial was located. As fate would have it, we saw a small herd that day. Liza spotted them first.

"Look, Dad! Over there! Just like grandpa said."

It was a truly beautiful sight. And a remarkable coincidence.

Sensing our presence, one of the beasts raised its head, and then tilted it slightly, as if wondering who we were and what we were doing there on such a cold day.

But despite the cold gusts, a sudden warmth passed over my body.

I could feel my father's presence.

He would've been pleased we were there.

PART THREE

ECHOES ACROSS TIME: *FROM DUBAI*
TO THE PHILIPPINES

CHAPTER ONE

Following a six-hour flight from Boston to London, a two-hour layover at Heathrow, another six-hour flight to Doha, a two-hour layover at Hamad International Airport, and finally a two-hour flight into the United Arab Emirates, I arrived slightly worse for wear, to say the least. But, as planned, Ramy was waiting for me at baggage claim, holding a sign with my name.

"Mr. John?" he said, looking at the photograph in his hand. "New principal of the Green School?" My new school's HR officer had a heavy accent, but I understood every word.

"Yes, yes, that's me," I replied flatly, so tired I could barely stand.

"As-salāmu alaykum," said Ramy, taking my hand. "Welcome to Dubai."

And so it began.

Located about fifty miles from Abu Dhabi along the shores of the Persian Gulf, Dubai was first established as a fishing village in the early eighteenth century by members of the Bani Yas tribe under the rule of Sheikh Shakhbut of Abu Dhabi. Following decades of tribal feuding, Dubai became an independent emirate under the rule of the Maktoum family, who would rule the city for the next two hundred years.

In the mid-twentieth century, the city established a free-zone port with no taxation on imports or exports. This, along with the city's geographical proximity to Iran, made it an important trading center for the region. Revenue from these trading activities was then used to build infrastructure. Private companies were established to build and operate the infrastructure, including the electricity grid, telephone services, and port operations.

Construction of Dubai's first airport began on the northern edge of the fast-growing town in 1959. This led to the city becoming a center for gold trade. By the late 1960s, more gold was being shipped from London to Dubai than almost anywhere else in the world.

Then came the oil boom.

Abu Dhabi discovered it first in the mid-1960s, followed by Dubai five years later, albeit in much smaller quantities. But it was still enough to further accelerate the city's development plans, which led to a construction boom that lasted throughout the 1970s and saw the city's population more than triple.

It was also the start of America's deep involvement in the affairs of the city-state.

As part of the infrastructure for pumping and transporting the newly discovered oil from the offshore Fateh field, two half-million-gallon storage tanks were built by the Chicago Bridge and Iron Company and placed near a beach which quickly became known as Chicago Beach. Soon, the Chicago Beach Hotel was built for the American workers and their families. Twenty-five years later it would be demolished and replaced by the five-star Jumeirah Beach Hotel, a place I frequented during my time in the city.

Along with America's involvement in the region, there was also a strong British presence as evidenced by the construction of Port Rashid in the 1970s, a deep water free-port constructed by the British company Halcrow. It was the first of many projects designed to create a modern trading infrastructure, including roads, bridges, schools and hospitals.

But British influence in the region was already on the downswing by that time.

For nearly a century, the British had provided security and mediated many disputes between the various city-states, including Dubai and Abu Dhabi. Once the British completely pulled-out, it left a power vacuum. Fearing that Iran would try to gain favor in the region, the various cities decided to unite under a common flag, and the United Arab Emirates was established.

Following the union, Dubai continued to grow, thanks to increasing revenues generated from oil and trade, even as the city struggled to handle the large influx of immigrants fleeing the Lebanese civil war. Many of them would never return home, instead choosing to settle in Dubai or one of the other emirates rather than return to the strife of war. Such was the case for my school's owner, Mr. Ahmad, whose father had come to Dubai in the early 1980s and had found success establishing a construction business, which he had then passed-on to his son.

The Gulf War of 1990 and the 2003 invasion of Iraq had negative short-term impact on the UAE's financial stability, as trade throughout the region was hindered. But by allowing the American military to use Emirati bases for refueling their bombers, the relationship between the two countries became stronger in the long term, with America all but replacing the British as the region's protector. But this infuriated many of the locals who saw America as infidels with no right to be on Arab land, especially given US ties to Israel.

"Thank you so much for everything, Ramy," I said as he dropped me at my apartment in a new section of Dubai called the Green Community following the half-hour drive from the airport along Sheik Zayed Road, the city's main thoroughfare. As we entered the front door, I took a look around the well-furnished, two-bedroom accommodation. "I didn't expect all of this," I said honestly. "Very nice."

"Marhabaan bik," said Ramy, smiling widely. "Anything for our new principal. I hope you'll be happy here."

"How long have you been at the school?" I asked, ready for bed, but trying to be as friendly as possible, despite the late hour.

"My wife and I both have three-year contracts. This is our third year."

"And then you'll leave?"

"We're not sure yet. My wife is from Syria and really wants to return home. But the situation there's getting bad."

"You're also from Syria?"

"No, Lebanon, like Dr. Saad," replied Ramy, referring to the school's director, the man who had initially interviewed and then hired me for the position of the school's principal.

"*Doctor*?" I replied, surprised. "I didn't realize he had a doctorate. Do you like working with him?"

Ramy hesitated, perhaps revealing his true feelings. Nevertheless, he remained professional. "He's very close to Mr. Ahmad, the school's owner, and they work together to be sure the school is profitable."

There was a lot to unpack in that statement, but I decided to let it go, as I could barely keep my eyes open. "I see. Well, I think I'll get some rest now, Ramy. Will I see you in the morning at the school?'

"Most definitely," he extended his hand. "I'll pick you up here at 8 am. It'll be good to work with you, Mr. John. Of all nationalities, I always like working with Americans best of all."

I smiled, not sure if he was being honest or sarcastic.

Over the course of the next three years, I would learn it was both.

My initial interview with Dr. Saad had only been a month earlier, via Skype. From the beginning, he had made it clear that he was intent upon hiring an American to oversee the school's American curriculum. Opened just a few years earlier, the K-12 international school was struggling to find its footing. Although Saad didn't provide many details as to why it was struggling, he did outline his goals for the school and wasn't shy in saying that one of those goals was for him to become the school's director, answering only to the owner, Mr. Ahmad.

Just a few days after that Skype conversation, Saad sent me the contract.

In retrospect, I should have been suspicious of the speed in which I was hired. But I wanted out of Maryland, and Saad had provided me with the means to do so.

As he had promised, Ramy picked me up at my apartment the morning after my arrival in Dubai and drove me the short distance to the school, passing by a number of new office buildings and apartment complexes under construction amid the barren, sandy landscape.

After passing through a few round-a-bouts, a Marriott hotel and attached mall came into view, its lush gardens and green lawns in stark contrast to the desert environment. As we made our way around the expansive property, I could see apartments and villas surrounding a central, man-made lake, complete with a large fountain at its center.

At the far end of the lake was the Green School.

I would come to understand that everything in Dubai was over-the-top. Each new construction in the ever-growing metropolis was meant to one-up the last one. Buildings became taller. Designs more elaborate. And landscaping more lush.

Schools were no different.

In the decade prior to my arrival, the number of international schools had grown exponentially, catering to expats from America, Canada, Europe, and the more developed nations of Africa and southeast Asia. Most of them, including my new school, were started by contractors who had made millions in the construction boom. Sometimes, it was their way of giving back. But more often, the schools were meant to be money makers. Unfortunately, my school was the latter.

As we approached the school, security guards promptly swung-open the main gates to allow Ramy to pull inside. They waved enthusiastically as we passed by their guard house, peering inside Ramy's Mercedes SUV to get a look at me.

I felt like a celebrity.

Ramy parked near the school's three-story, all-glass entrance façade in a parking spot designated for the school's owner. After we emerged from the SUV, two workers quickly appeared to begin wiping the dust off the vehicle which I then realized probably belonged to the school's owner, Mr. Ahmad.

Ramy then guided me inside the school's main lobby. It was a Saturday morning, so just a few local teachers and admin staff were present, including the school's secretary, Mr. Arvin. He warmly greeted me, his accent immediately revealing his Filipino nationality.

"Welcome, Sir John," he said, extending his hand.

Sir John? I thought. A bit much. But I would come to learn that it was the typical Filipino greeting to people in authority. Regardless, it sounded strange!

"You can call me John," I said.

Arvin hesitated, but then smiled. "Whatever you prefer, sir."

"How about a quick tour of the school?" offered Arvin. "You can then set up your new office."

"Sounds great!" I replied, still taking in the grandeur of the school's entrance lobby.

The floors were well polished. A model of the school's campus was displayed in a glass case in the lobby's center. Arvin's reception desk, complete with marble countertop, was off to one side, while a large sitting area with white, leather sofas on the other side, complete with a large screen TV displaying photographs of the school's students. At the far end of the lobby were some offices, including the owner's, Dr. Saad's, Ramy's, and mine.

Over the next thirty minutes, Ramy and Arvin gave me a tour of the sprawling campus which consisted of three main wings, each with three floors. Wing 1 included the early childhood classrooms of preschool, pre-kindergarten, and kindergarten. Wing 2 included the elementary class-rooms. And Wing 3 included both middle and high school classrooms and science labs. Each wing had its own library, computer lab, and cafeteria. Behind the three-winged main building was the gym, and behind that, a large outdoor sports complex with soccer fields, track, and tennis courts.

It was certainly a big step up from the little Catholic schools where I'd been working for the previous fifteen years in California and Maryland. Not to mention a far, far cry from Sister Agnes's mission in Africa or Doña Olga's school in Honduras.

Later in the morning, after setting up my office and introducing myself to many of the school's support staff which included the guards, bus drivers, and cleaners, I decided to take a few minutes to hang some international flags outside my office in the lobby. I'd brought them from the United States, so the pack included a flag of Israel, along with all of the other Middle Eastern countries. I'd simply thought they would add some nice color to the lobby, which was predominantly white.

Fortunately, the entire staff wasn't present that Saturday. But after I'd finished hanging the flags, the few who were there immediately expressed their shock.

"Allahu Akbar!" one of the teachers screeched.

She was soon joined by a few more, all of them wearing the tradi-tional head scarf of Arab women.

Both Ramy and Arvin came running out of their offices upon hearing the commotion.

"It's the flag, Mr. John," said Ramy, reaching-up to pull down the Israeli flag. "You shouldn't display it here."

I was speechless.

And then another screech. "Allahu Akbar!"

Ramy must have seen my shocked expression at the staff member's utterance. "It means *Allah is great*," he explained. "She's just expressing her shock at seeing the flag."

"I'm so sorry," I said to all of them. "I meant no disrespect."

But they would have none of it.

Before I'd the opportunity to explain myself, they were already out the front door. I could see one of them making a call on their cell phone.

"Uh oh," said Arvin, who was standing beside me. "I think she might be calling Mr. Ahmad."

"The owner?"

"Yes."

"Oh, shit," was all I could say.

CHAPTER TWO

Just a few years after the Nazis had nearly wiped them from the face of the Earth, the Jewish dream of establishing a state in their biblical homeland had come true. But their dream wasn't shared by those who had been living on that land for a millennium.

So, near the end of 1948, Israel's Arab neighbors invaded in an effort to destroy the new state. They failed miserably.

Following the war, nearly 750,000 Palestinians fled or were expelled from the land that became Israel, and were never allowed back. They would come to call it *al-Nakba*, the catastrophe.

Of course, that wasn't the end of the story.

For two decades, tensions between Israel and her neighbors simmered, then exploded again in the late 1960's with the Six Day War as Syria, Lebanon, Jordan, and Egypt joined forces in an all-out assault on the Jewish state.

Again, they failed miserably.

For a while, some Palestinians continued to fight using guerilla tactics that the Israeli's considered terrorism. Eventually, many of the fighters were either killed or jailed.

Mr. Ahmad's father was one of those who was jailed.

"I'm sorry we had to meet under these circumstances," Mr. Ahmad said to me, as we sat in his office in the late afternoon following my stupidity with the Israeli flag. He was a big man, in his late fifties, well-dressed in black slacks and a black coat.

"I'm afraid most of the people here do not even recognize Israel's right to exist" he continued in good English. "I know you didn't mean any harm. But it upset some of the staff."

"I'll apologize to the staff immediately, Mr. Ahmad. It certainly wasn't my intention to cause such a commotion."

"I know that," he replied with a wave of his hand. "Saad talks very highly of you. But it's going to take some time to . . . what do you Americans say? Mend fences?"

I nodded. "I understand. I'll do my best."

"I believe you will," Mr. Ahmad replied flatly without looking at me, instead shuffling the papers on his desk.

I then got up to leave, reached across his desk to shake his hand, and waited awkwardly for him to reciprocate.

He did. But the delay was undoubtedly his way of making a point.

It was his school, and he was in charge.

Regardless, the incident certainly wasn't the way that I'd wanted to begin my tenure at the Green School. Word of the incident had quickly spread through the staff, eventually reaching Saad who called me later that day to invite me to dinner with him and his wife. I guess he thought I could use some cheering up.

We met later that evening at the Al Qasr Madinat Jumeirah, a luxury beach resort about thirty minutes from the school. As my taxi entered the sprawling complex, I was immediately dumbstruck at the opulence. I'd read online that it was designed in the style of a sheikh's summer residence. So I'd expected some degree of grandeur. But my mouth dropped as the taxi approached the main building along a winding road that was bordered with tall palm trees, manicured lawns, dozens of flowerbeds, and beautifully sculpted Arabian horses in various poses.

The driver let me out in front of the main entrance, not far from dozens of luxury cars including Ferraris, Lamborghinis, and Rolls Royces that had clearly been strategically parked to attract the most attention possible.

As I walked inside, I looked up at the ceiling soaring above a central water fountain adorned with gold embossed sculptures of animals feeding around the water's edge, undoubtedly designed to mimic a desert oasis. Behind the fountain, I descended a massive staircase leading down to a lower level and a collection of high-end restaurants and a souk. Following Saad's directions, I stepped outside into the humid evening and gawked at the man-made canals that crisscrossed the property, complete with Venetian-like gondolas.

I saw Saad and his wife waving their hands to garner my attention. I'd only seen him once on Skype. He was a bit shorter and more portly than I'd expected. But well-dressed in khaki slacks and a dark blazer. His wife wore a flattering, but modest, dress.

"I think I'm underdressed," I said to them as I approached. "Should I have worn a jacket?"

Saad extended his hand, and his wife, Marie, gave me a big hug. "Not to worry," she said, her French accent immediately recognizable. "We thought you'd enjoy walking through the hotel. Quite something, isn't it? But we made reservations at a little cafe on the other side of this canal. It's much more . . . affordable," she added with a smile.

The cafe turned out to be near one of the resort's five pools, with a good view of the Persian Gulf waters. Some of the people around the pool wore traditional Western bathing suits, including skimpy, two-piece bikinis. But others wore traditional Arab attire of white linen kandoras for the men and the black abaya cloaks for the women.

It was an interesting scene, to say the least.

"Do you come here often?" I asked, sitting across from Saad and Marie with my back to the pool.

"Not as often as Marie would like," replied Saad with a smile, looking at his wife, who nodded her head emphatically. "But we try to go some-place different each weekend. There are so many resorts in the city that you can visit a different one each week, and still never see them all."

"So, you've been at the school for two years?" I asked Saad, just as a pretty Filipino waitress brought our drinks.

"Yes, we came here from Lebanon where I knew Mr. Ahmad, his son, and his father."

"Ramy told me that you worked in Russia for a while," I recalled.

"I didn't work there," corrected Saad. "But I went to school there for my doctorate while Marie was getting her master's degree in art. After that, we lived in France for a while, not far from Marie's home outside of Paris."

"Quite a journey," I said. "Where did the two of you first meet?"

"A few years earlier, in Beirut," answered Marie. "I'd just finished my undergraduate studies in France and was apprenticing for an artist who had a studio in the city. I was only supposed to be there for a few months. But I fell in love with the city and decided to stay for a while. And then I met Saad. He had just graduated from the University of Beirut and was teaching some classes there . . . European studies, I think." She looked at Saad, who nodded.

"And how did you get to know Mr. Ahmad," I asked Saad, wiping the sweat from my brow. Despite the shade and sea breeze, the temperature must have been well over a hundred degrees.

"Mr. Ahmad's son, Ayman, was one of my students at the university. I also met his father and grandfather a few times at some school events. They both apparently donated a lot of money to the university."

"It sounds like the family was a prominent one in Beirut," I said.

"Still are," replied Dr. Saad. "Construction business."

I happened to glance at Marie at that moment and noticed her shaking her head ever so slightly.

"If the family was that successful," I asked, "why did they come to Dubai?"

"Mr. Ahmad's father came here first, and then his son followed years later. But they always maintained homes in Lebanon, and all of the children went to school there," replied Saad. "The Dubai building boom of the early eighties attracted contractors from all around the region, especially from Lebanon, which was in the midst of a civil war. In those early days, there were few regulations about who could own property. Whatever you built, you owned. But by the time Mr. Ahmad had taken over his father's business in Dubai, the government had cracked down to ensure locals were given priority. These days, a foreigner can't even own property without a local partner."

"So does Mr. Ahmad have a local partner for the school?"

"He does," confirmed Saad. "But he rarely comes to the school."

"But he shares in the profits?"

"Yes," replied Saad. "I believe it's a flat fee paid annually."

"Is it unusual for a construction man to get into the education business?" I asked, trying to get a sense of everything.

Now it was Marie who answered. "Not really. Many of the schools in Dubai are owned by families who made their money in construction. But not all of them hire experienced educators like Saad to run the school. As a result, most are poorly executed."

"I wouldn't think there's much money to be made in the education business," I said. "Why do so many get into it?"

"I don't know about the others," answered Saad. "But Ahmad always told me he did it because his wife wanted him to. She was actually going to run it, but then became ill, so he hired Saad to assist."

"Just like that?" I asked.

Saad laughed. "No. After Beirut, Marie and I went to Russia to study, and then to France. But all the while, I kept in touch with Mr. Ahmad's family, both in Lebanon and in Dubai. We'd become good friends. At some point, Mr. Ahmad suggested an opportunity at a school in Abu Dhabi that was looking for an assistant principal. He knew the owner. So I took the job. But after I'd been there for a few years, he opened the Green School and asked me to be his principal, after his wife became ill. We jumped at the opportunity. Abu Dhabi wasn't our favorite place."

"Really?" I said. "I thought Dubai and Abu Dhabi were similar."

Marie scoffed at that. "No way!" she said, emphatically. "The two cities couldn't be more different. Abu Dhabi is a traditional Arab city. Dubai is much more . . . open."

"*Open*?" I asked.

"Less oppressive," answered Marie, herself wiping the sweat from her brow. "Compared to Abu Dhabi, Dubai is like an oasis of freedom—at least on the surface—in an otherwise oppressive, authoritarian part of the world."

It was a fascinating comment, and one that would stick with me throughout my travels around the Middle East. Over time, I came to agree with her.

"So you're happy here in Dubai?" I asked.

Again, I caught an expression on Marie's face which indicated her dislike . . . for something. Instead, it was Saad who answered. "Happier than Abu Dhabi, for sure," he replied. "But eventually we'll probably settle in France."

And with that comment, Marie smiled widely.

"And how about the school, Saad?" I asked, as our food arrived. "How is it doing?"

Saad shifted somewhat in his chair. "I think we'll get it straightened out," he said. "But it's going to take some time, for sure."

"What are some of the problems?"

"Mostly staffing," he answered immediately, as the waitress refilled our water glasses. She glanced at me, and I smiled.

"Most of the teachers we hire only stay for a year," continued Saad. "So we're constantly hiring and training new people. It makes it hard to establish a program with consistent quality."

"I can understand that," I agreed. "Why don't they stay longer?"

"Not happy," replied Marie, as Saad sat back in his chair, seeming displeased that Marie had cut him off. "I've talked with some of them and they think the accommodations and salaries are not good."

"How do they compare to other schools?" I asked.

Marie started to speak, but now Saad cut her off. "A little less. But not much."

I glanced at Marie and saw her shaking her head again.

Saad continued. "Of course we want to pay more. But it's a new school. It'll take time."

"What about the accommodations?" I asked. "Mine is very nice actually. Is it different for the teachers?"

"Very," said Marie quickly. "Ours is nice, too. But the teachers are not so lucky."

Sensing some tension between them, I decided to change the topic. "I gather many of the teachers are American."

"Yes," replied Saad, now sitting forward in his chair. He seemed relieved to change the subject. "Some Canadian and British, too. And a few South Africans."

"That must make it hard, too," I offered. "People coming from different education systems."

"Definitely," agreed Saad. "We need to provide more training. No question."

"So how do you want *me* to help?" I asked. "What should I focus on?"

Saad paused for a moment, clearly collecting his thoughts. "What we really need, John," he began, this time looking at Marie for approval, "is someone who can work with the Western teachers. Listen to them. Help them adjust. They don't always want to take direction from me."

"Why not?" I asked. "You have a strong background in education. And your English is probably better than mine."

The three of us laughed.

"It doesn't seem to matter to them," said Saad, now shrugging his shoulders. "They want things their way and don't like compromising."

Marie looked sharply at her husband, clearly not agreeing with that last comment. "They just want to be listened to, John," said Marie. "Really that simple. They don't think the ownership cares about them."

"Mr. Ahmad, you mean."

"Yes," confirmed Marie. "And when he's not there, Saad gets stuck with it."

"With what?" I asked, unclear.

"With their complaints," answered Saad quickly, generating another sharp look from Marie. "Don't get me wrong. I want to help them. But they have to understand that it's not always possible to do everything they want. Just not that simple."

I was trying to understand what Saad was getting at. "And what is it they want?"

Back to Marie. "For one thing," she began, "the school promises them things during the initial interview that are not provided when they arrive here."

"Such as?"

"The accommodations, for one," answered Marie.

I saw Saad rolling his eyes. It seemed the tension had returned.

"We don't lie to them, Marie," replied Saad, clearly agitated. "We *do* tell them that they'll be sharing an apartment."

Marie shook her head. "But they're led to believe it's a two-bedroom apartment, Saad. It's not. It's a one-bedroom with the living-room converted to the second bedroom."

"They each have their own room," argued Saad. "We're not lying to them."

"But perhaps they *feel* that way," I interjected.

"Exactly," agreed Marie. "They feel they're promised one thing, but then given something else. Same with the health insurance."

Saad was shaking his head more vehemently. "They all have health insurance, Marie. Same as you and me."

"But it's public health insurance, Saad. You can't expect these young teachers, mostly women, to go to a public clinic with Pakistanis and Bangladeshi. It's not even safe for them."

"Why isn't it safe?" I asked.

"Because they're all men," responded Marie. "Most of the laborers here are. You can't put a young American girl in the same waiting room with dozens of men who have been away from their wives for years. It's dangerous."

"I see," I replied. I didn't really, but felt uncomfortable with Saad and Marie's near-argument. "So you want me to be sure they understand the terms of the contract before they come here."

"I think the terms *are* clear, John," said Saad. "But I do agree that we need to provide better support when they arrive."

"And when are most arriving?" I asked.

"Soon," replied Maria, clearly still irritated. "I was at their accommodations with Saad yesterday. There is a lot of work to be done before they arrive."

"I'll do anything I can to help," I said, looking at both Saad and Marie. "After today's fiasco at the school, I want to do whatever I can."

"Don't worry too much about that," said Saad, taking a sip of his wine. "Mr. Ahmad will speak with the staff."

"He didn't seem too happy."

Saad shrugged. "He can be a difficult man, sometimes. But he's happy I was able to hire you."

"Because I'm American?"

Marie was nodding, but it was Saad who answered. "Because you're *qualified*. You'll do a good job here. I'm sure of it. But you have to remember that it's probably different from what you're used to."

"In what way?"

"You Americans are always trying to be collaborative. It's not always like that here," said Saad, who was smiling, clearly trying to make a joke. "Sometimes you just have to make a decision."

Marie, though, wasn't laughing.

"I see," was all I could say.

We finished our meal and enjoyed a few more glasses of wine, trying to keep the conversation as casual as possible. It'd already been a lot to absorb.

Following dinner, the three of us decided to take a walk along the beach toward Dubai Marina. It was a newer part of the city, much of it still under construction, including the man-made lagoon where dozens of luxury yachts would soon be berthed.

As we walked along the shoreline, I must have counted nearly a dozen high-rise structures under construction, most more than thirty stories high. And work was still going, even at that late hour.

"They're mostly Pakistani and Bangladeshi," said Marie, seeing me looking at the construction workers atop the buildings. "Most are working for less than a few thousand dirhams a month."

I did a quick calculation in my head.

"A few hundred dollars to work in this heat?" I said, flabbergasted. "Why not stay in their own countries?"

"Believe it not," answered Marie, "they can actually earn more here, and then send some home to their families. This city is built on cheap labor."

"And the worst part," continued Saad, "is the conditions in which they live. Sometimes ten men to a room, with hundreds sharing a single bathroom. The labor camps are really bad."

"No labor laws?" I asked, shaking my head. "Nothing to protect them?"

"Not really," replied Saad. "Laws here are designed to provide a lot of cheap labor and make it very difficult for the workers to leave the country until their contract is finished."

"Almost sounds like slavery," I said, watching the deathly thin workers trying to endure the stifling evening heat.

"They are being taken advantage of," agreed Marie. "No question about that."

We continued walking a bit farther down the beach until we arrived at another luxurious resort, the Mina Seyahi. Many local Emiratis were sitting near the beach smoking shisha.

"Do *they* work?" I asked Saad and Marie, nodding toward the dozens of kandora-clad men who seemed to be the majority of the hotels' patrons.

Saad and Marie both laughed.

"Most don't," he answered. "Some work as managers or are the owners of businesses. But every local receives money from the government. So, they don't really need to work. There's really only a few hundred thousand *locals* in the entire country. All the other people here are expats from other countries."

I'd only been in the country for one day, and had already learned so much.

As we entered the hotel to get a cup of coffee, I turned back to look at the construction of the marina and the workers that were making it all possible. A few of them were gazing in our direction, no doubt transfixed by the extreme wealth that was being flaunted right in front of them. The stark contrast between their world and that of the hotel's patrons was stunning, and it would be something that I'd struggle to reconcile throughout my time in Dubai.

CHAPTER THREE

Something else that I would struggle to reconcile was my own insecurity. It'd contributed to my failed relationship with Maria and my divorce from Gabriela, and had cost me the opportunity to have a good relationship with Andres and Fernando. And now, it'd driven me to the other side of the world in search of something that had remained elusive for nearly my entire life: contentment.

When I arrived in Dubai, my goal was to immerse myself in my job and hopefully gain some much-needed confidence. It was certainly not in my plans to date anyone or even to socialize much. But when the teachers began arriving for the start of the school year, I found myself attracted to their free-wheeling lifestyle. Most were much younger than I, having come to Dubai as much for the nightlife as for the job itself. And for people in their twenties and thirties, the lifestyle of Dubai could be seductive.

While the extravagant resorts such as the Madinat and Mina Seyahi were not within the budget-range of the teachers, there were certainly many other places for them to frequent. From gigantic malls complete with indoor ski resorts to a limitless supply of beachside bars to an equally limitless supply of nightclubs, Dubai had a lot to offer.

And the teachers of the Green School took full advantage.

The first few times they invited me to join them for a night on the town, I'd declined, feeling that it was inappropriate for the school's principal to socialize with the teachers.

But that position didn't last long.

By the end of my first month at the school, I was a regular member of the Friday Night Club, as we came to call ourselves.

I joined them for the first time during an outing to Barasti Beach, a seaside bar not far from the marina where I'd walked a few weeks earlier with Saad and Marie. It was a diverse group of people, to say the least.

There was Arvin, the school's secretary, who came from the Philippines and had been at the school for three years. There was Ray, the PE teacher, who came from South Africa and was starting his second year at the school. Judy, Ray's girlfriend came from Canada and was also in her second year at the school as a second grade teacher.

Curtis, also from Canada, was the high school's English teacher. He came with his girlfriend, Yule, who was South Korean and an airline hostess for Emirates airlines. And there was Trish, a Brit, who was the kindergarten director, and who came with her boyfriend, an oil rig diver.

"What do you think of Dubai so far," asked Kurtis, as we all sat together in a circle on a set of lounge chairs on the sand, the barista having just brought us a new round of drinks. "Is it what you expected?"

"I really didn't know what to expect," I said honestly. "I'd read about it, but I guess nothing can prepare you for experiencing it first-hand."

"I remember when I first arrived at the school and was living in those staff accommodations at International City. I was ready to quit right there," said Kurtis.

"Yeah, I remember that," said Ray. "I think we were all ready to quit."

"What's International City?" I asked, drinking my Heineken and trying not to compare my new group of friends with my drinking buddies from the Grand Hotel Sula in Honduras.

Everyone laughed.

"International *Shitty* is what we called it," said Judy. "Located right near a sewage treatment plant."

"Why would the school put you there?" I asked.

"Because the school is cheap," said Ray, unabashedly. "Ahmad doesn't care about the teachers. Just his family's profits."

I remembered what Saad and Maria had been arguing about during our dinner. "When were you moved to the current apartments?" I asked. "They seem better." I'd visited them a few days earlier, and while they weren't as nice as mine, they seemed acceptable.

"Oh, they're definitely better," said Arvin. "But when teachers are first hired, they're being told they'll share a *two*-bedroom apartment. When they arrive and see it's actually a one-bedroom."

I nodded. "With the living room converted to a bedroom."

"Exactly," said Judy. "Since we remember how bad International City was, we're okay with it. But for new teachers arriving to expect one thing and be given something different . . ."

"Not right," finished Ray.

"Maybe the school doesn't have enough money yet," I suggested, again remembering Saad's words. "It's still trying to build enrollment."

"Bullshit!" said Trish, sharply. "Ahmad is just a cheap bastard."

I took a bigger swig of my beer. "Then why do you stay?"

They all laughed.

"Because all of our visas are for three years," said Trish, downing a tequila shot. "During that time it's almost impossible to leave. Other companies or schools won't hire you until your visa expires."

"And it's even worse for the laborers," added Trish's boyfriend. "Their companies take their passports and don't give them back until the visa expires."

"How can they do that?" I asked. "Isn't it illegal?"

Again, the group laughed.

"All laws here favor the employer, John," said Kurtis. "Not the employee."

I thought about all of those workers I'd seen building the towers near the marina. *Hard life!* "And what about Saad?" I asked. "What do you all think of him?"

Dead silence, as nearly all of them took a drink.

"Saad is nothing more than Ahmad's puppet," said Judy finally. "He could probably do something about our accommodations, but he refuses to cross Ahmad."

"Afraid of getting fired?" I asked.

"Who knows," said Ray. "I know his wife hates it here and wants to go back to France. They'll probably leave at the end of this year."

"But I thought Saad was happy to be the school's director?"

"Ahmad wanted him to be director," corrected Trish. "Saad was happy with what he was doing last year. Principal and curriculum."

"Then why did he accept the position?" I asked.

"More money, I'm sure," answered Kurtis. "And more power. But I think he'll hate it."

"Why?"

"Because the teachers will now blame him for everything. They can't talk directly to Ahmad, so they'll harass Saad."

"Is that why Ahmad wanted Saad to be director?" I asked. "So he wouldn't have to deal with the teachers directly?"

And why Saad then wanted to pass on that responsibility to me, I thought.

"Mr. Ahmad is not even here most of the time," said Arvin. "Last year, he spent most of the year in Lebanon. In fact, the first time we saw him for months was when he came in to talk to you about the Israeli flag."

Everyone started laughing again.

"That was classic!" said Judy. "I thought for sure you'd be fired."

"Why wasn't I?" I asked sheepishly, looking around the bar at the growing crowd. It was close to midnight and the party was just starting.

"Because Ahmad wants an American to be the face of the school," said Ray. "It'll bring-in more students."

"Really?" I said. "I thought most of the people here hated Americans."

"The religious people do," said Ray. "But don't kid yourself. This place is much less religious than you think. The sheiks play the role of pious believers during the day. But at night, they're at Barracuda buying black-market alcohol with the rest of us."

"Barracuda?"

"It's this place on the edge of town that sells alcohol illegally," answered Kurtis, reaching for another beer in the bucket that was in the middle of us on the sand. "The government knows about it, but doesn't shut it down because so many of the local Emiratis get their alcohol there."

"I thought Muslims didn't drink," I said.

"Some don't," said Trish. "But many do. That's why so many Muslims vacation here from other countries. Here, they can get drunk and party and nobody knows them."

What happens in Dubai stays in Dubai, I thought.

"The hypocrisy here's stunning," said Judy. "But they have lots of money, so they can pretty much do whatever they want."

"Is Mr. Ahmad the same way?" I asked.

"He used to be a Christian," said Arvin. "And then converted to Islam because he thought it would be good for his business."

"The construction business?" I asked.

"And the school," said Kurtis. "Most of the students in the school are Muslim, and some parents would only send their kids to a school that was owned by another Muslim."

"Really?" I asked. "Why does that matter?"

"It's just part of the show," said Trish. "Everything here is a show. What lies beneath the surface is something else entirely."

I was starting to understand that.

"You said that Ahmad goes back to Lebanon a lot," I said. "Does he have businesses there, too?"

Another round of loud laughter from the group which was getting more and more inebriated. Judy was now standing, her sandals kicked-off, swaying to the music.

"What is it?" I asked.

The group looked at Arvin.

He shrugged. "We think the Lebanese government is trying to put him and his father in jail for corruption."

"You're kidding?" I said, thinking back on my short meeting with him. "I thought their family were these big shots in Lebanon."

"I'm telling you, the man is a shady character," said Trish, now standing beside Judy and starting to dance to the heavy bass of the music, their bodies glistening from the humid night. "Who knows how the family *really* made their money."

"Not in construction?"

"On the surface, maybe," continued Trish. "But I still think the school is a front for something else."

"A *front*?" Now I was really starting to feel like I was back in Honduras talking with the *contractors* at the hotel bar. "For what?"

"Nobody really knows for sure," said Kurtis. "But a lot of these schools are started by rich construction guys who have no background in education. And you can't tell me they're opening schools because they love kids."

"Then why start them?"

"Money laundering," blurted Ray, having joined Judy in the middle of our circle, grabbing her by the hips and pulling her close.

"You don't know that for sure," said Arvin, talking loudly to be heard over the music's incessant beat.

"Like hell, I don't," retorted Ray. "In the construction business, a percentage of their earnings must be given to the government. That's not so with the schools. I say they're running their construction profits through the school as a way to avoid paying the government."

"That's a stretch," said Yule, Kurtis' girlfriend.

"No it isn't!" persisted Ray, grinding against Judy. "You'll see. Someday it'll come out."

"What about Lebanon?" I asked. "How do you know the family is being investigated?"

"Saad," said Arvin, simply.

"*Saad* told you that?" I asked, disbelieving. "When did he say that?"

"One night when he was drunk," answered Arvin without hesitation. "Marie knows the story. It's another reason why she wants to go back to France. She doesn't want Saad working for Ahmad."

I remembered how upset Marie seemed to be during our recent dinner. Then, I couldn't quite put my finger on it. Now, it made some sense.

"It's all so confusing," I said, not wanting to reveal the details of my conversation with Saad and Marie.

"Welcome to Dubai!" said Kurtis, smiling, before guzzling another bottle of beer.

CHAPTER FOUR

In the weeks that followed, I wanted to confront Saad about what the teachers had told me. It all seemed so difficult to believe. But I also had to consider the possibility that some parts of the story might be true.

The question was, of course, which parts.

I also didn't want to ruin my relationship with Saad. We were working well together. While he focused on the business aspects of the school and kept Mr. Ahmad updated about the school's profit margins, I focused on supporting the teachers, both inside and outside of school.

Inside, I spent time in classrooms, facilitated training sessions, and met with parents to diffuse various disciplinary issues. Compared with the parents at my schools in the States, the parents of the Green School were definitely more difficult to manage, many of them displaying a strong sense of entitlement, which was understandable given the extreme wealth.

But it was the issues *outside* of school that occupied most of my time.

Despite my best efforts, the teachers—including the members of the Friday Night Club—remained very wary of Saad and Mr. Ahmad. They were unhappy with their accommodations and healthcare, still believing that they were not given what had been promised. The new teachers were also complaining about the length of time it took to process their employment visas, during which time the school retained their passports.

It was difficult, to say the least, to remain neutral. I completely understood the concerns of the teachers, most of whom were young women. They were far from home, in a part of the world where women were not considered equal. Back home, they were used to speaking their minds and fighting for their rights. But throughout much of the Middle East, men expected women to be obedient and submissive. It was a culture shock, to say the least.

But I could also understand some of the points made by Saad, and even Mr. Ahmad. For better or for worse, the school was designed to make a profit. And the enrollment wasn't yet high enough for that to happen. So spending was kept tight, especially with respect to salaries, housing, and healthcare, which constituted a large portion of the school's overall budget.

I was stuck in the middle.

But one thing that the teachers and I could agree on was the importance of always keeping the students' best interests at heart. Always supporting them as best we could. And the students—even the entitled ones—seemed to genuinely appreciate our efforts.

The cafeteria was a place where those efforts were often the most apparent. I enjoyed having lunch with the students and then playing a few games of ping pong. I wasn't that good, so the students gathered around the table always had a good laugh at my expense. But I didn't mind. It served to help break down those barriers between the Western teachers and the Middle Eastern students.

But I also had another reason for going to the cafeteria as much as possible.

A girl.

The last thing on my mind when I arrived in Dubai was another relationship. I'd failed twice, and didn't want to fail again. I wanted to focus on my job where I knew I could be successful.

But my father had always told me that I would find someone else.

And he was right. He usually was.

Her name was Jeana.

Saad had hired a catering company to provide lunches and snacks for the students and staff, and the manager of the company's business at the school was Jeana, a Filipino in her early thirties who had arrived in Dubai around the same time as me.

Jeana was simply gorgeous. Her almond eyes were piercing, especially when she brushed her shoulder-length black hair from her face. She was petite with mocha skin and - most importantly, she wore a constant smile. Although very shy, she would always walk around the cafeteria to see if anyone needed anything. It was Arvin who saw me staring at her one day and encouraged me to speak with her.

"Filipinos are always that way," he said. "Shy and reserved. You need to make the first move."

The *first move*, I thought. *Am I in back high school or something?*

Arvin saw my hesitation. "It's okay. We're just not used to interacting with . . . Westerners."

"There aren't any Westerners in the Philippines?" I asked.

"Some," replied Arvin. "But they're not always the best people."

"Really?" I asked.

"Most are older men who go there looking for younger women . . . *much* younger."

"Underage?"

"Often, yes," answered Arvin. "A lot of ex-military guys. It's the same in a lot of the Asian countries. Thailand. Cambodia. Vietnam."

"So she thinks *I'm* like that? Some sort of a pervert?" I asked, looking across the cafeteria to where Jeana was standing with her colleagues. "She thinks the same about all the white teachers?"

"Maybe," said Arvin. "You just have to earn her trust."

During my short time in Dubai, I'd come to understand that each nationality had specific roles to play. Most of the Indians, Pakistanis, and Bangladeshis were the construction workers, like I'd observed with Saad and Marie at the marina. The Americans, British, and Canadians were—more often than not—the teachers. And the Filipinos usually worked in the service industry, particularly hotels and restaurants.

I'd learned from Saad that salaries were also largely determined by nationality. If you were a white hotel manager, for example, your salary would be nearly triple that of a Filipino hotel manager, even if you were doing the exact same job. It was like a medieval caste system, nearly impossible to get a leg-up because you would always be judged by your nationality, not your work performance.

It was also unacceptable—at least in the eyes of the Arabs—to socialize with people not in your *group*. You would never see an Emirati befriending a Filipino, for example, and they couldn't understand why any American would want to associate with anyone other than another Westerner.

After a few weeks of just staring at Jeana, I finally built-up the courage to speak to her. I waited until everyone else had left the cafeteria, staying behind to help clean up the trash and trays that the students would inevitably leave scattered about, most of them used to having nannies and maids cleaning-up after them.

"You don't need to help us with those," Jeana said quietly, as I began stacking the trays near the kitchen. "We'll do it."

"It's okay. I'm sorry the students make such a mess. It's not your responsibility to clean-up after them."

She just smiled and continued cleaning.

"Arvin said you just arrived in Dubai. Is this your first job outside the Philippines?" I asked.

"You asked Arvin about me?" she said, still wiping the tables.

"Is that okay?" I asked. "I just wanted to know a little about you."

"Why?"

She still wasn't looking at me. I could see this wasn't going to be easy.

"We work together," I said. "So I thought we should introduce ourselves. My name is John."

"I know," she said, but not rudely. "You're the principal."

"True. But we can still shake hands, can't we?"

She finally looked at me, shrugged, and then extended her hand. "I'm Jeana."

"Nice to meet you,," I said, taking her hand in mine, and squeezing lightly. "Maybe you'd like to come out with us one weekend. Some of the teachers and I usually get together for some drinks. We'd love for you to join us."

"Oh, I'm not allowed to do that," she said, returning to her cleaning.

"Not *allowed*?" I repeated.

"We can't leave our accommodation after eight."

"Who says?" I asked, trying to understand.

"Mr. Haig."

"Who's that?"

"The owner of the catering company. He doesn't want any of us to go out at night, unless we have special permission."

I was dumbfounded. "That's not right," I replied, my voice rising a bit. "I'll have Saad talk with him."

Jeana stopped cleaning. "Please don't do that, Mr. John. I could get into a lot of trouble, and I need this job."

I reached out and grabbed Jeana's arm. "But he can't tell you what you can and can't do at night, Jeana. That's your time."

She pulled away from me. "It doesn't work that way for us. It's different for you."

It's different for you.

Those words stuck with me for days, and the more I thought about them, the more upset I became. I wanted to go directly to Saad, but resisted, not wanting to get Jeana in trouble. Instead, I talked with Arvin when we were together again with the Friday Night Club at Nasimi Beach.

"It's true," he said. "It's the same for a lot of the Filipino workers here. If they disobey, they'll be sent home."

"How can that be?" I asked. "Aren't there labor laws or something to prevent it?"

"Nobody will help. She's just a Filipino."

Just a Filipino.

Nasimi Beach is a beachside bar at the Atlantis hotel on the Palm Jumeirah, a man-made island just off the coast of Jumeirah Beach, connected by a tunnel running beneath the gulf waters. In the early evening, it was a place for smoking shisha and sipping beachy cocktails. Later in the night, it transformed into a riotous beach party packed mostly with sweaty expats hopping around to house music and looking to hook-up. As Arvin and I continued talking, Judy and Ray were already working up a lather, while Kurtis and Yume were necking on a lounger poolside.

"But you can go out whenever you want, Arvin," I said, drinking my Heineken. "Why is it different for you?"

"It depends on the owner," replied Arvin. "Ahmad and Saad don't care what we do with our own time. But Jeana's sponsor is different."

"Sponsor?"

"The guy who provides the work visa. In her case, Mr. Haig."

"But he doesn't *own* her," I said, barely able to control my anger. "He's just the employer."

"It's not that simple. We complain about Mr. Ahmad, but compared to most other owners, he's pretty good. Most are more like Haig."

"Did Saad know that when he contracted with Haig's catering company?"

"Saad had little to do with it," replied Arvin. "Haig and Ahmad are friends."

"You're kidding me."

Arvin continued puffing on his shisha nonchalantly.

I sat back in my chair and watched the crowd become progressively more raucous. But I wasn't in the mood to dance. Instead, I sat there for another few hours and got drunk. As I did, I thought about Maria and Gabriela, wondering if I was ready to go down a third road with Jeana. It wasn't why I'd come to Dubai.

But I also couldn't disregard what my father had told me following my divorce.

"You'll find someone else, Johnny," said my father. "So will Gabriela. You're both still young. The right person will come your way again. You just need to be patient and make smart decisions."

"Maybe," I said, skeptically. "But I think I need a break from it all, Dad. I'll just focus on my new job."

Dad smiled. "Nothing wrong with that," he replied. "But when you least expect it, love will come your way again."

"Was it that way for you after you divorced Ruth?" I asked, as we sat together on a stonewall, near my mother's grave, overlooking Crystal Lake, just a few days before I left for Dubai.

"It took a few years, but then I met your mother."

"In Boston?"

"Yes. I'd found a job teaching at the local high school here in Gardner, but still went into the city most weekends for the opera. It was what I enjoyed most."

"You met mom at the opera?" I asked, surprised. "I didn't think she liked that kind of music."

My father laughed. "That's true. She always preferred Sinatra. We actually met at the Veterans Affairs office in Boston. She was a secretary there, and I was doing some work for them helping the Korean veterans get re-settled. Like a financial advisor."

"I didn't realize you did that," I said. "I remember you working at the veterans office in City Hall here in Gardner when I was growing up, but I didn't know you had done something like it before in Boston"

"It was just for a year, and only a few hours each weekend. But it was my way of trying to put the war behind me and make some good use of my degree from Harvard. Almost twenty years later, when you were grow-ing-up, I ran the local Veterans Affairs office for a few years, but more as a favor to the mayor who had been a student of mine."

"I wonder if my work in Dubai will help me to finally put my expe-riences and Africa and Honduras behind me?" I said to my father, looking out across the lake.

"No way of knowing, Johnny. I didn't know that those weekends in Boston would make any difference. But they did. It helped me to put some of my demons to rest . . . and I met your mother. You just never really know where life will lead you. Luckily for me, it led me to your mother."

"Did you ever think of what your life would've been like if you had never met mom?"

"To be honest with you," replied Dad, "I never did. You have to be careful with things like that. Like Satchel Paige once said, *Don't look back because something might be gaining on you.*"

CHAPTER FIVE

It was the 1950s, and Boston had changed a lot in the nearly ten years since George had been at Harvard. Just as the construction of the highway cutting through Montana and Wyoming had dramatically changed life in that part of the country, the construction of Routes 128 and 495 around Boston had many of the same unintended consequences that completely changed the city's socioeconomic structure.

The men who had returned from the Second World War were now in their early thirties, married, and most with two or more children. Many had become stable members of a growing middle class—a predominantly white middle class—and were looking to improve their living standards even more.

The new highways had given them easier access to the suburbs, either to live or to work, or both. Businesses realized that they could leave the higher rents of the city and move their offices into the suburbs, knowing that the highways would still make them accessible to their employees. But the so-called *white flight* from the cities to the suburbs had left behind a mostly lower-income, minority population. This resulted in higher crime rates and a slow, yet steady, dilapidation of the city's appearance, as the focus of community improvements shifted to the suburbs.

Being more than an hour to the west of Boston, Gardner wasn't considered a suburb of the city, and George didn't frequently use Routes 128 or 495. But what he did notice was the city's changing appearance. While at Harvard, the city had been clean and reasonably safe to walk around at night. But now there were a lot of boarded-up storefronts, tenements in a continual state of disrepair, and the need to constantly look over your shoulder when walking to the subway station following an evening's show at the Schubert or Colonial Theatres.

Nevertheless, George looked forward to his weekend getaways in the city. He'd usually take the train from the West Street station in Gardner into Union Station on a Saturday morning, then take the Red Line to Government Center to work at the Veterans Affairs office on the third floor. His mother had helped to secure the job for him through a contact at her church who was also a veteran and also struggling to put his nightmares to rest. He had found some degree of solace in helping other veterans, and had suggested the same for George.

It became a godsend.

By helping Korean vets to organize their finances and re-enter society as contributing citizens, George had found a use for his finance degree from Harvard. He had found a purpose for being, something that made his horrible experiences in the war a little more bearable. It didn't pay much, but it didn't really matter. He would've done it for free. Anything to rid his mind of those blistering images that had infected his sleep for more than a decade. They hadn't completely abandoned him, but they had become tolerable. What remained, he could manage with some self-discipline, the specialty of his generation.

During his third month at the office, he had first met my mother. She typically worked weekdays as a receptionist in the main lobby of the same third floor, but had been asked to come in one weekend to cover for a sick employee. When that employee was unable to return, she had become a regular face on the Saturday shift. And to George, what a beautiful face it was.

"My name is George," he said to her, finally garnering the courage to approach her desk after staring at her for much of the morning.

"I'm Kathleen," she said, with a wide smile, her red hair falling softly over the side of her face, covering some of her freckles. "You work in the Veterans Affairs office, right?"

"Just started last month." replied George.

"You're a veteran, too?" she asked.

"I am. Second World War. Europe." It'd always been something that George preferred not to mention. But now, he was able to say it freely, and proudly.

"You're doing important work," said Kathleen. "It must make you feel good."

"It does," answered George. "I wish I'd done it years ago."

Kathleen nodded, her smile widening even further.

Following that first introduction, they had met a few times for coffee in the little cafe on the first floor, before finally agreeing to meet for dinner. It was a big step for Kathleen, who lived alone with her mother in Jamaica Plain and rarely dated, preferring to spend her free time with her close group of friends. There was also the fact that George wasn't Irish, nor Catholic, and was divorced, three points that she knew would displease her mother. But at nearly thirty years of age, she was ready for her first real boyfriend. And George seemed to fit the bill. He was smart, reasonably good-looking, if not a bit too thin, and had so far treated her with kindness and respect.

For their first date, George had purposely chosen the Union Oyster House on Union Street near Faneuil Hall marketplace. He knew that Kathleen would appreciate the fact that it was frequented by members of the Kennedy family who were idolized in Massachusetts, especially the younger Jack who was rumored to be considering a run for the White House in 1960. George didn't care much about politics, but knew that Kathleen did. When she saw the booth beside theirs adorned with the plaque *"Permanently reserved for members of the Kennedy family,"* she was suitably impressed.

"Maybe they'll come here tonight," she said, giggling. "I'd do anything to see Jack and his new wife, Jacqueline. She's so pretty."

"I thought you'd get a kick out of it," replied George, waiting for Kathleen to sit before he took his seat across from her in the booth.

The restaurant itself, located on the first floor, was the oldest in Boston, having been a seafood house since 1742. The first stirrings of the American Revolution had once occurred on the second floor of the building in the offices of *The Massachusetts Spy*, long known as the oldest newspaper in the United States. George smiled as he watched Kathleen admire the framed copies of some of those early editions that now hung from the walls of the restaurant.

"They say that the future king of France, Louis Phillippe, lived on the third floor of this building in the late 1700s after being exiled during the French Revolution," said George. "While here, he earned money by teaching French to many of Boston's wealthy families."

"It must have been an amazing time to live in the city," said Kathleen, looking around the restaurant. "I would've loved to have been a part of it."

"Didn't you say that your father helped to build the subway?" said George, remembering some of their earlier discussions. "He certainly played an important role in the city's history."

"He was just a ditch-digger," replied Kathleen. "But, yes, he did work on the Red Line after he arrived with my mother from Ireland just after the First World War."

"You should still be proud," said George. "The Irish built much of our eastern cities. Without them, and other immigrant groups like them, the country would be a completely different place."

"Better or worse?" asked Kathleen, smiling.

"Oh, much, much worse," answered George, knowing that Kathleen was joking. "I served with a lot of Irish in France. They were tough fighters, and always talked longingly about Ireland."

"My father had always wanted to go back, but died before saving money to return."

"Do you think your mother will ever visit?"

"Probably not," replied Kathleen, taking the menu from the waitress. "As a hospital cleaner, she'll never have enough money either."

"But she must be proud of you," said George.

Kathleen shrugged. "I suppose. But it was hard on her when dad died. They were always so close. Without him, she was really lost for a while."

"So it's good that you still live with her."

"Good for *her*, not for me," snapped Kathleen, then catching herself and calming down. "But it's all right. Eventually, I'll get my own place."

"Believe me, I know how you feel," said George, looking over his menu. "My mother and I don't always get along, either. But it's certainly better now than it was years ago."

"But you don't live with her."

"No, but for a while I did, when I returned from Montana. Then I found my own place near the high school where I work. But I still try to visit her each weekend. I know it's important to her."

"Do you think she would like me?" asked Kathleen, looking up from her menu. "She's not Catholic, right?"

George laughed. "No, she's *definitely* not Catholic. But I think she'd like you. If she knew I was happy, then she'd be okay with it." George wasn't so sure that was true, but figured it wasn't the time to discuss his mother's narrow religious views.

"You're not a regular churchgoer, I take it?" asked Kathleen.

"I go once in a while with my mother. But, no, Certainly not a regular."

"But you believe in God, right?"

George put down his menu. "I used to think very little about it. But I suppose the war changed that. On one hand, you wonder how a God could have let such devastating things happen. But on the other hand, you want to think that all those men who died went to a better place."

Kathleen looked at George. "It must have been such a horrible experience."

"It changed me," answered George. "That's for sure. And I'm only just now finding ways to process it all." He hadn't told Kathleen about Yvette, and had only said a few things about Ruth and Beth. "But it's a part of me now, like it or not. So I might as well use the experience to do some good."

"At the veteran's office?"

"Yes," replied George. "I'm so glad to have the opportunity. And without it, you and I would never have met."

Kathleen reached across the table and put her hand atop George's. "And I'm so glad we did."

George smiled. He was happy. Happier than he had been in quite some time.

CHAPTER SIX

After learning that Jeana was trapped by her employer—unable to enjoy a night out, and unable to look for a new job—I became solely focused on finding a way to help her.

Was it my place to do so?

Probably not.

Did I risk putting her in trouble?

Most definitely.

I also risked my own job because of her employer's friendship with Mr. Ahmad. But the situation was so wrong on so many different levels I just couldn't let it go.

I continued to learn more about the country's labor's laws—searching for a possible loophole that I could use to help Jeana—and continued to go to the school's cafeteria every day to see her.

It was always the high point of my day.

But our interaction was starting to draw the attention of other staff members, particularly the Islamic studies teachers who already didn't like me much because of the incident with the Israeli flag. At least I could understand that. But I just couldn't understand why they were so opposed to interracial relationships.

"The same thing happened to us last year," said Judy one day in the cafeteria when she saw me sitting alone at the staff table brooding. "Interracial relationships are looked down upon by most locals. When Ray and I started dating last year, we got all sorts of nasty looks from them."

"What did you do about it?" I asked, listening to Judy, but looking across the cafeteria at Jeana who was standing near the food-line smiling, as she always did, no matter the situation.

"In the beginning, it was hard," said Judy. "Ray wanted to respond. But I knew it would only make things worse. So we did our best to ignore it."

"Did their attitude change?"

Judy shrugged. "No. We still get some nasty looks. But not as many. Or maybe we just don't notice anymore."

"I try to ignore them, too." I said, drinking a bottled water. "But it's hard. Sometimes it just makes me so angry. It's none of their business."

"No, it's not," agreed Judy. "But you have to remember that it's their culture. We come from an open society. They don't. We can't really expect them to look at things the same way we do. They just don't know any better."

They just don't know any better.

On some level—despite my irritation—I found Judy's comment to be condescending. But I understood it. Tolerance is something learned, mostly through observation. If you're surrounded by intolerant people, then you're likely to be intolerant yourself. I couldn't expect them to change. I just had to ignore the criticisms and dirty looks. After all, I was living in *their* country, so I'd to follow *their* social norms.

But in doing so, it was like I was living two lives: one in public, and one in private. It certainly gave me a different perspective on what I'd previously considered to be hypocritical behavior.

By day, the sheiks—and their like—would appear to be pious believers of Islam who looked down upon drinking, dancing, and public displays of affection. Then by night, they'd buy their alcohol illegally, find a place out of public view, and exhibit the very behavior that they had shunned during the day.

But I had to remember that it was the result of a closed society. Inevitably, it created an underground culture, hidden from public view, but still very much a part of everyday life.

"Are you okay," asked Jeana, after everyone had left the cafeteria. "I saw you talking with Miss Judy." Jeana always wore her uniform. White shirt. Black pants. It was simple. And so was she. It was part of what attracted me to her.

"She was just trying to make me feel better," I replied, helping to clean-up the tables.

"Was she successful?" asked Jeana with a smile.

That smile! It always got me.

"I understood what she was saying. But it's still hard," I admitted, trying unsuccessfully to smile.

"Then maybe you should spend less time here. It just gives people something to talk about."

I stared at Jeana for a moment, not quite believing she had just said that. "But we're not doing anything wrong," I contested. "We're just talking."

"But to them, it's an American talking to a Filipino. They don't like it."

"I don't care."

Jeana stopped cleaning for a minute. "You have to care, John. It's not worth risking our jobs."

"Maybe it is," I said, honestly. "Maybe it's worth the principle."

"I don't understand."

"Some things are worth fighting for. Maybe this situation is one of them."

"But what can we do? I'm stuck with Mr. Haig," she said, with a sigh.

"I'm not so sure."

A few days earlier I'd met with an attorney who had been recommended by Marie, Saad's wife. I'd told her about Jeana and how unfairly she was being treated. Marie wasn't surprised, and suggested I meet with a friend of hers who understood Middle Eastern culture, but had studied law in the United States.

"It happens to so many workers here, not only Filipinos," explained the attorney to me the next day in his office in Deira, a poorer suburb of Dubai. "But most don't understand the law or have the money to hire an attorney. Or they're just too scared of being sent home."

"So what do you suggest?" I asked. "I want to help her, but don't know how."

The attorney studied me for a moment before continuing. "You like this girl, I can see that. But you need to be careful. The locals don't see things the way you do."

"But you understand how wrong it is, right? You've lived in the United States."

The attorney sat back in his chair. "Regardless of whether or not I lived in America, I agree it's wrong. But that doesn't necessarily matter."

"You're telling me there's nothing that can be done?"

"I didn't say that," he said, waving his hand. "Has her work visa been processed yet?"

"Processed?" I didn't understand.

"Yes. If she came from the Philippines, then she probably came here through an agent who provided a temporary visa. Once she arrived, she was hired by . . . what's his name again?"

"Mr. Haig."

"Yes. This Mr. Haig pays a fee to the agent and then needs to process her work visa. If she hasn't been with him for long, then the process is still probably ongoing."

"Meaning?"

"Meaning that another sponsor can still claim her," said the Lebanese attorney.

"Claim her?" I repeated. It sounded like human bondage.

"Another potential employer can offer her a job and process her visa," explained the attorney. "Does she still have her passport?"

"I believe so, yes," I confirmed.

"Then it's definitely possible. The visa can't be processed without her passport. Tell her to keep it, no matter what, and look for another employer. But you need to move quickly. The temporary visa will expire within ninety days of her arrival in the country and can't be renewed from within the country."

"She would need to leave the country?"

"Correct. Some go to Kish."

"Kish?"

"A small island in the gulf," replied the attorney. "It's actually part of Iran. Many Filipinos are sent there to renew their visas. But it's a bad place. You want to avoid it. How long has she been in the country?"

"Just a few months. Same as me."

"Then she has less than that to find a new employer."

"Is that enough time?" I asked, for the first time, feeling a glimmer of hope.

"It'll be hard," he said. "But there may still be a way."

As he explained it to me, I sat in my chair and listened carefully. It seemed like such a long shot. Yet, I was determined to give it a try.

CHAPTER SEVEN

Located south of downtown Boston along the subway's Yellow line, Jamaica Plain was first founded by Puritans in the seventeenth century. Originally part of the town of Roxbury, it became part of Boston in the late nineteenth century and was one of the first streetcar suburbs in America, allowing residents to work within the city's boundaries while still enjoying the more open spaces found outside the city.

By the early twentieth century, Jamaica Plain had a significant immigrant population, consisting primarily of Irish who settled in large numbers along Heath Street and South Street, part of the Forest Hills and Stony Brook neighborhoods. Many of the men, like Kathleen's father, worked on the subway lines under construction across the city, while the women either stayed home with the children or took domestic jobs.

With the presence of so many Irish, religion naturally played a significant role in the local life of Jamaica Plain during those early years. Many new Catholic churches rose, including Our Lady of Lourdes in the Brookside neighborhood where Kathleen's mother had long attended services each Sunday. With Irish families often consisting of three or more children, many of the churches soon built elementary schools that anchored the parish and also helped to ensure future generations of parishioners.

Kathleen had attended such a school.

In addition to religion and education, the churches also provided women's, children's, and missionary groups that brought together neighbors of different economic classes. In nearly all ways that mattered, the churches were the center of immigrant life.

Following Sunday sermons, many parishioners went to one of Jamaica Plain's many parks to enjoy an afternoon picnic and allow the children to run free, which was always a welcomed activity following a week of being cooped-up in the tenement houses where most of the residents of Jamaica Plain lived. The most popular parks included Olmsted Park, Jamaica Pond, the Arnold Arboretum and Franklin Park. Kathleen's favorite was Jamaica Pond, where you could skate in the winter and fish in the summer, an activity which she particularly enjoyed because it was one of the few she could do with her father.

"Were you close to him?" asked George, as he walked beside Kathleen along one of the many paths that crisscrossed the rolling hills around Jamaica Pond, a landscape that reminded him a lot of Crystal Lake near his childhood home in Gardner.

"Not really," replied Kathleen, wearing a knee-length skirt and blue blouse that accented her shoulder-length red, curly hair and freckled face. "He always seemed to be working. He would come home dead-tired at night, eat dinner, and go to bed. He even worked most Saturdays. Sunday was our day together."

"It must have been hard on your mom when he died," said George, remembering how hard it was for his own mother when his father had died.

"Without me to help her, I don't think she would've made it through."

"But you can't live with her forever," said George. "Eventually you'll need to get your own place."

"I know," admitted Kathleen. "Believe me, I wish I could get my own place right now. But it's still too soon to leave her. Maybe in a few more years ."

George nodded, understanding. "Your parents must have gone through a lot when they first arrived in the country. Did they talk much about it?"

"A little," replied Kathleen. "I pieced things together over time."

"When did they arrive?'

"1918," answered Kathleen. "They were only teenagers when they arrived in New York, eventually making their way to Boston. Ten years later, they had me."

Kathleen was just a few years younger than George.

"I know those early years were hard for them," continued Kathleen. "The Irish were not well-liked back then, most people felt they were taking away jobs from the Yankees . . ." Kathleen stopped suddenly. "I didn't mean your family . . ."

George laughed. "It's okay. I don't think my mother or father ever thought of themselves as Yankees, but I suppose they were. They were both from New England. I also heard that term a lot when I was in France during the war. The Brits and Irish always called me the *damn Yankee.*"

"That's horrible!" said Kathleen, as they continued walking slowly along the pond's edge.

"It's okay. They were probably right. Many of the original New Englanders thought of themselves as somehow superior to the new immigrants. Which they weren't, of course."

"I suppose your parents and mine would never have been friends," said Kathleen. "But maybe our generation will be different."

"It's already different. Your Senator Kennedy could never have run for president even ten years ago. The country wouldn't have accepted an Irish Catholic. But now . . ."

"I hope he runs, and wins. The country needs a young leader."

"It would certainly make the Irish community proud," said George. "Does your mother like him?"

"She doesn't really follow politics much. She doesn't have a television and can't read very well, so gets most of her news from her friends."

"She never went to school back in Ireland?" asked George.

"She never finished high school. Neither did my father."

"Where in Ireland were they from?"

"County Galway," said Kathleen, a tinge of pride in her voice. "My mother always said how beautiful it was there."

"I knew a soldier from Galway," said George, recalling a member of the unit that brought him into Lorient in the winter of 1944-45. "He said the countryside in Brittany reminded him of Galway. It sounded beautiful."

"I believe it was," said Kathleen. "My mother still considers it her home."

As two teenagers in love, Sean and Bridget took every opportunity to explore the countryside surrounding Tuam in County Galway, anything to get away from their parents and the seemingly endless grind of daily life.

It was a hard existence. No getting around it.

And ever since the potato crops began failing again, it'd only gotten harder.

Both kids had dropped out of school to help their parents, doing anything they could to earn some extra money for the family. Some days that meant working in the fields to harvest what they could of the family's potato crop. Other days it meant walking around their small town of a few thousand offering their services to anyone who could pay, whether it be cleaning horse stalls, hauling water from the wells, or babysitting children while their parents were in the fields.

But as hard as it was, it was still far better than being at home and seeing how depressed their parents had become.

Just a few years earlier, both Sean's and Bridget's families had been comfortable. Certainly not wealthy. But comfortable. Both families owned their land—which was unusual for the time—and both were able to grow enough to feed their family with enough left over to sell in the local markets.

But then came three straight years of unusually cool, moist weather causing much of those years' potato crops to rot in the fields. While it was nowhere as bad as the Great Famine of a half century earlier when nearly a third of the population had died, it was still bad enough, causing many small town residents to relocate to Galway City where a growing number of manufacturing jobs were available. But as those jobs were quickly taken, many left for the promise of America.

Sean's grandfather had gone in the years following the Great Famine, promising his family that he would make a new life in America and then bring them all across.

But they had never heard from him again.

There were always rumors of how badly the Irish were treated on the mean streets of America's eastern cities. So, the family had decided to do whatever it took to hang on to their life in the little town of Tuam. Their gamble eventually paid off when the potato crops came back and life returned to normal.

But a few decades later, it happened again.

"Do you think your family will leave?" asked Bridget of Sean, as they walked along the dirt roads of Tuam, heading home to their respective families after a long day of doing odd jobs.

"I don't think my father will leave," replied Sean. "He remembers what happened to my grandfather. He doesn't trust the Americans. Says it's better to take our chances here."

"What do you think?" asked Bridget, reaching for Sean's hand. "Do you want to stay here?"

"You know the answer to that," said Sean. "I want nothing more than to leave."

"To America?"

"Maybe," answered Sean. "But anywhere is okay, so long as it's not here. So long as we're together."

Bridget smiled and squeezed Sean's hand. "Me too."

CHAPTER EIGHT

Anchored by the Courtyard Marriott, the Green Community is one of Dubai's newer neighborhoods. As the city continued to expand southward along the coastline toward Abu Dhabi, new developments were springing-up, seemingly overnight. But few were as extensively planned as the Green Community, catering to the ever-growing expat population who were looking for more green spaces to remind them of home.

The Marriott and its attached mall had been built first, complete with a man-made lake around which villas and townhomes were soon constructed. Later came the track-homes in the style of southwestern American neighborhoods, extending outward like spokes on a wheel from the central hotel. When the project was done, the desert had been transformed into an oasis of residences, lawns, parks, soccer fields, and even a golf course, all kept green by means of recycled sewer water.

I'd been going to the mall regularly since I'd first arrived at the Green School, either to get some dinner in one of the many restaurants or to enjoy a drink with the Friday Night Club at the hotel's roof-top bar overlooking the lake.

But it was also where Jeana and I met for the first time outside of the school.

We'd been planning it for a few weeks, knowing that the school was scheduled to have an early dismissal for the teachers to attend an afternoon workshop. At first, she had been reluctant, fearing that Mr. Haig would find out. But her coworkers had promised to cover for her, giving us some much-welcomed time together out of view of the teachers and students to discuss the plans that I'd developed with the attorney who I'd met in Deira.

"What if someone sees us," said Jeana, looking around the Marriott's second-floor restaurant.

"Don't worry," I said. "The teachers are all at the school in training. There's nothing to worry about."

"Won't the teachers be looking for you?"

"I'll go back in a few hours to wrap up the meeting after they finish with the workshop facilitator."

She nodded, but kept looking over her shoulder.

After ordering some sandwiches from the Filipino waitress who smiled at Jeana, I began to explain the plan that the attorney and I'd crafted, the plan that would hopefully free Jeana from her contract with Mr. Haig. She listened, but seemed skeptical from the start.

"How can *you* be my employer?" she asked. "It doesn't make any sense."

"Expats in Dubai have maids and nannies, most of whom are Filipino. The Labor Department would just assume you were my maid or personal assistant. They wouldn't ask any questions."

"But Mr. Haig would never agree to that, especially if he knew you worked for Mr. Ahmad."

"He would never know. That's the beauty of it. Haig already paid the agent who brought you here from the Philippines. So he'll need to be paid back. The attorney can do that for us without ever revealing my identity. Then, since Haig hasn't processed your visa yet, another employer can still hire you. And that employer will be me. It happens all the time."

"Really?" she said. "I never heard other Filipinos saying that. They all think they're trapped."

"Because their visas are already processed," I explained. "Haig hasn't processed your visa because you're still in possession of your passport. That's your advantage. But we have to move fast. In another few weeks your tourist visa which was provided by the agent will expire and you'll need to leave the country."

"To Kish?"

"You know it?" I asked.

"Of course, a lot of Filipinos are sent there when their employers don't process their visas in-time. I know a girl who was raped there, went home."

I reached across the table to put my hand on Jeana's. "Don't worry, that won't happen to you. The attorney will meet Haig next week to pay back the fee, and will then help me process your visa to become my assistant. It's perfect. After that, you can find any job you want."

"But then *you'll* be my sponsor," said Jeana. "I won't be able to work for anyone else."

"Not true," I said. "The attorney explained to me that employees have six months to change employers after an employment visa is issued. It just rarely happens because the employer usually keeps their passport."

"Looks like you've thought of everything," said Jeana.

But I could tell that Jeana was still worried.

"It's not without risk, that's for sure," I admitted. "But the attorney seems confident that it'll work."

"I can't get sent home. As bad as things are here, at least I have a job and can send money home to my . . . family."

"I can help you do that for a while, Jeana, until you find another job." I was making alimony payments to Gabriela, which made it possible for her to stay in the same house and for the boys to attend a Catholic high school. But despite the payments, I was still able to enjoy a pretty good lifestyle in Dubai, and save some money.

"No!" said Jeana, her voice adamant. "I need to do this myself."

I admired her independence. "It'd just be for a while."

Jeana looked at me, her eyes watering. "There's so much you don't know about me. If you did, I don't think you'd feel the same."

I shook my head. "There's nothing that I could learn about you that would make me change my mind. I want to help. Please let me."

Another long moment of silence.

"Then let me tell you why I came to Dubai. Afterward, let's see if you still want to help." Her eyes continued to water, but her stare was hard.

"Of course," I answered, sitting back in my chair. "I want to know everything about you. But it won't change my mind."

We were poor, but it was still a good childhood. We all lived in the same compound in Cavite, near Manila. My brothers and sister, nieces and nephews. My grandfather was the one who kept the order. Everyone was afraid of him, except me. I loved being around him. Listening to his stories about the old days. He always said it was so much better back then. Before the crime and pollution. The American military bases at Clark and Subic were still open. And there were plenty of jobs for anyone who wanted to work.

Grandfather would give us all a small allowance each day to ride the jeepney to school and back, with enough extra to buy some Buko Pandan at the corner market on the way home. In the evening, all the families would eat together, play together, laugh together. We rarely left the compound, other than to go to school or the market. A trip into Manila was something special, something we all looked forward to. When we did go, I was always amazed by all the people, the cars, the noise. It was so different. But then we couldn't wait to get home. Home to familiar surroundings where everyone looked out for each other.

Jeana and I finished our sandwiches, rose from the table, and walked out to the pathway that meandered along the edge of the Green Community's man-made lake.

When I was in grammar school, I helped my grandfather in the little store he owned near the corner of the compound. Years earlier he had suffered a stroke and struggled to stock the shelves and give change to the customers. I would sit behind the counter doing my homework and helping grandpa as best I could with the customers. In return he would give me some candy or a coke. He was always so proud of me for making good grades in school. And he was always looking out for me. A few times I brought home friends he didn't like. He wouldn't say anything in front of them. But later in the evening he sat down beside me and said how important it was to choose friends carefully. How important it was to surround yourself with good people, people you could trust. People who respect you. I learned so much from him. I loved him so much.

When he died, everything changed. The families began fighting, and one by one they left the compound to start new lives. I stayed there with my brothers and sisters for a few more years. But then one day, our father came home to announce—in front of us all—that he had found a new woman and would be leaving. I remember how much my mother cried for days and days. She was never really the same again. Soon, we left the compound to live in this little house with just two rooms. I shared a mattress on the floor with my three younger siblings. Most nights we went to sleep hungry.

When things got really bad, I went with my younger sister to our father's house to ask him for help. Sometimes he gave us something, but most times he just said it wasn't his problem anymore. By then, he and his girl-friend had their own children. We didn't seem to matter to him anymore. We'd come home and tell our mother, and she cried for days on end, then got drunk, using the money that she should have been giving to us for food and transportation to school.

Jeana and I sat down on a bench along the water's edge, as other couples passed by.

As the oldest of my siblings, it was always my responsibility to be sure that Mom came home safely after one of her drinking binges. I remember being so tired some nights that I could barely keep my eyes open. But I would always wait for her to come home, then lock the door, and get a few hours' sleep before it was time to wake up my siblings and get ready for school. The neighbors often gave us money to take the jeepney to school, but it was rarely enough to buy food. I remember being so embarrassed when my friends would have enough money to buy something from the canteen, and I couldn't. Some days all I ate was a piece of bread and some water.

But somehow I finished high school and then got a job at KFC. I wanted so much to go to college, but someone had to work. Someone had to earn money. My mother couldn't do it. She was drunk most of the time, dating different men, and trying to forget my father. A few times she tried working overseas. First in Singapore, then Turkey. But each time she came back after only a few months. I never really knew why. I always thought she would leave and never come back. We never felt that she really loved us. But I guess she was missing us, in her own way.

Then, when I was eighteen, I started dating this guy. It was a mistake from the start. He never treated me well. But I didn't know any better. My grandfather had died. My father had left. And my mother didn't care. There was no one to tell me I deserved better. No one to sit me down and say that I should walk away. My brothers were too young to understand, and my sister had also started dating someone. We were all just so lost.

A year later I was pregnant with Ryan.

CHAPTER NINE

When I was growing up, I always looked forward to our family's summer trip to Chatham on Cape Cod. After my mother died, my father would take my sister and I, but it wasn't the same without mom.

Then one spring, the year after my sister had left for college, my father and I drove to Chatham for a long weekend to watch some Cape Cod League baseball games, considered one the best amateur leagues in the country. As we sat together watching a game between Chatham and Hyannis, Dad shared with me a story of the first time he had gone to Hyannis with mom.

"She loved the Kennedys and wanted to see their compound," he began, watching the game but clearly thinking back on a good memory from twenty-five years earlier. "Jack had already announced his run for the presidency, so the place had become quite a tourist attraction. He was more like a celebrity than a politician. But to a country that had always known older leaders, he represented something new and fresh. I can still remember the look on your mother's face as we stood outside the gates of the compound. She was like a teenager coming to see a concert."

"Did you also come here to Chatham?" I asked.

"We did," confirmed my Dad. "And went back many times after that, both before and after you and your sister were born. I never cared too much for Hyannis, but I thought Chatham was a very pretty town. I still do."

It was a beautiful night, as most were on the Cape. It was especially nice to be there with my dad, sharing the game of baseball which we both enjoyed so much. But I could tell that he was distracted that night. A few times I looked over at him, expecting to see him tracking balls and strikes on his scoresheet. Instead, he was looking out toward centerfield, beyond the ballpark, and into the night. I knew he was probably thinking about mom, but figured he needed to be alone in his thoughts.

"Thanks so much for bringing me here, George," said Kathleen, as they sat together on the grass slope looking down upon the game below. "I've always loved baseball. When I was little, my dad would take me to see the Boston Braves play. It was always cheaper than going to Fenway. It was so sad when they moved to Milwaukee. Did your father ever take you to a game?" asked Kathleen, enjoying her ice cream cone.

"No," replied George. "He wasn't much of a sports fan. He enjoyed his books most of all."

Kathleen was looking at George now. "Your father was much older, right? It must have been hard building a relationship with him."

"It was," agreed George. "But he did his best, I suppose. By the time he had met my mother, he had already lived another full life."

"He was married before?"

"He was, yes. I gather she was quite wealthy, too. They had a place in New York, another in Boston. And traveled throughout Europe. They even went to Egypt a few times, always traveling with servants."

"Wow," exclaimed Kathleen. "Where did the money come from?"

"His first wife was much older than him, having been previously married to some wealthy painter from New York. When he died, the money went to her. She then married my father and they were together for almost twenty years. But they never had any children. I guess they preferred to travel the world. When she died, most of the money went to the New York Public Library, as her first husband had indicated in his will. But my father received a little bit of it which he invested in the stock market. He also kept the brownstones in Boston and New York. When he met my mother, he was doing pretty well. They even had a few servants when they first moved into the house in Gardner. But it all disappeared shortly after I was born, in the crash of '29."

"Yes, that was hard," agreed Kathleen. "Do you remember having servants? That must have been really weird."

"I vaguely remember a maid. But I was only five when she was let go, shortly after the market crashed. My mother stayed in touch with her for many years after that, and ironically that maid was the mother of Mr. Gueran, the principal of my high school, who my mother convinced should hire me when I returned from Montana. Who knows, if his mother hadn't been my parents' maid, maybe I wouldn't have found a job in Gardner and you and I may never have met."

"That's quite a story," said Kathleen. "But Gueran sounds like an Irish name. Your family had an *Irish* maid?"

George had never considered that before. "I suppose. You have to remember, Kathleen, that a lot of wealthy people had servants in the 1920s. And in Boston and New York, most of the servants were immigrants, likely Irish. I don't think my parents treated her badly, otherwise Mr. Gueran never would've hired me."

"Oh, I'm not blaming your family," said Kathleen, not at all upset. "You're right. That's how things were back then. Fortunately, a lot has changed over the past thirty or forty years."

"Yes, they have," agreed George. "Just think of your Kennedys."

"Exactly," said Kathleen.

They sat together watching the game for another hour or so, and then walked back to their hotel near the Chatham lighthouse.

"It's so pretty here," said Kathleen, as they stood atop the cliff across from the lighthouse, able to see the waves crashing in the moonlight. "We should come back soon."

"Definitely," agreed George.

"I wish my parents could have come to places like this, but they never had the money."

"I know," said George, putting his sweater around Kathleen's shoulders as the wind blew in off the water. "But I'm sure they saw some beautiful places in Ireland before they came to this country."

Kathleen nodded, continuing to gaze out at the Atlantic. "Yes, I'm sure they did."

There was nothing quite as beautiful as a sunset over Galway Bay. And it was something that Bridget and Sean had longed to see together. But rarely did they leave their little inland town of Tuam. So when the opportunity arose to hitch a ride in the back of one of those new Mack AB trucks, they jumped at it. It was their first ride in a truck. In fact, it was one of the few times they had ever *seen* a truck. Few came to Tuam. Most people in the little town could only dream of owning one of the new machines. There were a lot in Galway and Dublin—most shipped across the channel from England—but horse and wagons still did the majority of the heavy hauling in little farming communities like Tuam.

"This is amazing!" yelled Bridget to Sean as they bounced along the dirt road between Tuam and Galway, the wind lifting her hair. "I feel so free!"

It was a rare moment of joy amid an otherwise hard life. To make things even harder, the Great War raged full-blown in France and Belgium, and some Irish had been conscripted to serve in the British Army. Sean's mother was fearful that he or one of his brothers might be called upon to serve.

At first, it was actually something that Sean welcomed . . . until he had fallen in love with Bridget. Now, there was no way he could leave her. They were committed to sticking together no matter what.

Still, so much was out of their hands.

The potato crops were coming back, but slowly. Yet, the small farming towns like Tuam were still being abandoned for the larger cities like Galway. When no work was available there, some people then left for America. Along with the war in France, it seemed almost too overwhelming for two teenagers to handle. But Sean and Bridget were tough. They were not going to allow the country's current hard times to rob them of a future together.

That afternoon, after arriving in Galway, Sean and Bridget had explored the town. Each had been there before, of course. But never together. It was different together.

They walked through the Latin Quarter and along Quay Street, fascinated by little shops, pubs, and street performers. People making money any way they could. They passed through both the Spanish Arch and the Caoc Arch, remnants of the old wall that once surrounded the city. They visited the docks where goods were arriving from other Western seaports, such as Sligo to the north and Limerick to the south. There was a constant bustle of people. Everyone seemed to be in a rush to get somewhere. It was so different from their little town where no one seemed to be in a rush to do anything, except grow old.

In the middle of Galway City was Eyre Square, known to locals simply as the Green. The park attracted families by day, and teens by night. It was their hangout. A place where they could get away from their parents for a few hours after completing their daily chores after school. When Bridget and Sean arrived, it was late afternoon and they knew they would have to soon find a way back to Tuam before their parents knew they were gone. But they were going to enjoy it for as long as they could.

"Where are you two from?" asked one of the kids who was sitting on the stone wall surrounding the square. "Don't remember seeing you before."

"We're from Tuam," replied Bridget. "Just down for the day."

"Really?" said the boy, maybe a few years younger than Sean. "I know some people from there. Do you know the O'Brien family? They came here last year. Or the O'Riellys?"

Bridget looked at Sean. "Maybe William O'Brien?"

"That's it," said the boy. "Bill was his name. Came with his parents. But I haven't seen him in months. Someone told me he may have gone to France to fight the Germans."

"Poor guy," said Sean. "It must be bad over there."

"Can't be any worse than it's here," replied the boy. "If I was a few years older, I'd go."

Sean and Bridget just nodded.

"Hey," said the boy. "You should both come with us to the river. It's the best place to watch the sunset. It's going to be special tonight."

"How far is it?" asked Sean, knowing that they needed to get back to Tuam.

"Not far," said the boy, jumping down from the wall and practically pushing Sean and Bridget along. "Follow me. You'll see. It'll be worth it."

Sometimes in Tuam, Bridget and Sean climbed to the top of Pete's Hill located just outside of town on the road to Belclare. From there, they watched the sunset over the fields. But that was nothing like the sun setting over Galway Bay. As the sun dipped below the horizon, the fleeting colors of dusk shimmered over the calm waters of the bay. A few fishing boats were quietly making their way back to dock, seemingly in no rush, her passengers undoubtedly standing on the boat's stern admiring nature's display.

"How far is America?" asked Bridget, looking across.

"Far," replied Sean. "Very far. Probably more than a week by boat."

"What do you think it's like there? Maybe like Galway?"

"Bigger," answered Sean. "Much, much bigger."

They stood there, hand in hand, for another few moments until Sean spotted a truck heading toward the northern road to Tuam.

"Come on," he said. "Let's see if they'll give us a ride."

He pulled Bridget's arm, but she didn't move. "I want to go there, Sean."

"Where?"

"America. I want us to go there together."

"How? We don't have any money," said Sean.

"Then we save. Whatever we make each day, we keep some. Put it away. And then someday . . ."

"That could take a long time," replied Sean.

Bridget turned around to look at Sean. "I don't care how long it takes. I want to go. I want to go with you. There's nothing for us here."

"But maybe there's nothing in America for us, either, Bridget. A lot of people have gone. Most never come back."

"We'll make it," persisted Bridget. "If we stick together, we can make it work. You believe me, right?"

Sean nodded. "Of course I do, Bridget. I believe you."

They stayed for another moment staring out across the waters of the Atlantic Ocean, dreaming of a land that seemed so far away. They turned and ran toward the truck. It was time to go home.

CHAPTER TEN

Before Ryan was born, things were already bad between his father and me. I suppose I was hoping that Ryan's birth would make things better. But it was stupid to think so. If anything, it got worse. The father became extremely possessive and wouldn't even let me see my friends or family. And then he started hitting me. I should have run away at that point, but I didn't. He was a police officer and knew a lot of people. I wasn't scared of what could happen to me. But I was scared that he would take Ryan away, and I'd never see him again.

As Jeana and I sat together on the lakeside bench, so many things were going through my head. I felt so bad for her and repeatedly had to wipe the tears from my eyes. But there was also a part of me that was thinking, "Do I really want to go down this road again? Do I really want to get involved with another woman who already has children?"

And the more she talked, the more complex my feelings became.

Two years after Ryan was born, Daniel was born. And things went from bad to worse, if that's even possible. By then, the father was using drugs and continuing to drink. I did my best to shield the boys from his behavior, and for the most part, I succeeded. We had a nanny, Grace, who was a big help. We became friends. Some days, she was the only person I saw. The only person I could talk to. If it hadn't been for her, I don't know if I would've made it through.

By the time Daniel was nearly two, I'd finally convinced myself that I needed to escape. With the help of Grace, I took the boys to my father's house who lived far enough away that the boys' father couldn't follow. I still hated my father for leaving my mother all those years before. But I didn't have any choice. He let me stay for a few months until I could make other plans with the help of my mother and brothers. But when those plans fell through, I found myself living under a bridge in Cavite. My youngest brother would take care of the boys during the day so I could work at Jolly-bee, bringing home chicken every night to feed the boys. It was a horrible few months. No running water. No electricity. The constant sound of cars passing overhead. But many of the people who lived beneath that bridge were kind to me, sometimes watching the boys when my brother couldn't.

Finally, one of my cousins who I'd grown up with in my grandfather's compound heard where I was living and came to help. At first, I was too proud to accept her help. But she persisted and I finally gave in. She had married a Chinese man who owned restaurants around Cavite, and he gave me a job. I soon worked my way up to become a manager at one of his restaurants, and from there, things got better.

At least for a little while.

"Did the boys' father ever come after you,'" I asked, as we stood up from the bench and continued walking around the edge of the lake behind the Marriott's poolside restaurant.

"At first, I heard that he was looking. But then he met another woman and lost interest. I'm sure the same thing happened to that woman, too."

"You never thought about going to the police?"

Jeana laughed. "The police don't do anything about that in the Philippines. Most are corrupt, and the boys' father was one of them. I'm sure they would've taken his side. Who knows what they would've done to me . . . or the boys."

"It must have been so lonely," I said.

"I'll always be grateful to my cousin for saving me from beneath that bridge. She gave me a second chance."

"You never married the boys' father?"

"No," answered Jeana. "But he created a fake marriage certificate that he filed with the courts so the boys would have his name. And he showed it to his parents so they would approve."

"Jesus."

"I know. He was a really bad guy. But one good thing came out of it all."

"What's that?" I asked, as we continued walking while throwing little pieces of bread at the ducks that swam by on the lake.

"Years later, the boys became close with their grandparents. And they still are to this day."

"Really? And their father didn't care? Didn't try to take the boys away?"

"He never really cared for them," said Jeana, looking straight ahead. "And he already had another child. I think even his own parents came to realize that he wasn't a good person."

"I'm so sorry for everything you went through. No one should have to endure that."

"Thanks. But I'm afraid I didn't learn much from the experience."

I suddenly stopped walking and turned to Jeana. "What do you mean?"

I was lonely

I worked as many hours as I could to support the boys, and spent all of my free time with them. Sometimes my mother would visit. Sometimes my brothers and sisters. I was still close to my cousin and her husband. But I was lonely. Then I met Miguel.

He was a regular customer at the restaurant, working as a dentist nearby. At first, I resisted his advances. But eventually I gave in and started dating him. He treated me well and seemed to really care for Ryan and Daniel. His family owned a large market in Santa Rosa, near Cavite, and after six months we moved in with him in his apartment above the market. My cousin kept telling me not to do it, but I didn't listen. I told her that he was a good person and could be a good father-figure for the boys. I'm not really sure if I ever really believed that, but I guess I convinced myself.

Jeana and I resumed walking.

For a year, it was good. Almost perfect. His career as a dentist was really taking off. We had plenty of money, mostly thanks to his parents. I was able to work in their store. We had two nannies. Everything was okay. But then he started talking about marriage. The problem was, since Ryan and Daniel's father had filed a fake marriage certificate, Miguel and I couldn't get married without getting my first marriage annulled through the courts. But we couldn't afford to do that without asking his parents for money, which he didn't want to do. His parents really seemed to care for me and the boys, but also desperately wanted a grandchild. His father was Chinese and it was an important part of their culture to have a male heir. Miguel was their only son. I'm not sure if he really wanted children of his own, but he was getting a lot of pressure from his parents. He knew they wouldn't accept a child born out of wedlock. So he had a fake marriage certificate made which he could show his parents.

And then I got pregnant.

Not just because of the parents, but because I really loved Miguel. Or maybe I was just in love with the idea of being in love. I don't know. I'm sure my grandfather would've seen through him. Would have told me to walk away, just like my cousin was doing. But, who knows. Maybe I wouldn't have listened to him anyways. I was twenty-five years old and thought I had all the answers.

A year later, Nadine was born.

A few days after that discussion with Jeana, I went out with the Friday Night Club. I didn't like talking with them about Jeana. But I needed some advice. So I shared some of Jeaana's story with them.

"If you really care for her, you'll stay with her," said Trish, as we all sat outside on the deck of *360°*, an upscale bar nestled at the end of the Jumeirah Beach Hotel walkway, past dozens of luxurious yachts owned by wealthy locals, and in view of the Burj al Arab, a seven-star hotel built to resemble a giant sail. "What matters is the present, not somebody's past."

I wasn't sure if it was quite that simple, but I understood what Trish meant.

Judy seemed to concur. "Everybody comes here for different reasons, John," she said. "You're here because you were divorced and wanted a new start. She's probably here to get away from her situation in the Philippines. Can you really blame her?'"

"No, of course I don't blame her for coming here," I said, leaning back on the outdoor sofa with my feet up on the coffee table where our drinks were spread-out. "But I just don't know about the kids."

"Does that really matter?" asked Kurtis, his arm around Yule. "You're both going to be here for a few years, so why not enjoy it. The future will work itself out."

Ray was nodding, as Judy had her head on his lap, her sandals kicked off, both of them sprawled out beside me on the sofa. "Anyways, isn't the visa the priority now," he said. "Even if you have doubts about the long-term, what matters *now* is that she can find a better employer."

I completely agreed with that.

But there was also a lot more to Jeana's story than I'd shared with the Friday Night Club.

For a while after Nadine was born, things were good. Ryan had started school and the nannies were really good with Daniel and Nadine. We even had some extra money which I used to start my own little food stall inside the parents' market, something they had encouraged. Miguel's dentistry continued to expand. He was working longer hours. But it was okay since I'd my own things to do in the store. Then, his parents started pressuring him to have another child, a boy. I was okay with having another child, but he didn't really want to. When Liza was born, everything changed.

In truth, it'd already changed. I just hadn't realized it.

Jeana and I sat down on the plush green grass that bordered the lake, as other couples continued to walk by and some children played soccer in the open space.

I found out from a friend that his dentistry business wasn't really doing well after all. In fact, he didn't even have a real license to practice. He had lied about all of it, even creating a fake certificate to show to his parents. On top of all that, he wasn't staying late to work. He was staying late to see another woman. At first, I didn't believe it. I'd been so sure that everything was real. But it never was. Even his parents' attitude toward me changed when Liza was born. They wanted a boy, and in their own twisted way, they blamed me for it.

Around the same time, my food stall started doing poorly. I was just so upset about everything, I didn't put any time into it. Miguel convinced his parents to help, which I think he did more to make-up for what he had done to me than because he really cared about the stall's success. His parents agreed to loan us some money. But when things didn't get better, we had to close the stall before we could pay them back. And that made them even angrier with me.

So many times I wanted to tell his parents what he had done, how he had cheated on me, but never did. I think I was afraid they wouldn't believe me. They thought he was the perfect son. But he wasn't.

She had had a hard life, there was no getting around it. But as she continued telling the story, what stood out was her strength. Despite it all, she had stayed positive. Didn't complain. Didn't blame others. But she was clearly looking for a new start.

Just like I was.

I don't want anyone to feel sorry for me. I wish I hadn't stayed as long as I did with Ryan and Daniel's father. But I did. And I should have left Miguel the minute I found out that he was cheating on me. But I didn't.

And then I got pregnant again.

She must have seen the expression on my face.

I know. You're thinking why didn't I use birth control? Why would I put myself in an even worse position? And to be honest, I don't have a good answer. My mother never talked to me about birth control. It just isn't something that parents talk about with their kids in the Philippines. The Church is totally against it, and the Church controls everything. Maybe things are changing now. I know that I'll certainly talk to my kids about it.

"I'm not judging you. Nobody can understand how difficult it was for you."

After Nathan was born, I tried as hard as I could to make it work. And even if I knew it was better to leave, where was I going to go with five children? Miguel's parents were at least treating me better because they had their male heir. But I knew it was only on the surface. I always felt like they were talking behind my back.

By then, Ryan and Daniel were old enough to understand some of what was happening, and I could see that it was starting to affect them. Miguel and his parents ignored them most of the time, or blamed them for things they didn't do. When they started having behavior problems at school, I knew I needed to do something. So I reached-out to their grandparents and asked if they could take the two boys. It was probably the hardest thing that I've ever done. But I knew it was the right thing to do. I was hoping it would only be a short time. I didn't really know. But I knew that every child had the right to live in a house where they were loved. Despite everything that had happened with their father, I knew the grandparents would show them that love.

And they did.

At that moment, I thought about my own failures with Andres and Fernando. They, also, had deserved to live in a house where both parents loved them. And I'd been unable to give that to them.

"Is that when you came here to Dubai?" I asked, turning to face Jeana who was lying back on the grass.

"A few months later, yes. But one more thing had to happen before I finally gave up."

"What was that?"

"He exposed himself to the nanny."

"What? You're kidding!"

I wish I was. I guess he'd done it before, but the nanny had been afraid to tell me. When she finally did, I left and went to live with my brother. My plan was to live with him for a while, save some money, and then get the three kids. But I knew there was no way that Miguel or his parents would let them go. They had more money than me and knew a lot of people.

A friend then suggested that I work overseas where I could make more money faster. At first, I hesitated, remembering that my mother had tried, and didn't like it. But I soon realized that it was probably the only way that I could save enough money. So I signed-up with this agency which sends Filipinos to Dubai. They were the cheapest, and with everything that has happened with Mr. Haig, now I know why. But I was desperate to get my kids back and didn't know what else to do. When I arrived here and started working for Mr. Haij, a part of me felt that I'd never see them again.

Then I met you.

CHAPTER 11

When I was growing up, another of our family's favorite summer destinations was Brattleboro, Vermont. Some years we'd spend a few days in the small town, enjoying its historic main street lined with art galleries and restaurants, or flying kites along the banks of the Connecticut River which cut through the town. Other summers, we'd just stop for lunch at my father's favorite sandwich shop on Canal Street on our way to Killington to stay at a chalet near the base of Pico Mountain.

A few weeks before I left for the Peace Corps in Africa, my father and I drove to Brattleboro to get some supplies at another of his favorite spots, the Brattleboro Co-op. For years, I wasn't sure why he liked the town so much. It was certainly a pretty location, located at the confluence of the West and Connecticut Rivers. It'd been a mill town through much of the eighteenth and nineteenth centuries until it transformed into an eclectic artists' haven in the twentieth century, particularly during the 1960s.

But my father's connection to the town ran much deeper.

"My great-grandfather on my mother's side of the family was a tailor here in the mid-nineteenth century. My mother often talked about the town when I was growing up, and I have vague memories of taking the train with her to see some of the family who had remained here," recalled my father, as we sat together having lunch at the Whetstone Restaurant overlooking the river.

"The tailor shop had apparently been located nearby, back when this restaurant was actually a woolen textile mill," he continued, pointing upriver along Main Street. "But when some of the mills closed down following the Civil War, my great-grandfather headed south and ended-up in Gardner, probably because it was along the Vermont-Massachusetts train line."

"Is any of the family still alive?" I asked.

"No. They're all gone, probably long ago. After my mother died, I didn't keep in touch with members of her family, which was too bad. Your mother and I came here a few times before we were married, and she liked the town. Probably because it was so different from Boston. She used to especially like coming in the Fall to see the foliage."

My life was about to change dramatically, as I prepared for my adventure in Africa. But for Dad, he seemed to be looking back over his life. Taking stock of things. In many ways, the past, present, and future had all come together for my father and I that day in Brattleboro.

"You always ask about my family," said Kathleen as she sat with George on a bench overlooking the Connecticut River near downtown Brattleboro, Vermont. "But you don't talk too much about yours."

"Maybe your family's more interesting," he joked.

"I doubt that. I'd like to know more about where you come from."

George and Kathleen had been dating for nearly two years and had even begun talking about marriage. But there were some significant challenges that needed to be overcome.

George liked living in the relative quiet of Gardner, and visiting Boston. Kathleen liked the bustle of living in Boston and visiting Gardner.

Kathleen's mother didn't much care for George, mostly because he wasn't Catholic. George's mother didn't like Kathleen, mostly because she *was* Catholic.

Kathleen was torn about leaving her mother. George had come to feel somewhat the same about his mother, particularly as her health had started to decline.

George liked the opera. Kathleen liked Sinatra.

George liked quiet walks through the woods. Kathleen preferred evening strolls along Newbury Street in Boston.

At least they both liked baseball.

"I don't really know too much about my father's side of the family before his first marriage. But after he died, my mother would talk quite a bit about her side. I think there were times she thought about coming back here to Brattleboro, but never did. She had become comfortable in Gardner and seemed resigned to the fact that she'd probably live-out her life there."

"What about you?" asked Kathleen. "Do you see yourself staying in Gardner?"

"To be honest," said George. "I do. My job's there. My mother's there. And my little house is there."

George had recently bought a small house in nearby Westminster. For a while after returning from Montana he'd lived with his mother, before renting a room from a widower—a situation that had reminded him of his time at Harvard more than ten years earlier. Finally, he had found the little house that met his needs and gave him some privacy.

"But to be honest with *you*, George," responded Kathleen. "I'm not sure I could do that. I'm comfortable in Boston. My mother and my friends are there."

"I understand that," replied George. "But my great grandfather left Brattleboro all those years ago not only because the mills were closing, but because he was following a woman whom he had met in Brattleboro who wanted to move away from her parents."

"I don't want to move away from my mother right now. She still needs me."

"All I'm saying," continued George, "is that people move to new places for unexpected reasons. When I was at Harvard, I never expected to end up in Montana. And when I was in Montana, I never expected to go back to Gardner. Life pulls you in directions which you least expect."

"When your great grandfather left Brattleboro to go to Gardner," said Kathleen, "was he able to find a job right away?"

"I don't know," replied George. "But he eventually opened a tailoring store on Parker Street in Gardner and kept it for the rest of his life before passing it on to his son, my grandfather. He had even more success with it, but died of tuberculosis when my mother was a teenager. The family moved away shortly after that."

"When did your mother return to Gardner?"

"After she married my father. But I don't think she expected to, or even wanted to. For a while after they were married, they lived in the brownstones in Boston and New York that he had inherited from his first wife. But when the markets crashed, they had to sell them. Soon they moved into the house where I grew up, just down the street from Crystal Lake."

"And now you want to settle there, too," added Kathleen.

"I suppose on some level we're always pulled back to familiar places. When we're young, we want to break out on our own and prove that we can make it without our parents. Then as we grow older, we're drawn back to the places that we once called home. Kind of like your parents. You said they always wanted to go home to Ireland, but never had the money. If they *had* had the money, don't you think they would've gone back?"

"Probably," agreed Kathleen. "Someday I hope I'll have the chance to go there."

"And I hope I can go with you," said George, looking intently at Kathleen.

"You mean that?'

"I do. It's part of who you are, just like Gardner is part of who I am."

As Kathleen listened to George, she watched the flowing waters of the Connecticut River, remembering the stories that her mother would tell about the beautiful rivers and lakes around Galway and Tuam.

Standing on a small, rocky island less than a hundred feet from the shores of Lough Corrib—the source of the River Corrib—lies Aughnanure Castle, built in the early sixteenth century by the O'Flahertys, one of Ireland's oldest and wealthiest families.

As one of the country's best-preserved tower houses, the castle includes the remains of a banqueting hall, watch tower, double bawn and bastions, and a dry harbor. Yet, its location wasn't well known to the few tourists who ventured north from Galway. Instead, it was a common destination for local teen lovers looking for a place to rendezvous near Tuam.

Sean and Bridget visited the castle by riding their bikes along Weir Road from Tuam, passing through Belclare, and continuing westward through the dairy farms toward the lake. It was an especially scenic route in the spring when the rolling hills were covered with flowering bluebells, lavender brooklimes, and purple butterfly-bushes. Occasionally, they'd drop their bikes by the side of the dirt road and hop over the low, stonewalls to lay in the fields and look up at the passing clouds. Clear days in western Ireland were rare, so any blue sky was a treasured sight. But no one was really bothered by the rain. Life carried on as usual.

On this particular day, Sean and Bridget enjoyed only sunshine, arriving after an hour's bike ride to the lake which extended north and south for nearly ten miles and was fed by a series of rivers and streams that originated in the mountains to the north. As they set down their bikes on the rocky shore and waded-out toward the castle, they were delighted to find themselves alone.

"It's so beautiful here," said Bridget, as they stepped out of the shallow water onto dry land and up the rocky embankment toward the castle walls. "I wish we lived closer."

"I bet they don't have places like this in America," said Sean.

"I'm not so sure about that," replied Bridget, passing through the arched entrance and into the banquet room, the far wall of which had partially collapsed. "We always hear such amazing things about America. Like it's some sort of paradise."

"It's no paradise, Bridget," said Sean, looking around the room, which included some graffiti on the walls. "A lot of good Irish have died over there."

"Yes, but many more made good lives for themselves," countered Bridget, both of them sitting down on two large stones from the collapsed wall.

Sean had brought Bridget to the castle to tell her about the conversation that he had had the previous night with his parents. More and more Irish were being called upon to serve in Europe, and his parents were afraid.

"Bridget," began Sean, a nervous knot in his stomach. "Two more of our neighbors have gone to France to fight with the English. My parents think that I'll soon be conscripted, too."

"What do they want you to do?" asked Bridget, the concern in her voice obvious. "You won't go, will you?"

"If I get the call, what could I do? Others have refused, and they've ended up in English prisons."

"We shouldn't have to do what they tell us," said Bridget, speaking of the English. "We're not their slaves."

"No, but we're part of the United Kingdom. If we're conscripted to fight, then we have no choice."

"At least for now."

Bridget was correct. Ireland was moving closer to complete independence from England. Rumor was that the south would achieve it first. There were many more nationalists in the south who were pushing for separation, while the majority unionists in the north were afraid that England might retaliate with higher tariffs.

"Nothing will happen until the war is over," said Sean. "For now, we're stuck."

"So what do your parents want you to do?"

"They don't believe in the war," replied Sean. "At least they don't believe in the Irish fighting for a cause that doesn't affect us."

"So?"

"They want me to go, Bridget."

"To America?" asked Bridget, excitedly.

"Yes," replied Sean, with less enthusiasm. "They say, when the war is over, maybe I could come back."

Bridget jumped up. "This is it, Sean! This is what we've been waiting for! We've saved some money, and now your family will help us with the rest. It's what we've talked about."

But Sean wasn't happy. "They want *me* to go. They don't even know about us. Neither do your parents."

"It doesn't matter," responded Bridget, undeterred. "They don't really care about me, anyways."

"That's not true," said Sean, adamantly. "Your parents love you very much. You know that."

"Maybe. But they care more for my brothers. They just see me as getting married and pregnant someday."

Sean knew that was true, but still tried to reason with Bridget. "But how would you go? You'd just leave home one day without telling them?"

"I'd tell them, of course. But what could they do? They can't lock me in the house."

Sean shook his head. "I don't know. Maybe it's better if I go alone."

"Alone?" repeated Bridget, her voice rising. "We've been talking about this for months, Sean. It was my idea. And now that we have a way to go, you're backing out."

"I'm not backing out," contested Sean. "I just don't want you to have a bad life. Who knows what will happen over there."

"It can't be any worse than it's here, that's for sure," said Bridget, pacing back and forth. "At least in America, we'd have some hope for a better life together. If we stay here, we'll be trapped in Tuam for the rest of our lives."

"I could go first, and you follow later?"

Bridget stopped pacing and stared at Sean. "You don't want me to go? You want to leave me here!"

"Of course I want us to go together, but . . ."

"But what?"

Sean began crying. "I don't want something to happen to you. You've heard the stories. Don't pretend you haven't. If you got hurt, I'd never forgive myself."

Bridget knelt down in front of Sean. "I can't stay here alone. Yes, I know the stories. But we'd be together. We always have to stay together. If we separate now, who knows if we'll ever see each other again."

"It'll be dangerous, you know. It's not the paradise you think it is."

Bridget grabbed both of Sean's arms. "I know that. I never thought that it was. But any place is better than here. Together, we can survive. Make a good life for ourselves. At least there's a chance there. Opportunity. We have none of that here. Not now."

It was Sean's turn to look hard at Bridget. "Why are you so strong?" he asked. "Why are you never afraid?"

"I didn't say I wasn't afraid."

CHAPTER 12

Lying on the east coast of the United Arab Emirates along the Gulf of Oman and the Indian Ocean, Fujairah is one of the seven emirates of the country, and the last to have joined the union in the early 1970s, having been a territory of Oman for centuries.

During those early times, its small population—isolated by the Hajar Mountains that divide the east and west coasts of the country—lived primarily by date cultivation and pearling. But as oil revenues began flooding into the new nation, improvements to infrastructure included the construction of new highways cutting through the barren, rocky mountains and opening up the east coast to development and eventually tourism.

As I drove over those mountains with my Springsteen CD blasting *Born to Run*, I had a lot on my mind with some life-altering decisions to make. I'd already met with the attorney to put into motion the plan to become Jeana's sponsor, allowing her to escape Mr. Haij and determine her own future.

But whether that future would include me, was still up in the air.

Understandably, she was hesitant to enter into another relationship following two tragically failed attempts. My track record was equally questionable. But her sole reason for coming to Dubai had been to work, save money, and put herself in a position to support her children without the help of their fathers. Those children were the focus of my thoughts as I descended the mountain and turned south to drive along the coast and into Fujairah.

Conventional wisdom dictated that I shouldn't pursue anything further with her than a good friendship. But I'd rarely made conventional decisions. Africa, Honduras, and now Dubai were drastic evidence of that. Yet, when it came to relationships, my failures were particularly conventional.

Like too many men, I took more than I received, always leading to an imbalance of emotions and commitment.

Maria had wanted to focus on her studies, and if I'd been secure enough with myself to let her do so, there could have been a chance. But I wanted more than she was willing to give at that point in time, so the relationship had been out of balance from the start.

Gabriela had wanted a proper father for Andres and Fernando, but my insecurities had again prevented me from fully committing myself to them. Once again, imbalance had led to failure.

Now I was presented with a situation that would require me to put the needs of others first. Not just the needs of two children, but the needs of five. Was I more secure in my own skin than I'd been ten years earlier? Was I more mature? And even if the answer to both questions was *yes*, there were still many practical questions that needed answering. Would the children come to Dubai? Would I go to the Philippines? In either location, could I support a family of seven?

So, as I entered the outskirts of Fujairah, passing by the massive Sheikh Zayed Mosque with its towering white minarets, I'd some soul-searching to do and had decided to check-in to the Al Aqah Resort. With panoramic views of the Indian Ocean on one side and the Hajar Mountains on the other, its isolation seemed to provide the ideal setting to focus my thoughts and decide.

The Friday Night Club had already encouraged me to move forward with the relationship, and while I respected their opinion, they had not lived through what I had. None of them had children of their own. And none of them had been divorced. So, it was my decision to make, and by the end of the weekend, I was going to make it, fully commit to that decision, and move forward . . . just as my father had always encouraged me to do.

Always move forward.

"My marriage to your mother was never a sure thing," began my father, as we sat lakeside during my visit to see him the summer when I moved from California to Maryland with Gabriela and the boys. "But once I made up my mind to do something, I always kept moving forward until I made it work. I was determined to get your mother to marry me."

"She didn't want to, at first?" I asked, talking loudly so as to be heard over the drone of the groundskeeper who was cutting the grass of the cemetery.

Dad smiled. "No, she certainly did not. I think I must have asked her three times before she agreed. And even then, it was uncertain."

"Why?"

"She never admitted it, but I always thought she had finally said *yes* because she really didn't believe I could find a Catholic church that would marry us. Back then, it was nearly impossible for a divorcee to marry within the Catholic church."

"But you did find one."

"I did," replied Dad, still clearly proud of his efforts all those years earlier. "But it took some time. In the end, it was actually my mother who helped. She didn't particularly like or trust the Catholic Church, but she knew that your mother made me happy. So her pastor had contacted the priest at Holy Rosary Catholic Church in Gardner. They were apparently friends. In the end, the priest agreed to let us marry in his church, but he had his associate pastor give the vows in an adjoining chapel, rather than the main church."

"How funny," I said. "Things have certainly changed a lot. I doubt my new boss, Father Lawrence, cares whether someone is divorced."

"Probably not," agreed Dad. "But back then, it was still a big deal. But even after we were married, the big question was where to live."

"Mom didn't want to come to Gardner?"

"Goodness, no!" answered Dad. "She liked visiting, but wanted to live in the big city. But my job was in Gardner, and I didn't want to leave. Which, in retrospect, was a mistake."

"Why was it a mistake?"

"Well, maybe not a mistake, but it was unfair. I wasn't willing to compromise. We could have looked for a place between Gardner and Boston. Between her mother and mine. But I already had the little house in Westminster and didn't want to sell it. So I made her come to Gardner. Those first few years were really tough on her. She didn't really find her footing until your sister was born a few years later. And that was another hard experience for her."

"Andrea?" I asked.

"The pregnancy itself was fine," said Dad. "But getting pregnant was difficult. In the end, she decided to use a medicine that increased her estrogen levels. But its use had posed a religious quandary for her, as the Catholic Church was opposed to any kind of family planning."

"Wow, I didn't know all that," I said. "Those first few years really *were* hard for her."

"Luckily, when we eventually moved to the new house on Bickford Hill, things got a little better for her. There were other women on the street who were her age and they eventually developed close relationships."

"Mrs. Atter and Mrs. Frie."

"Yes," said my father. "They remained close friends for nearly twenty years, right up until her passing."

I thought about what my father was saying, realizing that his stories were always told for a particular reason. "Dad, do you think it was a mistake for me to accept the job in Maryland?"

My father thought for a moment before answering. "It's not my place to tell you what to do, Johnny. You have to make the decision which is best for your little family."

"But . . ." I knew my father well.

"But . . . if Gabriela and the boys are comfortable in California, it'll make it that much harder to make things work in Maryland. Marriage is hard enough without making decisions that make it harder."

"But the new job pays more," I countered, without much conviction.

"Which is definitely a consideration," agreed Dad. "And that's why I say it's your decision to make. You know what standard of living is needed for the four of you to be happy. But if the marriage is already under stress, a big move can often have unintended consequences. Your mother eventually adjusted to living in Gardner, and I'm sure Gabriela will adjust to Maryland. But it'll take time."

I knew that my father, in his own way, was telling me not to go to Maryland. But it was already too late. I'd accepted the new job, quit my old job, and had rented a new house in Silver Spring. Nevertheless, I was fascinated to hear my father talk about those first few years with my mother in Gardner. And some of it would stick with me for many, many years.

"I made a lot of mistakes those first few years with your mother, but when you and your sister were born, I finally found my way," continued my father. "I'd failed as a father with Beth. But I was damned if I was going to fail again. You and your sister gave me the two most important reasons for moving forward. I needed to stop looking back at my failures with Ruth—not to mention my memories of the war and Yvette—and instead plan a future for the two of you. It gave me a purpose and a reason for being. And all of these years later, despite everything that has happened, even despite your mother's disease and death, what continues to matter most is the two of you. And I have come to understand that our most important role in this world is to be parents. To raise your children the best you can and watch them grow up to lead their own lives, hopefully better than you did. It's the so-called circle of life. But it requires putting aside your own shortcomings for a purpose higher than yourself."

I sat alone on the sand—a few miles down the beach from the hotel in Fujairah—looking out at the waters of the Indian Ocean. They were especially calm, save for some waves created by a few oil tankers passing in the distance, slowly making their way into the Strait of Hormuz and through to the Persian Gulf. Those waters had seen a lot over the past millennia, serving as one of the world's busiest and most important trade routes. The rise and fall of empires could be traced to those same waters, along with the current state of the world and its endless thirst for oil. But as I sat there—with the incoming tide slowly reaching my feet—the only history on my mind was my own.

It'd been quite a journey.

Africa, Puerto Rico, New Orleans, Honduras, Florida, California, Maryland. And now Dubai.

And something was telling me that there was still much more to come.

But the question that remained was whether I would continue that journey alone . . . or with Jeana and her children.

As I sat there, the waters lapping at my feet, I couldn't help but think of the many talks I'd enjoyed with my father since finishing college, and even before. He had always shared good wisdom, and I was certainly in need of some now. As I searched my memories, I drifted back to his words that had always been close at hand.

The circle of life.

I'd come to understand that it meant something more to him than merely the passing of the torch.

Something much simpler.

To him, it was the ability to move forward. Always forward.

And when you can move forward no more, and you look back on it all, what will you have to show for it?

My father had wanted more to show than a failed marriage and an estranged daughter.

What would I have to show? A failed marriage and two estranged children?

My life had to amount to more than that.

And I was suddenly determined to make it so.

CHAPTER THIRTEEN

I returned from Fujairah with a clear understanding of where I wanted things to go with Jeana. I'd no illusions about the immense challenges that lay ahead. At first, she still had reservations about our plans, fearing that it would somehow impact her ability to support her children in the Philippines. But we soon settled into a good groove that would continue for many months.

Unfortunately, my job never found a similar groove.

Mr. Ahmad and I'd gotten off to a shaky start following the incident with the Israeli flag, but had been able to work through it. For a while, we seemed to be getting along all right together. He would meet with Saad and I each Saturday in his office to sign checks and receive an update on academic and facility issues. At times, he would give his input. Mostly, though, he left it to Saad and I to resolve. But one area in which he always wanted to maintain control was staffing.

And on this issue, he and I rarely saw things in the same way. To me, it was important to treat employees with respect, pay them a fair wage, and make sure they were given suitable living accommodations. But on each of these three points, Mr. Ahmad balked.

I appreciated the fact that the school was still relatively new and continuing to build enrollment, so funds were tight. But the best way to build a good school was to have good teachers. Yet, if you didn't respect them by providing fair benefits, then they wouldn't stay long. That kind of instability would then make building enrollment nearly impossible.

Mr. Ahmad just didn't see it that way.

During my first year at the school, our differing points of view became an issue for sure, but not necessarily insurmountable. But as we began recruiting teachers for my second year at the Green School, it was clear that the issue was going to create considerable tension between us.

Like so many employers in the Middle East, Mr. Ahmad wanted to pay his employees primarily based upon their nationality, rather than their experience. If I was fortunate enough to find two good teachers with equal experience but different nationalities—perhaps one British and the other Indian—Mr. Ahmad would always want to pay the Westerner more. A few times I was able to find extremely qualified candidates who happened to be African American. But Mr. Ahmad wouldn't hire them because they were black, believing that the parents of the school wouldn't like it.

In the beginning, I tried to see things from his perspective, thinking that he knew his clientele and what they would or wouldn't find acceptable. It was a business, after all, and that required pleasing your clients, even if they showed racist tendencies. But as time passed, I was unable to rationalize his approach. Our employment offers had been turned down by many good teachers who were unwilling to accept a lower wage because of their nationality or race, and I knew this issue was keeping the school from reaching its potential.

So was the issue of staff housing.

Much of my time as the school's principal was taken up by various problems associated with the school's accommodations for the teachers, an issue that Saad didn't want to deal with. While he had come to agree with me that the school needed to be more transparent about housing during the recruitment process, Mr. Ahmad did not.

"We give them a free flight and a visa to come here, two thousand dollars a month, and a free apartment with free utilities. What are they complaining about?" he said one day as we were planning for the next school year.

"The teachers believe the contract is misleading, Mr. Ahmad. It promises a two-bedroom apartment and healthcare," I replied.

Ahmad shook his head, clearly irritated. "They *do* have healthcare," he responded, sitting behind his large desk in his office, off the school's main lobby. "And they each have their own room in the apartment. Why do we keep having the same issues?"

"But it's not the private insurance that some of the other schools are offering, and to them, a two bedroom apartment is different from a one-bedroom apartment with a converted living room."

"Those are bigger schools that have been operating for many years. They have more money than we do to spend on apartments and health-care," countered Ahmad.

"True," I agreed. "But our teachers feel their contract should indicate that the healthcare we're offering is not private and that the apartment is actually a one-bedroom. As it is now, if one of them gets sick, they need to go to a public clinic, and the female teachers are not comfortable with that. Some of them have been harassed at those public facilities."

Ahmad ignored that point, which he knew to be true. Instead, he focused on the apartments. "If we put in the contract that the apartment is a shared, one-bedroom accommodation, wouldn't they assume they were sharing the same room? They wouldn't accept the offer."

"Probably true," I said, trying to remain as agreeable as possible. "So maybe we could offer a few different options. A true, two-bedroom apartment to be shared by two teachers. A studio apartment for just one person. And a one-bedroom, also for just one person."

Ahmad laughed. "And how do you expect us to pay for that?"

"For those who wanted the one-bedroom, you could charge them for it. Some would definitely pay. Then you'd have happier teachers who would be more likely to perform well in the classroom."

"They are being paid to do a job, John. Their accommodation is a separate issue."

"I don't think they see it that way. To them, part of their payment *is* the accommodation and healthcare. If someone is not happy with it, it'll affect their performance."

More head-shaking. "If I hire an Indian or Filipino, I can save money, but then the parents are not happy. If I hire an American, the parents are happy, but the teachers don't like what we provide. Where does that leave us?'

I wanted to say that the real problem was racism. But I kept my mouth shut. "In my opinion," I said, "it's preferable to be as transparent as possible with the contracts. We'll have fewer unhappy teachers."

"Unhappy *Western* teachers, you mean" corrected Ahmad.

"Don't all people deserve to be treated fairly?"

Ahmad glared at me. "You think we're treating them unfairly?"

"It doesn't really matter what I think. *They* feel they're being treated unfairly. That is what matters."

There was a long moment of silence before Ahmad continued. "Your girlfriend thought she was being treated unfairly, too. Correct?"

I just about jumped out of my seat.

As Jeana and I'd planned, our attorney had already paid Mr. Haij the amount necessary to release her from his employment, allowing me to become her sponsor. But rumors of our relationship had already reached Haij even before the payment was made. Once it *was* made, he immediately went to his friend, Mr. Ahmad, to accuse me of manipulating the situation.

Which, of course, I had.

But they had no way of proving it, which was the advantage of using the attorney in the first place.

Despite my temptation to do otherwise, I remained calm when Ahmad mentioned Jeana. By then, she had moved in with me, something that was—believe it or not—illegal. So I did what I always tried to do with Mr. Ahmad: diffuse the situation.

"To be honest with you, Mr. Ahmad, many workers in Dubai feel that they're being treated unfairly. But I *do* appreciate everything that you're doing for *me*."

The conversation ended there.

A few days later, Jeana and I met Saad and Marie for drinks near the Jumeirah Beach Residences, a series of high-rise luxury apartments overlooking the Gulf. It was a short drive from the Green Community and one of Marie's favorite locations for dining and shopping, complete with a few French-style boutiques to remind her of home.

"I remember you telling me how important it was for the teachers to be comfortable in their accommodations," I said to Saad.

"It *is* important," agreed Saad, "but Ahmad is adamant that the teachers should just accept what they're given."

"Then maybe it's necessary to *push* him to understand," I suggested.

"I tried many times when I first arrived," he answered. "But nothing improved. Instead, he became more directly involved with the teachers' contracts. If anything, it got worse."

"He became more involved because he didn't trust you?" I asked, glancing over at Marie, who was nodding.

Saad saw his wife's reaction. "I don't know if it was because he didn't trust me or because he just wanted to save money. I'd secured new apartments for the teachers when I was handling it myself. But Ahmad thought they were too expensive. That's when he had his business manager take over the process of finding new accommodations."

"The teachers had been housed at International City, right?" I asked, remembering what the Friday Night Club had once told me.

"Yes. Those apartments were really bad," confirmed Saad. "Dirty and too far from the school. Where they are now is much better."

"So why not pay a little more money and make the teachers even happier?" I offered.

Saad smiled. "Happy?" he repeated.

"Yes," I replied. "What's wrong with that?"

"It's a very Western way of thinking. Ahmad will always resist that."

"I'm sorry, Saad. But I don't understand. What's wrong with making our employees happy? If they are, then won't they be more willing to work hard?"

"That's just the point," said Saad. "To Ahmad, you're negotiating for their effort. He thinks the effort should be there regardless of whether or not they're happy with their living conditions."

I leaned back in my chair. "But we're talking about mostly young women just a few years out of college. They are used to a certain standard of living."

Marie chimed in. "Employers here don't like that sense of entitlement. They think it's one of the negative parts of Western culture."

"What is?" I asked. "Wanting to have *good* living conditions?"

"No," she replied. "*Expecting* the same conditions here that you have in your home country. It would be like me expecting everything here to be like France."

"I think you're missing the point," I replied. "It's not a question of providing the same conditions. It's a question of transparency. If you're not going to provide something comparable to what the employees have come to expect in their own countries, then say so. But don't lie."

"Oh, I get it, John," responded Marie. "Believe me, I'm on your side. But what I'm saying is that *Ahmad* thinks that Americans are all entitled. He believes that Americans want every country to be just like America."

"I don't think basic human rights are peculiar to America," was my response, turning to Saad. "Don't people in Lebanon want good conditions? Or people in France? Or people in . . . wherever?"

"But to Ahmad, everything is compared to America," said Saad. "And he doesn't like that."

I took a deep breath, trying to stay calm. "What do *you* think, Saad? Do you also think that everything is unfairly compared to America?"

He laughed.

"I'm sure America is a wonderful place," he said. "But not every place in the world can be as wonderful. Other countries do the best they can."

Now it was Jeana's turn to jump in. "But I've talked to a lot of Filipinos here in Dubai, and many of them are treated just like Haij treated me. I don't think this country *is* doing the best it can. Why should Filipinos be treated worse than any other nationality?"

"In America, you always say that everyone is treated equally. But Arabs look at America and see that people *are* treated differently. Blacks, for example," said Saad. "So when America tells other countries that they need to do better with human rights, those other countries always think to themselves, *why don't YOU do better with your own human rights?*"

A part of me could see Saad and Marie's point. From my experiences in Africa and Honduras, I understood that much of the world considered America arrogant and hypocritical.

Yet all I was asking for was transparency. Two wrongs don't make a right.

If Mr. Ahmad didn't want to provide proper living conditions and healthcare, then okay. But don't promise people one thing, bring them half-way around the world, and then give them something completely different.

But I was beginning to understand that I was asking for something that would simply never happen.

Later that same night, Jeana and I met the Friday Night Club at Atmosphere, a bar on the 122nd floor of the newly opened Burj Khalifa, the tallest building in the world. It was our first time in the massive structure which was surrounded by a man-made lake and towered over the largest mall in the Middle East, the Dubai Mall, complete with an indoor amusement park and over twelve hundred stores and restaurants. On the opposite side of the lake from the Burj was one of the largest souks in the city, and behind it, newly built apartments and more hotels.

Each evening at dusk, the lake's fountains began dancing to the rhythm of a popular song that blasted from surrounding speakers, clearly an imitation of the water show at the Bellagio Hotel in Las Vegas. Like so much in Dubai, ideas were taken from other cities—mostly American cities, ironically—and then increased in scale to impress.

The entire area around the Burj was a new part of the city that had seemingly risen out of the desert overnight. But such was Dubai. Ever growing and expanding. Becoming more luxurious—and Westernized—by the day. But whenever I looked at all of those new buildings, I was always reminded of the workers that built them. Mostly Indian and Bangladeshi men, forced to live in horrible conditions, earning little more than a few dollars a day.

That was the *real* Dubai, the reality beneath the facade of wealth, luxury, and massive scale.

Our gathering at Atmosphere that night was also one of the few times that Jeana had joined the Friday Night Club. She wasn't a drinker, and didn't like to see me drinking. But she enjoyed the camaraderie of the group and became good friends with Yule, Kurtis' Korean girlfriend. As a stewardess for Emirates Airlines, she was paid well, so enjoyed a good lifestyle with Kurtis. But she knew how poorly Filipinos were treated around Dubai.

"It's just so unfair that one group of people is treated so differently. It's like the Arabs consider Filipinos to be their servants, or something," said Yule. "I don't know how you tolerate that, Jeana!"

"It's different when I'm with John," said Jeana. "But when I'm alone, yes, I feel they're looking down on me."

Ray was nodding. "Being a black guy in this city is like that. You always get these sideways glances from people. But I guess that happens in other countries, too."

"It does," I agreed. "But it feels different here. At least in the US people know it's wrong. Here, I don't get the sense that people really feel it's wrong."

"I also feel it when Ray and I are together," said Judy. "It's like people think I should be dating a white guy, and can't understand why I'm with Ray."

"Yeah. That really sucks," said Ray. "But it also depends where we go. If we're at a place like this," he said, looking around the bar, "then it doesn't seem to bother people. But if we go somewhere where there are a lot of local people, we definitely get those stares."

"Exactly," said Jeana. "If John and I are having brunch at a hotel, nobody looks at us twice. But when I was still working in the school cafeteria, the local teachers would look at us like we were doing something wrong. Just like that Dune Bashing trip we took a few weeks ago. They just kept staring at us and whispering behind our backs."

It'd been a last-minute decision to join the trip, organized by Asif, the school's technology director who was Pakistani. Ray and Judy had come along, but mostly it was the Arabic and Islamic teachers who joined. We'd met our safari guides at a local hotel, before splitting-up into groups of six people in each Land Cruiser which then took us about twenty miles outside the city and to the edge of the Arabian desert.

After the guides lowered the tire pressure in each truck, we headed-up into the dunes. From there, it was like a roller coaster, climbing to the top of one dune and then rapidly descending at top speed before roaring to the top of the next.

At one point, we stopped to enjoy the amazing sunset, the orange glow reflecting off the sand to create a dance of color. Our guides then took us to a nearby camping area where we were welcomed with traditional coffee and dates, followed by a barbecue dinner. Afterward, Jeana and I sat with Ray and Judy smoking shisha while a woman painted our arms with henna art.

As we enjoyed the experience, Jeana and I kissed. It wasn't until days later that we learned that such a display of affection had been unacceptable to the Arabic and Islamic teachers who were nearby.

"If you had kissed a white girl," said Kurtis, his back against the giant windows of Atmosphere, "their reaction would've been different, you know. What they can't understand is why a white guy is with an Asian. And to them, all Asians are the same. Inferior."

I took Jeana's hand, not wanting her to feel upset.

"It's not about you," said Trish. "They don't care about you as an individual. It's your nationality they don't approve. But even my boyfriend and I are careful when we're in public, and both of us are white. Remember that couple who were arrested for making out on the beach?"

We all nodded. They were a British couple on vacation and had been kissing on a public beach. Both were put into jail for nearly a week before the British consulate had finally secured their release.

"That's why the two of you have to be really careful about living together," said Judy to Jeana and I. "Ray and I *want* to live together. But we know the Islamic teachers in our building would report it to Ahmad. You're lucky that no other teachers live in your tower. But you still need to be careful. If Ahmad finds out, he'll put you both in jail."

It was so difficult to comprehend how a country in the twenty-first century could have such laws. Arab men were allowed to have multiple wives, but a boyfriend and girlfriend couldn't live together.

"Judy's right," said Yule. "It's why Kurtis moved-out of the school's accommodations to live with me. It's still a risk for us, but most of the other stewardesses are also Korean, so they don't care. But if someone reported us . . ."

Kurtis hugged Yule. "That's why we want to buy our own apartment," he said. "So we don't always have to worry about who is spying on us. But even buying an apartment is difficult because we're not married."

"It's so fuckin' crazy here," said Judy. "Look at this place." She looked out the window to the expanse of the city that lay nearly a half-mile below. "Probably the most modern city in the world, but their laws are from the seventeenth century, or something."

"Then why do you stay?" I asked. "You can get a teaching job in Canada and probably make more money."

"What about Ray?" she said. "It's hard for him to get a visa from South Africa to work in Canada. At least here, we can be together."

"What will you and Jeana do?" asked Kurtis. "Do you think you'll stay here in Dubai?"

Good question.

Jeana and I'd certainly talked about it many times since we started dating. But there was no simple answer.

Was Dubai an appropriate place for her children? And even if it was, their fathers would certainly not allow them to leave the Philippines.

America was an option. But getting a visa for Jeana would be a challenge, not to mention the same issue of getting the children out of the Philippines.

That seemed to leave the option of me finding a job in the Philippines. There were certainly many international schools in the country that might need a principal. But did I really want to return to a Third World country, following my experiences in Africa and Honduras?

A complicated situation, to say the least.

But it was about to become even more so.

CHAPTER FOURTEEN

Located on a plateau in the Judean Mountains between the Mediterranean and Dead Seas, Jerusalem is one of the world's oldest cities and considered holy to Jews, Christians, and Muslims, alike.

During its long history, it was destroyed twice, attacked more than fifty times, and sacked more than forty. Scholars believe that humans first lived in the area more than three thousand years before Christ. Two thousand years before Christ, King David conquered the city and made it the capital of his Jewish kingdom. His son, Solomon, built the city's first holy temple, which would become known as the Temple Mount. It was destroyed by the Babylonians about five hundred years later, and then rebuilt again. Alexander the Great took his turn in controlling the city in the centuries before Christ, followed by the Romans who settled in for centuries of authoritarian rule, some the stories of this period which are at the heart of New Testament lore, including the crucifixion of Christ at the hands of both Romans and Jews.

That single event, along with the Islamic prophet Muhammad's ascension into heaven from atop the Temple Mount in the seventh century, put the city at the crossroads of three major religions, the consequences of which continue to reverberate throughout the Middle East, and indeed the world.

Modern-day visitors to the city almost always visit the Wailing Wall, a small section of the ancient city's Western Wall which extends from the base of the Temple Mount, upon which was built the Al Aqsa Mosque in the years following Muhammad's ascension.

It was there that Jeana and I found ourselves on our first day of visiting the city.

As I approached the section of the Wall reserved for male worshippers, I looked over at Jeana who was approaching the female section. I knew it would be an emotional experience for her, having grown-up in a devoutly Catholic country which mostly believed in a literal translation of the Bible. Even though my feelings about religion were quite different, I also found the experience to be extremely moving, mostly because I knew how much it would've meant for my mother to have stood at that wall and touched the very foundations of her faith.

As you stand before the wall, you're able to insert a small piece of paper into one of the wall's many cracks and crevices. On my piece of paper, I'd simply written my mother's name. Jeana later told me that she had written the name of her grandfather.

So, what had brought Jeana and I to that wall?

You would think that I would've learned my lesson from the fiasco with the Israeli flag during my first week at the Green School and the subsequent backlash with the local teachers and Mr. Ahmad.

Jeana and I went to Israel partially to spite our bosses. Ahmad often referred to Israelis as terrorists, something he no doubt learned from his father and grandfather while growing up in Lebanon. Jeana's new boss, also Lebanese, often complained aloud in the office about the Jews, once saying that *all* of them should have been killed in the Holocaust.

But we also went to Israel to better understand where that hatred came from. How such a small piece of desolate land had influenced the lives of so many people across the region, around the world, and through time. But the trip wasn't without risk. Considerable risk.

"What if we can't get back to Dubai?" asked Jeana repeatedly as the trip began, knowing that immigration officers in Dubai often rejected passports with Israeli stamps.

"Don't worry," I always replied. "They'll never know we were here. The Israelis know not to stamp our passports."

We'd flown to Amman in Jordan where we hired a driver to take us across the Israeli border near Jericho. As we approached the frontier-crossing just a few kilometers from the Dead Sea, our driver was prepared to explain our situation to the young Israeli border agent who waved us to a stop. But before the driver could speak, the soldier grabbed our passports from the driver's hand and peered into the car.

"Americans?" he said, having looked at my passport first.

"I am," I replied. "My friend is from the Philippines."

His demeanor seemed to relax. "Where in America?" he asked in crisp English.

"My family lives in Boston."

He stared at me for a moment, and my heart skipped a beat. But then he said, "My brother and I live in Miami and will return this summer."

"Really?" I answered, surprised.

"We were born in America," he said. "But then came back here during the last intifada."

He must have seen my puzzled look. "The last Palestinian uprising," he explained. "I was called back to duty."

"You *had* to come?" I asked.

"No," he said firmly. "I *chose* to come. My father was born here but couldn't come because of his health. So my brother and I came instead. We're Israeli. It's our duty."

He continued flipping through my passport as I considered what he had just said.

"You're coming from Dubai?" he then asked.

Uh oh. But there was no use in denying it. "Yes," I replied, feeling my palms beginning to sweat. "We've lived there for a few years."

He nodded and then pulled out a pad of paper from his back pocket. "I'll stamp this paper instead of your passport," he said. "But keep the paper inside your passport until you return to Dubai. Then throw it out. They'll think you were only in Jordan." He handed back our passports, and added, "I don't think they'd appreciate your visit here."

"Thank you," I said.

The Israeli soldier nodded and then waved us along. As we drove away, I turned around and watched him through our rear window. As he carefully approached the next car, he certainly didn't seem like the terrorist that Ahmad had considered all Israelis to be.

During our five-day visit to the country, in addition to the Wailing Wall, Jeana and I visited such Biblical sites in Jerusalem as the Church of the Holy Sepulchre, the Via Dolorosa, and the Mount of Olives . . . all places that I knew Jeana would enjoy for their connection to Jesus's life and death.

We also traveled west to Tel Aviv to enjoy the Mediterranean beaches and north to the Sea of Galilee to see where Jesus was said to have walked on water. But one of our most memorable experiences was our visit to Bethlehem, located in the West Bank, a Palestinian territory. As the supposed birthplace of Jesus, it was one of the locations that Jeana was most excited to see.

But instead, it turned into a firsthand lesson on the realities of Israeli-Palestinian relations.

Our destination was the Basilica of the Nativity, the oldest major church in the Holy Land, built in the third century atop a grotto that is one of the oldest places of worship in Christianity, and considered by many to be the actual birthplace of Jesus. But just getting to Bethlehem to see the church was a challenge.

For all of our tours, Jeana and I'd used the same guide, an Israeli named Noam. His driver was Yousef, a Palestinian. Throughout our tours, Jeana and I listened to the two young men banter back and forth, switching among Hebrew, Arabic, and English with ease. At times we thought they were arguing. Other times they seemed to be the best of friends. But as we set-out from our hotel in Jerusalem to Bethlehem on our last day in the country, the true complexity of the relationship became more evident.

The actual distance between the two cities is little more than ten kilometers. But the journey took nearly two hours, not because of excessive traffic, but because of the need to pass-through an Israeli checkpoint at the fence that separates Israel from the Palestinian territory of the West Bank. As we waited our turn in line to pass through the gate, Noam explained the origin of the fence.

"The territory was captured by Jordan during the 1948 war with Israel and remained under their control until being taken back by Israel during the 1967 war. It remained under our control until it was given to the Palestinians as part of the Oslo Peace Accords of the early 1990s."

"But it was supposed to be *completely* given back, my friend," said Yousef to Noam. "Yet, people who live on the other side of the fence are basically prisoners, forced to pass through this gate every day to work in Jerusalem, and then pass through again to get back home."

"True," agreed Noam. "But Israel believes the fence is necessary. Before its construction, there were almost daily suicide bombings around Jerusalem. Since its completion a few years ago, the attacks have mostly stopped."

"But at what price?" argued Yousef. "It has created a jail for Palestinians."

"You live on the other side of the fence?" I asked Yousef.

"No. I live in East Jerusalem, on the Israeli side of the fence. But only because I can afford to. I'm lucky to have this job. But most of my friends make this crossing every day."

"You can see," said Noam, "that the fence has solved some problems, but created others. There really is no good solution."

"Why do Israelis and Palestinians hate each other so much?" asked Jeana, watching as some of the Israeli guards were yelling at a Palestinian family who was trying to cross through the fence. "You're both living on the same land."

"Do you have a few hours?" joked Yousef.

Noam laughed, as well. "First, I think Yousef and I are proof that the hatred is more political than practical. We're friends. We don't always agree on everything, but we've worked together for three years now, and our friendship has grown stronger."

Yousef nodded. "It's true. But there's no denying the root of the conflict: land. Palestinians lived here for hundreds of years when this region was part of the Ottoman Empire. When they lost the First World War, the British took over. And following the Second World War, they allowed the Jews who were coming from Europe to establish their own country. But the newcomers wanted the land for themselves, so expelled many of the Palestinians. Many went to Jordan and Lebanon. Later generations found themselves in such places as Dubai, where the two of you live."

I remembered Mr. Ahmad and his family.

"Why didn't the Jews want to share the land?" asked Jeana. "There seems to be a lot of empty land outside the cities."

"Because both sides claim Jerusalem," replied Yousef. "To both Jews and Palestinians, the city is a holy place and neither side wants to give it up. There are actually more Palestinians in the city than Israelis. But Israelis have the power. They have a stronger military, and can do what they want . . . such as building this fence."

As we continued to watch the Palestinian family trying to get back home through the checkpoint, it was easy to feel sorry for them. But as I remembered all those news reports about suicide bombers, it was also easy to understand why the Israelis wanted the fence.

It did seem like an unsolvable situation.

But our experience in Israel, particularly that day at the checkpoint to Bethlehem, helped me to better understand—if not sympathize with—the perspective of people like Mr. Ahmad. His family had fought the Israelis for control of the land and had lost. Now they were without a real home. How would I feel if I was unable to return to America? Or if Jeana couldn't go back to the Philippines to be with her children? It was a concept completely foreign to me . . . and to most Americans. But it was the root cause of so many problems in the Middle East. As Jeana and I returned to Dubai, I was hoping that our experiences would somehow soften my views about Mr. Ahmad and perhaps change the dynamics of our relationship.

They did not.

CHAPTER FIFTEEN

Our trip to Israel had only been possible because Jeana's visa indicated that she was my *servant*. Throughout the Middle East, it was common for certain nationalities, including Americans, to have nannies. Most often, the nannies were either Filipino or Indonesian. And since they were expected to travel with the families who employed them, it was reasonably easy to secure travel visas for them . . . to such places as Israel.

Jeana and I took full advantage of this during our time in Dubai, visiting Egypt and Italy, in addition to Israel. Places that were easy for Americans to visit, but difficult for Filipinos. While it was certainly a bitter pill for Jeana to swallow, to be referred to as a servant, she tolerated it, understanding that it'd freed her from Mr. Haij and provided the opportunity to travel.

Little did we know, though, that it was also paving the way for our future together.

When we applied for the travel visas to various destinations, it's likely that no one ever considered that Jeana was my girlfriend and not my servant. Mr. Ahmad knew, but could do little about it. He also likely knew that we'd visited Israel, but could never prove it since our passports had never been stamped. And he no doubt knew that Jeana and I were living together in the apartment that he was paying for, but hadn't yet tried to do anything about it.

As a result, the tension between us continued to grow as Jeana and I began our third year in Dubai. It was around that same time that we began giving serious thought to our next step. It didn't seem tenable to remain in Dubai beyond the completion of my three-year contract.

The question was, where would we go?

As that decision loomed, Jeana and I had both returned home. For her, it was her first visit with her children since leaving for Dubai more than two years earlier. For me, it was my annual trip home to see my father . . . and our pilgrimage together to mom's gravesite at Crystal Lake. By then, Dad was in his mid-eighties, but still strong and independent.

Yet, I knew that every visit with him was precious, never knowing when it would be the last.

"From what you've told me," said Dad, as we sat on his favorite bench and enjoyed the warm breeze that swept over the lake, "it would seem that Dubai is not someplace you should stay much longer."

I nodded. "I want to finish my contract," I said. "But then what? I really don't know."

"But you're sure you want to be with Jeana?"

"I am," I replied without hesitation. "I love her very much, Dad. I really think she's the right one."

"You realize that you'll become responsible for her children," said Dad. "You're sure that's what you want to do?"

"I made a lot of mistakes with Gabriela and the boys," I admitted, although not for the first time to Dad. "But when I married her, I was twenty-five. Now I'm forty-two. Hopefully, more prepared. More secure. And more mature."

"I think that's true," said Dad. "It was similar for your mother and me. All of my mistakes with Ruth in Montana had prepared me—in an odd sort of way—to make things work with your mother. But it would seem that Jeana's situation in the Philippines is even more complicated than Gabriela's in Honduras. How will you handle that?"

It was a question that had been continuously on my mind, and was the main reason why I'd wanted to come home: to get my father's opinion.

"I think the first step is to get her reunited with the children," I said.

"Which means you go to the Philippines," understood Dad.

"Yes," I confirmed. "I'm sure I can find a job there. I'll then have the time to get everything arranged for the next step. Someplace where she can be successful and the children will have more opportunities."

"Which means here."

I nodded. "It seems to make the most sense," I said. "But I know it'll be a long road."

"Like I think I've told you before, your mother didn't want to come here to Gardner to live. I forced it on her, and as a result, she had a tough first few years here. How do you know that Jeana will like it here?"

My father was always pragmatic.

"I think there may be a way to have her visit here first, see if she likes it," I said. "I'm still working on that part."

"Then you have one hell of a hard road ahead, Johnny. Are you sure you're up to it?" asked Dad. "Once you start down that road, you need to see it through. It would be unfair to them otherwise."

Dad was right, of course. He usually was. And that really was the bigger question. Would I see it through?

At the beginning of any long journey you never completely appreciate the many obstacles that you will need to be overcome. Most people hit those obstacles, and turn back. Would I turn back? Or would I have the wherewithal to keep moving forward.

Always forward.

As Dad had correctly pointed out, I realized that *even* if I was able to find a job in the Philippines, and even if we were successful in permanently reuniting Jeana with her children, how would we get everyone to America? And what if Jeana didn't like America? For her or for her children? It'd been a challenge to get Andres and Fernando out of Honduras, and that had been before all the changes to the immigration system following 9/11. Since then it'd become nearly impossible for a citizen of a Third World country like the Philippines to get an American tourist visa. They had to prove that they wouldn't stay in America, and the only way to do that was to show that they had a reason to return to their country, such as property or a large bank account. But Jeana certainly didn't own property and had little to no money in the bank.

But during our trips to Italy, Egypt, and Israel, it dawned on me that her servant visa might make it possible for us to get her an American visa. She could then accompany me home one summer, meet my father and sister, and see if America was a place she would want to settle someday.

When I returned to Dubai from my visit with my father, and Jeana returned from her reunion with her children, we made an appointment at the US embassy in Abu Dhabi. We walked in that day with low expectations. But walked out with an American visa stamped in Jeana's passport. The immigration officer had looked at me with a sly smile as we stood at his window, but hadn't said anything.

Did he know what we were doing?

I suspect he did.

But for reasons which only he knows for sure, he let it go, and gave Jeana her American visa. In doing so, set into motion a series of events that would play out over the following ten years.

Before we considered a trip to America, I wanted Jeana to accompany me on a trip to Ireland with my sister.

It was the twenty-fifth anniversary of a trip she and I'd taken a few years after our mother's passing. My father had wanted us to see where her family had come from in County Galway, so had planned the trip for us.

It'd been quite an adventure and one that set me on a completely different life-journey.

Before the trip, I'd been accepted at Emory Riddle University in Florida with dreams of becoming a pilot. During the trip, I decided instead to attend Mount Wachusett Community College in my hometown, living for two years with my father, before transferring to Bethany College in Kansas where I met the professor who would recommend the Peace Corps. The rest, as they say, is history. But if it'd not been for that trip to Ireland with my sister, my entire life would likely have been different. No Peace Corps in Africa. No Maria. No Honduras. No Gabriela. No divorce. No Dubai. No Jeana.

What had happened during that trip to change my mind so abruptly on where to attend college? A moment of quiet reflection on a dirt road outside of the small coastal town of Clifden in County Galway.

My sister often said it was mom's voice talking to me that day. I always said it was merely a moment of clarity during a time when everything seemed to be moving too fast. Things slowed down on that dirt road that day, and everything changed.

It wasn't until many years later when my father had shared with me a diary that had been kept by my mother's parents, Sean and Bridget, that the irony of my decision that day in Clifden was fully understood. I'd already learned that the decisions we make early in our lives almost always reverberate throughout our lives in ways that are only revealed as we go. But with that diary entry, I came to understand that those decisions indeed reverberate across generations.

CHAPTER SIXTEEN

A part of County Galway located to the west of Galway City, Connemara was once Ireland's largest Gaeltacht region in which the majority of its residents spoke the native Irish tongue. But the famines of the mid-nineteenth century had decimated its population. The turn of the century had seen a partial recovery, but most of the farmsteads of the region's glory days never recovered. Nevertheless, its bogs, lakes, and mountain vistas continued to attract residents of Galway who wanted to get away from the bustle of the ever-growing city.

Bridget's brother, Conor, had moved to the region a few years earlier to pursue a career as a painter, renting a room in the seaside town of Clifden. He and Bridget had often traveled there as children, enthralled by the wilderness and rugged coastline that surrounded the town.

Life was harsh, particularly during the winter months, and Conor struggled to make ends meet, finding that most Irish had little money to spend on luxuries such as art. So he had decided to try his luck in America, and he wanted Bridget to travel with him. He had suggested the idea to their parents, and had been slapped down hard for it.

But to Sean and Bridget, it was the opening they needed.

"Do you have enough money to go?" asked Bridget. "Sean and I have been saving for months, but we're still not sure it's enough, even though Sean's parents are helping him so he doesn't get sent to France to fight in the war."

"I have enough for the Atlantic crossing," replied Conor, who had lost a lot of weight since Bridget had last seen him. "When I get there, I'll figure it out."

"What if you can't find work?" asked Sean.

"I can't find work here, either," he replied with a sigh. "Maybe in America people will want my paintings."

Bridget and Sean looked around Conor's small room at the many landscapes he had completed, but couldn't sell. "These are amazing, Conor," said Bridget emphatically. "They really capture the beauty of the land."

"Maybe you could sell them in Galway," suggested Sean. "People have more money there."

"I know a few dealers there, but you really need to live there to have any chance," explained Conor. "If I have to live in the city, then why not New York or Boston. There must be plenty of opportunities there."

Bridget and Sean knew that there was no comparison between Galway and the big eastern cities of America. Like Conor, they wanted to try their luck across the Atlantic, not wanting to settle for a small town, Irish life.

"Have you told Mom and Dad yet about your plan to go together?" asked Conor. "Right now, they think it's just Sean and me going."

Bridget and Sean both looked at each other.

Conor smiled. "Not yet, huh?"

"It's hard," replied Bridget solemnly. "They won't understand. They don't even know we're dating."

"They need to know, Bridget. They deserve that. You can't just disappear."

Bridget knew her brother was right.

"When do you plan on leaving?" she asked her brother.

"Probably next month," he replied. "A friend works for the McCorkell Line and thinks he can get me a cheap ticket. Anything to save some money."

"Can he get two more?" asked Bridget.

Conor looked at his sister. "I'll ask him. But you need to talk with Mom and Dad. I don't want to get in the middle of that."

That night, the three of them went down to the pub beneath Conor's room to celebrate their time together. But as Sean and Conor nursed the one Guinness they could afford, Bridget took a walk down Beach Road which ran along the edge of the cove that gave the town its access to the sea. For the past year she had been keeping a diary about her relationship with Sean, and wanted to make an entry, maybe one that would help her find the right words to use with her parents.

It was good to see Conor again, but he looked so thin. I think life is hard for him here in Clifden. But I guess it's hard everywhere. He says that Sean and I can go with him to America, but only after I tell our parents. I know he's right. But I'm worried about how they will react when they know about Sean. I love him so much. When we're together, I feel complete. I can be myself. Mom and Dad were young when they married, so maybe they'll understand. I don't know. It's just so scary to think about a new life in America. What if something happens during the crossing? Or we can't find work? Or we get sick? But I know it's the right thing to do. There is nothing for us here. We can't spend our lives on a farm in Tuam.

"I want you to sell it, George," said Kathleen. "I want you to sell the farm. Use the money for the children's college. Please tell me that you will."

"I will, Kathleen. I promise," said George as he drove his wife to the hospital for what they both knew was the last time. She had fought hard, but was tired of the fight. The chemo had worn her down, and she'd had enough. A few months earlier she'd told George that she wanted to stop it. They both knew what that meant. But it was time to finally let go.

George had actually already sold the farm months earlier, but didn't want to overburden his wife with the details. They didn't need the money for the kids' college. That had already been taken care of from years of wise investing. But he did plan to use some of the money from the farm's sale to send John and Andrea on a trip to Ireland to see where their mother's family had come from nearly seventy-five years earlier. He wouldn't go. He wanted to, but knew that his leg would make it difficult for him to keep-up with the kids as they traipsed around the countryside of County Galway.

It'd all come as a surprise. A letter in the mail from an attorney in Galway. At first, they thought it was some sort of a mistake. Maybe the records had somehow been mixed-up. But in the months that followed, it became clear that Kathleen was the last living relative of her mother's side of the family who had come from County Galway. Her mother had passed away just a few years earlier, and all of her aunts and uncles had passed decades ago. A few had held-on in the *old country*, doing their best to keep the farm going. But with their passing, there was no one left.

Except Kathleen.

Over the years, Kathleen had told George many stories about her parents' journey from Ireland to America in the years following the First World War. He had always listened respectfully, knowing that Kathleen always yearned to see Ireland, but had been unable to because of her health. As he drove his wife to the hospital that day, he understood that the responsibility was now his to keep her family's history alive.

Sending John and Andrea to Ireland would be his way of doing that.

In the weeks following Kathleen's passing, he had gone through her belongings, most of which had been put into storage nearly twenty years earlier when they had first moved into the house on Bickford Hill. Perhaps Kathleen had gone through them over the years, but he had not. So when he came across the diary of her mother, Bridget, it was a revelation.

Written in Ireland in the years before her journey to America with the man who would become her husband, it detailed the story of a young woman with big dreams of a new life in America. The eventual reality of that life had probably not been as she had dreamed. But with the birth of Kathleen almost ten years after their arrival in the country as teenagers, they had started a new chapter in their families' history, one that would touch many lives throughout the twentieth century . . . and beyond.

CHAPTER SEVENTEEN

After spending a few days in London, my sister, Jeana, and I took the train north to Holyhead where we boarded a ferry to cross the Irish Sea to Dublin where we then took another train across the Emerald Island to Galway.

Twenty-five years earlier my sister and I'd done the reverse, wanting to see England after a summer of touring Ireland. It'd been a remarkable summer, exploring the country from east to west and north to south, from the mountains of Connemara in County Galway to the Cliffs of Moher in County Clare. From kissing the Blarney Stone at the medieval castle in County Cork to watching a Queen concert at Slane Castle near Dublin. But mostly it'd been about our mother's heritage, and visiting the family farm near Tuam.

Like my sister and I'd done nearly a quarter of a century earlier, the three of us stayed at a bed & breakfast in Tuam on High Street, near Saint Mary's Cathedral. During our second day, we hired a driver to take us to the farm on the outskirts of the town. Twenty-five years earlier, my sister and I'd actually hitchhiked our way there. But we weren't as brave anymore. Or maybe not as foolish.

Returning to the farm with Jeana was nearly as emotional as that first trip had been all of those years earlier. Sadly, the family who had bought the farm from my father just before our mother's passing had not been able to make a go of it, and was forced to sell in the years following our original visit. But the new owners had turned it all around, mechanizing nearly everything, and modernizing the main house of the farmstead.

Our grandmother had actually been born in an older structure on the property, one which had been abandoned even before my sister and I'd first visited. Back then, we'd entered the stone structure to see much of the original furniture from the turn of the century, covered in white sheets to protect it against time. Andrea and I'd made our way to the second floor and into a bedroom that had belonged to our great grandparents. Inside a drawer by the bedside we'd found an old dusty album of black and white photos that our grandmother must have sent home to her parents following her arrival in America, shortly after World War One. There were pictures of New York and Boston, of our grandfather working on the subway, and of our mother as a child in the 1920s and 30s.

Inside a closet in that same bedroom we'd then found a box with more photos, these of Andrea and I with our grandmother at Christmastime when we were small children, probably in the early 1970s. Our great grandparents had passed away before the Second World War having never left Ireland, but their sons had carried on with the farm, staying in touch with their youngest brother and sister, Conor and Bridget.

Sadly, when Jeana entered the house with Andrea and me, all of the furniture inside the house had long since been removed. But you could still feel their presence—our great grandparents and all those who followed them, those who had chosen to remain in the *old country*. They were like an echo from the past, reaching across time to touch us once again. The three of us cried that day in the bedroom, just as my sister and I'd cried twenty-five years earlier. And as I thought of those photo albums, I could imagine our great grandmother sitting on the edge of her bed, looking at those photos of her daughter in America.

She must have cried every day until the day she died.

The next day, Jeana, Andrea, and I rented a car and drove to Clifden. Of all the places I'd been in the world, none of them were quite as beautiful as Connemara on the west coast of County Galway. As we drove along the winding, two-lane highway from Galway westward, we passed one dairy farm after another, the properties still delineated by low, crumbling stone walls, all built many centuries earlier.

Rising-up in front of us were the Twelve Bens, a rocky mountain range that separated eastern Connemara from the Atlantic Ocean. As we passed-over them, we looked behind us to see an endless expanse of green stretching back toward Galway. And as we looked ahead, we saw the same ocean that Bridget and Sean would've looked upon as they dreamed of a new life in America.

Pulling into the small coastal enclave of Clifden, we parked near St. Joseph's Church and walked down Seaview Street until it crossed Beach Road. It was at that intersection—twenty-five years earlier—that I'd made the decision not to go to college in Florida, instead choosing the community college in my hometown of Gardner. And it was somewhere near that intersection—nearly a century earlier—that Bridget had written in her diary, searching for the words she would use to tell her parents that she would go to America, not only with her brother Conor, but also with her boyfriend, Sean.

That intersection, in that little Irish town, had changed the course of two young people's lives, separated in time, yet joined by blood.

"It's so important that both of you know your family's history," said Jeana to my sister and me as the three of us looked out across the waters of the Atlantic. "I don't know much about my family. My parents and grandparents never talked much about their lives."

"It was important to our father to keep our mother's memory alive," said my sister. "He talked more about her family than his own."

I nodded. "It's true. Sometimes he would talk about his time in Europe during the war. Maybe a little more about his time in Montana and Wyoming. But he always seemed more comfortable talking about our mother's family. And it all came alive when we spent that summer here all of those years ago." I put my arm around my sister.

My sister's journey had been very different from mine. After our mother died, we were both lost, taking very different paths in search of some sort of meaning to it all. But there were no clear answers. No rhyme nor reason why our mother had been taken from us. After graduating from college, she found a job in Boston, and never left. But over the years, she often struggled with anxiety and bouts of depression.

I, on the other hand, never stayed anywhere for long. Always in search of something elusive.

But despite our different paths, we'd always remained close. And that, perhaps more than anything, was what made our father proudest. To know that his two children could rely on each other. And to know that after he was gone, the family would carry on.

"It's hard to believe it's been twenty-five years," my sister said wistfully. "So much has happened."

And I knew that so much more was coming.

CHAPTER EIGHTEEN

A few months after that emotional trip to Ireland, Jeana came to America. The purpose of the trip was simple: Was America a place where she could see herself and her children settling someday?

It still seemed like a distant dream. But securing her American visa in Abu Dhabi had been the first step, and the visit to America the second. The third step had already become clear: relocating to the Philippines to permanently reunite her with her five children. The fourth and final step—many years down the road—would be to bring everyone to America.

But first, I wanted her to see my hometown . . . and Crystal Lake.

"Kathleen was my wife," said my father, pointing to my mother's grave with his cane, as I stood nearby with Jeana and my sister. "Actually, she was my third wife. I lost my first in the war, and divorced from my second."

"I'm so sorry, sir," said Jeana, always respectful of her elders. "John has told me a lot about his mother. She sounded like an amazing person."

Dad looked at me and nodded. "I'm glad Johnny has told you about her. I wanted both he and his sister to remember their mother in the best way possible. It was one of the reasons why I sent them to Ireland all those years ago, although I never knew the impact it would have, especially on Johnny."

"I loved it there," said Jeana. "It's so beautiful."

"Yes," replied my father. "Kathleen always wanted to see it, but just ran out of time." Dad paused for a moment, collecting himself, before continuing. "There's something about the Irish spirit that is exceptional. Maybe it's the centuries of struggle they went through, both here and in the *old country*. Maybe it's the land itself, so beautiful, yet so unforgiving. Like poet-warriors fighting an ancient enemy . . . time itself."

I'd never heard my father talk like that before. But he meant every word.

"Sadly, it was only after her death that I really came to appreciate it," said Dad, leaning on his cane and staring down at mom's grave.

"She told me many stories about her parents' arrival in this country, and stories of their lives before, in County Galway. She always described them as being so strong when they were young, before being beat down by years of struggle in this country. Toward the end of her life, Kathleen's mother came to live with us here in Gardner. She and I never got along very well. I think she always blamed me for taking her daughter away . . . her only child. But before she died, she told me something that I have never forgotten. She wasn't a particularly well-educated woman—probably never going much beyond a year or two of high school—but she understood her role perhaps better than I understood my own."

George, I came to this country as a teenager with big dreams. I thought Sean and I—god rest his soul—would become rich and famous. We were kids. What did we know? But when Kathleen was born, that all changed. It was no longer about us. It was about her. We accepted that we would never be rich, that we would never see much outside of Boston. But we had a new dream. An even bigger dream. We wanted Kathleen to grow up to do great things. Then, when Sean passed and Kathleen got sick, I had to find a new dream again: John and Andrea. And I think that's what it's all about, you know. Each generation doing a little bit better than the one before, until one day, the dream is finally realized.

"Imagine that," continued Dad, shaking his head and looking out across Crystal Lake. "There I was with my Harvard education being taught by an uneducated Irish immigrant. I'd spent the first half of my life trying to understand my role in this life, and she had laid it out in less than two minutes." Dad laughed, and turned back toward Jeana. "You have quite a journey ahead of you, don't you Jeana?"

"Yes, sir. I feel the same about my children. I want the best for them, even if I can't have it for myself."

My dad put his hand on Jeana's shoulder. "That's why you'll be successful here. This country works best for those who are willing to work hard and sacrifice for their children. And for those who understand the importance of education. But it takes time. Sometimes more than one generation. John and Andrea have done well for themselves. Your children can do well here, too."

"I hope so, sir. But John and I still have a lot to decide."

My father smiled. "You do. But it'll all work out all right, I believe. Just so long as you stick together."

Jeana began crying and fell into my father's arms, as my sister and I looked on, our own eyes watering up.

"It's okay, my dear. Kathleen would've loved you very much." He then grabbed her by both shoulders.

"Now, listen to me, Jeana. You and Johnny go back to Dubai, finish up things there, and then get those children out of the Philippines. From what Johnny has told me, they're in a tough situation there. Figure out a way to get them here, and then start over. They may find their way immediately, or it might take a generation or two." Dad looked down again at his wife's grave. "But of all the places in the world that you can go, it's this country that provides the best opportunities. No guarantees, mind you. And far from perfect. But good opportunities for those who can take advantage of them."

When my sister and I were young, we never thought much about our parents having their own dreams. Most children don't. But as I stood beside my father that day as he spoke to Jeana, it all became clear to me. Dad had left home at the age of nineteen because he dreamed of a life beyond the little town of Gardner, away from his mother and the memory of his father. Time chipped away at those dreams, first during the war in France, then in Montana, and finally with our mother's illness and eventual passing.

For years I couldn't understand how he had been able to live alone for all of those years following mom's passing. But at some point—perhaps just after her death, or maybe many years later—he came to the same realization as our grandmother. Namely that his role was to raise Andrea and I the best he could, and then watch us realize our own dreams. And in doing so, his own struggles would be given purpose. It was the circle of life that he had spoken of many years earlier.

But as I watched Jeana falling into my father's arms—perhaps thinking of her own grandfather who had been her role model when she was young—I wondered if I would be able to do what my father had found the strength to do: put my own dreams aside, and do whatever was necessary to give Jeana and her five children the opportunity to realize theirs.

CHAPTER NINETEEN

Our trip to America had been perfect.

Jeana had seen my hometown, met my father, and surveyed American culture. And when it was over, she knew it was where her children needed to be.

When I'd brought Andres and Fernando to America from Honduras, I was really too young to fully appreciate the advantages that America provided. But like my father had told Jeana, if you finish college, work hard, and have some luck, then you have a good chance of a fulfilling life in America. In the Philippines, like Honduras, opportunities were just too limited, and the cycle of poverty too entrenched.

But before we could even consider the children's future in America, there was a lot that needed to be done, and a lot of luck that needed to come our way. So, we returned to Dubai with a renewed focus on finding jobs in the Philippines.

And before we could even get started, another roadblock appeared.

A big one!

"I can't believe that someone broke into your apartment," said Trish. "What did the police say?"

"We didn't call them," I replied.

"Why not?" asked Judy, as we all sat around a table at the rooftop Buddha Bar atop the Grosvenor House Hotel in the Marina. Over nearly three years of hanging out with the Friday Night Club, it'd become one of our favorite spots, with 360-degree views of the ocean, marina, and city lights.

But not even our favorite watering hole could distract us from the current situation.

"Nothing was stolen, and they didn't really break-in. There was no sign of forced entry," I answered, with Jeana sitting by my side. "We think they had a key."

"What?" asked Kurtis, disbelieving. "Who has a key? Somebody from the school?"

"No doubt," I replied. "Probably Mr. Khalil sent someone."

"Mr. Khalil?" repeated Judy.

"Mr. Ahmad's accountant," I explained. "He's the one who leases the apartments. He has copies of everyone's keys in his office at the school."

"But they can't just enter whenever they want!" said Judy. "If he sent someone to my apartment . . ."

I cut her off, probably more abruptly than I intended. "What, Judy? What would you do? The apartments are all in the school's name and there's nothing in our contracts that say they *cannot* enter. You know the laws here. You all taught me that."

"He's right, you know," said Arvin to everyone. "I bet they were trying to prove that Jeana is living there." Arvin had become a really good friend to Jeana and me. Since he was Filipino, Jeana felt comfortable around him and they often spoke in their native language, Tagalog.

"You have to be very careful," he added, looking intently at us. "If they didn't already find something, they'll keep trying."

"Like what?" asked Yule, Kurtis' girlfriend. "What could they have been looking for?"

"Anything really," I replied. "Anything that proves that Jeana is living with me. Her clothes in my closet. Her make-up in the bathroom. Anything."

"Jesus Christ," exclaimed Ray, suddenly standing up. "That's is fuckin' crazy. We can't let them get away with this!"

We were in a bad spot. There was no getting around it. When Jeana and I realized that someone had been in the apartment, we'd thought about calling the police. But that would've just brought more attention to our living arrangement. So then we'd thought about confronting Khalid or even Ahmad. But to what end? What would've been the endgame?

There was no way we were going to come out on top.

Everybody sat quietly for a few minutes, with all eyes on Jeana and me. But we had no answers.

"I may have an idea," said Arvin finally. "A long shot."

All eyes shifted to him.

"When I first started working at the school," he continued, "they were still building the gym. And then the construction stopped for months. People figured that maybe Ahmad was short on money and couldn't get it finished. But one day this Russian guy came to the front office. Really angry. Demanding to see Ahmad."

"Russian?" I repeated. "Who?"

"Ramy later told me that he was a business partner of Ahmad's father who had helped to put up the main building of the school," remembered Arvin. "Maybe he was also involved in building the gym . . ."

"And something went wrong," finished Trish. "I remember hearing about that, too. Ramy's wife was really rattled by him."

"But how does that help us?" I asked.

"You need an ally, John," said Trish. "Somebody who's on your side. Somebody with some influence. Maybe this guy can help."

"I don't understand," said Jeana. "Why would a Russian help us?"

"If he and Ahmad had a falling-out," said Judy, "maybe he'd be willing to share some information. Something you could use against Ahmad. Worth a shot."

"What about Saad?" wondered Ray. "Could he help somehow?"

"This is crazy," responded Jeana, obviously very upset. "We just need to get out of Dubai. Now!"

"Where would you go?" asked Kurtis. "Back to the States?"

I looked at Jeana. "We've been thinking about going to the Philippines, so Jeana can be with her kids."

Everybody's eyes widened.

"Can you get a job there?" asked Kurtis.

"Probably," I answered. "There are some international schools. But I'd prefer to have something lined-up before going. I can't be without a job for long. I'm still making alimony payments to my ex-wife."

"You're in a hell of a spot, John," said Trish. "But maybe this Russian guy can buy you some time."

Maybe, I thought.

But first I would meet with Saad and Marie. Maybe they would have another idea.

"We're leaving this summer," said Marie. "After what happened at your apartment, we've had enough." Saad was sitting beside his wife, nodding his head. "Ahmad thinks he can control everything. We're sick of it."

The day after having drinks with the Friday Night Club at the Buddha Bar, Jeana and I met Saad and Marie at Costa Coffee inside the Green Community Mall. Jeana and I frequently went there for their Starbucks-like coffee and would then take a walk through the Marriott's gardens alongside the man-made lake. It was always a good way for us to relax and center ourselves. But as we sat on the patio outside the coffee shop with Saad and Marie, we were far from relaxed.

"They're just bad people," continued Marie. "The entire family is corrupt. We thought that it would be different at the school. But it's the same. Maybe worse."

"So you knew the family was corrupt before you accepted the job at the school?" I asked Saad.

He shrugged. "We'd always heard rumors, both in Lebanon and here. But we figured it was par-for-the-course in the construction business. Payoffs, bribes, and the like. But then I realized it was the same at the school."

"Arvin told us about a Russian guy who came to the school years ago, angry about something. Did you ever hear anything about it?" I asked, holding Jeana's hand.

Marie looked at Saad who was shaking his head, eyes cast downward. "They need to know, Saad," she said.

"What is it?" pressed Jeana. "You know him?"

After a long pause, Saad answered. "I don't know him personally, but I heard about the incident. I even asked Mr. Ahmad about it. He wouldn't answer, but I could tell by his reaction that he knew the man. So I asked a few people who worked for Mr. Ahmad at his family's construction business. One of them told me to just *let it go*."

"And did you," I asked, "let it go?"

"I'd no reason not to," replied Saad. "But I probably should have listened to Marie at that point." He looked up at his wife. "She never liked him."

"I wanted Saad to quit," added Marie. "But then Mr. Ahmad offered him the director position. It was a lot more money."

"And that's when you hired me," I understood.

Saad nodded. "Yes. He told me to hire an American. Said it would help us get more students."

"We should have told you all of this," said Marie. "But that's what Ahmad counts on. He thinks that if he pays people enough, they'll look the other way. But enough is enough."

"He crossed the line when he had someone go into your apartment," said Saad. "I can't work for someone like that."

"Who *did* go into our apartment?" I asked. "Khalil?"

"Probably not him," replied Saad, drinking his coffee. "Maybe one of his subordinates. But it doesn't really matter. If they'd go to that extreme, there's no telling what they'll do next."

"That's why you both need to leave Dubai," stated Marie firmly. "He wants to put you both in jail."

"Why?" I asked. "What did we do to him?"

"It's about control, John," answered Marie. "He wants to control everything and everyone. When you were able to get Jeana away from Haij, I'm sure they both plotted all of this. They don't like losing."

We all sat quietly for a few minutes, looking across the lake at the fountain that was shooting water more than fifty feet into the air. Beyond the lake, we could see a soccer game going on at the nearby sports complex.

"I just need a little time to find a job in the Philippines," I said finally. "Maybe a month. Do you think it's safe to stay that long?"

Marie answered immediately. "Not really. He's well connected in the Department of Labor. He could get you red-flagged at the airport, and then you wouldn't be able to leave."

"Red-flagged?"

"If there's an open case against someone, it'll show up when they try to leave the country. You could be detained."

"Do you really think he'd file a case against us for just living together?" asked Jeana. "We're not hurting anyone."

Marie reached-out to touch Jeana's hand. "I know, Jeana. But like I said, he doesn't like losing. Filipinos are not supposed to get the upper hand on Arabs. But you did. They won't let that go."

"So who's driving this?" I asked. "Ahmad or Haij?"

"In the beginning, probably Haij," answered Saad. "But when you went to Israel, that was crossing the line in Ahmad's mind."

"I told you we never should have gone there," said Jeana to me, loudly.

Saad waved his hand. "If it wasn't that, it would've been something else, Jeana. Once you're on his radar, he won't let it go until he wins."

"You keep saying that, Saad," I said, my voice rising. "Win. Lose. But it's not a game!"

"It is to him," said Marie. "A very dangerous game to you."

"Is there anything you think this Russian guy could do for us?" I asked. "Maybe somehow buy us more time."

"I don't know," admitted Saad. "Maybe. I could probably set up a meeting if you think it'd help. I believe his name is Anatoly."

"The Russians are dangerous people," cautioned Marie. "I'd stay away from them if I were you."

But somehow we needed to get Ahmad to back off, at least for a while.

"Set up the meeting," I told Saad. "I don't think we have any choice."

A few nights later, Jeana and I arrived at a dark and dingy, smoke-filled Russian bar called Muscovites in Bur Dubai, one of the older sections of the city. Although prostitution was illegal in the country, there were certain areas where it was allowed to flourish, if kept underground. That was Bur Dubai. Many of the prostitutes in the area were Russian, coming over from the Russian communities in Sharjah and charging exorbitant fees to satisfy their customers, many of whom were Arabs from other countries who came to Dubai to play hard and fast.

The moment Jeana and I entered the seedy bar, we were tempted to turn around and leave immediately. But we toughened up, still feeling that it was worth a shot.

Jeana and I crossed the bar, making our way through the crowd on the dance floor, as scantily-clad young women—mostly Russian—brushed up against us, moving suggestively to the Russian techno-pop music.

Anatoly had told Saad that he'd be waiting for us in a corner booth near the bathrooms. As we approached, Jeana stopped and squeezed my hand.

"Last chance to back out," she said, almost yelling to be heard over the music.

I looked at her and nodded, then pulled her gently forward.

The Russian was an older man, with a weather-beaten face and slicked-back hair. But he was well-dressed, his shiny shoes sticking out from beneath the table. He was surrounded by a bevy of young girls, which he promptly shoo-ed away as he saw us approach.

Saad had told us that Anatoly was most likely part of a growing number of Russians living in Sharjah who were taking advantage of the friendly visa rules to vacation and work. Many were involved in the import-export business, using the country's open banking system and many free-zones to cheaply move cash and goods in and out of the country. As their numbers grew, a subculture had developed, one where prostitution and drugs were rampant, and ties to the Russian Bratva back home were sundry.

The Russian motioned for us to sit down.

"Drink?" he asked, his eyes darting around the bar.

Almost on cue, a young waitress in a revealing little outfit arrived at our table to take our drink orders. I ordered two Heinekens, as the Russian studied us intently.

"Saad said you wanted to talk," he said in a thick accent. "So talk."

I leaned toward the Russian so he could hear me. "We were told that you worked for Ahmad when he was building the school. Did something happen?"

"I didn't work *for* that svolock," spat the Russian, saliva spewing from his mouth. "We only supplied materials. But he didn't pay us. So we filed a claim with the Ministry of Labor."

"What happened with the case?" I asked.

"Nothing," replied Anatoly. "The svolock has connections there."

"That was the end of it?"

"No," said the Russian, shaking his head and taking a shot of his vodka. "We had people look into his company."

"Really?" I asked. "Did you find anything?"

"We found a lot," replied the Russian, now with a sly smile across his face. "The family owes money to a lot of people here, and in Lebanon," explained Anatoly. "And he has connections with Hezbollah."

"Hezbollah?" I repeated, disbelieving. "The terrorist group?" I looked around to be sure no one had heard me.

Anatoly laughed. "You Americans consider them terrorists. A lot of Russians, too. But most Arabs don't, especially in Lebanon."

Hezbollah was founded in the late seventies as part of an Iranian effort to merge various Lebanese militias into a unified organization that would act as their proxy in operations against Israel. They were also believed to have attacked American soldiers in Iraq during the first and second gulf wars. But to Anatoly's point, they were also known to provide many social services in the poorest neighborhoods around Beirut.

I remembered the stories that Saad had told me about Ahmad's family, his father having fought the Israelis in the nineteen sixties. So it wasn't a stretch to believe that he had developed connections with Hezbollah. And maybe those connections had been passed on to his son.

But I couldn't see how any of it was helpful to Jeana and I.

"Did Saad tell you what happened at our apartment?" I asked.

"He did," responded the Russian. "What do you want me to do about it?"

"Jeana and I want to leave the country, but I need some time to find a new job. Saad seems to think that we should leave immediately."

"He's probably right," agreed Anatoly. "It seems dangerous for you here."

Just what Marie had said.

"Is there anything you can do to help us?" asked Jeana, speaking for the first time.

The Russian seemed surprised by this, a smile returning to his face. "I like Filipinos," he said. "They work hard. Honest. Good people." He then paused. "I'll see what I can do for you. If nothing else, it will be a way for me to stick it to that svolock."

Anatoly then summoned his girls to return to the table. The waitress soon reappeared, and more drinks were on their way. It seemed as though our meeting was over.

CHAPTER TWENTY

"Let's get married," said Bridget to Sean as they sat together by the docks of Galway, preparing for their journey to America in just a few days.

"What? Are you crazy?" replied Sean. "Our parents will never accept that. They're still recovering from the news that we'll be traveling to America together."

"You don't want to marry me?" asked Bridget, standing up and looking down at Sean.

"Of course I do, Bridget. But why now? Why not wait until we get to America, like we planned?"

They would be taking a ship called the Cedric from Galway to New York and then a train to Boston. Bridget's brother knew someone there, another artist, and he would help them to get started.

"Why *not* now? We don't have to tell our parents."

Sean looked up at Bridget. "I don't know if that's the right thing to do. They don't deserve to be lied to. This is all hard enough for them."

Bridget looked away toward the ocean. "We both know, Sean, that we'll probably never return here. When we say goodbye to them tomorrow, it'll be for the final time."

Sean knew she was right. But it was still hard to accept.

Bridget looked back at Sean. "I love you. I want us to be married *before* we go. If anything happens during the trip . . ."

Sean put his arm around Bridget. "Nothing will happen. We'll make it there. I'll find work. And everything will be okay."

The two teenage lovers embraced on the Galway docks, by the edge of the Atlantic Ocean, within view of the ship that would soon take them to America. They then turned, held hands, and walked toward the church only a few blocks away, resolute in their love for one another and in the hope of a brighter future in a far-away land.

"Your grandmother never liked me much," said my father as we walked together along the streets of Jamaica Plain, not far from where mom grew up. "In fact, she didn't even come to our wedding, something I knew hurt your mother deeply. But I understood. She'd had a hard life."

It was the summer of 1988. I'd just finished my two years at the community college in my hometown, living the entire time with my father. A few months later I would be going to Kansas to study at Bethany College. And a few years after that I would be in Africa.

That day—a typically humid summer day in Boston—we'd gone into the city to watch the Red Sox play the Yankees at Fenway. The Sox had won, with Roger Clemens pitching a three-hit shutout.

After the game, we drove over to Jamaica Plain. As children, my sister and I'd gone there a few times each year to spend time with our grandmother. But I hadn't been back for many years.

"It's sad, isn't it," I said to my father as we stood in front of my grandmother's old house, now occupied by a family from Puerto Rico. The area had become so run-down. "Sad how things change."

"That's life. Always changing. We all have a small part to play in it. We do the best we can with what we have and hope our children can do a little better than we did. In the end, your grandmother came to understand that. But it took many years. But without her part of the story, I never would've met your mother, and my own story would've been much different."

Dad and I continued walking through the neighborhood.

"As you get older you begin to see how things are connected," continued my father. "It's both sad and amazing, all at the same time. It's one reason why I wanted you and your sister to go to Ireland, so you could see where the story of your mother's side of the family began . . . and why they chose to come to America. I'm sure it was the hardest decision they ever made. To leave their homes. But so many immigrants in this country have had to make that same decision. Many who arrive here don't find the life they had wanted or expected. But they can still hope that someday their children will. That's America. That's the American Dream. It's generational."

My father and grandparents were on my mind as I drove north out of Dubai along highway-eleven, passing through the suburb of Sharjah before entering another of the country's seven emirates, Ras Al-Khaimah. Less wealthy and far more conservative than Dubai, it's known primarily as the agricultural region of the country due to its share of rainfall and underground water streams.

Passing through RAK and continuing north, you arrive at the Oman border, beyond which lies only a few towns, including Khasab. While not a place where most residents or tourists often travel, it was one of my favorite locations to go with Jeana.

Sparsely inhabited due to its rocky, mountainous terrain, there's little reason to venture into the region—known as the Musandam peninsula—other than to enjoy the outdoors, particularly snorkeling or scuba-diving in the warm waters of the Strait of Hormuz, the narrow sea-passage between Oman and Iran.

During one of our first trips to the area, we'd been fortunate to see the incredible sight of the American Seventh Fleet passing through the strait from the Indian Ocean on its way into the Persian Gulf and the base in Qatar. The imagery was enough to give us chills, as jet fighters from the fleet's carrier roared overhead announcing the American presence, followed by a line of helicopters flying along each shoreline, protecting the fleet from both known and unknown dangers. Looking through our binoculars that day from atop one of the many rocky mountain peaks that overlooked the strait, we watched in awe as the fleet slowly moved past, no doubt filled with soldiers and sailors tasked with fighting our Middle Eastern wars and keeping the shipping lanes open to ensure the flow of oil out of the Gulf and around the world.

Now we were back again, staying at the seaside Atana Khasab Hotel. The purpose of this trip was simple: take some time to reflect upon the previous three years, while also looking ahead to our next adventure . . . in the Philippines.

It'd happened much faster than expected.

After meeting with the Russian, I immediately began applying for jobs in the Philippines. Most of the international schools were in Manila, not far from Jeana's children. But a few were farther north in the province of Pampanga near the old American military base, Clark Airfield.

One of those northern schools, Clark International, showed immediate interest.

After speaking with the school's owner only a few times, I was offered the job. While it involved less money than I was making at the Green School, it was still a generous offer—given the country's Third World status—and included a nice accommodation, vehicle, and health coverage. At first, I thought back to how quickly Saad had offered me the job at the Green School. Not wanting another situation like that, I was momentarily hesitant to accept the offer from Clark International. But when I saw Jeana's excitement at the prospect of returning home, I realized that I'd be foolish to turn it down.

And so, I accepted the offer to become the school's next headmaster.

But there was still much to be decided.

First and foremost was how to leave Dubai. Ordinarily, I would inform my boss that I'd accepted a new position, provide proper notice, and then leave. But in Dubai, it's not that simple.

When I'd arrived in Dubai three years earlier, it'd taken the school a few months to process my employment visa. Consequently, the three-year visa in my passport didn't expire for another few months, later in the fall. Leaving an employer before a visa expired wasn't simple and often resulted in a penalty equal to the salary that you would've been paid until the visa did expire.

But I'd no intention of paying any such penalty to Mr. Ahmad.

Therefore, it would be necessary for Jeana and I to leave the country quietly. Not even the Friday Night Club could be told. And that's what bothered me most of all. They had been good friends, seeing me through some very difficult times. But something told me that they'd understand.

"I'll miss them," I told Jeana as we sat on the deck of a traditional Arabian Dhow sailboat with the sun beating down on our heads and the warm Arabian winds at our back.

"Maybe you'll see them again," offered Jeana.

"Maybe," I replied, but I doubted it. By leaving Dubai in the way we planned, we could never go back again. No doubt Ahmad would make sure of that.

"No second thoughts?" asked Jeana, studying me intently. "We could stay a while longer, you know."

"No way!" I answered emphatically. "We need to get out of here. It's just hard to leave behind people you care about."

"We'll meet new people in the Philippines."

"I know."

Jeana continued to look at me intently as we admired the stark beauty of our surroundings, the Dhow bouncing over the waves as a group of dolphins swam alongside.

"Are you sure you're ready for this, John?" she finally asked. "It's a big commitment."

"You mean with your kids?"

"Yes."

It was a big commitment. But I was ready.

The previous day, while Jeana was enjoying a well-deserved massage in the hotel's spa, I'd taken a long walk along the nearly deserted beach, stopping multiple times to sit alone on the white sand, staring out at the aqua-blue waters of the Persian Gulf. The last three years had been a whirlwind, but in many ways they had been the best years of my life.

Because of Jeana.

With her, I'd found what had eluded me for much of my life: fulfillment and purpose. I'd come to Dubai to start over, thinking it was meant only to be a period of transition. A time to find myself and my path in life. But it'd turned into so much more.

Like Sean and Bridget had found each other nearly a century earlier, I'd found my life-partner.

"I failed with Gabriela and boys for many reasons, but mostly because of my own insecurities," I said to Jeana aboard the Dhow. "I was unable to give myself fully to them. I wanted more *from* them than I was willing to give *to* them. I was selfish. Plain and simple. And I was too young. I suppose some men are able to be a father when they're twenty-five. I certainly wasn't. I wasn't even able to be a good husband."

"What's different now?" asked Jeana, as we moved to sit in the shadow of the dhow's sail to escape the sun's intense rays as we looked upon the stark beauty of the rocky mountains that dropped straight into the sea.

"You're different," I replied simply.

Jeana looked at me intently. "What do you mean?"

"I feel comfortable with you. I can be myself. I can let down my defenses. I'd never been able to do that with Gabriela. I always felt somehow insufficient with her, like I was never meeting her expectations. Like I never *could* meet her expectations. With you, I'm more confident, more sure that this is the right path."

"But I'm just a Filipino," said Jeana, almost embarrassingly. "Why not a white girl?"

She had actually asked me that same question before, and I'd come to understand that it was a point of insecurity for her. "You're the most amazing person I have ever met, Jeana. You have endured so much, yet you're so positive. Always smiling. Always patient. Always able to find something good in everyone."

It was true. I'd never met anyone quite like her before. But I also knew that she was incomplete, and the only way for her to become the person she wanted to be—the person she could be—was for her to be reunited with her five children.

Ryan. Daniel. Nadine. Liza. Nathan.

Believing that I could help her to realize that dream had also given me a sense of purpose that I'd never had before. Yes, I'd helped Andres and Fernando come to America. But it was different, because *I* was different. I didn't see Jeana's five children as some unwanted obligation that accompanied my relationship with her, as I'd sadly seen both Andres and Fernando. I saw them as five individuals who needed their mother, and a fresh start.

"You're the girl of my dreams, Jeana," I continued. "You're the person who I want to spend the rest of my life with. I have never been happier than I'm with you now."

Jeana put her arms around me and began to cry. "I don't deserve you," she said.

"No, Jeana. It's me who probably doesn't deserve you. I never really believed second chances were possible, never mind third chances. My father kept telling me that I would find someone again. But I didn't really think it would happen. At least not with someone like you. I don't know what I've done to deserve you, but I'm forever grateful."

"Do you think that feeling will be the same if we're able to get my children?"

"Not *if*. When. We *will* get them," I said confidently. "I promise you that. I don't know how long it'll take. But they will be with us as soon as possible."

"I don't expect you to love them as your own children. At least not in the beginning."

"I think those first few months with them will be the most important."

"Why?"

"With Andres and Fernando, I expected them to behave a certain way when they first came to America. My way." I explained. "But why should they have done that? It wasn't their responsibility to adjust to me. It was my responsibility to adjust to them. It started badly and never recovered. It'll be different this time. I promise."

"It's going to be a long journey," said Jeana. "Far beyond those first few months."

"Definitely," I replied. "The ultimate goal is to get all of you to America."

"One step at a time, I guess," said Jeana, still in my arms.

Yes, one step at a time.

The sun was starting to set as I lay atop that Dhow with Jeana in my arms. At that moment, I thought about my father and all of those words of wisdom he had shared with me over the years. He had always taught me to keep moving forward. To learn from my mistakes, but not to spend all of my time looking over my shoulder.

Learn your lesson, and then move on, he often said.

But now I was moving forward into completely uncharted waters. It was simultaneously scary and exhilarating. My heart was pounding, but I knew that my Dad would always have my back. Whenever things started to spin out of control, I could always lean on him.

Yet, the sun was also fast setting on my father's life as he neared ninety. I so wanted Jeana's children to make it to America while he was still alive. The circle of life would then be complete. But it was going to be a race against time.

CHAPTER TWENTY-ONE

Clark Air Base, located about a hundred kilometers north of Manila, was originally established as Fort Stotsenburg in the early twentieth century by the United States, a few years after they acquired the islands from Spain as a result of the Spanish-American War.

For nearly forty years it served as one of America's largest overseas air base until it was overrun by the Japanese shortly after their attack on Pearl Harbor, forcing General MacArthur—who lived on the base—to abandon the islands. The American soldiers who were left behind fought valiantly, but were massively outnumbered and eventually forced to surrender.

Months later, the American prisoners were marched past the main gate of Clark Air Base as their captors forced them to follow the nearby railway tracks northward toward their final destination at Camp O'Donnell. Very few survived what became known as the Bataan Death March. A long four years later, MacArthur returned to liberate the islands and return Clark to American control. But by then, much of the country's main cities, including Manila, had been destroyed.

For the next half-century, Clark Air Base continued to serve as one of America's most important foreign outposts, serving as a logistics hub during both the Korean and Vietnam wars. During much of that time, the Philippines was under the authoritarian rule of President Marcos, who was also an American ally against communism. But the people of the country eventually grew tired of his ruthless tactics and ultimately forced him from rule in the mid-eighties. The new, democratically-elected government wanted to separate themselves from Western influence and thus hesitated to renew America's lease of Clark Base.

While that dispute was going on, the nearby volcano, Mount Pinatubo, erupted, severely damaging the airfield and surrounding barracks. It was, in effect, the final nail in the coffin. In 1991, the base was officially closed and turned over to the Philippine government. As soon as the last American soldiers had departed, local citizens flooded through the main gates and looted whatever was left behind. The base was left abandoned for many years until it was gradually transformed into a commercial airport and free-zone.

But such changes did little to improve the conditions in nearby Angeles City.

As with most cities in close proximity to military bases, Angeles' prosperity—or lack thereof—had always been tied directly to the soldiers' interest in frequenting the local establishments. With that interest focused primarily on prostitution, the city became the center of the country's sex-trade, outside of Manila. But when the Army departed, the sex-trade didn't, simply finding new customers, often older American and European men in search of underage girls along Malabanas Road, the city's version of a red-light district.

It was certainly not a place I ever expected to be living, but it was where Jeana and I found ourselves after unceremoniously departing Dubai.

We had left literally in the middle of the night, not wanting to be seen by anyone who might report our sudden departure to Mr. Ahmad. Surprisingly, Anatoly had sent a driver to take us from our apartment to the airport. He had then stayed until we were through the gate, carefully surveying the airport to ensure we had made a clean getaway. We later learned that Anatoly had used his contacts behind the scenes to also ensure that getaway.

It was difficult not saying goodbye to our friends, including the Friday Night Club, Saad, and Marie. But in a sense, Jeana and I were breaking the law by not properly cancelling our employment visas or giving the necessary notice to our employers, and we didn't want any of our friends to be dragged down by our actions.

They were selfish actions. No question about it.

But we did what we felt we needed to do to achieve a fresh start. To reunite Jeana with her children. And to pave the way for their eventual emigration to America.

As my father had taught me, life is a collection of choices and decisions. Most are small and ultimately insignificant in the large scope of things. But some change the course of your life. Such was our decision to leave Dubai.

A few weeks after arriving in the Philippines, I informed Mr. Ahmad that I would not be returning. His reaction was as I'd expected.

"Don't return here, John, or I'll have you put in jail," he said in an email.

But we had no intention of ever returning.

I also reached-out to the Friday Night Club, Saad, and Marie. A few days later, Saad replied.

Dear John and Jeana

Marie and I'll be leaving for France tomorrow. Like both of you, we're starting a new life. Our experiences in Dubai were not always good. But we feel fortunate to have met both of you. We wish you all the best in your journey. Perhaps our paths will cross again. Stay safe. But most of all, stay happy together. You both deserve that.

Saad & Marie

My opinion about Saad changed significantly over the three years I knew him. When I'd first arrived in Dubai to begin working at the Green School, I considered him too fixed in his ways, unwilling to compromise with the teachers who had only wanted better working and living conditions. But over the course of those three years, he evolved in his thinking.

So did I.

Compared to Africa and Honduras, of course, Dubai was a much better place to live. But much of its appeal was only surface deep. Lurking not far beneath that surface was a culture that lacked tolerance. Where people were judged primarily by their ethnicity. Being an American, I was typically treated well. But it'd been different for Jeana. As a Filipina, she had been treated poorly. So, I knew that my memories of Dubai would always be closely linked with her experiences there. We'd been lucky to have found each other. But it was probably not a place we would've wanted to return to . . . even if it'd ended differently with Mr. Ahmad.

As for him, it would be easy to say that he wasn't a good person. But it's not that simple. It rarely is. He was a complex man living in a complex part of the world. Maybe Anatoly had been right. Maybe Ahmad's background was shady. But I'd also done some questionable things in my life in order to get what I wanted.

So, I was in no position to pass judgment.

Anyways, my focus had now shifted to our new life in Angeles City. I was back in the Third World. Was I prepared for it?

CHAPTER TWENTY-TWO

Like so many Third World countries such as the Central African Republic and Honduras, the Philippines is inextricably tied to its colonial history. The arrival of the Portuguese explorer Ferdinand Magellan in 1521 marked the beginning of Hispanic colonization which also resulted in Catholicism becoming the dominant religion, something which continues to play an intricate role in so many of the country's affairs.

But once America acquired the islands from the Spanish following the Spanish-American War, English became the dominant second-language and one that is still spoken by most Filipinos, with varying degrees of fluency. All schools, both public and private, provide rigorous English programs which make Filipinos very attractive overseas hires in places where English is widely spoken, such as Dubai.

My new school, Clark International, was one of the few international schools outside the capital of Manila. Catering to local, wealthy Filipinos and South Koreans who came to take advantage of the Free Zone of the old Clark Base, the school was built for a student population of five hundred, but struggled to maintain an enrollment of two hundred.

With a tuition rate similar to private schools in America, it was beyond the means of nearly all Filipinos, except the elite upper class. Many of the South Korean companies who sent their employees to the Clark Free Zone covered the cost of education for their dependents. Consequently, the tuition rate wasn't a consideration for them.

But the Free Zone had grown considerably more slowly than had been originally envisioned two decades earlier, mostly due to the country's poor infrastructure. Additionally, most of the wealthiest Filipino families were drawn to Manila where more modern—and Westernized— conveniences could be found. The same went for the South Korean families who were accustomed to a certain standard of living in and around Seoul, but didn't find any of those comforts of home in Angeles City.

In short, it just wasn't a particularly attractive place to live.

Nevertheless, Jeana and I made the best of things as we settled into our new surroundings, still looking ahead to a future in America, but remaining focused on our immediate situation.

Our accommodation—a single family house newly built within the Free Zone—was about a fifteen-minute drive from the school, passing through some of the city's worst slums and some of its most opulent subdivisions. And that was the Philippines. A country of extremes, like so many Third World countries, including the Central Africa Republic and Honduras.

Yet, the country still attracted some Americans, if not for the underage girls, then for the cheap cost of living. As a result, my school was able to attract a handful of American teachers.

There was Steve from Arizona and his wife Abigail from Guam. Mike from Ohio. And Billy from New York.

My predecessor was from Colorado, but had been too attracted to the teen girls of the Red Light District, one night getting his picture taken with one on his lap. When the photos were subsequently circulated online, the parental outcry was enough to force his exit from the school.

Jeana had been fortunate to also secure a job in the school as the front-lobby receptionist. We enjoyed meeting daily for lunch in the cafeteria and sitting with the other teachers, both Western and local. We couldn't help but be reminded of the Friday Night Club that we had left behind in Dubai. But we knew there would be less time for socializing in the Philippines. We had come for one reason: to reunite Jeana with her children.

Ryan. Daniel. Nadine. Liza. Nathan.

Our original plan was to take a few months to get settled before determining the best course of action to get the five children. But when

Jeana's mother indicated that their situation was becoming more and more unstable, we knew that we needed to move faster than expected.

When Jeana had first gone to Dubai, the three youngest children stayed with their father, while the two oldest were with their grandparents. But when Jeana had broken free from Haij and secured a better job, she was able to rent a small house in Cavite for her mother and youngest three. Their father had not protested since he had already acquired a new girlfriend. But when the relationship failed, he began pushing to retake custody of the youngest three. Nadine. Liza. Nathan

By then, the two oldest boys, Ryan and Daniel, had also moved in with Jeana's mother, reuniting the five children for the first time in many years. But with the reappearance of the youngest-three's father, the situation had deteriorated quickly.

It was particularly bad for Daniel, who had just turned fifteen. He felt unwanted by the youngest-three's father. Uncomfortable in the house, he stayed out late into the night, choosing a bad group of friends who quickly led him down the wrong path. Meanwhile, Ryan, the oldest, had started college. But without proper supervision, he was skipping classes and failing most of his classes. Jeana's mother did her best to maintain some sort of stability in the house, but with the father's constant interference, it was proving to be an intolerable situation. And it was made even worse by the sudden departure of the nanny that Jeana had hired to assist her mother. Apparently, the children's father has been harassing her for months.

It was all a mess, to say the least.

"I don't think we can wait," said Jeana, following a Facetime with her mother. "My mother is really worried about them. She found a new nanny, but the kids need stability. They can't continue like this. It's not fair to them." She began to cry.

"It's all right," I said, holding her close as we sat side by side on the couch in our new house's living room. "We'll figure out a way to get them as quickly as possible."

"Do you think that's possible?"

"Anything's possible, Jeana. We'll find an attorney and get some advice."

She looked up at me. "I can't do this without you, you know."

"And you don't need to. We'll get through this . . . together. We just need to move carefully and avoid mistakes which could be difficult to correct down the road. Everything we do must keep the door open to our eventual move to America."

One mistake that I knew we had to avoid was my direct contact with the children's fathers. I was tempted to handle the situation in much the same way as I'd handled the father of Gabriela nearly twenty years earlier, by having someone threaten him. But I knew that this situation was different. I didn't have any contacts or allies, and Jeana's other siblings weren't in a position to be of much help.

We were on our own. Pure and simple.

A couple of weeks later—following a few meetings with a local attorney—Jeana traveled to Cavite. If all went as planned, she would return to our house near Clark with the five children.

The question was, would the children's father try to stand in her way.

The attorney suggested using the nanny's harassment accusations as leverage by threatening the father with legal action if he didn't allow the kids to leave with Jeana. Reluctantly, the attorney had agreed to issue the threat herself by accompanying Jeana, a driver, and an armed security guard from my school on the trip to Cavite.

We knew full-well that the Philippine legal system would never actually prosecute the father. He could have raped the nanny, and they still would not have done anything. It was just the reality of life in a Third World country. But we were counting on the fact that the father would be temporarily frightened by the attorney's threat, just long enough for Jeana to take the kids out of the house and return to Angeles City. The father would have no way of knowing where they went. He would undoubtedly try to find them, but we would make sure that he'd be unsuccessful.

Everyone agreed that the most important part of the plan was my non-involvement. It was a bitter pill to swallow, but I knew they were right. My presence would only serve to rile up the father and make the situation more unstable, potentially putting the children at risk.

All I could do was watch as Jeana departed with her companions for the two-hour drive to Cavite, hopefully to return the next day with the children. As I waited, there was little else to do except to again reflect upon all that had brought us to that point . . . and all that lay ahead.

With the expectation that the five children would soon be with us, I'd been thinking a lot about all the mistakes I'd made with Andres and Fernando. I was intent upon doing things differently from the get-go with Jeana's children. I knew I needed to gain their trust. That I needed to move *toward* them and not wait for them to come to me. And that I needed to be patient and understanding.

After all, they had been through so much already.

I also knew that I needed to do things differently—in some ways, at least—from how my father had raised my sister and me. There were so many great memories from my childhood. Red Sox games at Fenway. Trips to the Cape and Maine. Backyard games of catch. Seeing my father behind the backstop whenever I was pitching in Little League all the way through high school. Dad helping me with my homework. With my model ship-building. And showing me how to become a man.

But there were also plenty of times when he yelled too much. When he didn't have enough patience. When he made me feel as though I was somehow in the way.

Over the years, I'd come to understand that he was also an inse-cure man and had passed that insecurity on to me and my sister through his sometimes-harsh actions and tone. As a result, I'd often felt unable to express myself in his presence, something that plagued me in relationships with Maria and Gabriela.

If my mother had lived, maybe it would've all been different.

But I'd finally reached the point in my life—thanks mostly to Jeana—that I no longer blamed anyone. Especially my father. He had done the best he could. Over the years, on that bench near Crystal Lake, I'd come to better understand him. And, ultimately, to forgive him. And that forgiveness would allow me to be a better father to Jeana's children.

I was determined to make it so.

CHAPTER TWENTY-THREE

We all have some vivid memories of our childhood.

For me, I still remember the grand-slam I hit to win a Little League game when I was twelve. Or when I struck out twelve batters to win the championship. Or when my dad took me to my first Patriots game in Foxboro. I also clearly remember that day on Cape Cod when my mother realized that she had breast cancer. Or when the hospital called my father to say that mom had passed away.

I also clearly remember the time when my mother and father returned from a parent-teacher conference with my seventh grade teacher.

They were not happy with what they had heard.

"Mrs. Lesnesky said that your grades are fine," my father explained, as my mother sat across from him at the kitchen table, with me in between. Any time I was called to sit with them at the table always meant bad news for me. "But she's not happy with your behavior in the classroom."

My mother chimed in. "We were embarrassed by what we heard, John." She was always direct and to the point. "She said that you laugh at other students and often speak out of turn." I could see my mother's hands shaking, she was so upset. "Why would you do that?"

"I don't . . ."

Dad cut me off. "Don't lie, Johnny," he said, calmly, but firmly. "Your mother is not happy with what she heard tonight. We didn't expect this from you. We've told you many times that your behavior is more important than your grades. Nothing is more important than how you treat other people, regardless of whether they're students or teachers."

"We never hear you talking rudely around the house," said my mother, her lecturing voice in full-throttle. "Why would you do it at school?"

Sixth grade had been a turning-point for me. Up until that point, I was a reasonably secure kid who got most of his confidence from excelling in sports. Other kids knew me because of that ability. I had some friends, mostly teammates from my baseball team. And a few others who lived in the neighborhood. The Atter's from across the street. The Gazettas from down the street.

But as we all made that awkward transition into our preteen and then teen years, I was somehow left behind. Those neighborhood friends went on to be the popular kids in high school, attending the proms, dating, and generally making the most of their high school experience.

Most of the time, I was home alone.

By the time I started middle school, my mother was very sick and would not live to see my eighth grade graduation. Understandably, my father's focus had been on caring for my mom and making sure that my sister made it to her high school graduation and into college. It wasn't that I was ignored or pushed away. But at a time when a kid needs the most guidance, there was little coming my way.

As a result, I became even more introverted than I already was. While she was still healthy, my mother had recognized that tendency and always made sure that I invited friends to the house. But as she became more and more overwhelmed by her illness, there was no longer anyone holding my head above water.

I began to sink. Fast.

At first, my insecurities surfaced in the classroom, just as Mrs. Lesneski had observed. I remember her talking to me the day following her meeting with my parents, knowing that they had probably taken me to task for my behavior.

"You know, John," she said to me in her classroom after school, "your parents want the best for you. They care for you so much. So do I. Sometimes when we're feeling lost or confused, we act-out in ways that are out of character. Others see it and will say something, if they really care about you. That's why I talked to your parents last night. I see you as a very kind person who doesn't always know how to express himself. So please know, if you don't feel that you can share your feelings with your family, you can always talk to me or another teacher."

Sadly, I never took her up on that offer. Other teachers also offered their support over the years. I always nodded politely, but never opened-up to them. Mrs. Lesneski had been exactly right. I didn't feel as though I could express myself at home, so I kept everything bottled-up inside, continuing to sink deeper and deeper within myself.

In many ways, I didn't resurface again until I met Jeana more than twenty-five years later.

Jeana struggled in much the same way, if not for different reasons.

While her family was always poor, her grandfather had been the glue that kept the family together. When he passed away, the family never recovered. Without his guidance, she was unable to finish college and was pregnant at nineteen. By the time she was thirty, she had five children.

At no time did she ever regret the birth of her children or consider them mistakes. Each one was a blessing. But if her grandfather had lived, her life would likely have been much different. But then, she may have never gone to Dubai, and we may never have met. As my father once said, things are connected in ways that we never really appreciate, until it all begins to unravel.

The tapestry of life.

Like me, Jeana had many good memories of her childhood. Summers with her grandmother in the province. Picking mangoes and running barefoot and free around the farm. Playing with all her cousins in the family compound in Cavite as her grandfather watched over them. And sitting in the front of her classroom, always raising her hand to answer the teachers' questions.

But there were most definitely some bad times. Besides the passing of her grandfather, there was the departure of her father from the house when she was only twelve. She had first shared the story with me during our first date in Dubai, and had often repeated the story in the years since.

I remember sitting on the couch in the living room next to my sister and brothers, with our mother sitting in a chair and our grandfather standing in the doorway. Then my father entered with this woman we'd never seen before. She was younger than my mother and didn't seem happy to be there. My father then announced that he was leaving us to live with this woman. I remember my mother almost falling out of her chair, then crying and screaming, before finally lunging toward him. My sister and brothers were all crying hysterically as my grandfather rushed over to grab my mother and then take her out of the room. My father explained that he would always love us, but he didn't love our mother anymore. And that was it. He left.

We sometimes saw him at Christmas or Easter. A few times, after my grandfather died, my sister and I would take a jeepney to his house to ask for money. He sometimes gave us some. Sometimes not. Mostly not. There were times I would go to school without any money for lunch. I would watch my friends as they ordered lunch. They would always ask me why I didn't have any money. I'd try to think of something different each day to tell them. Eventually, I think they understood and stopped asking, sometimes sharing their food with me. I also started sitting in the back of the class because I was embarrassed when my empty stomach would growl.

My mother was always away from the house, staying out late at night, drinking and playing cards with her friends. I would stay-up late to unlock the door for her and make sure she was in bed. A few hours later I'd wake-up to make breakfast for my sister and brothers. Then we'd all go to school. It was hard. But when I became pregnant with Ryan, I swore that I would be the best mother possible.

All of this was on my mind as I waited for Jeana to return from Cavite with the attorney, the driver, and the security guard . . . and hopefully with the five children.

I took a walk around our little neighborhood, down the road that led to the old Military Parade Grounds of Clark Base. It'd been turned into baseball and softball fields, although the grass needed some cutting. At the far end of the rectangular expanse of green was a large, white, turn-of-the-century house . . . the former residence of General McArthur. For the past twenty years it'd been used as a weekend retreat for the Philippine president, similar to Camp David in America. During the war years, the house had overlooked the Army barracks that surrounded the Parade Grounds. Now, those barracks were restaurants, real estate offices, and yoga studios.

The times had changed.

I continued my walk toward the little hospital that had once provided the most advanced healthcare in the country to the American soldiers stationed there. Now, it was in a sad state of disrepair.

Just beyond the hospital was the PureGold supermarket. In its heyday, it saw the constant flow of goods onto the base, much of it later to be resold in stores and shops that were constantly springing up like mushrooms along MacArthur Avenue that separated the base from Angeles City. But now the store had few customers, most preferring to visit the new mall that had recently been built near the airport.

As I walked, I kept my cell phone in my hand, constantly checking for a text from Jeana. When none came, I returned home, watched some TV, and then went out for another walk. This went on throughout the day until finally around eleven at night, the call came.

"We have them," said Jeana. "We have them all. We're coming home now. I love you so much."

The next stage of my life had officially begun.

CHAPTER TWENTY-FOUR

The Pamulaklakin Nature Park is located along the coastline of Subic Bay—an extension of the South China Sea—on the west coast of Luzon, the Philippines's most northern island, and its largest. The park was established in the 1990s by the Subic Bay Metropolitan Authority following the departure of the US Navy shortly after the closure of Clark Base.

School groups and families journeyed to the park from across the country, intent upon seeing the island's beauty as it was centuries earlier when the first conquistadors had arrived. They came to wander through the forest and marvel at such natural splendors as Ficus fruit trees, orange bush lilies, and nun's cap orchids. They came to listen to the sounds of nature's creatures, including the squawks of the macaque monkeys who swing freely through the high canopy cover.

It was to this park that I brought my new family for our first outing away from Clark.

A month earlier, Nadine, Liza, Nathan, and Daniel had started attending my school, while Ryan searched for a nearby college to continue his studies in computer science.

Nadine was in fifth grade, a bright, sociable, and pretty young girl with dreams of becoming a movie star in the Philippines.

Liza was a year younger. She struggled in school but never became discouraged or frustrated. Less confident than her sister, she never left the side of her brother, Nathan. They were inseparable.

Nathan was by far the brightest of the five children, and also the most gentle. He was clearly Jeana's favorite, although she never admitted it.

Daniel, Ryan's younger brother, was struggling the most when he arrived in Clark. But we also knew that a fresh start was exactly what he needed. He immediately joined my school's basketball team and became the starting point guard, something which gave him some confidence, as well as some much-needed new friends.

As the oldest, Ryan had been through the most. He was old enough to remember how bad things had been when he was little, living under the bridge with his mother and new-born brother. He had seen his father hitting his mother, and his stepfather cheating on her. He had watched her leave for Dubai, and now return with another man. But through it all, he had somehow maintained a maturity and level-headedness that was unusual for an eighteen-year old. He was a young man to be admired.

"Are you and mom going to get married?" he asked, as we sat together on a bench watching his siblings and mom feeding the monkeys.

"We've talked about it," I said. "How do you feel about that?"

Ryan thought for a moment before replying. "I can see how happy mom is with you. I want her to be happy."

"And I want all of you to be happy, Ryan. Everyone deserves the chance to be happy."

"Yeah, mom has never really been happy," he said finally. "It's hard for her to trust people."

"I can understand that, Ryan. A lot of people have let her down. But she always had you and your brothers and sisters to lift her up. It's what kept" her going. When I was with her in Dubai, she would always talk about the five of you. Many nights she would go to bed crying, thinking of you all. It means so much to her that all of you are together again."

"Thanks to you," said Ryan, looking at me sideways, with a smile.

"No," I replied immediately. "It's all because of your mother. She has sacrificed so much for all of you. Now it's her turn to be happy."

He was quiet again, for a moment.

"Will we go to America?"

"Do you want to go there?"

"I guess," he replied, still watching his mother and siblings playing together. "I just never thought it would be possible for someone from our family to go there. We've only seen it in movies."

"No matter what happens, Ryan, this will always be your home. But all of you need to be in a place where you can get a good education and have some opportunities to find a good job and live a good life."

"In America?"

"Maybe, yes. We'll see what happens."

Just then, Nadine came over and sat down with us. I could see Jeana looking over her shoulder at her two children who were sitting beside me. She smiled.

It felt good.

"What do you think of your new school, Nadine?" I asked her, knowing that she was still shy around me. "Do you like it?"

"It's okay, I guess." She wouldn't look at me.

"Harder than your last school?" I asked.

The three youngest children had been attending a small parochial school in their subdivision. Jeana had insisted upon it and had sent money from Dubai to pay for it. She had gone to mostly public schools, and wanted something better for her kids.

"A little," she replied meekly. "It's just different to have people speaking English all day."

I smiled. "It'll get easier for you, I'm sure. You just need to try your best."

"I wish I'd gone to an all-English school," said Ryan to his step-sister. "You guys are lucky."

Nadine shrugged.

Amazingly, the five kids all got along remarkably well together. The younger ones always referred to their older siblings as Kuya, a sign of respect in the Philippines. They all looked up to Ryan, and they all looked out for Nathan, the youngest. Despite their many challenges and struggles, they were remarkably polite, respectful, and smart kids.

Jeana was a truly amazing mother.

"Will we go to America?" asked Nadine. They all seemed to be thinking about the same thing.

"In time, probably we will," I answered. "But we'll stay here for a while and spend lots of time together. Does that sound okay?"

She finally looked at me and smiled. "Yes, I like it when we're all together."

For so many years their family had been torn apart. But now everyone was together, and I was determined to keep them together. They needed the stability. And so did I.

"Do you both like the house?" I asked. "You're comfortable in your rooms?"

Ryan shook his head. "We've never had our own rooms before. We've always slept together in the same room, usually just a mattress on the floor."

"And you can still do that, if it makes you feel safer."

"We feel safe," replied Nadine. "It's just . . . different."

"I understand. Lots of changes. It must be hard for all of you."

"Not hard," answered Ryan. "It's exciting. But sometimes we miss our friends in Cavite."

Nadine nodded.

"I wish I could say that you'll see them again. But I don't know if that will be possible. We need to be sure both your fathers don't know where you are. It's safer that way. At least for now."

"We know," said Ryan, shifting on the bench. "It's just hard."

"Maybe someday when everything is finished and you're all a little older, you can go back there. But not now. I'm sorry."

Jeana and I'd been meeting regularly with the attorney who had accompanied her to Cavite to get the kids the month before. She was honest in saying that it would be extremely difficult to get the kids out of the country without the father's approval.

Unless we were comfortable cutting a few corners.

Having been in Africa and Honduras, I understood full well how such things worked. To get things done, you had to be willing to pay for it. Usually by less than scrupulous means. I wasn't opposed to it, but I certainly didn't want to put Jeana or the kids at risk. But the more we listened to the attorney, the more apparent it became that we were going to have to take some risks.

But that was for another day.

As I sat there with Ryan and Nadine, I was just content to watch the family playing together and laughing together. I felt a sense of peace and satisfaction that I hadn't felt in a long, long time.

"I think you and mom should get married soon?" said Ryan suddenly. "I think she really wants to."

"What do you think about that, Nadine," I asked. "Would that be okay with you?'

She giggled. "I guess so."

Ryan elbowed his sister. "Mom is happy with Tito," he said, their name for me. "Let her be happy."

Nadine pushed her brother back. "I know. But . . ."

I understood. "It's okay, Nadine. Things are happening really fast. We'll take our time and be sure that all of you're comfortable with everything. No surprises. I promise. Okay?"

She nodded. "Okay."

Jeana and I'd indeed been talking a lot about getting married in America. But there were legal challenges which needed to be overcome first. Jeana had not married either of the children's fathers. But both had filed fake marriage certificates with the government to satisfy their parents. It would be a legal challenge to undo it. But our plans of emigrating to America depended upon our ability to get it done . . . at any cost.

CHAPTER TWENTY-FIVE

Later in the spring of 2012, as we waited for our attorney to find a way to annul Jeana's fake marriages, my sister visited from Boston to meet my new family. She had always been close with Gabriela and the two boys, but had also grown close to Jeana during our trip to England, Ireland, and America, and was now excited to meet the five children.

We all decided to pile into our minivan and head to the east coast of Luzon to a town called Baler, just north of the Aurora National Park. Getting there was a challenge, as we had to pass over the Mingan Mountains using unpaved roads. Luckily, the rainy season was over, so the road was passable, but still rife with dangers that came with its isolation.

Like much of the developing world, the Philippines had its share of revolutionaries who often resorted to kidnappings to replenish their bank accounts. Remote mountain roads were the perfect location for such activities, especially roads that led to a tourist destination such as Baler.

To make matters more uncertain, we'd made the mistake of leaving Clark too late in the day. By the time we passed over the mountains, it was already dark.

And it was most definitely *not* a place you wanted to be after dark.

At one point, we reluctantly stopped so the kids could pee by the side of the road. As they did, Jeana and I noticed a man on the ledge above us, seemingly holding a rifle. We ushered the kids back into the van and continued on our way.

More concerning still was that the area was also known as a bastion for members of Abu Saif, a terrorist group with close ties to Al Qaeda. With the help of the US military, the Philippine government had been fighting them for years, mostly with little success. In retrospect, it was probably a trip that we should not have taken. But as we finally pulled into the small town of Baler, it all seemed worthwhile.

We'd decided to stay at a resort atop Ermita Hill which offered pan oramic views of the coastline, Tibag River, and Baler Lighthouse which overlooked Dicasalarin Cove. Its crystal clear waters made it a popular spot for snorkeling. From the balcony of our three-bedroom suite, we could also look south toward Sabang Beach, a popular place for surfers to enjoy the waves of the Pacific.

Nearly forty years earlier, the same beach had been used to shoot the surfing scene from *Apocalypse Now*. When filming ended, the crew left behind a selection of surfboards. The locals took-up the sport and its popularity in the region quickly spread, with tourists coming from across Asia to enjoy the surfing culture.

"What do you think, Daniel?" I asked, as we stood on the porch together watching the surfers. "Want to give it a try?"

He shook his head. "I don't think I can do that," he replied. "It looks scary."

"Don't be afraid to try new things, Daniel. We'll get you and Ryan an instructor.

You'll prove to yourself that you can do it. It'll be fun."

"You'll try, too?

"Sure," I said, trying to sound as confident as possible, despite my reservations.

"We'll do it together."

Later that day, we did do it together. It was a great bonding experience. Jeana and the three younger children looked on from the beach, laughing uncontrollably as I continually fell from my board into the surf. I swallowed a lot of saltwater that day, but it was a good day. A good family day.

The next morning, we hired a boat to take us across the cres-cent-shaped bay to another resort which had some water slides that I knew the kids would enjoy. The ride itself was the real attraction, as we bounced along from one wave crest to the next. The kids were screaming the entire time, going back and forth between fear and exhilaration. Even Jeana seemed to be enjoying herself, her family's troubles a distant memory . . . at least for a while.

A few days later, on our way back to Clark, we visited Mount Pinatubo, site of the volcanic explosion three decades earlier that had changed so much of Luzon, and spelled the final death-knell of Clark Base as an American installation. We hired two guides with jeeps to take us across the lava-field, a bouncy, uncomfortable ride followed by a short hike up the side of the mountain until it opened-up into the volcano's crater. We descended into its mouth with our guides until we stood on the shores of the volcanic lake, the strong smell of sulfur permeating our nostrils.

After sticking their toes into the water, the kids turned their backs to the lake and joined arms, with Andrea at one end and Jeana at the other. I stepped back a bit and took the photo, one which would ultimately adorn our walls for many years to come.

They all seemed so happy that day. Together. Jeana's smile had never been so wide. Liza was snuggled into my sister's arms, holding on for pro-tection and comfort. My sister had begun calling her "my little magnet," a name which would remain through the years. She was a shy little girl, too skinny, too awkward. But since coming to live with us, she was starting to gain some confidence. Still, she rarely ventured far from her younger brother's side. Nathan was clearly her security blanket. Of the five chil-dren, he was the one who seemed to miss his father the most. But gradu-ally, he was growing more accustomed to my presence. I tried not to push too hard, taking advantage of opportunities like the visit to the volcano to reach-out to him.

"It's beautiful here, Nathan. Except for the smell," I said. "I always wanted to see this place. I'm glad we could all see it together."

He just stared across the lake. I wondered what he was thinking.

"I'm so happy that all of you are together," I continued. "It also makes your mother so happy. She loves all of you so much, you know."

He turned and looked up at me, but still didn't say anything.

"Your teacher, Mrs. Muna, says you're one of her best students. She says you always know the answer to any of her questions."

"I like her," he said finally. "She's nice."

I knelt down beside Nathan. "You know how proud your mother and I are of you, right? It's not easy being in a new school with new teachers and new friends, is it?"

"It's okay. Everyone is really nice."

I nodded. "Everyone cares a lot about you. We all want the best for you and your brothers and sisters."

We stayed there quietly for a few minutes until Liza came over, took her brother's hand, and they ran off together.

That night, we all stayed at a nearby hotel, ready to return to Clark the next day, and back to school a day later. After the kids and Jeana had gone to sleep, my sister and I sat together by the pool, drinking a few Heinekens and reflecting upon our life journeys. For two people who had been raised in the same house by the same parents, we were very different people. Yet, we shared one thing in common: insecurity.

"Are you sure you can pull this off?" she asked. "It's a lot."

"Probably a bit too late for that question now." We both laughed.

"But, yes. I believe I can pull it off. We're just at the beginning of things. For now, it's about building the family relationships and making everyone feel as secure as possible. But, yes. I believe it's all possible."

"And if you can't get them to America?" she asked.

"Then we stay here," I answered without hesitation. "Or go some-place like Singapore or Kuala Lumpur where they can go without a visa. But there's no question that America is the best place for them."

I could tell that my sister wasn't convinced. And that was okay. She had every right to be skeptical. She had seen how indifferent I'd been with Andres and Fernando. And she had seen my failures with Maria and Gabriela. Why should she think that I'd changed?

But I had.

"Jeana and I hope to get married this summer in Gardner so you and Dad can be there," I continued. "With that marriage certificate we can eventually process her green card. Once she's a citizen, the children auto-matically become citizens. But the immediate challenge will be to get the kids out of the Philippines. It usually requires the father's approval. So, we'll need to find another way."

"*Is* there another way?" asked my sister.

I smiled. "There's always another way."

Despite her own struggles, she had always been more comfortable in her life than I'd ever been in mine. I always needed to be on the move. Always needed new challenges to overcome. That restlessness, of course, was a double-edged sword. It'd sent me on many amazing adventures. But it was also the enemy of relationships. Yet, I'd finally come to feel more grounded and understood that the children needed stability and certainly could not be traipsing around the world, hopping from one Third World country to another.

"For now," I said, "we're taking things one day at a time. We don't know what the future will bring. But we have a very clear idea of what we want that future to be."

Which was true. But I was under no illusion that it was going to take many, many years to reach our ultimate goal: all five children graduating from an American college.

CHAPTER TWENTY-SIX

In the summer of 2012, our plans for the future took a giant leap forward as Jeana and I returned to America to be married. When I married Gabriela, it'd been in Honduras with neither of our families present.

This time, I was determined to do it differently.

It would've been ideal for Jeana's mother to be present. But getting her a visa to America was impossible, and marrying in the Philippines didn't make any sense since we needed the American marriage certificate to expedite the visa process for the children. But before we left for America, we had to address the issue of Jeana's fake marriage record.

Unlike the United States, the Philippines maintains a centralized database of marriages. Marriage certificates are issued at the local level, but then submitted to a national archive, called the National Records Office, where they're rarely scrutinized. Accordingly, fake *local* certificates are not uncommon. But whenever someone wants to marry, they must obtain a NOMAR certificate from the archives indicating NO MARriage exists. Since divorce is illegal in the Philippines and annulments are expensive, fake NOMAR certificates are common.

With the help of our attorney, we were able to receive such a certificate in a matter of days. For added security, we had the certificate notarized at the courthouse in Angeles City, near our house.

It was almost *too* easy.

With all the necessary documents now in hand, Jeana and I traveled to Massachusetts and went immediately to City Hall in my hometown to apply for a marriage license. The office clerk knew my father—as most people in Gardner did—so was willing to fast-track our license after we submitted all of the required documents—including the NOMAR certificate.

Three days later—the day after watching the Fourth of July fireworks with my sister on the esplanade in Boston—Jeana and I were married in the council chambers on the second floor of the turn-of-century City Hall, with my father and sister as witnesses.

It was an emotional moment as I put the ring on Jeana's finger, not only for all that lay ahead, but for all that both of us had been through in our lives. Everything—good and bad—that had brought us to that point. Two people with completely different backgrounds. Completely different life stories. Two people from opposite sides of the world, brought together, by chance, in one of the worlds' most opulent cities.

Fairy tale? Probably not.

But a pretty good story, nevertheless.

Following the little ceremony, the four of us went to lunch at the Old Mill restaurant in nearby Westminster, which had always been one of my mother's favorite places to eat. Set beside a lake, it'd been a sawmill through the early Twentieth century when small textile mills lined most of the rivers in New England. As we sat together enjoying our meal, I noticed that my father was tearing up.

'Are you okay, Dad?" I asked.

He nodded, trying to collect himself. "I'm fine. I just wish your mother could be here with us. It would've meant a lot to her."

"She is, Dad," my sister said. "She's here. I know it."

My father had aged quite a bit over the past year and had slowed down considerably, needing help getting in and out of chairs. But he still commanded your attention. He still had so much to give.

"I don't know if I believe that, Andrea. But it's certainly a nice thought," replied Dad. He then paused for a moment as he looked out the window at the lake and the still-functioning waterwheel. "Our little family has had quite a journey," he continued. "My side of the family, the so-called Yankees of New England. Your mother's family, from Ireland. My experiences in France and Montana. Your experiences, Johnny, in Africa, Honduras, and Dubai. And now the Philippines. Quite a journey, indeed."

"And with the five children, that journey will continue for many generations," I added.

It caused my father to smile.

"What is it?" I asked.

"The thought that the family will continue with five children from the Philippines. Remarkable. It could only happen in America."

It was true. I'd traveled enough of the world to know that only in America could our story be told. Only in America could immigrant children have the same opportunities as native-born children. But not only children. Adults too.

Such as Jeana.

She had been one of the top students in her high school. If given the chance to attend college, she undoubtedly would've excelled. But the opportunity was never provided. Yet, in America, she would have a second chance. And I'd no doubt that she would take full advantage.

But in the end, it was all about the children.

"So, what now?" asked my father. "Back to the Philippines?"

"Yes," I answered. "We'll spend a few days on Martha's Vineyard and then head back. Now that we're married, we can begin the process of getting the children here."

"Is that process a *legal* one?" asked my father, with a sly smile.

"As much as possible, yes. We don't want to be in the position of submitting fake documents to get the kids' visas. But we need to figure out a way of getting their fathers' names removed from the birth certificates. And that's likely going to be expensive. But we'll get it done."

"I probably don't want to know how you're going to do that, do I?" asked my father, still with a smirk on his face.

"Probably not," I replied. "Probably not."

"Just be careful, John," said my sister. "I'm sure the kids' fathers are not going to be cooperative."

"If we do everything right, they'll never know."

My father nodded.

He, of course, had married Yvette during the war without the Army's knowledge. And over the years, he had never been afraid to do what needed to be done. I guess I'd acquired that same perspective. It wasn't about ignoring rules or laws. It was about finding ways to open new doors once others had closed.

"Just promise me one thing, Johnny," added my father. "As you go through all of this, remember your mother and where her family came from. They emigrated to this country more than a century ago and also had to do what needed to be done to survive. Don't forget all that they sacrificed."

"I won't, Dad. No matter what I do, I'll always do my best to respect mom's memory. Her parents found a way to make it here. And so will the five children. I'm determined to make it so."

Before we departed Gardner, Jeana and I paid a visit to Crystal Lake. We sat together on the bench upon which my father and I'd spent so much time over the years. Where I'd gotten to know him. And where he had provided so much advice that had helped me find my way through life. We then walked to the top of the little hill where my mother had lay peacefully for nearly three decades. There was a place beside her waiting for my father. But he wasn't quite ready yet. He still had one last role to play.

Grandfather.

I'd deprived him of that opportunity with Andres and Fernando. But it would be different this time.

And then he could rest.

CHAPTER TWENTY-SIX

The Native Americans of the region called it *Kioshk*. The first English and Dutch settlers called it Gull Island, then Oyster Island. For a while it was a bastion for pirates operating along the eastern seaboard of the new nation. Then it became privately owned by a wealthy eccentric named Samuel Ellis. In the years before the War of 1812, it became federal property upon which Fort Gibson was built to protect the harbor from British invasion. But most famously, Ellis Island was a place where over twelve million immigrants arrived between the late nineteenth and mid-twentieth centuries.

Prior to 1890, individual states—instead of the federal government—regulated immigration into the country through such places as Castle Garden in the Battery section of New York City. From 1855 to 1890, approximately eight million immigrants passed through its doors, most escaping political instability, restrictive religious laws, and deteriorating economic conditions in western Europe. But it soon became apparent that places like Castle Garden were ill-equipped and unprepared to handle the growing numbers of immigrants arriving yearly.

The federal government then intervened and constructed a new, federally-operated immigration station in the middle of New York Harbor, on Ellis Island. But less than a decade after opening, fire burned through the wooden structure, razing it completely to the ground. No lives were lost, but state immigration records dating back half a century were gone forever. When it was rebuilt a few years later, the idea of using wood was logically abandoned. The subsequent structures would continue standing well into the twenty-first century.

In the first few decades of the twentieth century, up to ten thousand people passed through Ellis Island every single day. By then, most were coming from Eastern Europe, escaping the Great War and the fear of communism's spread across Europe following the Russian Revolution.

But from Western Europe, the Irish continued to come.

They didn't come in the massive numbers that had occurred in the years following the Potato Famine of the mid-nineteenth century. But still, they came. The sailing ships used for those first arrivals had long since been replaced by steamships which were faster and safer. But the Atlantic crossing from ports like Galway were still arduous, especially for the third-class passengers who were forced deep in the ship's bowels. Food was sparse and fresh water even sparser. Some passengers didn't even see the light of day for up to two weeks. But even that ordeal didn't compare to what awaited them following disembarkation in New York.

Anti-immigrant sentiment had increased dramatically following the Great War. New laws required a literacy test for new arrivals over the age of sixteen. They had to read fifty words in English . . . or be denied admittance. For the poorer, less educated passengers in third class, the test proved to be a heartbreaker, shattering many dreams of a better life.

It was all evidence that America had turned inward, just as it would many times again throughout the twentieth and early twentieth-first centuries. Nevertheless, it was into this lion's den that Sean and Bridget arrived in the summer of 1918. He was twenty. She only eighteen.

Their ship, the *Cedric*, pulled into New York harbor in the late afternoon of a hot and hazy August day. The city was blanketed by a thick layer of smog from the dozens of coal-burning factories that lined the Hudson and East Rivers, making it difficult for those who stood upon the ship's decks to see the city's famous skyline. Still, Sean, Bridget, and her brother, Conor, had pushed their way above deck, eager to catch a glimpse of what they had only seen in photographs: Lady Liberty.

"Sean! Look! Over there! That's it. The Statue of Liberty. I can see it!"

Sean put his arm around his new bride and pulled her close. "We made it. We actually made it. I can't believe it."

Conor stood behind them, equally in awe. "Amazing," was the only word he could summon as tears streamed down his gaunt cheeks.

Since Sean and Bridget's marriage in Galway a few weeks earlier, everything had been like a whirlwind. Neither of their parents had been approving of their union . . . or their trip together. But it didn't really matter. They were going to go no matter what. Someday, they hoped, their parents' feelings would be different. But both teenagers understood that it was entirely possible that they would never see their parents again. Only a few ever returned, usually the successful ones who had been able to earn enough money for the return passage. But Sean and Bridget were under no illusion that their joint lack of education would make financial success unlikely.

What they wanted most was a fresh start. A new beginning. A chance at something better. They respected their parents' commitment to their farms. But they didn't see a future in it. Few did. The countryside was emptying, as people bolted for the cities like Galway. Agriculture would always play a major role in Irish life. But it was diminishing. Fast.

Around the world, the new century had brought many changes, and many new opportunities. To foreigners, America seemed to be at the center of it all.

But America had also changed. And not necessarily for the better.

Nearly twenty years earlier, the country had started the century by acquiring territory overseas as a result of the Spanish American War. Places like the Philippines, Puerto Rico, and Cuba suddenly saw major American influence as progressive leaders like Teddy Roosevelt tried to make the country into a world power.

But then came the Great War.

Woodrow Wilson tried desperately to keep the country out of the war but eventually succumbed to pressure from within his own party. Soon, American boys were dying on the blood-soaked battlefields of France and Belgium. It was a horror beyond belief. And when it was over, the country retreated within itself, not to emerge for more than twenty years . . . following the attack on Pearl Harbor.

In short, the years following the Great War wasn't a good time to be a new immigrant in America.

As Bridget, Sean, and Conor disembarked from their steamship, each carrying a single suitcase, they fell in line with the thousands of other third-class pilgrims who had arrived that day from distant places across the globe. There were Poles. Russians. Germans. Czechs. Hungarians. Romanians. Bulgarians. And, of course, Irish.

First and second-class passengers were quickly processed on-board the ship, spared the need to stand in long lines for over five hours in the scorching sun, just waiting to get inside the Great Hall of the immigration station. Once inside, third-class passengers like Sean, Bridget, and her brother would have to wait another few hours, passing through more lines, including the English and physical exams.

"It seems like we're the only ones speaking English," observed Bridget, as they approached the registration desk, just inside the door of the cinder-block building.

"Is that a good thing?" wondered Sean.

They were about to find out.

Before their departure from Galway, Bridget and Sean had enlisted the help of their old English teacher to help them improve their reading skills. Neither had been in school for nearly two years, forced to drop out to help their families around the farms.

At first, they tried to keep up by reading at home. But when their chores were done each day, it was already dark, and reading my candlelight was hard. If they had known they'd have to pass a reading test to start a new life in America, perhaps they would've found a way to continue studying. But all they could do now was to try their best.

Never had a single test been so consequential.

Bridget stepped forward first to the desk and was met by a middle-aged, bespectacled man with thinning hair, his collar stained with sweat from the humid summer day. He had long ago lost any patience or sympathy for those arriving. It was just a job.

"Name and date of birth?" he said flatly, as he took Bridget's travel documents and glanced-up at her from his seated position.

Bridget replied.

"Port of origin?" the man continued.

"Galway," she said.

The man looked up again and shook his head. He had seen a lot of Irish pass by his desk in the twenty years he had worked on Ellis Island, almost since it'd first opened. He didn't care much for them.

He then slid a paper toward Bridget. "Read these words," he said abruptly

This is it, she thought to herself.

She read the words, tentatively at first, then more quickly and confidently. When she finished, she looked at the man and waited for his reaction. He again shook his head, sighed, but then produced a stamp.

PASSED.

He completed a few more documents and then waved her along toward the health-check booth.

She passed that, too.

Bridget had done it. She was an American immigrant.

She so wanted to scream aloud and jump for joy, but held herself in check, at least until they were all outside the Great Hall.

Her brother and Sean followed, each passing through without any problems. As the three of them exited the building and made their way toward the ferry port, they hugged, each wiping tears of joy. It was quite an accomplishment.

But now the real ordeal would begin.

After changing their Irish pounds into dollars at the money exchange near the dock on the island, the three new immigrants boarded the ferry to Manhattan. Their final destination was Boston. But to get there, they had to first find Penn Station where trains departed hourly to points both north and south. But for anyone who had grown up in a rural setting such as Tuam in County Galway, New York was nothing short of frightening, home to more than five million people, all seemingly in a rush to get somewhere.

Between the three of them, they had less than a hundred dollars in their pockets, just enough to get them to Boston and rent a room for a few weeks while they found work. They were in no position to spend any money in New York City for food or transportation. All they could do was to walk the long distance from the ferry docks in lower Manhattan, north along Broadway, passing by both Washington Square and Madison Square until they arrived at Thirty-Fourth street.

From there, they asked a policeman for directions to Penn Station, which turned out to be only a few blocks away. Many decades later, the majority of the city's police officers would be Irish. But in 1918, most found work as diggers, building the city's subway system. As Sean, Bridget, and her brother approached Penn Station, their ears perked up at the familiar sound of the Irish brogue. They soon passed a gang of diggers—all Irish— preparing to head home after a long day in the sweltering heat. They looked tired to the bone.

"I'm not sure I could do that work," said Sean, nodding his head at the workers. "That's harder than the work we were doing on the farm."

But Bridget's brother was looking in the other direction toward a collection of art galleries just across the street from the giant transportation hub. "That's where I want to be," he said. "You think a place like that would show my work?"

"I *know* they will, Conor," said Bridget, wiping the sweat from her brow. "You just have to think positively."

But the truth was that Bridget was also bone-tired. She hadn't eaten or drank anything for more than twelve hours. None of them had. She tried to be strong but was close to collapse. If they had needed to go any further, she may not have made it. But as they entered the cavernous main waiting hall of the terminal, she was able to find a seat on a wooden bench as Sean and Conor purchased their tickets. Less than an hour later they boarded the train bound for Boston. Within minutes of leaving the city, all three of them were sound asleep.

CHAPTER TWENTY-SEVEN

In August of 2013, nearly ninety-five years to the day after Sean and Bridget had arrived in New York, I landed at the San Francisco International Airport with Jeana and the five children. As they passed through the immigration line beneath the American flag which hung from the rafters above, I could barely hold back my emotions.

What a long journey it'd been.

Following our wedding in Gardner the previous summer, Jeana and I'd worked through the fall and spring with our attorney to amend the children's birth certificates. Since neither father was likely to grant approval for the children to leave the country, the attorney believed that our best option was to remove the fathers' names from the birth certificates altogether. Jeana would then become the sole decision-maker.

By law, Filipino mothers could choose not to list the father on the child's birth certificate if there had been no marriage. The NOMAR certificate—which had allowed Jeana and I to marry in the States—seemed the fastest means of using the law to our advantage.

But the attorney had disagreed.

"A request submitted to the National Record Office to amend a birth certificate will almost certainly be carefully reviewed," the attorney explained to Jeana and I a few weeks after we'd returned from getting married. We always met her at a coffee shop in Marquee Mall in Angeles City, not far from our house.

"In America, you use a person's social security number as the main means of identification.," she continued. "But here, a birth certificate is just as important. So they're always more scrutinized."

The attorney had helped many Filipinos to emigrate to America, including her own parents. Over the years, she had developed many contacts within the provincial governments. It was even rumored that she had acquired the cooperation of a few judges. Recommended by one of the Filipino teachers at my school, she seemed to be the right person for the job.

But it didn't come cheap, or without risk.

"It's possible that a NOMAR certificate could work," she continued. "But it won't work twice. Even if it worked with the oldest two children, we'd be foolish to try again with the youngest three."

"But the NOMAR allowed us to get married," I pointed out.

"True. But you were married in a little town, correct?" recalled the attorney. "They would have no reason to make a call to the National Records Office here. They probably never even heard of it. That certificate was the right move for your marriage. But it's too risky to use it to amend *both* sets of birth certificates."

"So then what's our alternative?" I asked.

"I suggest we get Jeana's first marriage annulled. That will allow us to remove the father's names from the two older boys' birth certificates. We then use the NOMAR for the youngest three, arguing that the father's name should never have been added."

"Since there was NO MARiage," understood Jeana.

"Exactly," confirmed the attorney.

"Then why didn't we get the marriages annulled in the first place?" I asked, trying to understand. "We could have used the annulment to avoid using the fake NOMAR certificate to get married."

The attorney smiled. "Time and money," she said simply. "Time and money. You wanted to get married immediately. An annulment takes time. And to annul *both* marriages at the same time would've been complicated, and risky. We don't want to draw any attention to your case."

"I never understood how both of Jeana's marriages could have been recorded at the National Records Office," I said. "Wouldn't they have rejected the second one?"

"Unlike birth certificates, marriage certificates are rarely scrutinized," explained the attorney. "And who knows, maybe the father used a NOMAR, just like you did."

I shook my head. "It's so complicated," I admitted.

"It is," agreed the attorney. "But that lack of scrutiny is what we're counting on."

"How so?" asked Jeana.

"Because the annulment won't be real,"

"What?" I said, disbelieving. "What do you mean, it won't be *real*?"

"It can't be," explained the attorney. "It would require the father to appear in court. We want to avoid that. All of this needs to be done without either father ever knowing."

"How is that possible?" asked Jeana.

Again, the attorney smiled. "Let me take care of that. The less you know, the better."

Over the course of the next year, we would meet with the attorney each month to get an update and pay any necessary fees, of which there were many. But we never hesitated, knowing it would all be worthwhile in the long run. As we waited for the attorney to complete her work, we took full advantage of the opportunity to explore the Philippines during school holidays, visiting such places as Baguio, Bohol, Cebu, and the beautiful island of Boracay. Each destination was a new adventure for the children who had never left Cavite before I'd entered their lives.

I felt good about being able to give them a good life. It gave my own life more meaning and purpose. For the first time in my life, I was doing things primarily for other people, instead of solely for myself. But I needed to be on the lookout for those selfish demons. They needed to be kept at bay if Jeana and the children were going to prosper.

But it was also necessary for Jeana to address some of her own demons.

When her father left the house to be with another woman, it was a turning point, not only for the entire family, but especially for her. In many ways, she had spent years trying to replace him. Two failed relationships were evidence of that. The passing of her grandfather only hastened the slide. Although I was hoping to provide some stability for her and the children, we both realized that sometimes it was necessary to look back before you were able to fully commit to moving forward.

"I think I need to see him," said Jeana, as we sat poolside at the Holiday Inn, one of the few hotels inside the Clark Free Zone. We often took the children there on weekends for the buffet dinner and a swim in their large outdoor pool. "If we do go to America, I don't know when I'll come back. If ever."

"Do you want me to come with you?" I asked.

She reached for my hand. "Of course, I do. We do everything together." She smiled and squeezed my hand.

Jeana and I'd decided to visit her father on the weekend, leaving the children with the nanny and our best friends, Gina and Garrick Sleight, both teachers at the school who also had two children of their own.

I'd worked with many teachers over the years, and Gina was one of the best. As Liza's fourth grade teacher, she had immediately recognized a learning disability that had made it difficult for Liza to process information. As the kids began their second year at my school, we'd followed Gina's recommendation to have Liza repeat the fourth grade. Years later, we would look back on that decision as a turning point in Liza's education.

The drive to Cavite from Clark takes about four hours. It's less than sixty miles, but the traffic through Manila is probably among the worst of any city in the world. I'd given up trying to negotiate the route myself, instead asking one of the school's bus drivers to drive me whenever I needed to go, usually for school conferences.

As we made our way to see Jeana's father, that same driver, Billy, navigated his way through the congestion of the city, passing through the Tondo district with its many slums, as well as Makate with its high-rise hotels and office buildings. The city of over fifteen million people was among the most densely populated urban centers in the world, and admittedly one of my least favorite.

We arrived in Cavite, just south of metro Manila, in the late morning with plans of visiting Jeana's father for only a few hours before heading back home. We'd decided not to tell him that we were coming, fearing that he would contact the children's fathers, which could have resulted in an awkward confrontation, not to mention the fact that we wanted to keep the kids' whereabouts a secret for as long as possible.

While Billy remained in the car—always with his gun in the glove compartment—Jeana and I knocked on the front gate of her father's modest house. As was common in the residential neighborhoods, the house was surrounded by a cement wall with a rod iron gate, and the windows all had bars.

A woman came to the front gate.

"I'm here to see Gustavo," said Jeana. "I'm his . . ."

"I know who you are," said the woman, cutting off Jeana. "I don't think he wants to see you."

"It's okay," came a voice from within the house. "Let them in, Angelica."

As we passed through the front door, an old slender man in shorts, sandals, and a faded t-shirt was there to greet us. It was Jeana's father.

The tension was immediate.

"Can we talk for a while?" asked Jeana, speaking Tagalog. "We won't take much of your time."

The man motioned for us to sit down, while the woman disappeared into another room.

"I wasn't sure I'd see you again," said her father, also speaking Tagalog. "Is this your new boyfriend?" he then asked, looking at me.

"This is my husband," replied Jeana flatly. "We married this past summer."

I nodded.

"I heard you had returned with an American. I guess congratulations are in order." He held up a beer, but didn't offer either of us a drink.

"I don't know if we'll ever see each other again," began Jeana. "So I wanted to speak with you now."

"Planning on leaving the country?" her father said with a smirk. "It'll be difficult to leave with the children, you know."

Jeana ignored him. "I know you have a new family, and it's not my intention to interfere. But I wanted to tell you, face to face, how much you hurt mom and my brothers and sister. You destroyed our family."

"It was a long time ago, Jeana. You should have moved on."

I sat beside Jeana, holding her hand, and could feel her beginning to shake with anger. But her voice remained even and calm.

"I know you don't care about us," she continued. "You probably never did. But we were your responsibility, and you let us down. Mom didn't get over you leaving for years. I had my grandfather for support, but my siblings had nobody. Our lives would've been so different if you had had the courage to stay."

"Your mother . . ." began her father.

Jeana cut him off. "I don't care about your excuses. And I don't really care about you. But I wanted you to hear how much you hurt us. After you left, my sister and I would sometimes come here asking for money. We just needed it for food and transportation to school. But you never gave us anything. We were still your children. But you never cared."

Jeana's father sat back in his chair, with his beer still in his hand. He had no choice but to listen,

"All of us were lost for years. My mother drank. My brothers used drugs. My sister and I married too young. None of us went to college. Kids need a role model. You weren't there."

I could tell that Jeana was trying so hard not to cry. She wanted to appear strong in front of her father.

"I have finally found someone who really cares about me." She looked at me. "And now my children will have the life they deserve. But if you had chosen to stay all of those years ago, we wouldn't have struggled for all those years. You ruined our family, *Dad*. You really did. But I won't let that happen to my family. I'm stronger than you ever were."

And that was it.

Jeana had confronted her father. She had been strong. Undeterred. Brave.

And now she could move on.

I'd understood a little of what she had said, the rest she had shared with me later. But one thing in particular that she had said, stuck with me. *Kids need a role model.*

My father had been my role model. He definitely wasn't the perfect father. But I'd come to understand that he was better than most. Simply because he was always *present*. He was always there for my sister and me. Maybe he was sometimes too gruff or too controlling. But the opposite of that is a father who doesn't care. Like Jeana's father. And that is the worst thing for children. Without a positive role model, kids are adrift, making decisions on their own without a parent's wisdom. The results can be devastating and irreversible.

For reasons which I still struggle to understand, I'd been drawn to women who had lost a male role model early in their lives. Maria's father had left. Gabriela's father had died. And Jeana's father had abandoned his responsibilities. Three women from completely different backgrounds, all with one thing in common: the lack of a father-figure. That missing piece had sent each of them on a long journey in search of a substitute. In many cases the substitutes were bad people who hurt them.

I would not hurt Jeana. More importantly, I would not hurt her children. I would be their father-figure.

CHAPTER TWENTY-EIGHT

Toward the end of my second year at Clark International School, as Jeana and I waited for our attorney to finish her work, I received an email from Father Lawrence, the pastor from my school in Maryland who had counseled Gabriela and I toward the end of our marriage.

Like Sister Agnes from the mission in Africa . . . Mr. Genco, my principal in New Orleans . . . Doña Olga the owner of the school in San Pedro Sula . . . and Sister Bridget, my principal in California . . . Father Lawrence had been one of my mentors. More significantly, he had become a good friend, following my journey to Dubai and now the Philippines. I'd recently shared with him my desire to return to America with Jeana and the children.

In his email he had suggested that I reach out to Father Kenneth, the pastor at a small Catholic school in Marin County in the Bay Area of California. His principal had recently left and he was looking for someone new. Knowing that Father Kenneth had traveled extensively in the Philippines doing missionary work, Father Lawrence thought it might be a good fit.

It was.

Within a few weeks, Father Kenneth and I'd already Skyped several times and developed a nice rapport, which culminated with an offer to become the new principal of his school.

Less than a week later, our attorney reached out with news that the children's birth certificates had been successfully amended. As I reviewed the annulment which had made the amendments possible, I noticed the signature of a judge from a province near Pampanga.

"How did you get him to sign," I'd asked the attorney.

Like she had told us a year earlier, "The less you know, the better."

Things were moving fast, almost too fast.

But one last step remained in order to get the kids out of the Philippines and to America where a new job was awaiting me in California:

Their US visas.

Did the end justify the means?

It was a question that I would ask myself time and time again over the years, including that day when I arrived in San Francisco with Jeana and the five children. In many instances, I cut corners. Took shortcuts. Bribed. And sometimes even lied to get what I wanted. What I needed. But my answer has always been the same.

You do what you have to do.

It was actually something my father had always said. *You do what you have to do to get by.* Does that mean he and I both lacked a moral compass?

I don't think so. But I'm sure many would disagree.

Perhaps they would cite Karma. And perhaps they're right. Perhaps someday it'll all come back around to get me. But that would be okay, because I accomplished what I'd set out to do. I'd brought Jeana and the children to America.

But it almost didn't happen.

With the children's birth certificates in hand, we were able to get their Philippine passports without any problems. We then all headed to Manila . . . and the US Embassy.

Built in 1946 along Roxas Boulevard within view of Manila Bay, it received tens of thousands of tourist visa applications every year. Nearly all of them were denied for a variety of reasons, most commonly a lack of sufficient *financial means*. In short, applicants had to show that they had a reason to return to the Philippines. A good job. Property. A large bank account.

Few Filipinos had *one*—never mind *all*—of these things. So their applications were almost always denied, as immigration officials assumed that they would stay illegally in America, overstaying the duration of their tourist visa which was typically six months or less.

Of course, many immigrants *gamed* the system and did just that. But even then, there was still a way to become an American citizen. So long as you entered the country legally, you could later apply for a *change of status* . . . from tourist to resident to citizen. And that was our plan.

But first, we needed to be issued the five tourist visas at the embassy.

For Jeana, there was no problem. She would continue to use the visa that was granted to her while we were still in Dubai. And for the youngest four children, it was also no problem because of Jeana's marriage to me.

But for Ryan—who was already eighteen—we were concerned.

Rarely were tourist visas granted to any dependent over that age because it was assumed that they would want to stay in America, find a job, and live independently from their parents.

So, we all sat nervously inside the embassy waiting for Ryan's number to be called. When it finally happened, I wanted to accompany him to the window to explain our situation to the immigration officer. But before I got a chance to say anything, the officer asked Ryan's age, and then instructed me to be seated.

My heart sank.

He was alone.

A few minutes later, our worst fears were realized.

Ryan's application was rejected.

That night at a nearby hotel, we all cried. Ryan insisted that we go to America without him. But that was simply not an option. We all went together . . . or not at all. The family would not be split up again.

"Tomorrow," I said, "Ryan and I'll go back to the embassy . . . together. If they will let me stay with him, I know I can convince the officer."

"Why?" asked Jeana, crying hysterically. "Why would it be different tomorrow? They will just say *no* again. We should just forget about it and go back to Angeles City."

"No," I replied emphatically, looking at Ryan and nodding my head. "We'll try one more time. It's worth a shot. If it doesn't work, we'll go back."

In truth, I really didn't think it would work. But if I could just speak with an immigration officer . . . just *maybe* there was a chance.

The next morning, Ryan and I walked the few blocks from our hotel to the embassy. At eight o'clock in the morning, there were already hundreds of Filipinos waiting in line. Waiting to fulfill a dream that would likely never be realized. Maybe they knew it. Maybe not. Either way, the pull of America was so strong that they were willing to try.

I flashed my American passport to the guard at the gate, and we passed by the line, all the Filipinos staring at Ryan with envy. Once inside, we took a number and waited our turn, finding a seat near one of the TV monitors showing CNN. We watched the images of the aftermath of the Boston Marathon bombing. It was disturbing.

"Is it really like that in America?" asked Ryan. "Bombings and shootings?"

I continued looking at the screen. "Sometimes it seems that way."

"Maybe it's safer to just stay here."

I knew the children were all apprehensive about going to America. It seemed so far away. So different from anything they had known. A few weeks earlier, Daniel had confided that he was worried about being bullied. Worried that he wouldn't be accepted in an American school. I'd told him the truth. It could happen. But I also told him that he'd never be alone. He would always have me and his mother to lean-on.

I turned to Ryan. "If this works," I began, "and we're all able to travel to America, it'll not be easy. In fact, it'll probably be the most difficult thing you'll ever do. But I believe you can do it, Ryan. I believe you can be successful there. But you have to remember something." I put my hand on his leg, just as my father had sometimes done with me.

"You and your siblings are just the beginning. It all starts with the five of you. But it doesn't end there. Someday you'll have children. So will Daniel. And Nadine. All of you, I'm sure. And for your children, it'll be a little bit easier. And for their children, easier still. Each generation will move a little farther ahead. But it'll have all started with the five of you. And as the oldest, you have the greatest responsibility. If we get that visa today, you need to be strong. Show your brothers and sisters that you're not afraid. Most importantly, believe in yourself. Believe that you can do this. *I* believe in you, Ryan. *I* believe in *all* of you."

At that moment, they called our number. I walked to the window with Ryan.

Window #201.

The officer behind the glass looked up at us. I expected him to tell me to step away. To return to my seat. But he didn't. He let me stay. He let me explain. I don't know why exactly. Maybe it was because he was Asian himself. Maybe because he was younger and perhaps more sympathetic.

Maybe . . .

Whatever the reason, that officer behind window #201 approved Ryan's visa that day. And in doing so, changed the course of one family's history.

As Ryan and I walked back to the hotel to give Jeana, Daniel, Nadine, Liza, and Nathan the good news, he grabbed my arm and stopped me.

"Thanks Dad," he said, hugging me. "Thank you so much. I'll make you proud. I promise."

I knew he would.

A few weeks later we all arrived in San Francisco.

America had some new immigrants.

And I'd finally found my purpose.

PART 3: EPILOGUE

Just a few summers ago, I took Jeana and the five children on a trip to the East Coast, visiting Washington, DC, Philadelphia, New York City, and Boston. By then, we'd been living in California for nearly four years. Ryan and Daniel were both in college. Nadine, Liza, and Nathan all in high school. They were all doing extremely well.

Jeana was working from home as a medical biller, and I was principal of a small private school just outside of Los Angeles. We'd stayed in Marin County for only two years, leaving after Father Kenneth's Catholic school closed and became a charter school. But southern California was working just fine. We were near the desert. Near the mountains. And near the beach. It couldn't get any better than that. It was a long, long way from Angeles City.

Even farther from Cavite.

Our visit to Washington was special, as the kids sat on the steps of the Lincoln Memorial, looking out over the Mall toward the World War II memorial which included a pillar for the Philippines, along with another pillar for the many American divisions that had fought in Europe following D-Day, including my father's.

We went inside the Capitol and toured the House chambers where so many of the country's immigration laws had been made. And the children stood in the shadow of the Jefferson Memorial, probably not quite realizing the significance of six new immigrants looking-up at one of the nation's forefathers.

But it was our visit to New York City which proved the most emotional . . . especially for me.

On our second day in the city, we took a ferry from lower Manhattan—not far from the 9/11 memorial—across New York Harbor, toward New

Jersey. The boat then began slowly turning, preparing to dock. From our location on the top deck, we turned back to see the incredible view of the New York City skyline. The kids were enthralled by the skyscrapers. The Chrysler Building. The Woolworth Building. One World Trade Center. And, of course, the Empire State Building which they had climbed to the top of only the day before.

But as the boat continued to turn, our objective came into view. Nearly one hundred years earlier, Sean and Bridget had passed by her, marveling at her size and beauty. Her arms forever open to the world's tired, poor, and huddled masses, yearning to breathe free.

The Statue of Liberty.

The children and Jeana turned toward her, their hands upon the railing of the ferry, leaning forward as if to touch Lady Liberty. It was all just too much for me to take, as I broke down in tears. It all seemed to flash before me. Kansas. Africa. New Orleans. Puerto Rico. Honduras. California. Maryland. Dubai. Philippines. What a long, incredible journey it'd been. And as I watched Jeana and children continuing to gaze upon the statue that was towering over the ferry as it made port, I knew for sure that it'd all been worthwhile. For so long, I'd felt that my life lacked meaning, lacked purpose. But not anymore.

I was truly blessed.

Perhaps my sister had been right all along. Perhaps Mom was watching over me.

We walked around Liberty Island for a few hours before boarding the ferry once again and heading to Ellis Island. In the years following my grandparents' arrival, the island's importance as an immigration station began to wane as American embassies around the world—such as the one in the Philippines—assumed responsibility for processing immigrants *before* they departed for America. By the time the Second World War came around, it'd become a detention center for enemy merchant seamen.

In 1965, President Johnson declared Ellis Island part of the Statue of Liberty National Monument. It was opened to the public in the late seventies before undergoing a major restoration, the largest historic restoration in US history. The Main Building, where Bridget had first passed her language exam, was reopened to the public on September 10, 1990, as the Ellis Island National Museum of Immigration.

As I entered the Great Hall with Jeana and children, we walked forward to the area on the far side of the hall that maintained the Port of New York Passenger Records, more than sixty-five million arrival records dating from the early nineteenth century through the mid-twentieth century.

The historical manifests had been transcribed into a vast digitized archive of ships passenger lists where information about each passenger had been written down and used to examine immigrants upon arrival in the United States . . . including Sean, Bridget, and her brother Conor. Once again, I became choked up as the computer screen displayed their names and the details of their arrival in August of 1918 aboard the *Cedric*.

After leaving New York, the three of them had made it to Boston by train. Within a few weeks, Sean had found work as a ditch digger building the city's newest subway line, the Green Line, which would extend the city's network to include an area called Jamaica Plain. Bridget found work as a cleaner at a local hospital. Her brother, Conor, was eventually invited to show his work at a local gallery, but died only a few years later of pneumonia. In 1927, Bridget and Sean gave birth to Kathleen and moved into an apartment on the second floor of a tenement building in Jamaica Plain.

Following our visit to New York, Jeana, the kids, and I took a train to Boston, getting off at South Station to meet my sister and then taking that same Green Line to Jamaica Plain. We all walked down Boynton Street and stood in front of my grandparent's home where they had lived together until Sean's passing in 1954 from lung cancer, the same disease that had taken my mother from me.

When they had first moved into the neighborhood in the twenties, it was predominantly Irish. Then the Latinos moved in, followed by the Vietnamese, Cambodians, and even some Filipinos. The melting pot of America.

You wondered who would be next.

The last leg of our trip was to Gardner to see my father. He had met his grandchildren for the first time a few years earlier and continued to enjoy our visits, usually for Thanksgiving or Christmas. But he was ninety-three now, his heart and kidneys weakening, but his mind still sharp. He most enjoyed sitting on the front doorstep of his house on Bickford Hill— where he had lived for nearly sixty years—watching the five kids cutting his grass and trimming his bushes.

"They're good children, Johnny," he would always say. "You and Jeana have done a fine job."

A trip home to see my father was never complete without a visit, of course, to Crystal Lake. On our last day in Gardner before heading to Boston for our return flight to California, my father and I once again sat on his favorite bench within a few feet of the water, his back to the hill atop which was buried my mother.

"You've done well for yourself, Johnny," he said, adjusting his cap to shield his bald head from the summer's sunshine. "Far better than I ever did. And that's the way it should be."

"And the children will probably do better than me," I said.

"Indeed. That could only happen here, you know. In America. We have lots of problems. Some of them are unsolvable, I'm afraid. But it has always been a land of immigrants. And it always will be. That'll never change. People will try, mind you. But they will fail, simply because history is against them. The tide of history has washed upon these shores from across the world for many centuries, bringing first the West Europeans, then the East Europeans, then the Latinos, and now more and more the Asians from such places as the Philippines. It's a remarkable story, and I think there's many chapters yet to be written."

I looked at my father as he gazed over the waters of Crystal Lake. What a remarkable life he had lived. What remarkable lives his generation had lived. The Greatest Generation. They did everything that was asked of them, and so much more. And one by one, they were passing into history. Soon to be remembered only in books . . . and in the hearts of their children.

I wanted my five children to remember him, as well. So I'd taken them to Harvard Yard to see where he had gone to college. I'd taken them to Montana and Wyoming to see where he had lived in the years following Harvard. And I'd taken them to Europe to retrace his steps in the months following the D-Day landings.

As they grew up and had their own children, I wanted them to pass on their grandfather's story. It is, in the end, one of the main roles of a family. To remember the deeds of one generation by passing on the stories to the next.

My father passed away quietly in his sleep a few months following our visit. We all returned to lay him to rest beside my mother along the shores of Crystal Lake. It was, of course, a very sad day. But as my sister and I watched his grandchildren wiping their tears, we knew our father's memory was in good hands. His legacy now extended beyond my sister and I, and into the distant future, like an echo across time.

The torch had been passed. The story would continue . . .

ABOUT THE AUTHOR

George John Black was born in Massachusetts. Throughout his thirty-year career in education, he has lived and worked in the United States, Africa, Honduras, the United Arab Emirates, and the Philippines. His father served in France during the Second World War. Following the war, he attended Harvard and lived in Montana before returning to his hometown in Massachusetts. He passed away in 2019 at the age of 94. George currently resides in California with his wife and five children.